"YOU'RE INTERESTED IN THE POSITION?"

There was a hopeful upturn in Andy Leitner's voice as it came through the phone. "I was wondering if the store owners had taken my note down."

Rhoda's heart raced. "*Jah*, I'd like to talk to you about it," she gushed. "But ya should understand right out that I don't have a car, on account of how we Amish don't believe in ownin'—I mean, I'm not preachin' at ya, or—"

She winced. "This is comin' out all wrong. Sorry," she rasped. "My name's Rhoda Lantz, and I'm in Willow Ridge. I sure hope you don't think I'm too *ferhoodled* to even be considered for the job."

"Ferhoodled?" The word rolled melodiously from the receiver and teased at her.

"Crazy mixed-up," she explained. "Confused, and—well, I'm keepin' ya from whatever ya need to be doin', so—"

"Ah, but you're a solution to my problem. The answer to a prayer . . ."

More Seasons of the Heart books by Charlotte Hubbard

Summer of Secrets

Autumn Winds

Published by Kensington Publishing Corporation

WINTER
Of
WISHES

Seasons *of the* Heart

Charlotte Hubbard

ZEBRA BOOKS
KENSINGTON PUBLISHING CORP.
http://www.kensingtonbooks.com

ZEBRA BOOKS are published by

Kensington Publishing Corp.
119 West 40th Street
New York, NY 10018

All Kensington titles, imprints, and distributed lines are available at special quantity discounts for bulk purchases for sales promotion, premiums, fund-raising, educational, or institutional use.

Special book excerpts or customized printings can also be created to fit specific needs. For details, write or phone the office of the Kensington Special Sales Manager: Attn.: Special Sales Department. Kensington Publishing Corp., 119 West 40th Street, New York, NY 10018. Phone: 1-800-221-2647.

Zebra and the Z logo Reg. U.S. Pat. & TM Off.

ISBN-13: 978-1-4201-2171-1
ISBN-10: 1-4201-2171-5
First Printing: September 2013

eISBN-13: 978-1-4201-3272-4
eISBN-10: 1-4201-3272-5
First Electronic Edition: September 2013

10 9 8 7 6 5 4 3 2

Printed in the United States of America

For Darla, who knows how to live, laugh, and love!

Acknowledgments

Thank You once again, Lord, for guiding this story and sending me wonderful ideas each time I needed them. Your sudden inspirations are always better than my deliberate plotting and planning.

As always, working with Alicia Condon, my editor, and Evan Marshall, my agent, has been such a pleasure. Thank you both for sharing your excitement and your ideas with me as this series progresses through the seasons of our hearts.

Special thanks again to Jim Smith of Step Back in Time Tours in Jamesport, Missouri, as I continue to write Amish stories and ask him questions about Old Order ways. Blessings on you for helping me even as you fought the good fight—and won!—your battle with cancer.

Thanks to Martha Johnson, author and colleague, for answers to questions about all manner of Amish details.

Special blessings and love to you, Neal, for knowing when I needed entertainment and comic relief as I wrote this one. Your application for sainthood is being processed.

Matthew 19:16–26

*And, behold, one came and said unto him,
Good Master, what good thing shall I do, that I
may have eternal life?*

*And He said unto him, Why callest thou me good?
there is none good but one, that is God: but if
thou wilt enter into life, keep the commandments.*

*He saith unto him, Which? Jesus said, Thou shalt do
no murder, Thou shalt not commit adultery, Thou
shalt not steal, Thou shalt not bear false witness,*

*Honor thy father and thy mother: and thou shalt love
thy neighbour as thyself.*

*The young man saith unto Him, All these things have
I kept from my youth up: what lack I yet?*

*Jesus said unto him, If thou wilt be perfect, go and
sell that thou hast, and give it to the poor, and
thou shalt have treasure in heaven: and come and
follow me.*

*But when the young man heard that saying, he went
away sorrowful: for he had great possessions.*

*Then said Jesus unto his disciples, Verily I say unto
you, That a rich man shall hardly enter into the
kingdom of heaven.*

*And again I say unto you, It is easier for a camel to
go through the eye of a needle than for a rich man
to enter into the kingdom of God.*

*When his disciples heard it, they were exceedingly
amazed, saying Who then can be saved?*

*But Jesus beheld them, and said unto them,
**With men this is impossible; but with God all
things are possible.***

Luke 1:46–53

And Mary said, My soul doth magnify the Lord,

And my spirit hath rejoiced in God my Saviour.

For he hath regarded the low estate of his handmaiden; for, behold, from henceforth all generations shall call me blessed.

For he that is mighty hath done to me great things; and holy is his name, And his mercy is on them that fear him from generation to generation.

He hath shewed strength with his arm; he hath scattered the proud in the imagination of their hearts.

He hath put down the mighty from their seats and exalted them of low degree.

He hath filled the hungry with good things; and the rich he hath sent empty away.

Chapter One

As Rhoda Lantz stood gazing out the window of the Sweet Seasons Bakery Café, her mood matched the ominous gray clouds that shrouded the dark, predawn sky. Here it was the day after Thanksgiving and she felt anything but thankful. Oh, she'd eaten Mamma's wonderful dinner yesterday and smiled at all the right times during the gathering of family and friends around their extended kitchen table, but she'd been going through the motions. Feeling distanced . . . not liking it, but not knowing what to do about it, either.

"You all right, honey-bug? Ya seem a million miles away."

Rhoda jumped. Mamma had slipped up behind her while she'd been lost in her thoughts. "*Jah, jah.* Fine and dandy," she fibbed. "Just thinkin' how it looks like we're in for a winter storm, which most likely means we won't have as many folks come to eat today and tomorrow. It's just . . . well, things got really slow last year at this time."

Her mother's concerned gaze told Rhoda her little white lie hadn't sounded very convincing. Mamma glanced toward the kitchen, where her partner, Naomi Brenneman, and Naomi's daughter, Hannah, were frying sausage and bacon for the day's breakfast buffet. "Tell ya what," she said gently.

"Lydia Zook left a phone message about a couple of fresh turkeys still bein' in their meat case. Why not go to the market and fetch those, along with a case of eggs—and I'm thinkin' it's a perfect day for that wonderful-*gut* cream soup we make with the potatoes and carrots and cheese in the sauce. I'll call in the order, and by the time ya get over there they'll have everything all gathered up."

"*Jah*, Mamma, I can do that," Rhoda murmured. It meant walking down the long lane with the wind whipping at her coat, and then hitching up a carriage, but it was something useful to do.

Useful. Why is it such a struggle lately to feel useful? I wish I knew what to do with my life.

Rhoda slipped her coat from the peg at the door, tied on her heavy black bonnet, and stepped outside with a gasp. The temperature had dropped several degrees since she'd come to the café an hour ago. The chill bit through her woolen stockings as she walked briskly along the gravel lane with her head lowered against the wind.

"Hey there, Rhoda! *Gut* mornin' to ya!" a voice sang out as she passed the smithy behind the Sweet Seasons.

Rhoda waved to Ben Hooley but didn't stop to chat. Why did the farrier's cheerfulness irritate her lately? She had gotten over her schoolgirl crush on him and was happy for Ben and Mamma both, but as their New Year's Day wedding approached, they seemed more public about their affections—their *joy*—and, well, that irritated her, too! Across the road from the Sweet Seasons a new home was going up in record time, as Ben's gift to her mother . . . yet another reminder of how Rhoda's life would change when Mamma moved out of the apartment above the blacksmith shop, and she would be living there alone.

As she reached the white house she'd grown up in, Rhoda sighed. No lights glowed in the kitchen window and no one ate breakfast at the table: this holiday weekend, her twin sister Rachel and Rachel's new groom, Micah Brenneman, were on an extended trip around central Missouri to collect wedding presents as they visited aunts, uncles, and cousins of their two families. Rhoda missed working alongside Rachel at the café more than she could bear to admit, yet here again, she was happy for her sister. The newlyweds radiated a love and sense of satisfaction she could only dream of.

Rhoda hitched up the enclosed carriage and clapped the reins across Sadie's broad back. If Thanksgiving had been so difficult yesterday, with so many signposts of the radical changes in all their lives, what would the upcoming Christmas season be like? Ordinarily she loved baking cookies, setting out the Nativity scene, and arranging evergreen branches and candles on the mantel and at the windowsills. Yet as thick, feathery flakes of snow blew across the yard, her heart thudded dully. It wasn't her way to feel so blue, or to feel life was passing her by. But at twenty-one, she heard her clock ticking ever so loudly.

God, have Ya stopped listenin' to my prayers for a husband and a family? Are Ya tellin' me I'm fated to remain a maidel?

Rhoda winced at the thought. She gave the mare its head once they were on the county blacktop, and as they rolled across the single-lane bridge that spanned this narrow spot in the Missouri River, she glanced over toward the new gristmill. The huge wooden wheel was in place now, churning slowly as the current of the water propelled it. The first light of dawn revealed two male figures on the roof. Luke and Ira Hooley, Ben's younger brothers, scrambled like monkeys as they checked their new machinery. The Mill at Willow Ridge would soon be open to tourists. In addition to regular wheat flour and cornmeal, the Hooley brothers would offer specialty grains that would sell to whole-foods stores in Warrensburg and other nearby cities. Mamma was already gathering recipes to bake artisan breads at the Sweet Seasons, as an additional lure for health-conscious tourists.

But Rhoda's one brief date with Ira had proven he was more interested in running the roads with Annie Mae Knepp than in settling down or joining the church anytime soon. Both Ira and Luke were seemingly happy to live in a state of eternal *rumspringa.* Rhoda considered herself as fun loving as any young woman, but she'd long ago committed herself to the Amish faith. Was it too much to ask the same sort of maturity of the men she dated?

She pulled up alongside Zook's Market. The grocery and dry goods store wouldn't open for a couple of hours yet, but already Henry and Lydia Zook were preparing for their day. Rhoda put a determined smile on her face as the bell above the door jangled. "Happy day-after-Thanksgivin' to ya!" she called out. "Mamm says you've got a couple turkeys for us today."

"*Jah*, Rhoda, we're packin' your boxes right this minute, too!" Lydia called out from behind the back counter. "Levi! Cyrus! You can be carryin' those big bags of potatoes and carrots out to Rhoda's rig, please and thank ya."

From an aisle of the store, still shadowy in the low glow of the gas ceiling lights, two of the younger Zook boys stepped away from the shelves they had been restocking. "Hey there, Rhoda," ten-year-old Levi mumbled.

"Tell your *mamm* we could use more of those fine black-berry pies," his younger brother Cyrus remarked as he hefted a thirty-pound bag of potatoes over his shoulder. "That's my favorite, and they always sell out. Mamm won't let us buy a pie unless they're a day old—and most of 'em don't stay on the shelf that long."

Rhoda smiled wryly. Cyrus Zook wasn't the only fellow around Willow Ridge with a keen interest in her mother's pies. "I'll pass that along. *Denki* to you boys for loadin' the carriage."

"Levi's fetchin' your turkeys from the fridge," their *dat*, Henry, said from behind his meat counter. "Won't be but a minute. Say—it sounds like ya had half of Willow Ridge over to your place for dinner yesterday."

Again Rhoda smiled to herself: word got around fast in a small town. "*Jah*, what with Ben and his two brothers and two aunts—and the fact that those aunts invited Tom Hostetler and Hiram and his whole tribe to join us—we had quite a houseful."

"Awful nice of ya to look after Preacher Tom and the bishop's bunch," Lydia said with an approving nod. "Fellows without wives don't always get to celebrate with a real Thanksgiving dinner when their married kids live at a distance."

"Well, there was no telling Jerusalem and Nazareth Hooley they *couldn't* invite Tom and the Knepps," Rhoda replied with a chuckle. "So there ya have it. They brought half the meal, though, so that wasn't so bad."

"Tell your *mamm* we said hullo." Henry turned back toward the big grinder on the back table, where he was making fresh hamburger.

"*Jah*, I'll do that. And *denki* for havin' things all set to go."

Jonah Zook stood behind his *dat*'s counter trimming roasts. Rhoda met his eye and nodded, but didn't try to make small talk. Jonah was a couple of years younger than she, and had driven her home from a few Sunday-night singings, but he had about as much sparkle as a crushed cardboard box. And goodness, but she could use some *sparkle* about now . . .

Rhoda glanced out the store's front window. Levi and Cyrus were taking their sweet time about loading her groceries, so she wandered over to the bulletin board where folks posted notices of upcoming auctions and other announcements. No sense in standing out in that wind while the boys joshed around.

The old corkboard was pitted from years of use, and except for the sale bills for upcoming household auctions in New Haven and Morning Star, the yellowed notices for herbal remedies, fresh eggs, and local fellows' businesses had hung there for months. Rhoda sighed—and then caught sight of a note half-hidden by an auction flyer.

> NEED A COMPASSIONATE, PATIENT
> CARETAKER FOR MY ELDERLY MOTHER,
> PLUS AFTER-SCHOOL SUPERVISION
> FOR TWO KIDS. NEW HAVEN, JUST
> A BLOCK OFF THE COUNTY HIGHWAY.
> CALL ANDY LEITNER.

Rhoda snatched the little notice from the board, her heart thumping. She knew nothing about this fellow except his phone number and that he had an ailing mother and two young children—and that he was surely English if he was advertising for help with family members. Yet something about his decisive block printing told her Mr. Leitner was a man who didn't waffle over decisions or accept a halfhearted effort from anyone who would work for him. He apparently had no wife—

Maybe she works away from home. Happens a lot amongst English families.

—and if he had posted this advertisement in Zook's Market, he surely realized a Plain woman would be most likely to respond. It was common for Amish and Mennonite gals to hire on for housework and caretaking in English homes, so if she gave him a call, she could start working there, why—as soon as tomorrow!

How many of these notices has he posted? Plenty of Plain bulk stores to advertise in around Morning Star, plus the big discount stores out past New Haven. And if he had run ads in the local papers, maybe he'd already had dozens of gals apply for this job. But what could it hurt to find out?

Pulse pounding, Rhoda stepped outside. "You fellas got all my stuff loaded, *jah*?" she demanded. Levi and Cyrus were playing a rousing game of catch with a huge hard-packed snowball, paying no heed to the snow that was falling on their green shirtsleeves.

Levi, the ornerier of the two, poked his head around the back of the buggy. "Got a train to catch, do ya? Busy day chasin' after that Ira Hooley fella?" he teased. "Jonah, he says ya been tryin' to catch yourself some of that Lancaster County money—"

"And what if I have?" Rhoda shot back. "Your *mamm* won't like it when I tell her you two have been lollygaggin' out here instead of stockin' your shelves, ain't so?"

Levi waited until she was stepping into the carriage before firing the snowball at her backside. But what would she accomplish by stepping out to confront him? Rhoda glanced at the two huge turkeys, the mesh sacks of potatoes, carrots, and onions, and the sturdy boxes loaded with other staples Mamma had ordered, and decided she was ready to go. "Back, Sadie," she said in a low voice.

The mare whickered and obeyed immediately. Rhoda chuckled at the two boys' outcry as she playfully backed the buggy toward them. Then she urged Sadie into a trot. All sorts of questions buzzed in her mind as she headed for the Sweet Seasons. What would Mamma say if she called Andy Leitner? What if a mild winter meant the breakfast and lunch shifts would remain busy, especially with Rachel off collecting wedding presents for a few more weekends? Hannah Brenneman had only been helping them since her sixteenth birthday last week—

Jah, but she got her wish, to work in the café. And Rachel got her wish when she married Micah. And Mamma got more than she dared to wish for when Ben Hooley asked to marry her! So it's about time for me to have a wish come true!

Was that prideful, self-centered thinking? As Rhoda pulled up at the café and parked the buggy, she didn't much worry about the complications of religion or the Old Ways. She stepped into the dining room, spotted her cousins, Nate and Bram Kanagy, and caught them before they went back to the buffet for another round of biscuits and gravy. "Could I get you boys to carry in a couple of turkeys and some big bags of produce?" she asked sweetly. Then she nodded toward the kitchen, where Hannah was drizzling white icing on a fresh pan of Mamma's sticky buns. "Ya might talk our new cook out of a mighty *gut* cinnamon roll, if ya smile at her real nice."

Nate rolled his eyes, but Bram's handsome face lit up. "*Jah*, I noticed how the scenery in the kitchen had improved, cuz—not that it isn't a treat to watch you and Rachel workin'," he added quickly.

"*Jah*, sure, ya say that after you've already stepped in it." Rhoda widened her eyes at him playfully. "Here's your chance to earn your breakfast—not to mention make a few points with Hannah."

Rhoda went back outside to grab one of the lighter boxes. Then, once Nate had followed her in with bags of onions and carrots, and he was chatting with Hannah and Mamma, she slipped out to the phone shanty before she lost her nerve. Common sense told her she should think out some answers to whatever questions Andy Leitner might ask, yet excitement overruled her usual practicality. Chances were good that she'd have to leave him a voice mail, anyway, so as her fingers danced over the phone number, her thoughts raced. Never in her life had she considered working in another family's home, yet this seemed like the opportunity she'd been hoping for—praying for—of late. Surely Mamma would understand if—

"Hello?" a male voice said over the phone. He sounded a little groggy.

Rhoda gripped the receiver. It hadn't occurred to her that while she'd already worked a couple of hours at the café, most of the world wasn't out of bed yet. "I—sorry I called so early, but—"

"Not a problem. Glad for the wake-up call, because it seems I fell back asleep," he replied with a soft groan. "How can I help you?"

Rhoda's imagination ran wild. If this was Andy Leitner, he had a deep, mellow voice. Even though she'd awakened him and he was running late, he spoke pleasantly. "I, um, found the notice from an Andy Leitner on the board in Zook's Market just now, and—" She closed her eyes, wondering where the words had disappeared to. She had to sound businesslike, or at least competent, or this man wouldn't want to talk to her.

"You're interested in the position?" he asked with a hopeful upturn in his voice. "I was wondering if the store owners had taken my note down."

Rhoda's heart raced. "*Jah*, I'd like to talk to you about it," she gushed. "But ya should understand right out that I don't have a car, on account of how we Amish don't believe in ownin'—I mean, I'm not preachin' at ya, or—"

She winced. "This is comin' out all wrong. Sorry," she rasped. "My name's Rhoda Lantz, and I'm in Willow Ridge. I sure hope you don't think I'm too *ferhoodled* to even be considered for the job."

"Ferhoodled?" The word rolled melodiously from the receiver and teased at her.

"Crazy mixed-up," she explained. "Confused, and—well, I'm keepin' ya from whatever ya need to be doin', so—"

"Ah, but you're a solution to my problem. The answer to a prayer," he added quietly. "For that, I have time to listen, Rhoda. I need to make my shift at the hospital, but could I come by and chat with you when I get off? Say, around two this afternoon?"

Rhoda grinned. "That would be wonderful-*gut*, Mr. Leitner! We'll be closin' up at two—my *mamm* runs the Sweet Seasons Bakery Café on the county blacktop. We can talk at a back table."

"Perfect. I'll see you then—and thanks so much for calling, Rhoda."

"*Jah*, for sure and for certain!"

As she placed the receiver back in its cradle, Rhoda held her breath. What would she tell Mamma? She felt scared and excited and yes, *ferhoodled*, because she now had an interview for a job! She had no idea how to care for that elderly mother . . . or what if the kids ran her so ragged she got nothing done except to keep them out of trouble? What if Andy Leitner's family didn't like her because she wore Plain clothing and kapps?

What have ya gone and done, Rhoda Lantz?

She inhaled to settle herself, and headed back to the café's kitchen. There was no going back, no unsaying what she'd said over the phone. No matter what anyone else thought, she could only move forward.

And wasn't that exactly what she'd been hoping to do for weeks now?

Chapter Two

Andy pulled into the parking lot beside the Sweet Seasons and switched off his ignition. He'd stopped here a couple of times for a sack of muffins or cinnamon rolls but never for a sit-down meal. He was always on the run, in a hurry, it seemed. He admired the work ethic of the mother and daughters he'd seen cooking and waiting on tables, and he'd noticed how a lot of local folks ate here—which, in small towns like Willow Ridge, meant the food was excellent and the prices were right.

Rhoda Lantz had sounded like a delightful young woman over the phone, bubbly and cheerful. That was exactly the sort of caretaker his mom and kids needed. *Oh, don't lie to yourself*, he thought as he climbed out of the car. *You're tired of having to be the cook and the maid and the dad and the mom and—*

Andy paused at the door, reminding himself that if he carried his frustrations inside, he'd frighten Rhoda away. As he stepped into the Sweet Seasons, heavenly aromas of roasted turkey and stuffing still lingered after the lunch shift. Inhaling deeply, he gazed around at the sturdy tables and chairs . . . the homey calico curtains at the glistening windows. Two mature women and a young girl back in the kitchen chattered happily, wearing aprons over their dresses of deep green and blue, with their hair tucked up under their head coverings. Another young woman turned from the glass bakery case near the cash register, where she was taking out pies.

"*Jah*, and how can we help ya today?" she asked as she approached him. "Did ya come for a bite of lunch? Or would ya just happen to be the Mr. Leitner I jabbered at this morning?"

Andy couldn't help himself: for the first time in weeks he was smiling from the top of his head to the tips of his toes, listening to this young woman's lilting German accent. He held out his hand, gazing at her face . . . so fresh and open. Even without makeup she was remarkably attractive. "And would you be Rhoda? It's wonderful to meet you."

"*Jah, jah*, that's me." She glanced at the women in the kitchen and lowered her voice as she steered him toward a back table. "But I'll tell ya straight out that I haven't had the chance to mention this interview to Mamma," she confessed with a nervous laugh. "So if she comes back to check on us, she'll be in for a big surprise."

Andy pulled out a chair for her and sat down across the table. He wanted to hire her on first sight—could already see she was exactly the sort of caretaker he'd had in mind—but he didn't want to get crossways between mother and daughter, either. "Is it permissible for a Plain girl to work for me? To watch my kids and—"

"*Jah*, that's not a problem! It's just that, well—" Rhoda again glanced toward the kitchen, her cheeks turning pink. "When I saw your note in Zook's Market, it was like the sign I'd been waitin' for, that I was to move along into something new for myself. What with my twin sister gettin' hitched, and my *mamm* marryin' the new farrier come New Year's, and Naomi's girl comin' to work here, and all the fellas either treatin' me like I'm invisible, or—well, never mind about that part! I'm jabberin' at ya again."

Andy studied her face, sensing her hesitation. He didn't know any Amish folks as friends, but he respected their faith and didn't want to get her in trouble with her church leaders. "Rhoda, if you have reservations about working in a non-Amish home—"

"No, no—that part's fine and dandy," she blurted with an apologetic smile. "It's just that I've not done any caretakin' before, and—well, here comes my *mamm*, so the cat's gonna get let out of the bag."

Andy watched the woman who was approaching from the kitchen, drying her hands on a towel. She had energy about her, a liveliness he enjoyed before she even opened her mouth. He stood up, smiling because he couldn't help it: this was the coziest, friendliest place he'd been in a long while.

"And what can we feed ya?" she said, her gaze flowing from his face to her daughter's. "We're closed for the day, but we've got—"

"Oh no, Mrs. Lantz, it's not lunch I've come for," he replied. "But, wow, this place smells just like Thanksgiving dinner! I missed out on all that wonderful food this year because my mom's not up to the cooking anymore."

Rhoda stood up, her expression tight. "Mamma, we've been so busy here today—and I didn't want to say anything in front of Naomi and Hannah, but—well, I saw a note on the Zook's bulletin board, for a job takin' care of this fella's *mamm* and his two kids. So I called him about it. This—this is Andy Leitner, from over around New Haven."

"And I'm pleased to meet you, Mrs. Lantz," Andy said.

"Oh, call me Miriam or I sound old enough to be your *mamm*," she replied with a chuckle. "Except, thanks be to God, I'm healthy and happy and able to cook those turkeys you're smellin'. Real sorry to hear your mother's not doin' so well. Puts a damper on everything."

"Thank you," he murmured, immediately sensing this woman's compassion. "Mom had a stroke a while back, and while the therapy is helping, she still doesn't have full use of her right hand and arm. She's home when the kids get out of school, but . . ." How did he explain his situation without sounding like he was pleading for pity?

"The good fairies aren't showin' up to cook and clean, so things are lookin' untidy," Miram finished quietly. "And what sort of work do ya do, Mr. Leitner?"

Instinct prodded him to follow her earlier lead. Miriam's face looked so pleasant and fresh it was hard to judge her age. She could easily be Rhoda's older sister, considering how Amish women were often still having children when their firstborns got married. "Please, call me Andy," he insisted, "or you'll have me feeling old enough to be your father."

Their laughter rang around the dining room, a sound that lightened his heart. After an ICU shift that had drained him, it felt wonderful to be here where their happiness rejuvenated him. "I'm almost finished with my internship, due to graduate with my nursing degree at the end of this semester."

Their eyes widened, but he was used to Midwestern people who still considered nursing a female occupation. Yet he saw no derision on their smooth, sweet faces.

"What a wonderful gift, to be a healer," Miriam said with a reverent nod.

"*Jah*, there's never enough doctors or nurses to go around, especially in farmin' areas like Willow Ridge," Rhoda remarked. "It's lucky for your *mamm* that ya probably knew what was goin' wrong when she was havin' her stroke."

Andy vividly recalled how he'd found his mother unable to get out of bed, with her face already gone slack on one side so she couldn't speak clearly. "Mom's better now, but she has a long way to go and . . . well, with the kids in school and me working shifts, she gets depressed—"

"And ya don't feel right leavin' her by herself, wonderin' what might go wrong." Miriam's face took on a thoughtful glow. "I'll let you two talk out the details of this job. Be sure and stop by the kitchen before ya leave, though."

And what did she mean by that? Andy noted the quickness of Miriam's step and realized how long it had been since he'd spent time with a woman who knew her purpose and carried it out with humor and dignity. Why, even when he and Megan had first been married—

Megan has no place in this conversation. But she'll have to be explained sooner or later, won't she?

"Well, now." Rhoda smiled shyly as she took her seat again. "That went better than I figured. Didn't mean to catch ya betwixt the two of us kitty-cats—even though Mamma and I rarely show our claws."

Andy delighted at her turn of phrase. "That's one of the reasons I believe you're the right person to restore order in my home and to—to care for everyone." He cleared his throat, deciding to lay his cards on the table. "I'm divorced, Rhoda. I know your church frowns on that, so if it'll cause a problem—or if you or your mother feel uncomfortable about it, I'll understand."

Rhoda studied him, her hands clasped on the table. He saw the eagerness in her blue eyes, the desire to be helpful and to try a new job despite her inexperience. "When we lost my *dat* a couple years back," she said in a low voice, "Mamma and Rachel and I kept goin' here at the café by doin' some things the bishop didn't think was quite right—

mostly because he wanted to marry Mamma himself," she added wryly.

"I can certainly understand that."

A sparkle came out to play in Rhoda's eyes, as though she, her sister, and her mother had become adept at working around permission issues. "So as long as ya explain how ya want things done with your kids and your *mamm*, and ya allow for my mistakes—and so long as I'm not alone with ya in situations that might raise the preachers' eyebrows," she added in a purposeful voice, "it won't be any different from what a lot of other Plain gals do to earn some income."

Why did her reply pique his interest in ways it shouldn't? Andy sat back, reminding himself that this interview with Rhoda was strictly business. "We need to talk about your pay. I've not hired anyone in this capacity before, so—"

"I don't have the foggiest notion what other caretakers make," she admitted. "Truth be told, I'm not considerin' this job because I need the money. I just wanna try somethin' *different*, ya know?"

Her refreshing attitude appealed to him. "That's exactly why I got into nurse's training after being a teacher. My wife had just left me, so the timing wasn't the best," he admitted. "But our school in New Haven's so small, I would've been my daughter's fourth-grade teacher next year. So—"

Rhoda chuckled. "I wouldn't have wanted my *dat* for a schoolteacher," she agreed. "And for you, the lines might've blurred between bein' a parent and then puttin' on a whole different hat once ya got to school, dealin' with everybody else's kids."

Oh, but this young woman was a breath of fresh air. Insightful and articulate, too—the right example for his kids. And Rhoda Lantz wouldn't be bringing her boyfriend over to fool around or to help himself to the fridge, as some of their babysitters had done.

"Tell you what, Rhoda. Maybe the next step should be introducing you to my family. Letting you look around the house, before we seal the deal," Andy suggested. "That way you'll see what you're getting into. And if Taylor or Brett or Mom seem uncomfortable with you—which I can't imagine— we'll know it's not the right thing to do."

"*Jah*, I can do that!"

Andy suspected there weren't too many things Rhoda Lantz *couldn't* do. Her enthusiasm was contagious. "I can take you there now, or—"

"Ah, but then I'm ridin' in an English fella's car, with neither of us bein' married," she pointed out. "Best for me to take down your address. I'll call a driver—"

"But I hate that you'll have to pay someone to come over."

Rhoda shrugged. "It's how we Amish get around . . . unless ya want my horse poopin' in your yard. Now *that* would be a chore like your kids've never had, cleanin' it up."

Andy got carried away on a belly laugh like he hadn't enjoyed for months. "All right, but I'll pay for your ride and we'll work such an allowance into your wage. It's only fair." He took a pen from his jacket pocket and wrote his address on a napkin.

When Rhoda's gaze wandered toward the café's kitchen, a secretive grin twitched at her lips. "How about if I show up around four thirty or five? That'll give me time to line up my ride, and you can warn your family about somebody Plain comin' to look them over."

"Hah! It'll give us time to scramble around and clean things up, so you won't think we're total slobs." He stood up, extending his hand. "Rhoda, it's been a pleasure. See you in a couple hours."

"*Denki* for givin' me a chance at this."

Again her rhythmic way of speaking tickled his ear, and

when Andy turned to go he had another pleasant surprise. Miriam was coming from the kitchen with a large pumpkin pie in her hands.

"Not the same as a Thanksgiving dinner," she said, "but I'd like your family to have it, Andy. God bless ya. Especially your mother as she's recoverin' from her stroke."

His eyes misted over. "What a wonderful gesture," he murmured, barely able to get the words out. "And please let me know if my hiring Rhoda, or her hours or traveling back and forth—or *anything*—doesn't set right with you, Miriam."

"*Jah*, I can do that, Andy." She put the pie in a cardboard box.

Rhoda's earlier words took on a different tone when her mother spoke them, but all was still well. As he drove away from the Sweet Seasons with a fragrant pie on the passenger seat, lilting Amish voices and open smiles replayed in his mind. He had no doubt that the Lantz women could do anything they decided to, and for the first time since Megan had walked out on him, Andy felt that he could accomplish wonderful things, as well.

"Bye, now—and thanks for makin' it a real *gut* day, Hannah," Miriam said as Naomi and her daughter put on their coats. "If you want to keep workin' with us, I'm thinkin' it would be just fine."

"*Jah*, I'm likin' it," the young blonde replied with a smile that resembled Naomi's. "See ya tomorrow."

Miriam waved at Ben Hooley, who was loading equipment into his big horse-drawn farrier's wagon. Then she closed the café's back door against the cold wind. Powdery snow had blown up against the phone shanty, giving it a bit of sparkle around the edges in the afternoon's last rays of sunlight . . . similar to the sparkle on Rhoda's face while she'd been talking to Andy Leitner. Miriam decided to tread carefully, for—just like the surfaces of the ponds hereabouts—the ice was thinner, more fragile, than it looked.

"So are ya gonna tell me more about wantin' this job?" she asked quietly.

Bless her heart, Rhoda was leaning against the counter with her hands clasped. She'd looked this way when she was a child who'd tried something mischievous and only admitted to it when she'd been caught. While Rachel had usually escaped discipline by reporting the pranks everyone else had pulled, Rhoda had been more adventurous . . . more willing to take the dares and then own up to them. Her cheeks were pink, but she met Miriam's gaze. Her blue eyes twinkled like her *dat*'s had, so much so that Miriam sometimes wondered if this was Jesse's way of keeping in touch from heaven.

"I was pokin' around at the Zooks' store, waitin' for Levi and Cyrus to load the carriage, and a little note on the bulletin board caught my eye." Rhoda shrugged, her grin edged with eagerness. "It seems like somethin' new to do, what with you hitchin' up with Ben, and—"

"I know we bother ya with our flirtin'," Miriam said gently. "And ya miss your sister, and now that she's hitched, ya miss bein' in the big house ya were born in. All manner of things have changed these past few months." She sighed, choosing her words carefully. "And it grieves my heart that the local fellas pass ya up for girls who don't have half your smarts or your *gut* nature."

"Oh, Mamma, I didn't mean for ya to think I've been unhappy or—"

"A mother's eyes don't miss much, honey-bug. Truth be told, it might be *gut* for ya to try out this new type of work—as long as ya figure out the comin's and goin's, and ya realize that everything we do brings on consequences we can't always predict."

"*Jah*, there's that," Rhoda agreed. "I'll call Sheila Dougherty to take me to the Leitners' this afternoon. I hope she and I can work out my rides, once I know what my hours'll be. And—"

"Sheila's a *gut* woman. Always gets me where I need to go."

"—I thought I'd take some supper along to go with that pumpkin pie ya sent," Rhoda continued in a rising voice. "We've got some turkey left, and stuffing and yams. And the green bean casserole'll taste a whole lot better tonight than if we warm it over to serve tomorrow!"

Miriam opened her arms. "How can I object if ya want to share with a family who missed out on Thanksgiving dinner?" she murmured. "I'm pleased ya thought of them. But then, you've done me proud all your life, Rhoda. Truly ya have."

"Oh, Mamma."

As they hugged, Miriam reveled in the solid warmth of her daughter's body, thankful they could share such affection. She would miss chatting with Rhoda at meals and as she cleaned her new house and did laundry, or as she sat down to darn stockings or crochet for an evening—not that Ben hadn't invited Rhoda to claim a room in their home across the road. But life marched on. Miriam was stepping lively these days, engaged to a fine man a few years younger than she, and for this new love in her life she was ever so grateful to God.

Rhoda would find her way. Miriam had never doubted that. And maybe this caretaking job with an English family would open up a new world of possibilities none of them could have foreseen. The Lord often worked out His purpose in unusual ways.

"Well, then," she said as she released her daughter. "Let's see about that day-after-Thanksgiving dinner. Better to take it in pans ya can slip into their oven, so's ya don't have to find cookin' equipment in a strange kitchen, ain't so?"

Rhoda's smile shone like a rainbow after a downpour. "That's what I was thinkin', too, Mamma. Thanks for understandin' what I meant—what I needed—before I could find the way to say it."

Chapter Three

"Denki, Sheila. I'll call ya when I'm ready to go home." Rhoda pulled a five-dollar bill from her coat pocket and tucked it into the console of the van. "Nice talkin' to ya on the way over."

"Good luck as you look things over," her driver replied. "I take several ladies to jobs like this, and you'll be especially good at tending those kids, Rhoda. That dinner you brought smells so good, how can they help but love you?"

How can they help but love you?

Sheila's words boosted Rhoda's confidence as she followed the narrow sidewalk toward a house that stood shoulder-to-shoulder with other homes built in a bygone era. The neighbors seemed too close for comfort—why, you could pass a pie from your kitchen window to the one next door. But then, she'd grown up on a farm . . . and she wasn't here to judge how the Leitners lived. She was here to help.

Rhoda was raising her hand to ring the bell when the door opened. Andy stood there smiling at her. "Rhoda! You found us!"

"Jah, your directions were perfectly—"

"Dad, is it her? Is it Rhoda the Rodent?" a young boy called out.

"Brett, stop it! That's disgusting!" a girl replied indignantly. "If she doesn't stay, it'll be all your fault!"

Andy's expression waxed apologetic. "Welcome to my world, Rhoda. Anything and everything can be said or done, at any given moment."

"Isn't that the way of it, when you've got little children?" she said as she stepped inside.

"Who's little? I'm seven and a half—and bright for my age, too!" A boy with a mop of dark curls gazed at her from behind glasses that would have made him look like a serious scholar if it weren't for the plastic eyeballs dangling on springs.

Rhoda laughed. "So, Brett the Baryonyx," she challenged. "Your *dat*'s told me all about how ya terrorize your sister and play tricks on your poor grandma. Ya might be a killer dinosaur who's thirty-two feet long with claws of nearly twelve inches, but ya don't scare me one little bit."

Brett yanked off the funny glasses to gawk at her. "You know about dinosaurs?"

"For sure and for certain." Rhoda glanced at the girl, a little older, who assessed her from behind Brett. "It's nice to meet you, too, Miss Taylor. Does it smell so *gut* in here because you're bakin' cookies?"

She nodded cautiously, which made the ponytail at her crown bob in its pink ribbon. "You talk kinda funny."

"Depends on whose ears are doin' the listenin'," Rhoda said with a shrug. "Everybody I know talks this way on account of how we all learn German—we call it Pennsylvania Dutch—at home. Didn't speak English until I started to school, ya see. Ya might want to check your cookies, ain't so?"

Taylor's eyes widened and then she dashed toward the

back of the house. Brett scurried behind her, hollering, "I'm not gonna eat the burnt ones, Tay! Those'll be all for you."

Andy squeezed the bridge of his nose. "Most times they're not quite so, um, *charming*. But you handled them like a pro, Rhoda."

Heat crept into her cheeks as he took her coat. "I grew up dealin' with all manner of cousins and neighborhood kids, ya know. The fellas on the Willow Ridge school board asked if I'd be their teacher, but that was right after Dat had passed and Mamma was startin' up the Sweet Seasons."

"Any second thoughts about leaving the café to help us out? No hard feelings if you want to keep working there," he said, watching her reaction. "But I really, really hope you'll stay and take care of us."

Rhoda's heart skittered in her chest. "What a nice thing to say. I—"

"A man in my position, working crazy shifts and finishing his degree, can't just be *nice* when he's hiring someone to care for his mom and keep his kids out of reform school. I'm watching out for my own sanity." Andy glanced at the big picnic hamper she'd carried in. "That smells so good, do I dare to hope it's dinner? I could offer you frozen pizza, but—"

"We had turkey and the fixin's left from our lunch shift today. Mamma wanted ya to have a little Thanksgiving dinner because, well—" She smiled up at him, noting how he stood head and shoulders taller than she did. "Every day's a chance to be thankful, for every little thing God's given us, ain't so? And I'm thankful for this chance to check out your kids and a whole new way to spend my days."

Andy gazed at her with eyes of the deepest, darkest brown she'd ever seen. "You're awesome, you know it? The answer to a prayer—when I didn't think I had a prayer," he added with a sigh. "Come on back and meet Mom. She's feeling a little puny today."

"How about if I tuck these pans into the oven first? I'll just be a minute."

Was it too nervy, heading off in the same direction Taylor and Brett had disappeared? Through the front room she went with her basket, noting various shoes and schoolbooks scattered around furniture that was showing some wear . . . smelling cookies that had indeed spent too long in the oven.

She stopped in the kitchen doorway. The countertop was strewn with a hand mixer, a dough-smeared bowl, and the ingredients Taylor had used. The poor girl was scraping blackened cookies off a baking sheet with a knife nearly as big as she was. Tears dribbled down her cheeks.

Rhoda slipped an arm around Taylor's shaking shoulders. "Ya know," she murmured, "if I had a perfect cookie for every one of them I've burned—mostly because something interesting distracted me for too long—why, I could open a bakery with them! Just takes practice and patience, honey-bug."

Taylor, somewhere around nine years old, was a thin little pixie and, bless her, she'd styled her hair herself . . . because who could help her, if her mother was gone and her grandma could hardly hold a comb? "Dad says you do have a bakery. I—I just wanted to make something for when you came—"

"And isn't that thoughtful? I can't recall the last time somebody made cookies because I was comin'." Rhoda picked up the blackened half of a chocolate-chip cookie that had fallen to the counter, but when she raised it to her lips, Taylor snatched it.

"Don't eat that yucky one! I'll make you a good one, Rhoda."

Rhoda grinned at her. "Now there's a better idea! Would it be okay if I tucked some pans in your oven first, though?

So we can share some turkey dinner and get to know one another?"

"You brought turkey dinner? Like, for Thanksgiving?" Taylor's eyes lit up behind her tears.

"*Jah*, today at the café we cooked turkey and green bean casserole and yams and stuffing—"

"Oh, I love all that stuff. But since Mom's been gone . . ."

Rhoda's heart tightened painfully. How could any woman leave such a precious daughter? "Things change for everybody. And sometimes it's all we can do to figure out what comes next," she remarked. "I bet you've been tryin' to cook and clean up, now that your grandma's sick, and it's a big job for a little girl, ain't so?"

Taylor nodded somberly.

"Can ya clear the table and set out plates for us, while I meet your grandma?"

"Uh-huh. I set the table all the time."

"See there? You're takin' care of the family, doin' what needs to be done," Rhoda assured her as she slipped her pans of warm food into the oven. "Your *dat*'s mighty proud of ya, too, for holdin' up your end when times get tough."

The little girl's eyes widened, another set of deep, dark eyes like Andy's. "He told you that?"

Rhoda closed the oven door. "He didn't have to," she replied as she leaned down to whisper in Taylor's ear. "I can read his mind, ya see. I know what he's thinkin'."

"You do?" Taylor considered this for a moment. "Mom used to always be yellin' about how he was so impossible to figure out. Or to live with."

"Oh, honey-bug, I'm sorry." Rhoda rested her forehead on Taylor's, wondering if she'd opened a tricky can of worms, talking as though she really knew what Andy Leitner—or any man—was thinking. If that were true, would she still be single at twenty-one, feeling pinched about her possibilities for marriage? "I'll see your grandma real quick, and then we'll put dinner on. If I take this job, I'll need your help findin' things around the kitchen. And I'll want ya to tell me how the house should look, and—"

"I'll be the best helper you ever had, Rhoda. Promise!" Taylor nodded decisively. "Go see Gram, and when you come back, everything'll be ready for dinner—mostly because Brett left when he saw all the cookies were burnt."

Rhoda squeezed her shoulders. "See there? Every cloud has a rainbow, ain't so?"

As she left the kitchen, she glanced at what her family would have used as a dining room. Computer desks stood against two of the walls . . . most likely one computer for the kids and one for Andy. Family portraits on the wall showed the four Leitners fairly recently, as well as when Taylor was a toddler and Brett couldn't have been a year old.

Rhoda stepped closer, to see what sort of woman Andy's wife had been. She seemed sleek and blond and glamorous— at least by Plain standards—yet she was focused in a different direction from the others, her eyes not looking toward the camera like the rest of her family's.

"Those photographs stab at me," Andy said softly. "But I don't have the heart to take them down. It's all the kids have left of their mom."

Was Andy feeling guilty about the breakup of his marriage? It wasn't a topic Rhoda wanted to get into, even though she was curious about why the children lived with their dad instead of their mother.

"I can't fathom how that must feel," she said with a rueful smile. "We Amish don't believe in divorce, so I've not known anybody who's gone through this—well, except for Preacher Tom. His wife ran off with a fella in a fancy car, without so much as a how-do-ya-do. But his kids are all grown and married, so that's a horse of a different color."

Andy's smile went lopsided. "Well, the good news is that Mom wanted to meet you badly enough that she got out of bed. She's resting in the living room."

Rhoda hoped she didn't appear anxious or fearful. Would she be able to assist a lady who'd suffered a stroke? The only disabled person she knew was Naomi's husband, Ezra Brenneman, who'd fallen through the roof of a house he'd been building. Ezra was confined to a wheelchair, and because of phantom pain in his missing legs he was an unpleasant man most of the time. "I feel honored she's made such an effort on my account."

Rhoda preceded Andy into the front room. The woman seated in an armchair wore a deep pink robe that had come untied, and her slippers were on the wrong feet. Yet her smile looked so hopeful . . . at least on the side of her face that hadn't sagged. Oh, how hard it must be for the kids to see their gram this way. And how difficult it must be—how frustrating—for this poor soul to be trapped inside a body that had betrayed her.

"Mom, this is Rhoda Lantz, the Amish girl I was telling you about," Andy said loudly. "Remember that little bakery in Willow Ridge where we got those fabulous cinnamon rolls? She and her mom run that place!"

"Oh, that's so . . . nice," the woman said with obvious difficulty. Her eyes brightened, though, and she reached out the hand that still functioned properly.

Rhoda's heart knotted in her throat. She knelt as she grasped that outstretched hand, so Andy's mother could focus on her better.

"This is my mom, Betty Leitner," he said. "She came to help us out after Megan left, and well . . . stuff happened. But she's a lot stronger than she was last month at this time."

"And I'm happy to hear that part," Rhoda responded, grasping the withered hand between hers. Was Betty sixty or

ninety? With her uncombed hair sticking out in tufts and the
dry skin on legs that weren't quite covered by her robe, it
we s difficult to judge.

But what did it matter how old she was? Rhoda smiled up
at her. "What would any of us do without our mothers and
grandmothers?" she mused aloud. "My *mamm* sends ya her
best—along with some Thanksgiving dinner! Can ya smell
it in the oven?"

Betty inhaled deeply. "Ohhhh. Stuffing."

"I bet those mashed yams and green beans'll be just the
thing. And if we have to help ya cut your turkey, well, that's
easy enough to do. Ya like turkey and stuffing?"

"Yup."

Rhoda released Betty's hand and stood up. "Taylor said
she'd have the table set for us when we got back to the
kitchen. Shall we see how she did?"

As they started toward the kitchen, Rhoda watched Andy
offer his mother an arm . . . observed how he helped her up,
yet let Betty stand and then walk by herself. The thunder of
fast footsteps descending the stairs announced Brett's arrival, but he carefully went around his grandmother before
darting past Rhoda.

"Rhoda the Raptor," he teased under his breath.

"Brett the Brontosaurus," she replied in the same low
voice, pleased the boy had responded to her dinosaur game.
This back-and-forth would be to her advantage when she
had to give him some discipline—and that day would come
as surely as the sun would rise tomorrow.

Rhoda stepped into the kitchen ahead of Andy and his
mother. She flashed a big smile at Taylor. "What a perty
table, with all the plates at their places and your handprint
turkeys as our centerpiece," she said. "*Denki*, Taylor—which
is *thank you* in our language."

"No problem," the girl replied with a grin.

Rhoda paused before opening the oven door. "Ya know, I hear English folks say that in the café, and I'm not sure it fits," she said in a pensive tone. "When ya tell me it was no problem to do somethin', it makes me feel like it *was* a problem—or at least an inconvenience to ya—but ya managed to rise above it."

"Yup," Betty joined in as she shuffled toward a place near the end of the table. She smiled at Rhoda with one side of her face. "Always make . . . the other person . . . feel welcome. Important."

"Good call, Mom," Andy agreed as he held out her chair. "Making people feel important is, well—*important*. Respect never goes out of style, even when you're dealing with your brother or sister . . . or the person cooking your dinner." He looked directly at Rhoda until she returned his gaze. "And dinner smells fabulous, Rhoda. Thank you so much for your thoughtfulness."

Rhoda flushed. "You're welcome," she replied happily. "My *mamm* says it's her mission to feed people. I'll pass along your thanks."

Brett had followed this conversation with a wary expression as he took his seat. "So what's *your* mission, Rhoda the Raccoon?"

Now there was a question she hadn't expected from a boy Brett's age! And she'd learned not to dodge an important issue when a child asked about it.

"Well, Brett the Bear," she answered as she placed a steaming pan of sliced turkey on the table, "I believe I was born to help folks, whether it be cookin' for them or gettin' them to laugh off their troubles and keep goin'. We all have a lot of *gut* reasons for bein' on God's earth. And the sooner we figure out what our purpose is, why, the easier it is for us to be truly happy with our life."

"And are you happy with your life, Rhoda?" Taylor asked

as she carried the basket of fresh bread to the table. "I . . . I don't think I'd like wearing dresses like yours, or having that funny little hat on my head all the time."

"Taylor, that's enough of such talk," Andy warned, but Rhoda kept smiling. She took the chair Taylor had gestured toward, pleased that it was the seat beside hers.

"Most English folks—those are families like yours, who aren't Amish or Mennonites," she explained, "have a hard time understandin' Plain ways. Sometime I'll tell ya whatever ya want to know, all right? But for now, I'm hungry, for sure and for certain. Shall we pray?"

Brett's eyes widened, but Taylor bowed her head and pressed her hands together at her chin.

"God is good, God is great," the girl recited. "Let us thank Him for our food. Amen."

It pleased Rhoda that prayer was already a part of the Leitner family's mealtime. And who wouldn't be gratified at the way these children dove into the mashed yams and green bean casserole? Betty was slowly feeding herself with her good hand, opening her mouth as best she could, and Andy . . . well, Rhoda had watched a lot of fellows eat at the Sweet Seasons, but none of them had worn an expression of such utter bliss. With each bite he took, the man at the head of the table closed his eyes to savor the juicy turkey . . . the stuffing with its apples and pecans . . . the creamy green bean casserole . . . the warm, chewy bread he slathered with the butter she had brought.

"Now *this* is Thanksgiving dinner," he murmured when he'd eaten about half the food he'd taken. "I think I speak for all of us when I say I hope you'll come here to help—"

"Yeah, do it, Rhoda! Please and thank you!" Brett piped up.

"We really, really need you," Taylor murmured earnestly.

"—but even if you decide it won't work," Andy continued

quietly, "you've blessed us with your food and your presence today, Rhoda. And for that we're thankful."

"Amen to . . . that," Betty rasped as she reached for another piece of bread.

Now that they'd all pleaded for her to stay, how could she not take this job? Rhoda swallowed hard. Ordinarily she discussed important decisions with Mamma or Rachel, but they weren't here, were they? And she couldn't possibly replay this shining moment for them later.

But this wasn't a position she could agree to today and then decide, in a week or two, that it wasn't her cup of tea. If she said yes, she'd be committing herself . . .

Four sets of eyes held her hostage. Wasn't it a fine thing that this family had so immediately accepted her—said they *needed* her—without having to confer among themselves? For months she'd been feeling like a fifth wheel on a buggy, out of balance and superfluous, yet in less than an hour with these folks she'd found a way to be *useful*. At the Sweet Seasons, she took orders and wrote the menu on the whiteboard and cleared tables, only to do it again and again. Here she could make a difference—she could make life better for every one of these people.

"Jah," she said. "I'd like to come work for ya."

"YAY!" Brett hollered, while beside her, Taylor clapped her hands. Betty's face took on an endearing smile of gratitude even though half of her features remained slack.

And Andy . . . Andy let out a sigh and closed his eyes. "Thank you, God," he whispered.

The kitchen went still. It felt like a holy moment as they all considered what had just happened.

Lord, Ya brought me here for this very reason, ain't so? Rhoda prayed as she met each of the Leitners' eyes. *Please help us all remember this special day—this special feeling— when things aren't goin' so gut.*

"I promise I'll be your best helper," Taylor vowed.

"And I won't call you Rhoda the Rodent ever again," Brett declared solemnly. "Cross my heart and hope to die."

"Ya can't die, Brett," Rhoda replied with a straight face. "Think how the house will smell—what a mess you'll make when the maggots start munchin' on your guts. I for one refuse to clean it up."

"Eeeewwww," Taylor said with a grimace.

A snicker made Rhoda look up. Lo and behold, Betty was quivering with the effort it took for her to giggle.

"Not a pretty sight, Son," Andy agreed. "But we all appreciate the sentiment behind what you said. And we're all ecstatic that Rhoda thinks she can put up with us."

He gazed at her warmly, his smile framing his eyes and lips with laugh lines. "Can you start tomorrow?"

Chapter Four

Saturday morning Miriam watched Sheila Dougherty's van pull away, and she let out a concerned sigh. Rhoda had come in before dawn, as always, to set up the tables and help get the breakfast shift going, but now that the Brenneman boys and her nephews were on their second trip to the buffet, while Tom Hostetler; Gabe Glick; her fiancé, Ben; and a few other regulars were eating at their usual tables, service was starting to slip. Bless her heart, Hannah had only been on the job for a few days, and it was clear she did better at cooking than she did at waiting tables.

Grabbing a carafe from the coffeemaker, Miriam saw that another batch of coffee hadn't been set up—something the twins did like clockwork during the morning rush. As she was pouring in the water, the bell above the door jangled. Eight folks from the senior center in Morning Star shuffled in out of the cold.

"Be with ya in two shakes of a tail," she called over to them. Hannah had an anxious look on her face, because none of the remaining empty tables would seat that group.

Ben, bless him, realized her predicament. He signaled to Seth and Aaron Brenneman and together they scooted three small tables together. Hannah scurried to set bundles of silverware in place. "*Gut* mornin' to ya!" Ben said as he gestured for the group to be seated. "Nice to see everybody out and about on such a cold mornin', ready for a hot breakfast!"

Miriam flashed Ben a grateful smile. Hannah hadn't made it around to refill any coffee mugs—but there was only the one of her when most times both Rachel and Rhoda bustled about taking care of such jobs.

Lord, help us stay cheerful, she prayed as she approached the table where the two preachers sat. *And bless my Rhoda as she starts her new job, too. It was so* gut *to see the sparkle in her eyes when she told me about the Leitner family.*

Gabe Glick, the oldest preacher in Willow Ridge, held up his mug as she approached. "You seem to be shorthanded this morning, Miriam. Hope Rhoda's not under the weather."

She poured his coffee and refilled Tom Hostetler's, as well, considering her reply. When the church elders heard why Rhoda wasn't here, they might ask all manner of questions. And of course they would share their information with the bishop, Hiram Knepp. "Thanks for askin'," Miriam replied breezily. "She's tryin' out a new job, takin' care of an English gal who's had a stroke—a lot like Doris Hilty and the Wagler sisters do, caretakin' and housekeepin'," she remarked.

Hearing his name, Matthias Wagler glanced in their direction. "Rhoda'll be right *gut* at that," he remarked. "My sisters never seem to run out of places to work, once English folks get word of how dependable Amish women are."

Preacher Gabe, who nowadays looked older than his eighty-some years, bowed his head. "Gonna have to get a gal like that for my Wilma, most likely," he murmured sadly. "Gettin' so I can't help her outta bed anymore."

Preacher Tom was following this topic with great interest.

"I had an aunt who worked at that sort of job for years, cleanin' mostly," he said. "What with Rachel off collectin' wedding gifts, it sounds like the chicks are all flyin' from your nest at the same time, Miriam."

"*Jah*, you could say that. Can I get ya anything else?" When the bell jangled again, Miriam saw how flustered Hannah was looking as she seated the English couple who came in. Only two empty tables remained.

"We're fine, Miriam." Tom gazed around the dining room. "Your café's gettin' busier all the time, like more folks are hearin' about this place."

Miriam headed over to the table of eight from the senior center. Could it be that the website her other daughter had set up was already attracting more customers? Rebecca, raised English after she'd been lost downriver as a toddler, had caused quite a stir when she'd returned to Willow Ridge last summer. Her advanced schooling in computers and graphic design would probably increase traffic at a lot of Plain businesses in Willow Ridge.

"And what can I get for you folks on this fine mornin'? Who's ready to start?" she asked as she fetched an order pad from the front counter. Most of these seniors came here a couple of times a month to eat, and even though the menu choices hadn't changed since the Sweet Seasons opened, they still took a long time to decide.

Their driver, Connie, winked at Miriam. "It might take us a minute."

"Somebody'll be back in a few, then. You folks take your time," Miriam insisted. "Cold as it is today, the hens won't lay your eggs until you're *gut* and ready!"

A few chuckles followed her into the kitchen, where Naomi was loading plates into the dishwasher—yet another task Rachel usually took care of. "Is it me, or are we chasin' our tails and not catchin' them this morning?" Miriam murmured.

"*Jah*, only eight o'clock," Naomi replied, "and I'm cookin' up a bunch more sausage to make another pan of breakfast casserole." She glanced toward the dining room. "Tell me straight-out, Miriam. Will Hannah be able to handle all this commotion, or should we be lookin' to hire another girl or two for out front? If you and I can't keep cookin' and bakin', why, runnin' outta food's gonna be a problem like we've not had before."

"Ya got that right, partner." Miriam helped Naomi carry the chubs of bulk sausage over to the stove. It was a tricky question to answer, because the two of them had been close friends since long before they opened the café together. "Hannah's doin' the best she can," she finally replied. "Another week or two of waitin' tables with Rhoda and Rachel would've been better, but there's no help for that."

When the timer dinged, Miriam grabbed hot pads and removed two large pans of sticky buns from the oven. As she stirred milk into a bowl of powdered sugar to make a glaze, she glanced out the pass-through window into the dining room.

Once again Ben had come to her rescue: he stood at the checkout, ringing up bills as Tom, Gabe, and Matthias got ready to leave, because Hannah hadn't yet mastered the cranky old adding machine.

Lord, I thank Ya for bringin' Ben Hooley into my life, she prayed as she drizzled glaze on the hot rolls, *but he's got his own work. We need to solve this problem mighty quick—not that I'm ungrateful that You've made the café so successful*, she added.

After all, how many times had she talked to God when they had first opened, wondering if anyone from outside of Willow Ridge would ever find them? They fed Naomi's sons and Miriam's nephews each morning as payment for her sister Leah Kanagy's gardening and Naomi's working here, so it took a lot of paying customers to compensate for what those five strapping young fellows devoured each day.

Hannah burst into the kitchen, ready to cry. "All the tables are full," she whimpered, "and those old people from the senior center are takin' *forever* to decide, so I can't wait on the ones who just came in and everybody's gettin' impatient about coffee refills, and meanwhile Nate and Bram and my brothers are sittin' there with tables fulla dirty dishes, eyeballin' me like I've got two heads and—"

Miriam squeezed the girl's shoulders. Poor Hannah looked like a mouse cornered by so many cats she didn't know which way to turn. "Take it easy, honey-bug," she said in a soothing voice. "Do just one thing at a time. If you pour coffee and water for everybody, I'll take the orders. We'll get through this shift and when folks're gone, we'll figure out who else can help us, all right?"

Hannah glanced doubtfully at her mother. Miriam suspected that if Naomi hadn't given her daughter a steady, stern look from where she stood frying up three skillets of sausage, Hannah might have raced out the back door never to return.

The young blonde drew a shuddery breath and nodded obediently. She headed for the coffeemaker.

"*Denki*, Hannah," Miriam murmured as she strode out to take the orders. "You're a *gut* girl and we're glad you're with us."

As Miriam returned to the table of eight, the bell above the door jangled again and in strode the bishop. Hiram Knepp cut an imposing figure as he stood surveying the crowded dining room in his broad-brimmed black hat and overcoat.

The chatter quieted. The bishop was under the ban for his secret ownership of a car, so Plain folks weren't to eat at the same table with him until his confession and reinstatement, come mid-December. He was still a customer in her café, however, so Miriam couldn't ignore him. "Mornin' to ya, Hiram," she called over. "I'll be right with ya."

Once again Ben came to her rescue. At his whispered suggestion, the two Brenneman brothers and the Kanagy boys stacked their dishes into the dishpan Ben brought over. Bram grabbed a rag to wipe down their tables and then cleared the one where the two preachers had eaten, as well.

"Quite a crowd today," the bishop remarked as he hung his coat by the door. "Are Tom and Gabe already gone?"

"*Jah*, they left a few minutes ago. What can I bring ya?" While Miriam figured Hiram could wait his turn, same as everyone else in this crowd, she knew she'd hear about it after his ban had been lifted.

"I'm meeting with a buyer for some of my Belgians in half an hour. I'll help myself to the buffet." Hiram took the outer aisle to avoid squeezing between the crowded tables, nodding rather than speaking to members of his congregation.

No doubt the bishop would wonder why Ben and the other fellows were bussing tables, but Miriam couldn't be concerned about that: she patiently wrote the orders for the senior center table, all of them on separate checks. After she greeted the customers who had just taken a seat, she took the long list of new orders back to the kitchen.

"How's my Hannah holdin' it together out there?" Naomi asked as she drained sausage on paper towels. Stirred-up eggs and milk waited in a big glass pitcher, and cubed bread had already been sprinkled with cheese in a steam-table pan. Miriam smiled gratefully at her partner's efficiency.

"I think we'll keep her through today's lunch, anyway," she replied. "But we need *gut* help and mighty quick, in case this rush keeps up. I'd best go out and speak to Hiram. He'll be askin' where Rhoda is."

Miriam plated orders for two of the tables and then

stepped out into the dining room with her loaded tray. Even if the morning was hectic, wasn't it a fine thing to see every chair filled? As she set steaming food in front of a young English couple, their expressions gratified her. "Enjoy your breakfast now, and have a real *gut* day," she said as she left the tab on the table.

"We found your café online and couldn't wait to try it!" the young woman remarked.

"Yeah, this looks fabulous!" her husband said as he grabbed his fork. "Getting this much home-cooked breakfast for such a great price sure beats the chain places. Makes it worth our drive."

"I'll pass that along to the young lady who designed our website," Miriam replied with a pleased nod. After she delivered orders to another table of four, noting how Ben was ringing up the folks who were leaving, she considered what she would say to Rebecca. Was the website bringing in more business than they could handle? The bishop's expression told her to refill his coffee next. Hannah was dutifully setting up the cleared tables for more customers, probably too intimidated to pour the shunned bishop's coffee—or afraid she'd spill it on him.

"And how are things at the Knepp house this morning?" Miriam asked as she approached his table.

"Jerusalem insists that the kids arrive at the breakfast table on time, and that I preside over the meal," he remarked with a rise of his dark eyebrows. "All well and good, but I still have a business to run. And despite my ban, I need to see Tom and Gabe occasionally to keep abreast of our members' concerns."

Miriam smiled to herself: after a month of being shunned, Hiram was putting his own spin on the *Ordnung*'s rules for interaction with other folks. Jerusalem Hooley, Ben's aunt, had taken it upon herself to corral Hiram's unruly children while her sister, Nazareth, had restored order and tidiness to his home. Hiram was tolerating the *maidels'* assistance more patiently than most folks had figured he would. "Can I bring ya some eggs to go with your biscuits and gravy?"

Glancing up as the bell jangled again, Hiram shook his head. "What I've got here is fine, thanks. Looks like you're short a couple of daughters today, but your third one just came in."

Miriam flashed Rebecca a grin, pleased that her non-Amish daughter headed on back to the kitchen as though she felt completely at home. "Rachel and Micah are visitin' with the kin around La Plata this weekend," she replied as she stacked the bishop's dirty dishes. "Makin' the most of their time as newlyweds, you see. Have a *gut* rest of your day, and give my best to your family."

Before Hiram could quiz her about Rhoda, Miriam wove her way between tables, asking folks how their food was. So many of these guests she'd never seen before . . . was it because she usually stayed in the kitchen, or because these people had recently discovered the Sweet Seasons online? As Miriam returned to the kitchen with two more orders, she smiled at Rebecca. It gave Miriam a special sense of sweetness when this daughter came to spend time with her. And what a relief that she'd stopped wearing black fingernails and leather bracelets with chains!

"You're lookin' perky in that aqua sweater, honey-bug," she remarked as she bussed Rebecca's cheek. "And I'm hearin' from a lot of folks out there that they found us on their computers, thanks to your website."

Rebecca grabbed an apron from the pegs on the back wall. "Looks like you could use another set of hands. Is Rhoda okay?"

"Oh, bless your heart," Miriam murmured. "Rhoda's

startin' a caretaker job for a fella over by New Haven. Sure seems excited about it, too."

"Seriously?" Rebecca gaped. "So with Rachel gone on weekends, and Hannah just starting out—"

"We're feelin' a little pinched, *jah*," Naomi chimed in. She poured the egg-and-milk mixture over the sausage, bread, and cheese she'd arranged in a big steam-table pan. "My Hannah's hoppin' around like a scared rabbit, not used to this kind of bustle yet. We'll be findin' another girl or two to help us out front, soon as we can."

Rebecca slipped an order pad into her apron pocket. "Where can I sign on? I don't have classes on Fridays or Saturdays this semester, and I graduate next month."

Miriam nearly dropped the tray of sticky buns she was carrying to the glass bakery case out front. "Oh, but I couldn't expect ya to quit what you're doin' and—"

"We couldn't pay ya what you'd make for your computer jobs, either," Naomi said with the same concern in her voice.

Rebecca hooked her arms around both their shoulders. "Just feed me some of your wonderful food." She kissed Miriam's cheek with loud enthusiasm. "You're my mamma, and I'm so glad I found you. I couldn't possibly work for pay."

When Rebecca scurried out to the dining room, Miriam exchanged a startled but ecstatic look with Naomi. "Now what do ya think about that? Seems God's answerin' prayers mighty quick today, ain't so?"

Chapter Five

Andy sat at the kitchen table watching a miracle: his kids were eating breakfast! Together, and without squabbling. The twinkle in Rhoda's eyes when she had lured them to sit down should've been his first clue that this young woman did indeed know how to handle children.

"It's Special Saturday," she announced as she stirred up a bowl of batter. The bacon was already arranged on a plate, which was the only invitation Andy needed to take his place. As though Rhoda sensed his son was the pickier eater, she wore a secretive smile as she poured batter onto the griddle.

"It's a B!" Brett exclaimed when she flipped the first pancake onto his plate. "And it's for me!"

"And here comes a T for your sister," Rhoda replied. "Seems to be an A on the griddle, too—but let's don't start eatin' until we've had a word with the Lord. Since ya got served first, will ya say our grace, Brett?"

Guilt flickered in Andy's chest. Years had passed since they had blessed their food. And why was that?

We so rarely sat down to a meal together when Megan was here.

But he couldn't blame everything on his ex. The sound of his son's voice repeating the grace he himself had said as a child made him vow to do better in the God department.

After the quick *amen*, both small hands grabbed for the syrup bottle, but Brett withdrew his. "After you, Taylor the Toad," he said in a debonair voice.

His sister's eyes widened as they did when she was ready to protest her brother's teasing, but then she demurely removed the bottle's cap. "Why, thank you, Brett the Baboon," she replied in a honeyed falsetto. "How very kind of you to wait."

Andy glanced down the table. Rhoda was smiling—and smearing peanut butter on her pancake, followed by some of the apple butter she'd brought from home. "May I please have the peanut butter when Rhoda's finished with it?" he asked.

Taylor poked a large bite of pancake into her mouth. "Who ever heard of peanut butter and jelly on pancakes? And you're gonna eat that, too, Dad?"

"Never hurts to try new things," he replied. "Adds some protein and fruit, instead of pouring on straight sugar. Is that the Amish way to eat pancakes, Rhoda?"

"It's the way I eat them," she said as she passed him the apple butter. "But then, my sister Rachel has always made fun of me for doing it, too."

One bite made a believer of him. The peanut butter added a richness, wonderfully complemented by apple butter that was darker and spicier than any he'd ever tasted. "Maybe we could entice Mom to the table for this—but don't wait on us," he added. He plucked a strip of bacon from the platter as he rose from his chair. "Might take her a while to come out if she's still asleep."

Andy realized he was feeling more lighthearted than he

had in a long, long time. No dull ache hovering behind his eyes. No knots in his stomach from juggling work and classes and fussy kids and an ailing mom. As he opened the downstairs bedroom door, another pleasant surprise awaited him, too: his mother sat in the chair beside her bed, putting on her slipper socks. Her hair looked like a gray haystack caught in a windstorm, but she'd gotten up without his nagging at her about eating regular meals.

She glanced at him. "Bacon?" she asked in a hopeful voice.

"It's the real deal, Mom," Andy replied as he stepped in to help her. "Rhoda's making pancakes. She's already got the kids eating out of her hand, too."

A clipped laugh escaped her. "Sounds . . . messy."

His brow furrowed—and then he got it! His mother had caught the old play on words and she'd played back. Andy slipped an arm around her as she started up out of her chair. "Actually, Rhoda straightened the kitchen and wiped down all the surfaces before she started to cook. *Messy* might be something that disappears from this house now. Can you imagine that?"

"Nope. Too hungry."

Andy's eyes widened. Here was yet another minor miracle: his mom wanted to eat! Was it wishful thinking, or was she walking a little faster, with more confidence, as they headed toward the kitchen?

"Gram, look! Alphabet pancakes!" Taylor crowed as they approached the table. "I got a T and then an L, for my initials!"

"I got a B and B, for Brett the Baboon!" his son chimed in. He was spreading peanut butter on his pancake, and he had fetched the grape jelly from the fridge.

"*My* pancake!" Andy's mother teased, pointing a wrinkled finger at Brett's plate.

"B is for Betty." Taylor glanced toward Rhoda, who was already pouring more pancakes. "But I don't think Brett's gonna share this one, Gram."

Andy took his seat again, content to watch this peaceful scene . . . letting the anger that had once filled this room fade from his memory, along with the vicious words his wife had hurled at him before she walked out. Megan had been a reluctant cook, at best. He could have tolerated her lack of culinary interest had she been more patient with the kids. More honest with him.

Wasn't it her brutal honesty that punched you in the gut? Things seemed comparatively easy when she lied about where she was really spending all those nights away from home.

As Rhoda approached him with more pancakes on a plate, Andy let go of the rancor such memories called up. How could he remain bitter when a kindhearted young woman was flipping an A and an L onto his plate, and a fancy cursive B onto his mother's?

His mom chortled with delight. And wasn't it the most wonderful thing, that her interest in everyday living had returned—at least for this meal?

"Thank you so much, Rhoda," he murmured as he watched his son jam another bite of pancake into his mouth. Even the smears of tan and purple around Brett's mouth seemed something to be thankful for—not to mention the way Taylor carried the bacon platter to her grandmother.

"You're quite welcome," Rhoda replied.

And weren't the simplest exchanges, the quiet niceties, fulfilling in themselves?

Why was making someone else's beds and cleaning someone else's bathrooms more fun than doing those same chores at home? Rhoda put the final load of clothes in the dryer, marveling at how quickly laundry got done when she didn't have to run the clothes through the wringer and hang them on hangers or a clothesline—and then fetch them inside frozen stiff. Although it hadn't taken but a moment for Andy to explain the controls on the electric washer and dryer, she reminded herself not to wish for such luxuries at home. She peeked into the room where the computers were, gratified to see Taylor dusting while her brother organized their games and something they called DVDs in the hutch where the children's computer sat.

"Rhoda, shall we talk for a moment? It's almost four o'clock and I need to pay you." Andy stood in the kitchen doorway, waiting for her.

"Where has the day gone? I'll start your dinner while we talk, if that's all right."

"All right?" he teased. "That's just the latest of the wonderful ideas you've had since you set foot in my home."

Rhoda glowed from the many compliments he'd paid her today. "Well, I won't be here tomorrow, ya know. Sundays are for spendin' time with the Lord and your family, even when there's no preachin' service."

Andy's eyes widened. "You don't go to church every Sunday?"

She shook her head as she chopped an onion over the hamburger she was browning in a large skillet. "Services'll be held at our house tomorrow, so we've been reddin' up the rooms and cookin' for the common meal that follows the preachin'. Might have a hundred-fifty folks there, so it takes a little gettin' ready."

"How on earth do you fit so many people into your home? And how do you feed them all?"

While his questions sounded incredulous, Rhoda sensed Andy Leitner was sincerely interested in her day-to-day life.

"When Amish folks build a home, a lot of the downstairs rooms have partition walls that come down," she explained. "That way, we can fit in all the pew benches and the tables where everybody eats afterwards. And believe me, after about three hours of church, sittin' on those hard wooden benches and kneelin' on the floor now and again, we're ready for movin' around while we set out the food!"

He was leaning against the counter, watching her stir the sizzling hamburger as he considered the Sunday morning ritual that had been a part of her life forever. "Three hours?" he murmured. "So where are the kids all that time? They surely don't sit through—"

"Oh, *jah*, they do," she said. "We're raised up to be quiet and prayerful during church, nappin' on our *mamm*'s or *dat*'s lap when we're wee little. As we get older, we listen to the preachin'. Or at least we figure out how to sit so folks *think* we're payin' attention!"

Andy's laughter filled the kitchen. "Your sense of humor surprises me, Rhoda. Most of us non-Amish people associate your plain, dark clothing with a stern personality."

Rhoda enjoyed the light that shone in his deep brown eyes. "We've got ya fooled, Andy. We Amish are really very happy people, for we find joy in every little task. And we work together instead of tryin' to do everything by ourselves."

His expression softened then. "Now there's a worthwhile idea," he reflected. Then he watched as she placed the cooked hamburger into a soup pot that already held chunks of cooked carrots and potatoes. "When did you find time to prepare this food, Rhoda? And how did you figure out what to make for us?"

She shrugged. "It's no different from goin' to the fridge in the Sweet Seasons of a morning, seein' what we've got on hand or what we need to use up," she remarked. "Ya had the meat in your freezer and the veggies handy, and a big can of tomato juice. Should be enough soup here for your supper tonight and another meal tomorrow, I'm thinkin'. I'll leave it simmerin' real low, so don't forget about it!"

His sigh made her look up. While it wasn't her place to speculate about Andy Leitner or his personal life . . . those had made for interesting topics to ponder while she'd been cleaning. He pulled his wallet from the hip pocket of his well-worn jeans.

"Would it be feasible for you to work weekday after-noons, so you'll be here when Taylor and Brett get home from school?" he asked. "Mom needs a nap by then. I'd feel a lot better if you were here to keep the kids from killing each other—or so my son won't blow up the kitchen with experiments from his favorite science kit."

"*Jah*, that's perfect! I can help Mamma at the café morn-ings, and come here to redd up and make sure you've got meals in the fridge that just need warmin'."

Once again Andy's expression told her of his relief and gratitude. "Rhoda, you're a godsend," he murmured. "You have no idea how you've lightened my load—not to mention how you've gotten my kids to cooperate. And you've made my mother smile."

When had anyone ever complimented her so profusely? While Rhoda knew better than to expect such praise for doing everyday tasks, she couldn't look away from Andy's earnest expression. He was an attractive man, head and shoulders taller than she, with thick brown hair trimmed well above his collar. He was seeking care for his ailing mother and trying to raise his children right, while completing his nursing degree. What a hardworking, honorable fellow he was . . . so why would any woman leave him?

None of your beeswax. Nor should ya think about keepin' him company.

And where had *that* thought come from? Rhoda focused on the soup she was stirring. He would be at the hospital most of the time she was here with his family, after all. That was for the best, because Hiram Knepp would be asking about this new job, deciding if it was proper work for her to do as a young, unmarried woman.

As Rhoda accepted the money Andy handed her, she let out a gasp. "Oh, my stars, this can't be right! I only—"

"Is that not enough?" He reached into his wallet again. "You were here eight hours today, and with minimum wage being more than seven dollars, I haven't even paid you—"

"Stop!" Rhoda pressed his hand down to keep the rest of his money in his wallet. "Fifty dollars is more than I've ever earned for—well, I'm *ferhoodled* at the thought you'd pay me this much!"

He relaxed. Smiled at her until little crinkles framed his chocolate-colored eyes. "There's that interesting word again," he said quietly. "Crazy mixed-up, are you? Well, to me you seem like a very sensible, industrious young woman, Rhoda. You earned every bit of this money today, what with helping Mom shower and style her hair, and getting the kids to eat and clean up their rooms, and—well, I stand in awe. Truly I do."

Rhoda's cheeks prickled and she looked away. "You're too kind, sayin' such things."

"I meant every word." He placed the money on the countertop . . . maybe so he wouldn't touch her again?

Does Andy feel little jolts through his system, too, when ya touch him? Or are ya bein' silly, gettin' a crush on this fella because he's so different from the Amish boys you've known all your life? If she was to continue working for Andy Leitner, she would have to keep closer watch on her feelings—and her imagination. "I'll call my ride now, if I may use your phone, please."

"Whatever's in my home is yours to use, Rhoda. Shall we set your hours at two o'clock until around seven, when I'll be home from my shift at the hospital?"

"*Jah*, that'll work just fine."

His smile warmed her like a cup of cocoa. "Thanks again. You have no idea how you've brightened my life."

And wasn't that a worthwhile accomplishment? All the way home, Rhoda replayed his words in her mind while Sheila drove her down the snow-packed blacktop.

It was wonderful-gut, *a fine day in so many ways, Lord*, she prayed between their bits of conversation. Rhoda gazed out the van's window as the Lantz place came into view, across the road from the new house Ben was having built for Mamma. *And I thank Ya for work that has made me so happy.*

Chapter Six

"This is such a cool apartment, Mamma!" Rebecca gazed at the pastels . . . soothing blue and green bedrooms and a sunny yellow in the kitchen. "These walls that roll on tracks to form different rooms are awesome! And to think Micah got his inspiration from watching a little movie clip on my iPad last summer."

"*Jah*, that was quite a time, honey-bug," her mother replied as she put on the teakettle. "We found *you*. And then we weren't quite sure what to do about it, when Micah caught trouble from the bishop for visitin' with ya."

"I'm glad that part's behind us," Rhoda joined in as she studied the contents of the refrigerator. "Rachel and I are real happy about how ya turned out to be our sister."

Closing her eyes, Rebecca reveled in the sincerity of these two accented, musical voices. While she had felt close to the mother who had raised her, it had been wonderful to discover her real roots. "I was quite a shock to your systems, showing up in my black clothes, with a tattoo and spiked hair," she recalled with a chuckle. "Just lucky you saw beneath my surface, when I felt so betrayed by my folks . . .

thought I had nowhere to turn, after Mom died and couldn't explain to me about that little pink dress I'd found."

"Oh, it was the hand of God at work, daughter," Miriam said with a firm nod. "His hand saved ya from drownin' when ya washed away in the river's current as a wee little toddler. And His hand led ya to find that dress—"

"And then to find *us*. And to like us, too!" Rhoda continued. "From what Mamma tells me, ya stepped right in, takin' orders during this morning's breakfast rush like ya were an old hand at it."

Rhoda flashed her a wide smile, so much like the one Rebecca saw in her mirror these days. She'd hidden her emotions behind the black hair dye and the pale Goth makeup that she, as Tiffany Oliveri, had believed was so dramatic, so flattering—until this Plain family had accepted her with their unconditional love. The name *Rebecca* felt more comfortable now, too—more in tune with who she was becoming, now that she'd gotten away from her former friends.

"Truth be told," she said, imitating their Pennsylvania Dutch version of English, "I waited tables while I was in college. So taking orders and clearing tables is no big deal to me."

"Well, I was mighty relieved to see ya step in that way," Mamma assured her again. "Poor Hannah was tryin' her best, but she works better in the kitchen with her *mamm*."

"She's young yet," Rebecca noted. "It's mind-boggling to juggle all those little waitressing tasks, until you're used to it."

"*Jah*, and I bet her older brothers Seth and Aaron, not to mention our cousins Nate and Bram Kanagy, were givin' her a hard time, too." Rhoda emptied a quart jar of home-canned green beans into a pan and sliced an onion into it. "They've got no idea how long they take—or how much they eat! And their chatter about their dates gets irritatin' when they go on and on as though I'm not in the room, too!"

"That sounds infuriating." Rebecca watched her sister's expressions as she vented. "So who does that?"

"Are ya talkin' about Ben's brothers?" Mamma gazed earnestly at her other daughter. "Ira and Luke've been gettin' nervy that way when they've come to the house, too. I was ready to say something to them on Thanksgivin', so I'll bring it up to Ben—"

"It's no bother, Mamma," Rhoda assured her quickly. "They can brag all they want about takin' Annie Mae Knepp and Millie Glick out. I've got bigger fish to fry!"

Rebecca laughed as she set three plates on the small table in the apartment's tidy kitchen. Rhoda had a freer sense of humor than their sister Rachel, and her spirit seemed more mischievous than Rebecca had expected of an Amish girl, too. "So how's your new job? Was it scary to work with a lady who'd had a stroke? Did the kids help you around the house, or were they a pain in the butt?"

Rhoda's smile defied description: a pinch of mystery and a dash of satisfaction mixed with a heaping helping of happiness. "Oh, Betty—Andy's *mamm*—is such a sweet lady, even if half her face is droopy," she said with a little shrug. "After I washed and combed her hair today, you'd have thought I made her face muscles snap back into place."

"No matter how hard Andy might try, it's not the same as havin' your hair fixed by somebody who halfway knows how." Mamma looked up from the platter of fried chicken she was about to warm in the oven. "The two kids are probably glad to have somebody lookin' after them, too, seein's how their *mamm*'s not around."

"*Jah*, I can't imagine how any woman could leave them." Rhoda shook her head. "They were so excited when I made pancakes in the shapes of their initials, like nobody had ever done that for them."

Rebecca considered that . . . because it was a clever idea that Rhoda had carried out as second nature. Nobody had ever made alphabet pancakes for *her*, either. It was her sister's kitty-cat grin that made her speculate, however: Rhoda seemed very happy about working in that English household, not to mention surprisingly tolerant of the way Ben's brothers had bragged about their conquests. "So what's the dad like? Did you say he was a nurse?"

"Almost finished with his schoolin', *jah*," Rhoda replied. "I'll have to ask him not to go on and on about the *gut* work I do for him, though. It's just not our way to get caught up in so many compliments, you see."

Oh, but Rhoda's grin was shining like a clean window-pane, at the mention of the man who had hired her. Rebecca filled their glasses with water. Whether she knew it or not, Rhoda was showing all the signs of a crush like the ones she'd had on a couple of her better-looking teachers in high school. Rebecca could well imagine what Hiram Knepp, the taut-jawed bishop, would say if he caught a hint of this . . . just as he would raise some pointed questions about her own private plan to return to Willow Ridge.

"I liked Andy, though," Mamma continued matter-of-factly. "Busy as he is, tryin' to finish his nursin' degree, he sincerely wants to take care of his kids and his *mamm*. Nothin's more important than faith and family, and Andy Leitner's got a boatload of faith even if he doesn't go around talkin' about it."

Faith and family . . . if ever there was a lead-in to what was on Rebecca's mind today, her mother had just handed her a key to what she hoped would be a new door for all of them. Rebecca closed her eyes, gathering her strength. *It would be a wonderful thing if You'd give me some convincing*

*words here, Lord, even if I'm not so good about praying
except when I want something.*

"This family idea has been on my mind a lot since I've
gotten to know the three of you Lantzes," she began tenta-
tively, "so . . . well, what would you think if I wanted to
move to Willow Ridge? Say, around the first of the year?"

Her mother's brown eyes lit up. "And what's bringin' this
on?" she asked, barely containing her excitement. "I hope
your *dat*'s doin' all right—"

"Oh, he's fine! But he's selling the house, to move into a
condo where he won't have yard work in the summer or
snow to shovel in the winter—"

"Well, there's a fine idea!" Rhoda remarked as they sat
down to their dinner.

"—and, well . . . I think Dad might have a girlfriend he's
not saying much about yet. He's getting out more, and he
seems pretty happy about it."

The whole room vibrated with Mamma's suppressed
laughter. "*Jah*, we parents who're lookin' to have a social life
can be a real mystery—or an embarrassment—to our kids,"
she remarked with a grin for Rhoda. "So we know how
you're feelin' about now. Like things aren't such a *gut* fit
anymore, while your home situation seems to be changin'
faster than you're ready for."

How was it that this Plain woman had such a handle on
the way she was feeling, even though she hadn't grown up
as Miriam's daughter? Rebecca relaxed.

"I hope that means you'll want to bunk with *me*!" Rhoda
chimed in. "Now that the Hooley brothers have moved into
their apartment above the new mill, and Rachel's in the big
house with Micah, and Mamma's gettin' a new home across
the road, well—" Her arms opened wide to encompass the
apartment they now sat in. "We've got us a cozy nest
here, Rebecca, and a nice blue room for ya. If ya think ya

can stand livin' in such close quarters with the likes of *me*, that is."

Rebecca's hand fluttered to her mouth. Her eyes welled up with tears. Why had she thought it would be difficult to make such a request of Miriam and Rhoda? Time and again she'd seen these women welcome newcomers to their table and into their lives. "I—I wasn't sure how I might fit in, or who might already plan to live in the main house, or—"

"You're family, honey-bug," her mother said with a sweet smile. "Not a one of us would turn ya away, even if all of us—includin' Ben and his brothers and the two Hooley aunts—were gonna live in that house. I'm just so tickled ya want to come here, Rebecca!"

"*Jah!* So . . ." Rhoda studied her over a chicken leg. "Does this mean you'll want to waitress at the café all the time? I thought you were doin' computer work."

"And I am," Rebecca replied quickly. "But my dream is to develop my own graphic-arts business. It will take a while to build up enough clients to live on what I make. I don't want to be a mooch—"

"Ya don't have a moochin' bone in your body, child," Miriam whispered as she reached across the table for Rebecca's hand. "Your folks raised ya right. And besides that, ya come from Amish stock and some of those workin' ways are bred right into ya, like it or not!"

Again Rebecca got goose bumps. Oh, what a wonderful thing it was, to be so loved and accepted by these women. "I like it just fine, Mamma," she breathed. "I hope my living here won't cause you any problems with Hiram Knepp, or—"

"Puh!" Her mother reached for a second piece of chicken. "What with the bishop bein' put under the ban for hidin' that fancy car, he's learnin' humility like the rest of us. And have ya ever known me to knuckle under just because Hiram thought he knew what I needed better than I did?"

Rebecca laughed. Such a feisty spirit this woman had beneath her prayer kapp and apron. "You certainly proved that when my dad bought your building, and again when you decided to marry Ben instead of the bishop."

"So there ya have it!" Rhoda crowed.

"For sure and for certain!" Miriam declared, grabbing her hand again. "For *gut*, and forever, Rebecca."

"*Jah!* For *gut* and forever!" her sister echoed as she completed their circle around the little kitchen table.

Rebecca held her breath, overwhelmed by the love that filled this room . . . by the pulse that connected them with an inexplicable bond. It called to mind the morning of Rachel's wedding day, when she had dressed like her sisters: they'd obviously been triplets on the outside, yet the three of them were even more deeply unified on a level she'd never experienced. While being raised as the only child of Janet and Bob Oliveri had been a wonderful life, this coming together with her kin moved her deeply. Blood *was* thicker than water—and the love of Miriam, Rachel, and Rhoda Lantz had certainly proved stronger than the river current that had carried her away as a toddler.

"Thank you so much," she whispered. Then she grinned. "I think Dad might be just as tickled as I am about this, when I tell him where I'm moving."

"He'll know you're in *gut* company, amongst family," her mother agreed as she helped herself to another slice of bread. "It'll free him up to make his own move forward, just like it'll give ya a way to start your computer business without goin' out on too much of a limb. Once again, it's the hand of God nudgin' everybody the way He wants us to go—just like He's done for Rhoda."

Rebecca considered that as she helped herself to more of this simple, delicious meal. "I guess I always thought of Amish women as stay-at-home mothers who mostly kept up the house and did the gardening, and who expected their daughters to do the same. I'm glad I was mistaken about that!"

"Oh, what you're sayin' is true," Miriam replied, "because the Old Ways haven't changed for centuries. But losin' the head of the household puts a whole 'nother twist into things for a widow. I could've lived with my brothers' families in Jamesport or Clark, or asked some of Jesse's family to take me in. But Willow Ridge is my home."

A delightful smile lit her mother's face. "Once I decided to bake, and Naomi jumped in with me—on account of how her Ezra can't work at his carpentry, after his accident—why, all sorts of doors opened up. Now I'm wonderin' if we're gettin' more business than we can handle. But we'll work it out," Mamma insisted quickly. "After all, here *you* are, Rebecca, takin' on some of the table-waitin' like a pro. God'll provide whatever we need, whether it be gettin' more help . . . or decidin' that the new website is stretchin' us beyond where the Sweet Seasons is meant to go."

Rebecca's eyebrows rose as she passed on what her teachers had impressed upon her. "Well, Mamma, nobody goes into business to get smaller—"

"That's English thinkin'. We Plain folks don't believe our livelihoods should overtake our lives." Mamma clasped her hands on the tabletop, her expression firm yet loving. "While Derek Shotwell at the bank would sure enough loan me money to expand—and to convince your *dat* to add on to the building—that's not gonna happen. My faith and my family come first. And what with gettin' hitched and startin' up in a new home with a fella a few years younger than me, well . . ." Once again a grin lit up her mother's face. "Let's just say I'm lookin' forward to bein' a bride again."

Miriam Lantz radiated a passion for love and life—and for Ben Hooley. And why wouldn't she? Ben was a wonderful man, not to mention attractive. In the months since the blacksmith's arrival, he'd contributed a lot to the Willow Ridge community.

"If you think your website needs to come down, Mamma, that's the way it'll be," Rebecca said. "It's wonderful, seeing you this happy! You're a good example for me to follow, when I finally meet a guy I'd consider marrying."

Her mother shrugged. "That's what *mamms* are for."

Wasn't it just the best thing, that after she had lost one mother, she'd found Miriam? *God's hand, leadin' ya where you're supposed to go . . .*

Rebecca went warm inside. She'd spent the last couple of years wishing, figuring out what to do with her life . . . trying out dreams she wanted to make a reality. And today at the Sweet Seasons, a major chunk of her future had magically, effortlessly, fallen into place.

Pretty awesome, God. Thanks!

Chapter Seven

Ben sat in the church service Sunday morning smiling, trying not to be obvious about peering between the heads of the older fellows seated in front of him. When Miriam's eyes found his from across the crowded room, his heart fluttered. Maybe their game of peekaboo wasn't appropriate for Sunday worship, yet who could fault him for loving the woman he intended to marry?

Meanwhile their deacon, Reuben Riehl, stood up to read from the large Bible. "From the thirteenth chapter of Romans, the day's Scripture lesson," the burly redhead announced. "'Let every soul be subject unto the higher powers. For there is no power but of God: the powers that be are ordained of God,'" he said in his clear voice. "'Whosoever therefore resisteth the power, resisteth the ordinance of God; and they that resist shall receive to themselves damnation. For rulers are not a terror to good works but to the evil . . .'"

As the reading ended and Jeremiah Shetler rose to preach, Ben sensed the Morning Star bishop's words would be aimed partly at Hiram Knepp: because of his shunning, Hiram sat in the front row of the men's side with his head bowed as a sign of humility and repentance. From what Ben had heard from his aunt Jerusalem, however, Hiram was champing at the bit and more than ready to get his final two weeks of separation behind him so he could resume his role as the bishop of Willow Ridge. He wasn't a man known for letting anyone else take the lead or take control.

And sure enough, after a three-hour service focused mostly on the theme of obeying a higher power—be it God, or those chosen by God—Hiram abruptly stood up and stalked out. Miriam's kitchen door slammed in his wake, raising the eyebrows of those in the huge room. After a moment, the men rose to rearrange the room, as usual, while the women got the food ready to serve.

"Well, there you have it," Seth Brenneman murmured. "Hiram's not allowed to stay for today's common meal, nor to talk much to members while he's shunned, but he's sure enough been chattin' up those of us who haven't yet joined the church."

Ben turned to face the two brothers who, with Rachel's Micah, had completed Willow Ridge's new mill in record time so they could build his house for Miriam by year's end. "*Jah?* How so?" he asked.

Naomi's brawny blond sons looked at each other as they shifted the long wooden pew benches into place for the meal. "Oh, he seems real interested in what-all species of wood ya chose for your cabinets and stairs," Seth remarked. "And he's askin' about what the place is costin' to build—"

"And if it's bein' financed by Derek Shotwell's bank," Aaron joined in with a shake of his head. "I was glad Micah was there with us when Hiram came along to quiz us, on account of how I didn't know much about those particulars."

"Nor did we think—even though Hiram's the bishop—he

had any call to be keepin' account of your new house," Seth added.

"Now why am I not surprised?" Ben murmured as he looked around the crowd of men who were setting up tables. "When was this goin' on? Just lately?"

"*Jah*, he was there yesterday morning. After we left the café."

"*Denki* for lettin' me know. Something tells me he might've been chattin' up my brothers, as well, if he was over at the house." Ben spotted Luke and Ira near the kitchen door, where Annie Mae Knepp and Millie Glick stood ready with plates and silverware. Now *there* was fuel for Bishop Knepp's fire, as Luke had been spending plenty of his evenings with the bishop's eldest daughter.

Ben made his way toward them, considering how to speak to his brothers without involving the girls. He reminded himself that as their bishop, Hiram had the authority to warn them about becoming too worldly or so heavily indebted they couldn't keep up with their bills. But this latest visit to his future home—talking with the carpenters rather than with him—raised a red flag.

"Say, fellas," he said as he clapped his brothers on the shoulders, "I'm wonderin' if I can pull ya away from these perty girls to help me for a few."

Ira looked ready to smart off, but Luke smiled gallantly at Annie Mae and then followed Ben through the kitchen to Miriam's front porch. "What's goin' on, Bennie?" he asked as they stepped outside into the brisk wind. "Have Aunt Jerusalem and Aunt Nazareth been waggin' your tail—waggin' their tongues—about my keepin' company with Annie Mae?"

Ben gestured toward some boxes of food to be carried into the kitchen, pies and salads that wouldn't fit in Miriam's fridge but had stayed plenty cold enough out here on this late November day. "*Should* they be tellin' me things?" he countered playfully. "Like, about how Hiram thinks you're leadin' his daughter astray, keepin' her from bein' baptized into the church?"

"Oh, that subject's come up, for sure and for certain!" Ira replied with a laugh. "And Hiram was bendin' our ears about that—amongst other things—the other day when we were settlin' into our rooms above the mill."

Again, Ben noted that the bishop had made his visit while he wasn't there. "Funny you should say so," he remarked in a lowered voice. "He didn't by chance ask ya how much the mill was costin'? Or tell ya he thought the Brenneman boys made the place fancier than it needed to be?"

Luke's and Ira's exchanged glance told Ben these subjects had indeed been discussed.

"Truth be told, Hiram did seem to be snoopin'," Luke said. "Didn't want to bother ya with this, knowin' how he's been keepin' such close tabs on you and Miriam."

Ben smiled to himself. Luke was adept at selling prospective farmers and storekeepers on the idea of raising specialty grains and carrying the milled flours in their stores: his head for business had earned him enough money to fund the Mill at Willow Ridge without needing a loan—no small accomplishment for a man who'd recently turned thirty. "So ya handled the bishop's questions all right? Didn't get riled up about him nosin' into your business?"

Luke shrugged. "First time we met Hiram, his feathers were ruffled about us buildin' the mill on Miriam's land, maybe cheatin' her out of property that had been her husband's," he recalled. "So from the get-go, I figured him for a fella who'd make it his business to watch my business."

Ben nodded. "Which, most likely, is why you're seein'

Annie Mae. Keeps things more interesting than if she was an ordinary man's daughter, ain't so?"

His brothers snickered. They both had a bit of the daredevil in them, like Dat, and they refused to be intimidated by bishops or other men who told them how to behave. "That's partly it," Ira admitted as he grabbed a picnic hamper with each hand. "But there's also the way Annie Mae's been known for galavantin' around with a certain Yonnie Stoltzfus, who's supposedly up to no *gut*, as well."

"So I haven't left her any time to see Stoltzfus these past few weeks," Luke continued. "A man's gotta do what a man's gotta do."

Once upon a time Ben, too, had talked with such a swagger in his attitude. That was the way of it while Amish fellows were still in their *rumspringa*, or running-around years. "Next time Hiram comes around askin' questions, feel free to refer him to me. I'd just as soon squelch whatever schemin' Hiram might be doin'." He glanced down the long lane lined with carriages, toward the skeleton of a new house across the county road. "That place is my gift to Miriam, and I don't want her happiness spoiled by a fella who's peeved that she's marryin' me instead of him."

"See there?" Ira teased. "We're not the only ones stirrin' the pot! You're way ahead of us at doin' that, Bennie-boy."

As they stepped back into the heavenly warm kitchen, which was bustling with women, Aunt Jerusalem met them. "*Denki*, boys, for bringin' this stuff inside," she said. She took a triple pie carrier from Ben and set it on the nearest table. "Seems Hiram's gone off in a snit again, despite my talkin' to him about showin' more humility during his shunning. But it is what it is, his attitude," she added with a touch of starch in her voice. "Miriam's invited us all for Sunday dinner next week, bless her heart. If he refuses to sit at his own little table, as he's supposed to during the ban, he'll miss out on a wonderful-*gut* meal."

"*Jah*, he wasn't keen on his separate seating at Thanksgiving," Ira recalled.

"None too thankful, for sure." Luke glanced toward the bustling front room, where the younger girls were setting out plates and silverware. "But enough about Hiram. Any time Miriam invites us over to eat is a day to be thankful that Ira's not cookin'."

Their steely-haired aunt laughed heartily as she cut the three pies. "Miriam's mighty excited about havin' everybody. Her Rebecca'll be joinin' us—and she's soon to move upstairs with Rhoda, above the smithy. She's ready to start some sort of computer business, and meanwhile she's helpin' at the Sweet Seasons," Aunt Jerusalem went on with a rise in her voice. "*That*'ll be somethin', havin' her English daughter livin' with them after all those years they'd figured she was gone forever."

Ben nodded. Miriam was indeed ecstatic that her lost-and-found daughter wanted to live with her Plain family. Meanwhile his two younger brothers exchanged a purposeful look, as though they had their own ideas about what Rebecca's presence in Willow Ridge might mean.

As he carried two pies out to the tables, Ben smiled. It seemed *stirring the pot* was becoming everyday behavior among the Hooleys and the Lantzes. But then, from the first time he'd laid eyes on Miriam, he'd known his life would never be dull again.

Rhoda was placing silverware alongside the plates Annie Mae had set on the long tables, when she heard thundering footsteps and loud laughter upstairs, a sure sign that some of the kids had slipped away to play. Not that playing was a bad thing, but there was a time and a place for it. As she headed for the stairway, she couldn't help thinking that Brett and Taylor Leitner would never make so much racket indoors—

Or maybe ya haven't seen that side of them yet. Kids'll be kids.

She smiled as she pictured Taylor's mop of flyaway curls and Brett wearing those glasses with the dangling fake eyeballs. Had they gone to church today? Was Andy home with them, or did he have to work a shift at the hospital? While it wasn't the Plain way to labor on the Lord's day, hospital patients depended on Andy and their doctors every day of the week.

Rhoda stopped at the top of the stairs, crossing her arms. Sure enough, Josh and Joey Knepp were positioning themselves to race down the long hall while Levi and Cyrus Zook egged them on. "There's plenty of room outside to be runnin' your races, boys. Snow or not, you've got no business horsin' around in other people's homes," she stated.

"Better get outta our way," one of the twins challenged, "or we might just run ya down, Rhoda Lantz!"

"*Jah*, you can save your orders for those English kids you're watchin'," his brother joined in. "Dat says you oughtn't be workin' for that fella in New Haven."

Rhoda set aside the bishop's opinion. If anyone had boys who needed a firmer hand, it was Hiram Knepp. "That's neither here nor there. You boys can take your game outside with the other kids—"

"And I'm just the man to escort ya there." Ben ascended the last two steps and stood beside Rhoda in the hall. "Let's go, boys. When I tell Jerusalem you were runnin' races down the hallway, *she'll* make sure ya know better than to do it again, ain't so? The four of ya can gather up the dirty dishes and carry them to the kitchen after we eat, instead of makin' the girls do it."

The five-year-old twins rolled their eyes, but they knew not to sass Ben or to test Jerusalem Hooley's patience. The Zook boys, who were plenty old enough to behave better, followed Josh and Joey down the stairs.

"Thanks, Ben," Rhoda murmured. "Rachel and Micah have brought home a lot of nice wedding gifts from their weekend visits to family, and I saw no need for those four monkeys to break anything."

"I wasn't so different at their age," he recalled, "but my *dat* would've smacked my backside had I been racin' down the hallway or snoopin' around somebody else's house."

As Rhoda returned to the expanded front room, where the tables were nearly ready for folks to be seated, she again wondered about the Leitner family. Did Andy discipline his kids? If she corrected them, would he support her or take the kids' side? No doubt that situation would arise one of these days . . .

As she took her place at a table between Annie Mae and Nellie Knepp, Rhoda wondered how much their *dat* had discussed her new job at the Leitners'. These two girls, Hiram's oldest, had been raised with a firm hand while their mother was alive. They'd taken over most of the baby tending when Hiram's second wife, Linda, had borne the twins, Sara, and Timmy in rapid succession before she died—which probably explained why Annie Mae showed no inclination to join the church so she could marry and start a family of her own.

After Bishop Shetler called for the silent grace, Annie

Mae caught sight of Luke Hooley across the crowded room. She wiggled her fingers at him.

"So what's your *dat* say about ya goin' on dates with Luke?" Rhoda asked.

Annie Mae, who was nearly eighteen, let out a short laugh. "What *can* he say? *Rumspringa* is for tryin' wild and crazy things before ya settle down—and Luke Hooley is one wild and crazy thing!"

On the other side of Rhoda, Nellie shook her head. "My sister'll catch a cartload of trouble for tellin' Dat and Jerusalem she won't sneak out anymore, only to do that very thing that very night," she muttered. She stabbed a slice of ham and passed the platter to Rhoda. "She'd do better comin' to our crochet club instead of temptin' a devil Luke's age. My stars, he's *thirty* and still hasn't joined the church."

"Ya think he's mighty cute, Sister," Annie Mae retorted as she grabbed the bread basket. "And you'd give your eye teeth to be goin' out with Ira—or anybody who'd give ya a second glance."

"When I'm sixteen and out of school, I'll do just that!" Nellie fired back.

Rhoda knew better than to take sides when these two sisters unsheathed their claws. She and Rachel had rarely bickered . . .

What'll it be like when Rebecca moves into the apartment? What if she dates all sorts of fellas and I'm left at home, while Rachel and Micah are spendin' their evenings here and Mamma and Ben play the newlyweds in their new house?

But then Andy Leitner's handsome face came to mind . . .

his low, pleasant voice echoed in her ears as he told her what good work she'd done for him.

Rhoda smiled. No harm in thinking about Andy this way, keeping her special daydreams to herself. Tomorrow afternoon she'd be going there again, and she couldn't wait to see him! She had just the right surprise in mind.

Chapter Eight

After a harrowing stint in the emergency room, Andy entered the house and fell against the front door to shut it. Images of two teenagers who'd been riding tandem on a motorcycle still haunted him: when they had skidded through an icy intersection and spun out, it was a miracle they'd both lived . . . if *living* was what they'd do after all of their internal injuries became evident. Sometimes surviving such an accident wasn't the luckiest thing.

He'd vowed not to bring such tragedies home with him, though, so he stood for a moment, listening for the kids . . . getting a sense of whether his mom was up and around.

Cookies. He inhaled the sugary-cinnamon scent that filled the room. *It smells like absolute heaven in here.*

When Andy started toward the kitchen, craving all the sweetness he could get his hands on, Rhoda peered out the kitchen doorway. "I was hopin' that was you comin' in," she teased. "Better join us, or there won't be any left!"

It was a fine sight that greeted him. His mother sat at the table, spooning up cookie dough with her good hand and pushing it onto a cookie sheet with the spoon in her weaker hand. Taylor and Brett stood at the counter measuring flour into another bowl.

Nothing short of a miracle, he almost said, but that would ruin the mood Rhoda had once again set so effortlessly. Total cooperation . . . his kids working together while his mother regained her motor skills and manual dexterity.

When Rhoda approached him with two chunky, warm cookies, all Andy could think of was how sweet she was. Unassuming and compassionate, as though she'd known exactly what sort of therapy he needed. "Oatmeal raisin," he murmured. "Wow, do these look awesome."

"Rhoda's oatmeal cookies!" his son exclaimed as he looked up from reading another recipe. "What do you think, Dad? Did we do good?"

Andy bit into the soft, chewy cookie, still warm, and let out a low moan. "You did good, kids," he replied, but his eyes were on Rhoda. "Can we keep a copy of this recipe? It's not an old family secret, is it?"

"Puh!" Rhoda waved him off. "I make these a couple times a week for the Sweet Seasons. Got the recipe memorized, but I can write it down, if ya want."

"Tell me! I'll write it," Taylor said as she scrambled for paper and a pencil. "Rhoda was teachin' us about fractions while we were measuring out all the stuff for these cookies. Kitchen math is a lot funner than doing it on paper for school."

"I bet she's doing a better job with fractions than I could, too," Andy admitted. "That wasn't your favorite math lesson, last time we tackled it."

Right now, however, math—and highway catastrophes—seemed miles away. As he bit into his second cookie, Andy poured a glass of milk and sat down beside his mother. She looked delighted to be helping with these cookies even though she'd never been one to bake a lot. How it soothed him to listen as Rhoda patiently dictated her recipe and then helped Taylor spell the ingredients. And was that *Brett* so carefully pouring vanilla extract into a measuring spoon? Ordinarily, his son flitted from one activity to the next, not finishing what he started—and definitely not doing girlie stuff in the kitchen.

"So what are you stirring up there, Brett?" Andy asked.

"These ones are gonna be chocolate chip cookies! Rhoda says it's just as easy to bake a couple batches, while we've got the stuff out, so we can freeze some," his boy replied with a big grin. "Then, whenever we're ready for homemade cookies, they'll be ready for us!"

"Sounds like a great plan." Again Andy marveled. While engaging his kids in making cookies, Rhoda had given them lessons in fractions, home economics, and working together as a team. It was something Megan had never—

Let her go. No use in rehashing the past.

Andy blinked. It seemed such messages came to him a lot these days, thoughts about moving forward rather than dwelling on a marriage that hadn't been happy for more years than he cared to count.

"And for supper," Taylor chimed in, "we're makin' pizza, Dad! Well—Rhoda's makin' the crust and we get to put on the toppings. Rhoda says if we use some whole wheat flour and put on lots of sauce and veggies, pizza can be a healthy meal with all of the basic food groups."

Rhoda says . . . Rhoda says . . . Andy didn't even mind that his kids were showing more enthusiasm for their new housekeeper than they did for him most days. Rhoda Lantz, in her wine-colored dress, white apron, and pleated white kapp, with her hair pulled up into a bun and not a hint of makeup, was turning his house into a home again. And for that, he was so thankful his eyes stung.

He blinked back tears. It wouldn't do to get all emotional, because that led to floundering in doubt and fear and inadequacy, as he had when Megan had walked out. He had no time for that. He had an internship to complete and exams to pass and—

Rhoda's smile made him forget those pressing obligations. "What do ya like on your pizza, Andy?" she asked. "So far, we've got sausage and cheese and green peppers and black olives. We'll make two big pizzas, so ya can warm up what's left over for another meal tomorrow."

"Pizza for breakfast," he murmured before he even thought about it. "Now there's a treat! Can we put bacon on one of them?"

When her eyes twinkled with approval, Andy realized they were the same blue as a springtime sky.

"Now you're talkin'!" She removed two sheets of cookies from the oven and then slid in the two sheets his mom had just filled. "Rachel and Mamma and I make one with bacon and onions and extra cheese, and another with bell peppers and sausage—"

"Say no more!" Andy closed his eyes in ecstasy. "We're talking about waaay too much fat and cholesterol, but I'm going to enjoy every bite!"

A couple of hours later, as he raised his first slice of bacon pizza to his mouth, Andy thought he'd died and gone to heaven: tender, chewy crust . . . thick, gooey cheese . . . salty-sweet bacon . . . tomato sauce seasoned with garlic and herbs. As the kids and his mother were oohing and aahing, he held Rhoda's gaze across the table.

"Thank you," he mouthed.

She smiled shyly. *You're welcome*, came her silent reply.

It occurred to him that after only two visits, he was hooked on this young woman in a dangerous way: if for some reason

Rhoda had to stop coming, returning home to find his kids fighting and his mother lying despondently in bed again might well overwhelm him. He'd already grown so accustomed to the order and harmony this young woman had brought into his home that he couldn't—didn't want to—consider his life playing out any other way.

Andy snatched a piece of the sausage and veggie pizza—because if he devoured all of the bacon pie, he wouldn't be able to have any for breakfast, would he? Wouldn't be able to savor this deliciousness again tomorrow morning as he anticipated what wonders Rhoda would work after she arrived on Tuesday . . .

An hour later as she dried her hands, satisfied that the kitchen was tidy enough, Andy took her aside. The kids were in their rooms choosing their clothes for tomorrow—yet another fine idea Rhoda had suggested—and his mom sat on the couch watching TV, so he had a few private moments while she waited for her ride.

"Rhoda, we really love all the cooking you do, but—" Andy barely stopped himself from laying his hands on her shoulders. "Well, I never intended for you to work so hard, or to see that we had meals for the next day, or—"

Rhoda's brow furrowed. "*Ach*, I've done nothin' but what I'd be doin' at home. If ya don't want me to cook—"

"Oh, please don't stop!" He took money from his wallet. "But you're spoiling us. We—we could get by with canned soup or frozen lasagne or—"

Her crestfallen expression told him he'd just made a mess of this conversation. Andy sighed. "It's just that you work so hard at putting the house to rights, and paying attention to my kids, and—"

"When I'm doin' that here, for you, it doesn't seem like work," she murmured. Her sincere blue-eyed gaze nailed him. "I feel like I'm helpin' your family. I feel like I'm . . . needed here."

And I do need you, Rhoda. More than you know, his heart whispered.

He clenched his teeth to keep from saying that. It would be totally inappropriate to imply any personal interest in this open, ingenuous Amish girl because it would get her into trouble—and cause him more heartache than he could handle. Andy handed her the day's pay, relieved that a van's headlights flooded the doorway with light.

"Thanks for another great day," he said in a more businesslike tone. "We'll see you tomorrow."

Chapter Nine

Miriam stepped outside Tuesday morning to discover an inch of fresh snow on the ground, and the dark sky was thick with huge flakes like down feathers that had burst from a pillow. She raised her face to catch some on her tongue, giggling as they tickled her cheeks. The hills around her place and the Brennemans' lay blanketed in a whiteness that glowed in the moonlight and muffled the sound of a car passing cautiously along the county blacktop.

Well, Lord, it's December first. If this snow isn't a sign that it's time to start some holiday bakin', I'm not payin' attention, ain't so? Miram hurried toward the back entrance of the Sweet Seasons, and within minutes she had flipped on the kitchen lights and had the ovens preheating.

What a joy it was to revel in Christmas again! Last year—before she'd met Ben—the holidays had still held a tinge of sadness, even though she'd put on a happy face for the girls. This morning she had a new reason to rejoice: a month from today, she'd be getting married! Miriam stepped into the pantry, thinking the lunch crowd might be lighter on this wintry Tuesday—a perfect day for soup! It seemed yet another sign from above that just last week she had stocked up on dried split peas. A few minutes later she had a big stock pot of them on to boil.

A rapping on the kitchen door made her look up. "Ben! Get yourself in out of this weather," she said as he stepped inside. His shoulders and broad-brimmed hat were coated with snow. "You're out mighty early this mornin'."

"I'd kiss ya," he teased, "but my face is as cold as—"

"And ya think I don't know how to fix that?" With a mixing bowl still in the crook of her elbow, Miriam slipped an arm around Ben's neck for a fine, satisfying start to her morning. She'd been happy with Jesse, but it was a delight to be marrying a man who kissed her and held her like he never wanted to let her go.

"Watch out now," he murmured, his hazel eyes alight. "You'll have me tryin' for something you won't want your girls and Naomi to walk in on. A man can only resist temptation for so long, ya know. What's smellin' so *gut* already?"

Miriam kissed him again and slipped out of his embrace. "I've got split pea soup simmerin' for the lunch buffet, and Irish brown bread in the oven to go with it. And we've got fun stuff for breakfast, too. Sausage-and-cheese biscuits, and the special banana muffins I make at Christmastime—which ought to be about ready." When an oven timer dinged, Miriam pulled out two tins of fruit-studded muffins.

Ben looked ready to grab one and burn his fingers. "My word, what-all's in those?" he asked, inhaling deeply. "I sure hope those aren't for somebody's special order."

"Nope. You can be my tester, Ben. Want a couple eggs with them?"

He settled onto the tall stool at the back counter to watch her move around the kitchen. It was a different sensation, having a man who openly adored her and chatted with her while she baked, and Miriam suspected she would never tire of it. "Only if you'll join me," he replied. "Why do I suspect you've been hard at it since before three, without a break?"

"Because I love my work?" she asked. "And on account of how excited I am that Christmas—and our wedding's—comin' up?"

"It's *gut* to see ya so happy, after the way things went last weekend when Rhoda started her new job and Hannah looked like a deer in the headlights."

"Perty sure we won't have that problem today." Miriam glanced outside. The snowflakes looked bigger and thicker than they had an hour ago.

"I'm here to clear your walk and parkin' lot so's Preacher Gabe and your other folks won't break any bones," Ben said. "My Pharaoh's a fine horse for pullin' that vee-shaped plow in the smithy. Figured I'd clear Naomi's lane so Ezra's driver can pick him up to work at the hospital today, too. I'll do that right off, after I eat."

Miriam smiled at him as four eggs crackled in the cast-iron skillet. "*Denki*, Ben. What would I do without ya?"

Ben snatched one of the warm muffins as she removed them from the tins. "You'd probably cook a lot less without my brothers and me gobblin' up your fabulous food. Oh my word, Miriam, I'm seein' red cherries and chunks of orange . . . nuts and melty little chocolate chips," he murmured as he studied his muffin. "This looks more like dessert than breakfast. Not that that'll stop me!"

As he took his first big bite, Ben's expression made Miriam's heart sing. His long lashes fluttered down over his clean-shaven cheeks, and he smiled as though he was the happiest man on God's good earth. She loved him so much she nearly burst at the seams.

Oh, but I wish I could bear this man's children.

But there was no call for getting upset about what wasn't going to happen. God had His reasons for every little thing, and hadn't He already blessed her with more joy than she had ever imagined?

The back door whooshed open and Rhoda came inside, coated with snow. "*Ach*, there must be three inches out there already!" she exclaimed as she stamped her feet on the rug. "Rachel probably won't get here until Micah gives her a ride down that long lane!"

"That would be her way of handlin' this snow, *jah*." Miriam smiled. Why wish for more children when the three daughters God had given her blessed her every day? And they would be giving her grandchildren to delight in, too!

"Soon as I finish here I'll be plowin'," Ben replied. "*Gut* morning to ya, Rhoda. The snow's put roses in your cheeks and a sparkle in your eyes."

Rhoda surveyed the baked goods on the counter and then snatched a biscuit rich with crumbled sausage and cheese. "If I had my way about it, I'd hitch up the sleigh and go ridin' today. But I'm workin' two jobs now—the responsible adult, ya know," she added with a chuckle. "What can I do for ya, Mamma? You've been bakin' up a storm already, even if we might not have many customers today."

"It never goes to waste," Miriam said as she scraped the last of her egg from her plate. "Want me to fry ya some bacon or—"

The bell on the wall jangled, which meant the phone was ringing in the shanty behind the café. Miriam wondered who might be calling at this early hour. Had the three Schrocks decided not to open their quilt shop today?

"I'll grab that." Rhoda dashed out the door without her coat.

"Here's my chance for one more kiss," Ben whispered as he rose from the stool. "Better get these lanes and your lot cleared out."

"You're a fine man for lookin' after us this way, Ben."

Miriam savored the feel of his lips on hers. "Come inside every now and again to warm up. I'll make some cocoa for ya."

"I love ya ever so much, Miriam," he murmured.

"*Jah*, and don't I know it! You're a lucky man," she teased softly.

As he stepped outside, Rhoda came in on a gust of snowy air. "That was Andy Leitner, sayin' their school's been called off," she reported. "He asked if I could be there so his *mamm* won't have to keep track of the kids all day. Hope it's all right that I went ahead and called Sheila."

"Well, *there's* something we Plain folks don't worry about. Our Willow Ridge scholars'll be walkin'—or their *dats*'ll hitch up the sleighs and drive them to the schoolhouse— like it was any other day." Glancing outside again, Miriam spotted two bundled figures coming down the Brennemans' lane. "For sure and for certain Hannah and Rachel can handle anybody we'll have eatin' here today, so don't you worry about it, honey-bug. Get your things together, and tell Sheila to take her time on the roads, hear me?"

"*Jah*, Mamma, I'll do that." Rhoda bussed her forehead with a kiss. "*Denki* for understandin'. If my workin' for the Leitners causes ya problems, just tell me straight-out, all right? It's not my intention to leave ya shorthanded."

"Go on with ya now," Miriam said, waving her off. "It's *gut* that Andy cares enough about his kids to have ya there. I've heard tell that a lot of English parents have no idea where their youngsters go after school, or what sort of mischief they get into while their *mamms* and *dats* are away at work. Askin' for trouble, they are."

The door closed against the snow with a *whump*, leaving Miriam in a kitchen that was silent except for the hum of the big freezers and fridges. She savored the hush of this fragrant kitchen where she had found a whole new life since Jesse had passed.

Jah, Lord, Rhoda's ready for a new life, too, she prayed. *And meanwhile, I ask Ya to be with her and Sheila and Andy—all the folks who have to run the roads today. I'm ever so grateful to be workin' right here on my home place, doin' what I love with a fella Ya created just for me.*

As Rhoda walked up the driveway toward Andy's house, along a cleared path the width of a snow shovel blade, she sensed the kids might show their naughtier sides today because they'd been given an unexpected vacation. As Andy let her inside, she was glad she could help him out. He hadn't even driven to work yet and he looked weary.

"Rhoda, you're a lifesaver," he murmured. "A couple of the other interns went home with the flu yesterday, so I'm going in early to cover some of their patients. When Taylor and Brett heard school was called off, they jumped back into bed, so you'll have some peace and quiet for a while."

When she caught a movement in the hallway, Rhoda waved at the woman who was shuffling slowly behind her walker. "Ah, but your *mamm's* outta bed. Betty and I'll have a nice cup of tea to start our day. Don't worry about a thing, Andy."

The lines on his face nearly disappeared as he smiled at her. "I so appreciate all you do for me, Rhoda—and for my family," he added quickly.

Was there a new intensity, a wistfulness, in his reply? Or was she hearing Andy's words with wishful ears?

Don't let me get all wrapped up in Andy's kindness, thinkin' he's interested in me, she prayed. She watched his car back into the street and then fishtail on the packed snow. *Keep him safe, Lord. A lot of folks depend on him.*

Rhoda went into the kitchen then, saddened by the way Betty labored to walk. She quickly pulled out a chair so the poor old soul could land in it. Betty's white hair stuck out in tufts and her chenille robe looked as if she'd eaten a few meals with unsteady hands. "It's *gut* to see ya up and about on this snowy morning," she said in a cheerful voice. "Will ya have a cup of hot tea with me? Maybe some eggs and toast or a bowl of oatmeal?"

Betty's face brightened. "Snow?" she mumbled.

"*Jah*, the kids're home from school today, but they're sleepin' in. So it's just you and me for a while." Rhoda stooped to smile directly into Betty's eyes, pleased to see that her inner lights were burning even if her muscles couldn't fully show it. "You'd feel better if we got ya showered and into a clean nightgown and robe, ain't so?"

Andy's mother held her gaze, maintaining the connection between them for as long as she could. Then she looked down at Rhoda's shoulders. "I . . . like your dress," she said with some difficulty. "No . . . buttons."

Rhoda's eyebrows rose. "Are ya sayin' you'd wear day-time clothes if ya could fasten them easier?"

Betty nodded eagerly, fingering Rhoda's sleeve. "I've got . . . a sewing machine. Fabric, too."

Rhoda's heart thumped faster. Andy's *mamm* seemed to be emerging from behind the damage her stroke had done, back into being interested in everyday life. "I sew all my own dresses, ya know. I could make ya somethin' simple—"

"Like your dress. Apron, too." Her eyes were shining and clear, alert to this new idea. "Mother . . . always wore aprons . . . at home."

"So you're wantin' a Plain dress? I could make ya some of those in my sleep." Her mind raced, eager to begin this worth-while project. "And if ya have snaps, I could put them down the dress front so ya could put them on yourself, ain't so?"

Oh, but Betty smiled! While Rhoda suspected it would

take a lot of time and therapy before Andy's mother could fasten her clothing, who was she to dampen Betty's excitement by saying so? The two of them ate their eggs and drank their tea faster than she would've thought possible. Once they got to Betty's room, Betty showed Rhoda a walk-in closet that held bins of neatly folded fabrics, spools of thread, and a console sewing machine that hadn't been opened for a long while, judging from the stuff sitting on top of it.

"Now we're cookin'!" Rhoda slung her arm around the older woman's shoulders. "Let's get ya cleaned up first, and then we'll sew up a new dress!"

Betty moved much faster as she got cleaned up, excited about having something new to wear. While she was in the shower, Rhoda chose some fabric pieces large enough for winter-weight dresses. She found some coordinating prints and colors that would work for aprons, too. It intrigued her, the bright array of colors and bold patterns Andy's mother had chosen when she was sewing for herself.

"Rhoda?" a little voice spoke behind her.

Rhoda turned and then giggled: Taylor stood in the closet doorway, her light brown hair forming a wispy halo around a face still groggy with sleep. Her flannel pajamas were bright pink with some sort of white cartoon cat on them, and she held a well-loved stuffed dog. "Mornin' to ya, honey-bug. Did ya sleep *gut* after ya heard ya didn't have school today?"

Taylor nodded sleepily, glancing at the fabrics Rhoda had chosen. "Whatcha doin'? Gram brought all this stuff when she moved in with us, couple of years ago."

"And did she sew lots of perty clothes, back before she had her stroke?" It wouldn't do to be nosy, but Betty's grand-daughter would have quick answers to things that didn't add up . . . like why, for instance, most of the clothing hanging in Betty's other closet looked dull and shapeless and, well . . . depressing.

Taylor shrugged. "She wore sweats mostly, after Paw-Paw died. Didn't come out of her room a lot, 'coz she and Mommy didn't get along too good."

And wasn't that a sad situation for two young children to witness? And for Andy to be caught in the middle—tryin' to keep his wife happy while doin' the right thing, givin' his widowed *mamm* a home? From what she'd seen of English ways, it seemed the generations of their families often lived separate lives, splintered off from each other like strips of bark fallen off the family tree.

"So . . . was Gram gonna make clothes from these wild designs?" Taylor reached into a bin of colorful fabrics to get a better look at them.

Rhoda decided to take this conversation a bit further while Betty was still in the shower. "Does that surprise ya, that she used to sew up such bright, perty pieces?"

"Jah," the girl murmured, unaware that she'd picked up on some Amish dialect. "Look at that awesome purple with the bright pink polka dots, Rhoda! Now, can't you see *me* wearing that instead of Gram?"

Rhoda chuckled. "Maybe if ya ask her real nice, she'd let ya have that piece."

An exasperated sigh escaped the girl. "But I don't know how to sew!"

"Hmmmm," Rhoda said with an exaggerated roll of her eyes. "But *someone* in this closet does. Maybe if ya asked her real nice—"

"You mean it, Rhoda? You'd make me a dress from that? Pretty pleeeease?"

Rhoda's heart swelled as she held up the polka-dot fabric. "If ya don't want a lot of pleats or ruffles or what-not—"

"Yuck! Not ruffles!"

"—there's enough here for a dress or a jumper, *jah*. But you're askin' Gram about that before ya get your heart set on it, ain't so?"

Taylor's head bobbed happily.

"And if you'll be in charge of breakfast for you and your brother—and keep him outta here while I'm dressin' your gram—I'll be happy to sew ya something," Rhoda replied. "But your gram's dresses come first, so she can start to dress herself of a morning. She's all excited about gettin' new clothes, ya see."

The little girl's eyebrows rose slowly. "So . . . how will you know what size to make them? And how to sew the kind of dress she wants?"

"Truth be told, she asked for a Plain-style dress like I'm wearin', so she can snap it shut in the front." Rhoda pointed to the way her own dress was pinned beneath her vee-shaped cape. She watched Taylor's reaction to that, considering that most English women wouldn't ask for an Amish dress even if it was an easier style to fasten. "She wants aprons, too. Her own *mamm* wore them to do her housework, and an apron'll keep her dress cleaner when she eats, too."

"That would be a good thing," Taylor replied matter-of-factly. "She tries real hard, but sometimes the fork doesn't stay in her hand, or she can't keep the food in her mouth too good." Her brows puckered. "I thought Amish ladies didn't wear bright colors or designs."

"Well, I wear brighter solid colors in the summer than this green I've got on, but Mennonite ladies wear prints. They use the same basic Plain patterns for cuttin' out their clothes as we Amish do, though." Rhoda shrugged. "Your gram wants a simpler way to take care of herself. I think that's a real *gut* idea, and I know you'll help her all ya can, Taylor."

Rhoda wondered if Taylor would quiz her about the differences between Mennonites and Amish, but the girl glanced up at the ceiling, listening. "Brett's up," she murmured. "I'll get him into the kitchen real quick. See ya later, Rhoda."

"*Jah*, I'll be there in a few, honey-bug."

Taylor turned in the doorway of the closet, grinning as though they shared a fine secret. "You talk kinda funny, Rhoda, but it's cute, you know it?"

Over the next hour and a half the two kids behaved like angels. While Rhoda wasn't keen on the way they watched television and played with little gadgets in their hands, at least they weren't aggravating each other. So she focused on sewing their grandmother's new clothes.

Using a dress Betty said was still a good fit, Rhoda laid it on newspaper pages on the kitchen countertop to draw a paper pattern. As she allowed for the differences between this dress's style and the Amish type she herself wore, she became aware that Taylor had sat down beside her grandmother at the kitchen table.

"Whatcha doin' now?" the girl asked.

Rhoda smiled. Any time a young lady seemed curious about sewing, it was an opportunity to show her a skill she could use all her life. "Once I have paper pattern pieces for the dress and the sleeves, I'll pin them on the fabric and cut them out," she explained. "Which dress shall I sew first, Betty? I'll make one, and then we'll check the fit before we cut into another piece of fabric."

Betty, now wearing clean sweats, with her hair neatly combed, leaned eagerly over the three lengths of fabric they'd chosen. "Red poppies," she declared, pointing with her good hand. "Christmas'll be here . . . before we know it."

Rhoda smiled. "Ya want to save that piece for the second dress, after we try out our pattern on another fabric to be sure it's right?"

"Nope. It'll be . . . perfect if you . . . make it, Rhoda."

Rhoda's breath caught. Could she live up to such an expectation with her makeshift pattern? When the pieces were all cut out, the three of them went to Betty's room. She and Taylor pulled the sewing machine out of the closet, and with Betty's gestures and halting suggestions, Rhoda set it up. "I'm not used to an electric machine, ya know," she said as she threaded the needle with red thread. "So I just press my foot on that pedal, and the needle moves?"

"Yup. Old machine, but . . . still runs good." Betty took a seat in her overstuffed chair, while Taylor bounced onto the bed to watch.

After a few wild, racing starts that made the three of them giggle hysterically, Rhoda got the feel for feeding the fabric under the needle. When the main seams were basted in with long loose stitches, Taylor showed her where the iron and ironing board were—again, a new experience with an English appliance. Rhoda marveled at how easy it was to press the seams open with the steam that came out of the light-weight iron.

"It's time for your fittin'," she announced. "Ya ready for this, Betty?"

Taylor went out to check on Brett, who was watching a TV show about animals. As Rhoda helped Betty slip out of her sweats, she felt little tremors of anticipation in the older woman's limbs. The red poppies brightened the whole room, and as Rhoda pinned the front panels of the dress together, she got caught up in Betty's excitement.

"So how's it feel to ya? It drapes real nice in the back,"

she said as she went around to look. "Let's check the mirror, and see how long ya want it."

When they positioned the closet door so Betty could step in front of the full-length glass, the older woman's expression stopped Rhoda's heart: Betty's mouth opened and closed, but no words came out. Slowly she turned from one side to the other. She stood taller and squared her shoulders, as though she had someplace to go—perhaps recalling younger, happier days. As Betty smoothed the fabric at the shoulders, a sigh escaped her. "So . . . perty, Rhoda," she murmured. "Thank . . . you ever so . . . much, dear."

Rhoda wiped away a tear. When Betty reached for her with shining eyes, she stepped into a hug that took her by surprise with its intensity. How long had it been since this sweet old soul had worn something new? Had Betty endured long, lonely weeks, staying out of the way while Andy and his wife had ended their marriage? Did she feel that she was imposing on her son—especially after she'd lost the use of one side of her body? Sadder yet, had Betty resigned herself to just hanging on from one day to the next, without any hopes or hobbies?

Rhoda pressed her cheek to Betty's, sharing a kind of love she'd never expected, from a woman she barely knew. When she had told Andy that she felt *needed* here, she'd had no idea how much truer that statement would become . . . or how deep her emotions would run.

As they eased apart, Rhoda blinked back a last tear, noting the shiny streaks on Betty's face. "Well, now," she murmured. "Ya had faith in my sewin', so we're off to a real nice start. I was thinkin' that piece of bright green would make a *gut* apron—"

Betty's smile shone like the Christmas star as she nodded.

"—and I'll make a white one from that piece of twill we found," Rhoda continued as she unpinned the bodice.

"While I'm doin' so *gut* on the machine, I'll hem this dress and start another one. Which fabric do ya want for it?"

Betty considered the other large swaths they'd pulled from the bin and pointed to a piece of textured tweed in blues, yellows, and greens. "After this one . . . Taylor wants something from the purple . . . with the pink dots."

"*Jah*, so she's told me!" Rhoda said with a laugh. Then an idea occurred to her. "Do ya know if she's ever done any hand sewin'? Might be a *gut* chance for her to learn, on these nice big snaps that'll go down the front of your dresses."

Betty's eyes widened. "Good idea. I'll go get her."

Was it her imagination, or had Andy's mother said "*gut* idea"? Rhoda laughed at herself: with the morning nearly past and a new dress to show for it, her happiness was surely coloring what she saw and heard.

After their lunch, Rhoda agreed that Brett could play games on the computer while Taylor tried her hand at sewing the snaps on her gram's poppy-print dress. Taylor sat very still, holding her mouth just so, focused on jabbing thread through the needle's tiny eye the way Rhoda had shown her. Then Taylor observed closely as Rhoda made small stitches in each of the first snap's openings.

It was a gratifying sight, to see Betty giving encouragement as her granddaughter carefully circled each snap with her stitches. This meant Rhoda was free to cut and sew the tweed dress, knowing her paper pattern was an accurate fit.

This has to be Your hand at work, guidin' mine, Lord, she thought. An hour later, the tweed dress hung on the door awaiting snaps where she'd marked its front edges with pins.

At the sound of a loud sigh, Rhoda looked up. "Gettin' tired of that hand sewin', Taylor?" she asked gently. "Go on and play with Brett, if ya want. You've been a real big help."

"My stitches are so big, compared to yours," Taylor said in a dejected tone.

"Oh, don't ya worry about that, honey-bug!" Rhoda exclaimed as she looked at Taylor's work. "For your first time, ya did mighty fine—"

Betty was nodding emphatically, hugging Taylor's shoulders.

"—and ya know what?" Rhoda continued. "Your grandma's gonna smile every time she puts on this perty red poppy dress, because the color makes her *almost* as happy as lookin' at the snaps ya sewed on for her today."

"Real . . . proud of you . . . Taylor," Betty agreed.

Rhoda stopped sewing for a while to figure out what to cook for their supper . . . a dish that could simmer until Andy got home, probably in an hour or so. She put some frozen chicken breast tenderloins on to boil. When they were cooked, she would combine them with noodles and a can of cream of chicken soup for a meal everyone would like.

When she glanced out the window, she grinned at the snowman Brett and Taylor were making in the backyard. It was good to see them outside playing, much like Willow Ridge kids would be now that school had let out for the day. Fat flakes of snow were still coming down. She'd been so focused on sewing for Betty, it seemed like a whole day had passed since this morning when she'd talked with Mamma and Ben in the café.

Rhoda went into the front room. Her mother and Naomi would be cleaning up the Sweet Seasons kitchen by now, so if she called—

The jangle of Andy's phone startled her. Betty awoke from the nap she'd drifted into while sitting on the couch.

"Shall I answer?" Rhoda asked. Betty nodded, so she picked up the receiver. "*Jah*, hullo? This is Rhoda, who's takin' care of Andy Leitner's kids," she said, thinking the caller might be confused unless she identified herself.

"And how are Andy Leitner's kids?" a familiar male voice asked. "They'd better be behaving for you, Rhoda."

"Andy! Oh, *jah*, they've been busy bees today. They're makin' a snowman out back," she replied in a rush, "while your *mamm* and I, well—we've been sewin' up some new dresses. Ya want to talk to her? She's sittin right here."

There was a pause, filled with a tired sigh. "I have a huge favor to ask," Andy said. "We're understaffed today, and we've had a steady stream of patients coming in from car accidents on the icy roads. We've gotten word of a school bus full of kids that got broadsided by an eighteen-wheeler—"

"Oh, Andy, how horrible!"

"—so I'm hoping you can stay at the house while we patch up those kids. It's going to be really late before I get home, so if you need to call your driver—"

"I'll stay right here," Rhoda insisted. "If the roads are that bad, I don't want Sheila comin' for me. We're snug as bugs in a rug, Andy. Truly we are."

"Thank you so much," he murmured. "Here comes the first ambulance from that bus crash—but we'll get you home eventually, Rhoda. We'll figure it out when I get there."

In the background Rhoda could hear tense voices and a lot of commotion before Andy said, "Tell Brett and Taylor there's no staying up late tonight. The snow's letting up and the salt trucks are out, so they'll have school tomorrow," he explained. "Stretch out on the couch if it gets late, all right? You've had a long day."

"You have, too," she replied as his words set her thoughts to spinning. "Be careful drivin' home, Andy. Things get tricky when you're drivin' after dark and you're tired."

"Thanks, Rhoda," he breathed. "You're the best."

As the phone clicked off, Rhoda tingled. *You're the best.* When had anyone ever told her that? She returned the receiver to its cradle. "Andy's going to be really late," she told Betty. "A busload of school kids is comin' to the hospital, after they got hit by a big semitruck—"

Betty gasped. "Glad . . . our two are home . . . safe. Call your mother, Rhoda."

Rhoda lifted the receiver again. "After I talk to Mamma, we can cut out the aprons for your new dresses," she suggested. "Amazin' what we've accomplished today, Betty! The snow's been a problem for a lot of folks, but not for us."

Chapter Ten

Andy shut off the ignition and sat in the dark car, rubbing his eyes. While eighteen-hour shifts would be necessary now and again when he became a registered nurse, he prayed days like today would be few and far between. He'd been beyond exhausted when they'd received word about the bus wreck, yet he'd called upon a strength he hadn't known he possessed. Even so, the images of those kids, some of them with crushed, mangled limbs, would live in his memory for a long, long time.

As he glanced at the living room window, however, he smiled: Rhoda had left the lamp on, so its glow would welcome him home.

Get real. She doesn't want to stumble in a dark house if she gets up from the couch. She's worn out, too.

Andy stepped carefully out of the car, grateful to the neighbor who had cleared the driveway with his garden tractor and blade. Where would he be without good friends like Milt Rodgers and the Gaines family across the street, who had helped him through tight spots with the kids while Megan's presence had been so unreliable? So unpredictable.

You'll never associate such words with Rhoda, he thought as he headed for the door. *Rhoda the Reliable. Rhoda the Resilient. Rhoda the—*

"That you, Andy? *Gut* to see ya made it home!"

Andy's thoughts raced like the chaser lights on the house next door: as the porch light illuminated the falling snow and made Rhoda's white kapp glow above her warm smile, it occurred to him that he'd seldom known such a wonderful welcome. His weariness lightened with each step he took toward the young woman who held the door for him.

Man, do I wish this could happen every day.

"Saved ya back some chicken and noodles," Rhoda was saying as he came inside. "The kids and your *mamm* have been in bed for a while. We all had a real *gut* day."

Andy gazed at her, at a loss for words. How did she perform such magic? How had she won over his kids and taken his mother under her wing and turned his house into a comfortable, cozy home within a week? Rather than rhapsodize over the miracles Rhoda had worked—because his praise would surely cross the line his thoughts had already ignored—he focused on the matter at hand.

"But if I eat, you'll be even later getting home," he reasoned. "And I've been wondering about how to work that situation. I hate to have you call your driver at all hours of the night, but I'm not allowed to drive you. Am I?"

Rhoda clasped her hands demurely at her waist. "*Jah*, that's one of the rules. Especially when it comes to me bein' unmarried and you bein' English."

Oh, but he had stray thoughts about how to fix that situation. He followed Rhoda to the kitchen, where aromas of seasoned chicken still lingered. As he settled tiredly into his chair, she took a plate from the fridge and placed it in the microwave. The countertop was cleared. The sink drainer held no dirty dishes. All was calm, all was bright.

"You know how to use a microwave?" he asked, figuring it was a safe subject.

Rhoda's grin tickled him. "Taylor showed me how it works. She did some hand sewin' today, too. Puttin' snaps on your *mamm*'s new dresses."

"Taylor used a needle and thread?"

"*Jah*, she did! We didn't let a moment get by us today, sewin' on your *mamm*'s machine," the young woman said with a smile. She set a plate in front of him that was loaded with noodles and chunks of chicken, laced with seasonings. Then she took the chair beside his.

"My God, but this smells wonderful," he murmured without thinking about it.

"Sounds like the perfect table grace." Rhoda leaned her head on her hand, gazing at him. "I think your mother came a long way today, Andy. She's excited about havin' two new dresses, and aprons to go over the top of them—like her *mamm* used to wear, she told me."

Andy had a flash of memory—Grandma Whitney had considered an apron part of her everyday attire as she'd baked bread and cleaned and kept the household running . . . just as Rhoda Lantz did in this day and age. Something about that connection of past and present felt right to him, even as he knew he should concentrate on what this young woman was telling him. "Let me know what I owe you for that, Rhoda. Mom needs new clothes, but I'm not so good at taking her shopping—"

"Puh!" Rhoda said as she grabbed his wrist. "It was somethin' for us to do together—with Taylor—and she already had the fabric." She drew back her hand then, her eyes widening with sudden realization. "It—it was no trouble at all, Andy. Truly."

Andy took a bite of the creamy chicken and noodles, every nerve ending in his body a-jangle. Rhoda had touched him. She, too, had felt the jolt of awareness jump between them. "How am I supposed to get you home without getting you in trouble? I assume your mother knows you've stayed here this late?"

"*Jah*, she does." Rhoda glanced at the wall clock. "Won't be but a couple of hours and she'll start her day's bakin'. We Amish are *gut* at seein' the practical side to what the *Ordnung* says we're to do—not bein' sneaky, understand. Just gettin' things done without makin' a fuss. So, since it's all right for us to *pay* English fellas to drive us—and since it'd be wrong to get Sheila outta bed at this hour—"

"You're not going to pay me, after the day you've put in!"

"*Jah*, I am! Or we'll have Mamma do it," she said with a decisive nod. "That way, if our bishop, Hiram Knepp, gets wind of the situation, you and I kept it all business between us. Mamma knows about doin' that, from when Rebecca's English *dat* bought the café building out from under Hiram last summer."

His shoulders shook with silent laughter. "I suppose Amish women have to be resourceful sometimes—"

"*Jah*, that's Mamma. Resourceful. Smart."

"—but do you really think it's all business between us, Rhoda?"

As her eyes widened, Andy groaned. Had he really opened that can of worms? "I'm sorry," he rasped. "I'm too tired. I shouldn't have said that."

Rhoda glanced away. Then her blue eyes shone with determination in the low light of the kitchen. "It's usually the words we try to keep to ourselves that most need sayin', ain't so?" she murmured. "I love bein' in your home, and bein' with your kids, Andy. And I love—"

"Don't go there." He gazed at her more sternly than he wanted to. She couldn't use that *love* word. If her feelings for him were on the tip of her tongue—if she uttered those

three little words—they'd be in an even stickier situation. "It's too soon to have these feelings, and we both know it."

Rhoda sighed plaintively. "The heart always knows best. Mamma says so herself."

Andy swallowed. How had he gotten into this pickle? And now Rhoda was in it with him, and using her mother to validate it.

No, you *are grasping at straws, trying to justify your feelings. You're lonely and tired, and Rhoda's filling in all the gaps in your life. Get her home. Get over it.*

"I have tomorrow off, so you won't need to come. Meanwhile, let's get you back to Willow Ridge." Andy hoped he sounded honorable rather than peeved at her. Poor Rhoda hadn't done anything but answer his ad and connect with his kids and befriend his mother. Not her fault that in her Plain clothes, without makeup, she appealed to him with her openness, her candor . . . the absence of schemes and mind games.

"*Jah.* I'm ready."

Oh, but that innocent response teased at him as they got into the car and started down the dark county highway. He regretted the silence that hovered like a cloud as black as Rhoda's coat and bonnet . . . all because he hadn't kept his mouth shut.

"Must've been hard on ya, seein' those kids after that bus wreck," Rhoda said quietly. She was gazing out into the night as they rolled past hillsides blanketed in ten inches of snow that glistened in the moonlight. "We Amish believe that everything happens for God's own *gut* reasons, but I still hate it when folks get hurt real bad. Especially kids who couldn't do anything to help themselves."

It wasn't the time to quiz Rhoda about her beliefs—partly because his own faith had gone by the wayside after Megan left him and their kids. But she had introduced a safe topic of conversation. It was slow going, even though the plows had been out, because the black ice was impossible to spot until the car was already fishtailing on it.

"It seemed as though they came in an endless river of crushed legs and broken arms and bloody faces," Andy murmured, trying to maintain an emotional distance from the vivid images of those kids. "Made it worse that they were from northern Missouri, on their way home from a school event south of here, where the weather hadn't been an issue. Think of all those parents, getting calls late in the night that their kids were injured."

"Andy, I'm so sorry." Rhoda's whisper filled the car with her sorrow, not to mention her concern for him. "But think how much worse it would've been had ya not been there. Seems to me you'd be the calm in the storm, the voice of reason in that room full of pain. Those kids were terrified, but you were there to put them back together. And what a blessing for their parents, too."

Andy forced himself to focus on the road. How had Rhoda formed such a noble picture of him, sketching him as he would *like* to be seen? Especially since she'd probably spent little time in a hospital or at the scene of a disaster. "Thank you," he rasped, raw with the terror that had filled the emergency room.

Rhoda smiled. "We Amish have a real respect for doctors and nurses, on account of how our members don't get enough schoolin' to practice medicine. We have the occasional midwife among us, but she gets her trainin' from other midwives."

It was an intriguing idea. But not a topic to discuss while he was steering the car along an icy road at a snail's pace. "It's sweet of you to say that . . . to be concerned for the way I'm handling tonight's crisis," he said quietly. "Frankly, there were times I wanted to walk away from it. To ditch nursing and find an easier livelihood."

"Ah, but when you're a healer, there's no turnin' your back on the misery—or on your God-given skills, ain't so?" Rhoda squeezed the hand he'd kept on the gearshift knob so he could downshift on the hills. "That would be like tellin' God to go fly a kite. I can't see ya doin' that, Andy. There's too much love in ya."

Even through the gloves on her hand and his, he felt compassion pouring out like a balm to his battered soul. "Rhoda, if you knew much about love, you wouldn't be saying that. You're looking at a refugee from a failed marriage, whose family got split apart by—"

"How can ya think such a thing?" She sat taller in the passenger seat. "You're actin' as God's healin' hands on this earth. The Bible teaches that God is love, and that we're all His children, which means we're made of that same love. Can't be any other way, as I see it."

He had no choice but to ease the car to a stop on the edge of the road. They had just reached Willow Ridge, where the farmsteads and shops lay sleeping beneath their blankets of snow. The only light was a quarter of a mile away, at the river bridge . . . and at this hour no one else was out. Rhoda's hand felt like a branding iron, searing him with her innocent passion. Her *faith*. Here she was talking about love again, but in a way no man could construe as making a pass or mistake for feminine wiles. Rhoda Lantz didn't know about wiles . . . did she?

As the moonlight shone through the windshield, her face took on an ethereal glow. Her black bonnet accentuated the pale purity of her skin . . . her sweet, unassuming features.

Do Amish girls know about kissing?

As soon as the thought flitted through his mind, Andy dismissed it. Of course Amish girls didn't go around kissing—

So explain the fact that their families average six to ten kids.

Andy closed his eyes and tried to think of anything but kissing Rhoda. Sure, she was in her twenties . . . had a boyfriend, for all he knew. But wasn't this thundering in his soul about more than kissing her? From what he'd learned this past week, Rhoda Lantz was precisely the kind of woman he'd always wanted: a helpmate, a listener, a mother to his children. A kick in the pants when he needed it.

Before Andy's hand found Rhoda's face, she was leaning toward him. There was no explaining it or preventing it: despite his better judgment he was kissing Rhoda Lantz, in the middle of the road in the middle of the night.

And yes, Amish girls knew about kissing.

Again and then again he tasted her sweet, eager lips. As he eased away from her, fighting to regain his sense of reason, Rhoda's sigh filled the car with the same yearning he'd known on a daily basis of late . . . the wishes he wanted to come true. The happily-ever-afters she dared to believe in. "Rhoda, I—"

"*Jah*, not the smartest thing," she rasped, "but I can't un-kiss ya now, ain't so? And why would I want to? Those were the nicest kisses ever, Andy."

He exhaled, focusing his frantic thoughts. He would drop her off at her house now. He'd call her tomorrow, and she would understand why it was best that she not work for him anymore. Never mind that the kids and his mother would be heartbroken—

It's you that would feel shattered, man.

Andy eased his foot onto the accelerator again. "It was wonderful, kissing you," he agreed tiredly. "But we just caused a whole set of new problems, didn't we?"

A grin twitched on Rhoda's lips as they turned off the highway beside the Sweet Seasons Bakery Café. "Kissin's been causin' problems since Adam and Eve. But if everything happens as a part of God's will, then that shines a whole new light on us, ain't so?"

Andy shook his head, knowing when he'd been out-classed in the reason and religion departments. "Good night, Rhoda," he said firmly. "And thank you for . . . everything."

As she clambered out of the car and then leaned down to beam at him, Andy knew that for better or for worse, he would forever remember the expression on Rhoda's beautiful face.

Chapter Eleven

"Well, Brother, you'll never guess who I saw in the wee hours this mornin', kissin' an Englishman in his car, no less!"

Ben stopped cracking eggs for their breakfast so he could listen to his twenty-eight-year-old brother Ira, speaking from the bedroom he shared with Luke. In the apartment they'd just completed above their new gristmill, the walls still echoed with the emptiness of the rooms and the lack of furniture and rugs. Maybe Ira's swaggering tone meant he was stretching the truth a bit, coaxing Luke to take his bait. Still, Ben's heart clenched.

"And what were ya doin' that ya witnessed such a thing?" Luke shot back. "And how do ya know who it was? Were ya on the hood of that car holdin' a lantern?"

"Puh! It was Rhoda Lantz, because she got out at the Sweet Seasons and hurried into the smithy!" Ira replied. "Millie and I both said her name at the same time. Saw it all from the sleigh we were ridin' across Preacher Gabe's pasture, right near the road where the car had stopped."

Ben was already striding down the short hallway, quickly considering his words. He stopped in the doorway of his brothers' bedroom. "That's not something to spread around," he said sternly. "It was late and dark last night, so ya might be mistaken."

Ira and Luke turned toward him, their eyebrows riding high. They were putting on their heavy flannel shirts, preparing for another day of plowing the snow-covered lanes around Willow Ridge.

"There was a full moon," Ira replied pointedly, "and with it glowin' on the white snow, it was almost as light as day. Perfect night for a sleigh ride, too. When we saw a car stopped on the road, I headed the horse in that direction, thinkin' they might be havin' trouble."

It was a plausible enough explanation, but it still didn't set right. Surely Rhoda wouldn't have put herself in such a compromising position. She'd only worked for that Leitner fellow about a week.

"And *jah*, you're gonna ride my rear again about bein' irresponsible, not yet joinin' the church," Ira challenged. "But Rhoda *is* a member. And she knows better than to be ridin' in a car with that English fella she's workin' for, let alone kissin' him."

"Might've been her. Might not've been him," Ben insisted, yet he sensed he was clutching at straws. "Could be she called a different driver, rather than askin' Sheila Dougherty to fetch her at such a late hour—"

"And she was *kissin'* him?" Ira retorted. "I don't think so, Bennie."

Ben stepped into the untidy bedroom, wishing he didn't have to mention this to Miriam first thing this morning. But Millie Glick was a close friend of the bishop's daughter, Annie Mae, and Hiram would be calling on the Lantz women as soon as he got a whiff of this. "My point is, little brother, that shootin' off your mouth can only bring trouble to a family who's been awfully *gut* to ya. Ya wouldn't have your mill if it weren't for Miriam settin' up the transaction with the bank, and standin' up to Hiram when he was none too happy about this land changin' hands," he said, crossing his arms. "And Rhoda's sister is gettin' your website up and runnin'—without you even havin' to ask her. Or pay her."

"Are ya sayin' I'm supposed to lie?" Ira asked in a tight voice.

"No harm in keepin' what ya know to yourself. It'll be you in the hot seat one of these days, Ira," Ben pointed out. "And if ya upset the applecart with Miriam and her girls about this incident, they might not be so happy to help ya out anymore. Just sayin'."

Ira dropped his suspenders over his shoulders to hook up his pants, apparently done discussing this subject. Luke had finished dressing, so he followed Ben back to the kitchen, where a thin trail of smoke was rising from the bread toasting in the oven. While Ben rescued the bread, swishing the air with a towel, Luke reached for three of the plates on the new shelf.

"What do you make of Ira's story?" he asked quietly. "If Millie talks to Annie Mae, there's no tellin' how much further it'll spread, no matter how Ira and I insist the girls keep this under their kapps."

"*Jah*, there's that," Ben agreed. "And if Rhoda was caught in the act, there's no changin' what she did, either. I just hate for Miriam to catch any more heat from Hiram. Things've been perty quiet with him under the ban, but he'll see it as his duty to keep Rhoda from strayin' off the path. And rightly so."

When Ira joined them at the small kitchen table, the three of them ate buttered bread and the eggs Ben had scrambled. They shared little table talk except to agree that breakfast at the Sweet Seasons seemed the better way to start their mornings, even if it meant a hike over there before returning to the mill. No dishes to wash that way, and no burnt smell lingering in the apartment.

But tossing the three pieces of black toast to the birds was the least of Ben's concerns. He hitched Pharaoh to the Lantz's plow blade, waving as his brothers headed to the eastern end of town to help clear the unpaved roads Willow Ridge kids walked to reach the schoolhouse. As Ben re-plowed the shoulder of the county blacktop so Plain folks had more room to drive their buggies, he thought about how to mention last night's incident to Miriam . . . especially be-cause Preacher Tom's rig was parked at the café, along with several others, even though it wasn't yet fully light.

Ben pulled up in front of the smithy, which was directly behind Miriam's bakery. Through the back door he went into the kitchen, figuring his fiancée would be pulling something fabulous from her ovens or helping Naomi refill the steam table with fresh muffins or biscuits. As he stomped the snow from his boots, Miriam's eyes lit up—and oh, how those eyes warmed him like hot cocoa as she came over for a quick kiss.

"Mornin' to ya, Ben," she murmured. "You've got a way of showin' up just in time to sample things. I took chocolate date bread outta the oven a while ago, and I recommend a little cream cheese or honey butter on it."

Naomi wiggled her fingers at him from the stove, where she stirred a pot of fragrant chili they'd be serving for lunch. Hannah was out front waiting tables. "Rhoda not feelin' up to snuff this morning?" he asked as he joined Miriam by the back counter, where she'd been slicing loaves of dark, sweet-smelling bread. The *swish-swish* of the dishwasher would mask their talk.

Miriam handed him a honey-buttered slice of the chocolate bread, her expression tight. "Rhoda stayed late at the Leitners' last night, while Andy patched up a bunch of kids after their bus got hit by an eighteen-wheeler," she murmured. "All well and *gut*, that part. But when I quizzed her about why his car had stopped in the road . . . well, her moony-eyed smile told the tale. I'm not one bit happy about it, either."

Ben let out the breath he'd been holding. "*Jah*, well, I'm afraid ya weren't the only one who figured out what she and her driver were up to," he replied beneath the noise of the dishwasher. "Ira and Millie Glick were out sleigh ridin'. Thought the folks in the stopped car might be havin' trouble— and then saw what they were doin' in there. Knew it was Rhoda gettin' out, too."

Miriam closed her eyes in distress only a mother would know. "Oh, but I hate to hear that. Millie can't keep her mouth shut to save her soul—but then, it's Rhoda's soul we need to be concerned about, ain't so? Much as I respect Andy Leitner for becomin' a nurse, nothin' *gut* can come of this. And Rhoda talks on and on about his kids and his *mamm*." She blinked rapidly, determined not to cry. "Hearts are gonna get broken, but there's no way around it. She can't keep workin' for him. And she'd best go straight to Preacher Tom and confess before he—or Hiram—hears about it second hand."

Rhoda opened her eyes and gawked at the clock on the yellow kitchen wall: 7:30!

Mamma had told her to get her rest after such a long day—no sense in dropping dishes or burning herself on the stove from being exhausted—but she couldn't recall the last time she'd been in bed this late. She washed up at the bathroom sink, scrambled into clean clothes, and wound her hair into a fresh bun.

But when Andy's face flashed in her mind, she came to a complete standstill, suspended in her memories . . . recalling the way he had reached for her at the moment she had leaned toward him in the darkness. Their souls had connected in some inexplicable way until sheer joy had shimmered between them.

Then Rhoda hung her head. How could kisses that had felt so right, so beautiful, be so very wrong?

Andy said it wasn't his intent to get me into trouble, Lord, and I knew better than to kiss him, too, and yet . . . it happened. Even if Mamma figured out what we were doin', I can't feel sorry about that kiss. I just can't!

Much as she didn't want to enter the Sweet Seasons and deal with the disapproval in her mother's eyes, there was nothing to do but show up for work. By the looks of the buggies in the lot, several folks were eating breakfast this morning.

Has Mamma told Naomi? Has she said anything to Rachel?

It would be just as difficult to face her twin sister as it was to handle Mamma's disappointment. Rachel had been properly courted by an Amish boy, both of them already members of the church. True enough, their sister Rebecca's dramatic return had made some waves in their relationship last summer, but Rachel had never doubted that Micah Brenneman was the right man for her. They'd grown up next door to each other and had been sweethearts for most of their lives.

I wish it were simpler to find the right man, the right path, Lord.

Rhoda wrapped her shawl around her shoulders for the dash between the smithy and the back door of the café. Was it wrong to express such wishes to God? Did He get tired of her whining? It had been easy enough to assure Andy last night that God was love, and that all people were His children, made of that same love . . . but it was another thing altogether to justify their behavior with that statement today. No matter how she felt about those kisses, or about Andy Leitner, she knew better than to cross the line between Amish and English.

Rhoda stepped inside the kitchen and stomped the snow from her high-topped shoes. The warmth from the ovens wrapped around her as the fragrances of bacon and cinnamon filled her soul with their sweet richness.

"Mornin' to ya!" Naomi called over from the fridge. She was taking out several pounds of ground meat, which would go into the soup for today's lunch, so Rhoda grabbed the fridge door and steadied the heavy pan as Naomi lowered it. "Sounds like ya had a mighty long day yesterday, Rhoda, but it's *gut* ya were there with Mr. Leitner's kids when he had to stay so late at the hospital."

How much did Naomi know? Even though her tone and smile were as warm as ever, Rhoda again realized the weight of last night's behavior . . . how it would affect every little conversation until her sin was out in the open. The only cure was to confess. Because Bishop Knepp was under the ban, he wouldn't be the man she'd go to, but it wasn't any easier having to tell Preacher Tom what she'd gotten herself entangled in. Even though Tom Hostetler was a good friend, he might require her to kneel in confession in front of the whole church.

I can't deal with that this morning. Not until I've sorted out my feelings . . . and maybe enjoyed the fact that Andy thought I was worth kissin', for just a little longer. Is it a sin to feel gut, to feel perty, after the way so many local fellas have passed me by?

Rhoda blinked away her musings. "*Jah*, I think Andy's *mamm* was glad to have me there, too," she remarked as she hung up her shawl. "I was real surprised she wanted me to sew a couple of dresses—Plain, like we wear—so's it'll be easier for her to dress herself without any buttons. And she wanted aprons, too!"

"Well, what do ya know about that? Bet she was real happy to have those new clothes," Naomi replied. "Fresh colors always lift your spirits."

Rhoda saw Rachel and Hannah out in the dining room, which was about half full. Her mother stood at the back counter drizzling white glaze over a pan of cinnamon-raisin sticky buns. "Mornin', Mamma," she said, with what she hoped sounded like her normal cheerfulness. "*Denki* for sayin' I should sleep later. I feel all the better for it."

Her mother's smile appeared tight. Downright grim. "Always best to start the day with a clear mind, well rested," she remarked. Then she gestured for Rhoda to follow her. "Need some help gettin' our Christmas cookie decorations down from the shelf, before ya get busy."

Rhoda's thoughts began to spin. While the big plastic bin of sanding sugars, jimmies, and paste food colors was bulky— tucked away until December—it seemed odd that Mamma would ask her for help.

"We need to talk." Mamma slipped an arm around Rhoda's shoulders to bring her closer. "Seems I wasn't the only one who noticed how the car stopped on the road last night."

Rhoda's heart thudded. What were the chances, after one o'clock in the morning on a cold, snowy night, that anyone else would've seen Andy kissing her? "Who else, then?" she breathed.

"Ben says his brother Ira was out sleigh ridin' with Millie—"

Rhoda grimaced, already sensing what would come next.

"—and when they thought ya were havin' car trouble, they came on over," Mamma continued in a rapid, worried whisper. "They saw what ya stopped for. And after they went on their way, they saw ya gettin' out of the car to come inside, of course."

Why did it have to be Ira Hooley who had spotted her? Ira, who had flirted and acted interested in taking her out but had taken Millie Glick instead.

"Oh, Mamma, I had no idea . . . it was just this one time." Rhoda covered her face with her hands, wishing her frightened thoughts would stop spinning so fast. "It only lasted a few seconds—"

"*Jah*, well, you're no stranger to our ways, Daughter," her mother said softly. "What's done is done, but there's the consequences to face. Better to come clean with Preacher Tom sooner rather than later, so he'll know you're sincerely tryin' to stay right with the Lord and the *Ordnung*. And since Millie and Annie Mae are pretty thick, be ready for the bishop to come callin', askin' for your answers, as well."

Rhoda sighed heavily. She stepped on the folding ladder they kept handy and grabbed the awkward bin full of Christmas cookie decorations from the top shelf. "Here ya go," she said, aware of how dead her voice sounded in this tiny room.

"Preacher Tom left a bit ago. With his milkin' done for the mornin', and after all the snow plowin' he did around his dairy barns yesterday," her mother said, "he's probably gonna spend a quiet day in his warm house."

With a resigned sigh, Rhoda put away her thoughts of savoring Andy's kiss just a little longer. "Does Rachel know? Or Naomi?"

"Not the details. Only that ya came back real late from New Haven," Mamma said with a shake of her head. "It's not my place to tell them, ya see. But this little tidbit won't stay under Millie's kapp for long, even if Ira doesn't gossip about it."

Rhoda gazed into her mother's doelike eyes, sorry she'd been the cause of the doubts and worry that now clouded Mamma's usually cheerful nature. "I'm on my way over to Tom's, then."

Chapter Twelve

Rhoda pounded loudly on Preacher Tom's front door. She waited for what seemed like forever . . . Maybe he was out in his barns working on his milking equipment. Maybe she should scuttle on home rather than admit to kisses that still seemed more wonderful than anything she'd ever known. The wind whipped the edges of her bonnet, chilling her.

You'll have to come back again, if ya leave now. Mamma won't hear of it, if ya haven't confessed and made good on your promises as a member of the church.

Then she heard a familiar voice inside the house. "*Jah*, I'm gettin' there! Don't go away!"

When the door opened, Preacher Tom gazed at her over rimless glasses that were ready to slip off the end of his nose. "Well, now! This was worth comin' to my door for," he said with a smile. "Come on in! But you'll have to tell me if you're Rachel or Rhoda."

Oh, but for a moment she was tempted to give her sister's name! Except Preacher Tom would see through that lie in a heartbeat once she told him why she'd come. "I'm Rhoda," she murmured as she stepped into his big kitchen. "And I'm real sorry to interrupt whatever you're doin', but . . . well, I've gotta talk to ya, Tom."

"Been paintin' on a Nativity set," he said as he led her through his cluttered kitchen and into the sunny front room. A large worktable sat by the picture window. "Keeps me busy on these cold days. Seems that for every set I sell to tourists in Zook's Market, I get orders for three more."

"That's because ya do *gut* work, Tom." Rhoda picked up a wooden figure still awaiting paint—a wise man with a broad-brimmed hat and a beard, holding a big apple as his gift for the baby Jesus. Brett and Taylor would love such a Nativity set. What a perfect gift, to help them understand the Amish culture and the way Plain folks celebrated Christmas.

But she hadn't come to ooh and aah over Preacher Tom's crafting. Rhoda removed her bonnet and coat, suddenly warmer than she wanted to be.

Tom perched on the wooden stool he sat on to paint, gesturing toward the rocking chair nearest his table. He was a few years older than Mamma, with just enough silver in his hair and beard to resemble tinsel. His clothes looked rumpled, on account of how he didn't always get them pressed: his wife, Lettie, had run off with an English fellow last spring. And while Ben Hooley's aunt Nazareth now seemed to be carrying a torch for Tom, it wouldn't be proper for her to spend time here in his home. Lettie had divorced him, but the *Ordnung* stated that Tom wasn't free to remarry until she died.

"And what might be on your mind on this cold, snowy mornin', Rhoda?" he asked gently.

She knew that confession was the way to handle what she and Andy had done last night, but she felt flustered. Suddenly tongue-tied. This was the first time she'd done anything she needed to confess. Rhoda clasped her hands in her lap, finding a worn spot in the rug to focus on. "I guess ya know I'm workin' for an English family," she began.

"*Jah*, your *mamm* talks like it's goin' well. You're well suited to that sort of work."

Oh, but that stung like a paper cut! "Andy's a fine man, devoted to his nursin' work, and, well—we both knew better," she mumbled, "but last night he had to stay at the hospital real late, so he drove me home. We . . . kissed in his car."

Tom's eyes widened. "Oh my. That's not the way to—"

"We won't let it happen again!" Rhoda blurted, her eyes stinging with tears. "But we were stopped alongside the road—had no idea Ira Hooley and Millie Glick saw us while they were out in a sleigh. And Mamma noticed the car had stopped, too . . . and she guessed what had happened from the look on my face."

Tom sighed wearily. "Ya won't like hearin' this, but ya have to quit workin' for this fella, here and now. You're only puttin' yourself in temptation's way if ya keep goin' to his home."

Her heart clenched. Preacher Tom had said what any leader of the church would say, and much more gently than Bishop Knepp would've handled it. But it tore at her soul to think about not seeing Taylor's and Brett's bright smiles anymore. And poor Betty was starting to show some real recovery . . .

"*Jah*, you make a *gut* point, Preacher Tom," she said with a sigh.

He gazed pointedly at her. "But?"

Rhoda met his eyes and saw great concern but great compassion, as well. "What if I believe I . . . belong in his family?"

"Oh, Rhoda, it's way too soon to be thinkin' such a thing, even if it is right!"

"But—but I took to his kids right off. And his *mamm* is comin' out of her shell, recoverin' from her stroke, and—" Rhoda nipped her lip, knowing her thoughts were headed down the wrong road. But if she were to truly confess, didn't she need to lay all her feelings out in the open? "Andy's a special man, Tom. Not like any of the fellas I've been on dates with."

"Rhoda Lantz, if ya take up with an Englishman—if ya forsake the vows ya made when ya were baptized into the church—we'll have no choice but to excommunicate ya," the preacher said earnestly. "And that would break your mother's heart. Take it from a fella who lost the one he loved when she kept thinkin' the grass was greener on the English side of the fence."

She sighed. "I know that. I had to say it out because I didn't want to lie to ya."

"All well and *gut*," Preacher Tom affirmed. "But you've been taught obedience—to God and to the *Ordnung*—from the cradle. There's right and there's wrong here. No middle ground."

Rhoda closed her eyes against tears she didn't want him to see. Why was this so difficult? What he had said was absolutely true: there was no middle ground. And if she entertained the wild idea of giving up her Plain life—even though she wasn't nearly at that point—it would make Mamma look like an ineffective parent who had lost the most basic control over her child . . . even if that child was twenty-one years old.

She clutched at another straw. "It wouldn't be right to just up and quit, though," she murmured. "The kids need an adult there after school, because Betty's not strong enough to keep track of what-all they're doing."

Preacher Tom's gaze didn't waver. "And ya really think one kiss won't lead to another?" he demanded. "Anybody could see why a fella would be attracted to a young woman who keeps his house runnin' while he's away, and English men don't understand what they're gettin' into when they flirt with an Amish gal. They've no idea what trouble they make for her, pretendin' to care for her when there's no *gut* direction for the courtship to go."

Andy was doing more than pretending to care. Even after such a short time, Rhoda believed he was as sincere about his feelings, his needs, as she was.

"If ya promise me here and now, Rhoda, that ya won't go back there—that you'll call this fella first thing when ya get home, tellin' him ya can't sacrifice your soul to work for him," Tom said earnestly, "then this confession between you and me'll be the end of it. Ya did right by comin' here. But I can't keep this under my hat if your relationship goes any farther. Then you'll have to confess at a Members' Meeting— a kneelin' confession that might lead to puttin' ya under the ban."

"*Jah*. That's the way of it."

"Use my phone in the barn, then. Make the call right now."

Rhoda's jaw dropped. While it was the right thing to do according to what the church demanded, it felt like a betrayal of a decent man, a responsible father who was depending on her. "I—I don't know the phone number."

"Even so, I can see your answer in your eyes," he murmured. Tom sounded disappointed yet determined to help her through a difficult situation. "I know a little about fallin' head over heels for somebody special—love at first sight, if ya will. First time I ever saw Lettie, I knew I had to marry her."

Rhoda and everyone else in Willow Ridge knew how that had turned out—even though Tom and Lettie Hostetler had been married long enough to have four kids who were now married themselves. The rumors and signs of Lettie's involvement with that English fellow had popped up all along the way. It wasn't like she'd left Tom on a whim, with a stranger.

"I'm real sorry that happened to ya," she murmured. "Everybody is."

"Well, *sorry* hasn't put my life back together," he said with a sigh. "I'm warnin' ya about such things, Rhoda— about such *pain*. We Amish believe that everything that happens to us is God's will, but that doesn't make this empty house any easier to live in."

Rhoda picked up her coat, wishing she could do the right thing effortlessly, but every muscle in her body resisted walking out to his phone. And it would be a lie to tell him she'd call from the Sweet Seasons.

Tom stood up with her. "If ya get in that bind again, where ya have to stay late workin' someplace and ya don't want to call Sheila for your ride, call *me*, Rhoda," he insisted. "Might sound silly or pathetic, but I've got a bell in the house here, in case the phone rings in the barn. Sure, it's the way my milk haulers keep in touch with me, but truth be told, if Lettie needs me to come and get her, I'll know it right off. Just promise me ya won't go back to this Andy's house."

Her throat went tight. How sad, that this fine man lived at the ready to fetch his runaway wife, even though she had divorced him. "Might not look like it, but I really appreciate what you've been tellin' me, Tom. I—I'll let ya know when I've made that call."

Rhoda stepped outside, tying her black strings to keep the wind from snatching her bonnet. She wasn't ready to return to the café, where Mamma would once again know how she'd fallen short, so she walked down Preacher Tom's long lane to the county road instead of taking the shortcut through the fields. Even though the big plows had driven past, clearing the snow and spreading cinders and salt, the pavement had a lot of icy patches that made walking tricky. She picked her way along, head down against the wind, wondering how to resolve this problem about Andy and his kids . . .

When she looked up a while later, Zook's Market was just a few minutes ahead. She was unaware of how she'd gotten this far along, but ducking in out of the wind seemed like a fine idea, even if she would need a plausible reason for being there instead of at the Sweet Seasons helping Mamma. Had Henry and Lydia heard about last night's escapade? How strange it felt, wondering if she was already being talked about—being judged—by folks she'd known all her life. What would she tell the Zooks if they asked any difficult questions?

When she stepped inside Willow Ridge's general store, however, she saw the perfect inspiration: one of Preacher Tom's Nativity scenes was on display near the door. Along with a manger watched over by an angel and a star, Baby Jesus and His family, three bearded wise men, two shepherds, and an assortment of sheep, cows, and a donkey completed the scene. Men in Bible times didn't wear black broad-brimmed hats, nor did the animals in that long-ago stable have colorful Amish quilts for blankets, but such artwork that depicted Plain folks at the manger appealed to tourists. And it was still a way to spread the joy of Jesus's birth.

If I take this along tomorrow, Taylor and Brett—and Betty and Andy—will know how much they mean to me. Even if I have to leave them.

Rhoda read the little sign:

AMISH NATIVITY, HANDMADE
BY LOCAL ARTIST—$150.

She swallowed hard. Few Plain folks would pay such a price—but then, they often made their own Nativity scenes or handed them down from one generation to the next. Wasn't this the perfect way to spend the money Andy had paid her?

Rhoda looked between the tall white shelves of the store, which was very quiet this afternoon. She was relieved to find Katie Zook over by the cutting table where they sold fabrics. "Katie! Will ya box up this Nativity scene by the door for me? Meanwhile, I'm gonna pick up a few cookie-makin' supplies, too. It's time for that kind of bakin'."

Her friend smiled up at her, looking as though she'd heard nothing about Rhoda's kisses in a car. "Would this be for those kids you're watchin'?" she asked as she took a box from under the cutting table.

"Jah," Rhoda replied, pleased she didn't have to explain anything further. "They're curious about our beliefs, and this'll be a *gut* gift for keepin' Christmas the way it was meant to be."

She chose flour and butter, along with four colors of sanding sugar and a box of food coloring, and by the time she left Zook's Market with her packages she felt much better. Rather than not showing up without an explanation for Betty and those dear children, she would spend just one more day with the family she'd grown so close to. Surely it wouldn't be a sin to say a proper good-bye . . . to give Andy more time to find her replacement . . .

Chapter Thirteen

Andy sat gazing at his computer screen, clicking and reading . . . leaning closer to study the menu items on the Sweet Seasons Bakery Café website. He'd spent the entire morning cramming for his exams, and after warming some of Rhoda's soup for his mom and himself, he'd allowed his overstuffed mind a few moments away from the complicated world of prescription drug interactions and nursing procedures. Rhoda's sweet smile and lilting voice had been in the back of his mind while he'd studied, and with the kids at school and his mother napping in front of her TV, he gave in to his craving for information.

The site's descriptions of sticky buns and fresh fruit pies were making him ravenous, so he clicked the link for the new Mill at Willow Ridge. The ads for Amish shops listed along the side of the screen made it easy to keep clicking and reading, and then on a whim he typed "Amish" into Google and did a search.

What must I do to become Amish?

When that question popped up on his screen, Andy immersed himself in the various online sites that provided answers. While he had no intention of making that huge lifestyle change, the Lantz family and the town of Willow Ridge had taken on a new fascination for him. What would life be like without computers and cell phones . . . without a car and electric lights and appliances? His classes on medical technology, the legal ramifications of life support, and the confidentiality of patient information made the Plain life seem very down-to-earth and inviting. Even though nursing—healing people—seemed a noble calling, there was something to be said for allowing God to decide matters of life and death in a world where insurance coverage often dictated the care a patient received.

Andy rubbed his aching eyes and kept reading. Becoming Amish went much deeper than wearing home-sewn clothing and giving up modern conveniences, of course. It required learning the Pennsylvania Dutch dialect and attending Plain church services to eventually be baptized into the faith. And it wasn't enough for an outsider to aspire to the Amish lifestyle and faith: once you were walking the walk and talking the talk, the Amish community voted on whether to accept you as one of them. In recent years, many English had expressed interest in the simpler Amish life but couldn't get past the nitty-gritty of following the *Ordnung*'s rules . . . couldn't give up the competitive, capitalist mindset they had been raised with and embrace living fully in the faith that Jesus had taught. So while they remained friends with the Plain community, they weren't accepted as true members of it.

Why do Amish practice shunning?

Andy clicked on this question and held his breath as he read some of the reasons Amish folks might be ostracized by family and friends as punishment for wrongdoing. Sin, a glossed-over concept in many present-day churches, had to be followed by sincere public confession and repentance before the erring member was restored to good standing in the Old Order faith. If a member avoided the consequences of his or her wrongdoing and didn't comply with the rules of the ban, as prescribed by the bishop, he or she could be excommunicated . . . cast out of the membership and considered ineligible for the salvation Jesus promised his followers.

Andy let out the breath he didn't realize he'd been holding. This was serious stuff. No-frills Christianity, without praise bands or pretty pictures of a God who welcomed all of His children home. It occurred to him then that although Rhoda had insisted on paying him to drive her home last night, to comply with her beliefs, money had been the last thing on their minds after they had kissed. If Rhoda were shunned, would Miriam really seat her daughter at a separate table for meals? If no one from the community could do business with Rhoda or accept anything from her, that meant she couldn't serve meals at the café, which would cause a quandary for the whole Lantz family.

Andy's stomach churned. Their kisses had been so simple, so brief, yet his moment of unconsidered affection had thrust Rhoda into a situation with serious consequences if anyone found out about it . . . or if guilt compelled her to confess. He had a sudden image of her sweet face, reddened and wet with tears, as she admitted her sin to Miriam, for Rhoda impressed him as a young woman of intense sincerity and the desire to do the right thing.

Was she in hot water today? At odds with her mother, and possibly everyone else at the café, because she'd broken a basic rule the moment she'd gotten into his car? He and Rhoda had used icy roads and the late hour to justify her ride home, but Andy sensed that if her church leaders got wind of her forbidden activities, those justifications would hold little water with them.

Andy had the sudden urge to call her, to see if she was all right. Yet that might tip the scales even farther against her—especially if her mother or sister answered the phone and thought he was too interested in Rhoda. He was damned if he did call, and damned if he didn't.

And if he showed up at the café to check on her, he might compound her problem even more. Never mind that he didn't want to wake his mom to say he was leaving. His mother had been so pleased this morning when he'd peeked into her room to find her wearing a new dress covered with bright red poppies. Andy didn't want to ruin her happiness. She was excited about Rhoda sewing her new aprons tomorrow, but maybe that wasn't going to happen.

Maybe Rhoda was already forbidden to come here again.

Andy clicked out of Google and stood up. His imagination might be taking him for a ride, for Rhoda was probably as resourceful as her mother. Maybe none of the dire consequences he'd envisioned had happened, and she was waiting tables and smiling at folks in the café, as usual. And yet, if there was a chance she couldn't work for him any longer, he needed to know that. He wanted to prepare his mom and the kids for her absence . . . which meant he'd have to have an explanation ready for *why* Rhoda wouldn't be coming over anymore. Something other than admitting he'd kissed her.

How would he face his family's disappointment? Brett, Taylor, and his mom were every bit as wrapped up in Rhoda's charm and caring, efficient ways as he was.

Andy glanced at the clock. If he slipped quietly out to the car for a quick run to Willow Ridge, he could be back before the kids got home from school—before his mom awoke—

The ringing of the phone made him jump. "Yeah, hello?" he said as he raised the receiver of the phone in the living room.

"Andy?" There was a pause. "Andy, it's—"

"Rhoda," he breathed. How had she known to call him at this very moment? Had she felt his anxiety all the way from Willow Ridge? "Are you all right? I—I've just realized, after reading on the computer, how much trouble I might've gotten you into and I'm so terribly sorry if—"

"*Jah*, there is trouble." She cleared her throat, sounding resolute. "Preacher Tom has insisted I have to quit workin' for ya—"

Andy closed his eyes against a welling-up of regret. This was his fault, and Rhoda was suffering the consequences. If her preacher already knew what had flared between them last night . . .

"—but I'm gonna come tomorrow afternoon. I've got a gift for the kids, and . . . it'll give ya more time to find somebody else to be with them and your *mamm*. I'm sorry it's such short notice."

"No, *I'm* sorry," he rasped. His mind raced over what Rhoda was saying . . . and not saying. "How did your preacher know about us?"

Rhoda let out a rueful laugh. "Well, Mamma sent me to his house straightaway this morning to confess, after she saw the look on my face when I came in last night . . . and after a couple folks in a sleigh saw us parked alongside the road, too."

Andy swore under his breath. In a town the size of Willow Ridge, this juicy tidbit would spread faster than Miriam's apple butter had covered his toaster waffle this morning.

"So I guess I'm doin' the right thing by quittin'," she continued with a shuddery sigh, "but that doesn't mean I feel any too *gut* about it."

"Rhoda, I never intended for you to be in trouble with your mom or the preacher. I had no idea anyone saw us—"

"Me neither. But that full moon on the new-fallen snow made it the perfect night for sleigh ridin'," she replied wistfully.

What an image filled his mind, of a horse-drawn sleigh crossing open moonlit fields . . . Rhoda bundled up beside him in the seat, smiling up at him. But that sweet idea was never to be, so he might as well get it out of his head.

"Too bad it was a couple of my chatterbox friends thinkin' we might be havin' car trouble," Rhoda continued. Then she cleared her throat. "Well, I gotta get back to waitin' tables. Just wanted ya to know what's goin' on, Andy. I'll see ya tomorrow."

As he hung up, Andy dropped onto the couch and fell back, scowling. While there was no damage control strong enough to prevent the consequences of their being seen in his car, or to relieve Rhoda of whatever penance her church required, his mind was whirling in such a high gear that studying for his exams was impossible. The real questions for him now didn't involve medicine or hospital procedure. What would he say to his son, his daughter, and his mother about Rhoda leaving them? What could he do to set things right for Rhoda—and with her family and the leaders of her church?

How would he concentrate on his exams, which began tomorrow, when his mind was filled with the cadence of her accented voice . . . her gentle humor . . . her open, trusting smile?

It was too soon to have such strong feelings for Rhoda Lantz. But that hadn't stopped him from kissing her, and it wouldn't keep him from missing her.

That evening as she and Mamma finished the dishes, Rhoda again felt the tightening of her insides: their crochet club met this evening over at the Knepp place. Hiram wasn't one for hanging around during their weekly hen parties, but if he'd talked with Preacher Tom or had heard the rumors from his daughters, he would delight in pouncing on her about the kiss she'd shared in Andy's car.

"You're quiet tonight," her mother remarked. "Did your talk with Preacher Tom not go well?"

"Went fine." Rhoda tied on her black bonnet, steeling herself for more of Mamma's questions—and then for Rachel's. Never in her life had Rhoda kept anything from her twin . . . but then, never had she done anything that defied the ways of their faith, either. "Not lookin' forward to bein' at the bishop's tonight. Tom assured me my confession would remain between him and me, since I went over and talked to him immediately, but . . ."

"*Jah*, Hiram's just itchin' to find a reason why ya shouldn't work in an English home," her mother replied. "But there's no controllin' how this story will play out. That's why it's best to avoid gettin' into trouble in the first place. Talkin' to folks is easier when ya don't have to watch every word ya say."

Mamma's tight tone was one more reminder of how guilt affected relationships. Through the window they saw a carriage coming from the main house, so they went downstairs. As they went outside and clambered into the backseat, Rachel smiled at them over her shoulder. "Micah's brothers are meetin' him at your new house tonight, Mamma," she remarked. "He says while we gals are gossipin', the three of them will set your kitchen cabinets in place, ready to install tomorrow."

"Mighty nice of him to be workin' such long hours," Mamma replied.

Rhoda glanced at the new structure when her sister steered the horse past it, noting how their mother didn't sound nearly as happy about such news as she ordinarily would have. *Because I've caused her such worry . . . put a damper on her happiness by fallin' for a man I can't have . . .*

"So how's it goin' over at the Leitners'?" Rachel asked. "Are those kids behavin' themselves?"

Rhoda nipped her lip. It would be so much easier to leave Taylor and Brett if they were ornery or lazy—just as it would be easier to answer her twin if she and Andy had behaved as well as his children had. "The kids are doin' fine," she hedged. "But with their *dat* workin' late shifts at the hospital, it's not *gut* to be callin' my ride home at all hours of the night. Not like I can park a horse and buggy in their yard and drive myself home, either. So tomorrow's my last day."

Rachel swiveled in the front seat. "Oh my. You've been so happy with that job, too, Sister. Smilin' brighter than I've seen ya for a long time."

Mamma found Rhoda's hand and squeezed it beneath the layers of their heavy coats, but it was small comfort. "That's the way of it in the nursin' profession," Rhoda replied with a halfhearted shrug. "Probably best to find out now, before . . . before we all get real attached to each other."

It wasn't a lie, but it wasn't the whole truth, either. While she should have been able to share last night's happenings with her twin, Rhoda didn't feel like opening that can of worms when they were only minutes from the bishop's house. If things worked out right—if Millie and Ira and Tom kept quiet—maybe this whole episode would vanish into thin air like the vapor of the horse's breath on this frosty night. After all, their sister Rebecca's existence had remained a secret for eighteen years—and wonderful love had come from her reappearance last summer. God had picked just the right time to reveal her presence to them. So maybe years from now Rhoda could reflect on how kissing Andy had been a great lesson in her life. A positive turning point.

They had barely removed their coats in the Knepps' kitchen, however, before Annie Mae's gaze told Rhoda the bishop's daughter *knew*. And she wanted to hear a whole lot more. Nellie Knepp and Nazareth Hooley poured steaming tea into their cups before the seven of them headed toward the front room with their bags of bright-colored yarn.

"So if we're startin' a new afghan tonight, who shall we give it to?" Nellie asked as they all settled into chairs and sofas. "Ben got the first one—"

"And he's usin' it on his bed in the mill apartment, too," Mamma remarked as she pulled a half-used skein of magenta yarn from her bag.

"Hiram's got our second afghan folded over the rockin' chair in his office," Jerusalem chimed in. Her fingers flew around the center clusters of a new granny square. "Saw him with it wrapped around his shoulders yesterday, when I wasn't supposed to know he was nappin'."

As they all laughed, Rhoda caught Annie Mae looking purposefully at her and then toward the kitchen door.

"Am I the only one who noticed a drafty spot in Preacher Tom's front room when we had services there?" Nazareth took a long sip of her tea. "Seems to me any fella on his own would enjoy something cuddly to curl up in. And he does so much for us, being our preacher." Her girlish smile gave away her feelings for Tom—but Rhoda was more aware of their hostess holding her gaze.

"Silly me, I forgot about that tray of cookies Nellie and Jerusalem made," Annie Mae said as she rose from her chair. "Believe me, there'd be none of them left if we hadn't hidden them away from the twins."

"And where are the kids tonight?" Rachel asked as she started a row of deep green around the fuchsia center she'd crocheted.

"Dat took the four of them out in the sleigh," Nellie said with a big grin. "I told him to go clear on over to Morning Star and all that fresh night air would surely put the little ones to sleep before they got back!"

As more laughter filled the front room, Rhoda got up to

help Annie Mae. She and the bishop's eldest daughter had become better friends of late, so it might be best to humor her now . . . and find out how much she knew about last night. When Rhoda entered the kitchen, Annie Mae was beckoning her into the pantry. As the door swung shut behind them, Rhoda wasn't so sure this was a good idea.

"So is it true, what Millie told me?" Annie Mae whispered. "Did ya really kiss that English fella in his car? Was he any *gut* at it?"

Rhoda's cheeks burned in the darkness. "Ya can't be lettin' on to folks about—"

"Dat says he's divorced—"

The bottom dropped from Rhoda's stomach. "And why'd ya go tellin' your *dat* about—just because Millie thought we were kissin' doesn't make it true, ya know!"

Annie Mae's hands found her shoulders in the darkness. She laughed softly. "Lord a-mercy, *no*, I wouldn't tell my *dat*, ya silly goose," she replied. "I'm just amazed that *you* would be doin' such things, when it's *me* everybody's been shakin' their heads over, for runnin' with Yonnie Stoltzfus and now datin' a fella Luke's age."

"*Jah*, but you're still in your *rumspringa*—"

The pantry door swung open and bumped Rhoda's shoulder, which made her and Annie Mae jump toward the back shelves. But there was no escaping the stalwart figure silhouetted in the doorway: Jerusalem Hooley gazed at them pointedly. "Thought maybe ya hid those cookies so well ya couldn't find them," she remarked dryly. Then she let the door swing shut again.

Rhoda's heart pounded painfully. How long had Jerusalem been listening outside the pantry? There would be no escaping judgment if she'd overheard. The former schoolteacher had been the one to insist Bishop Knepp confess and serve out his shunning for hiding a car in the barn. When Annie Mae pulled the string of the battery light on the pantry wall, to find the large platter of cookies she'd hidden in a blue enamel roaster, Rhoda saw the dread sketched around her eyes.

"I promise ya, I won't breathe a word," the bishop's daughter murmured.

Ya might not have to, Rhoda thought desperately. But she didn't have the heart to say that to Annie Mae.

Chapter Fourteen

Andy left the theater-style lecture hall Thursday afternoon feeling totally drained. He had no idea how he had performed on his written phlebotomy exam, but going home sounded a lot more fulfilling than locating good veins or drawing blood. When he pulled his cell phone from his pocket, however, a text message awaited him.

"Phooey," he muttered as he reread the words from Dr. LaFarge, his hospital supervisor. He'd so hoped to spend Rhoda's final afternoon in his employ immersed in whatever magic their Amish caretaker might be working, but once again duty called. On his way to his car, he phoned home.

"Hello?" Brett answered breathlessly.

"Hey, buddy, what's going on?"

"Dad! We're decoratin' Christmas cookies we made with Rhoda—"

Oh, but Andy could taste a sugar cookie . . . lots of creamy frosting and sprinkles that crunched slightly between his teeth. Rhoda probably baked them soft and chewy, the way he liked them.

"—and when you get home, she says she's got a present for us! So you've gotta get here," his son gushed.

Andy closed his eyes. "Yeah, well—eat a star cookie for me, and put Rhoda on, will you?" he replied. "I'll see you as soon as I can."

Brett sighed. He'd heard it before, about how the hospital had called his father to work an unexpected shift. "Sure, Dad. Just a minute."

During the pause, Andy swore he could smell cookies baking . . . heard Taylor and his mother laughing in the background . . .

"*Jah?* Andy? How'd your big test go?" Rhoda asked.

Her voice—her interest in his activities—made him smile in spite of the reason he'd called. "I'm so brain-dead I'm not sure," he replied with a rueful chuckle. "And I've just gotten called in to cover a shift in the oncology ward."

"Ah. What's that?"

"Um, cancer care. Not a happy job, but necessary. So, as much as I'd hoped to spend the afternoon with you and the kids," he continued, "it might be late again. I'm really sorry, Rhoda."

"Well, ya gotta do what ya gotta do. I'll keep ya a bowl of our chili for when ya get home."

Andy closed his eyes against a wave of yearning. "Thank you so much. Everything going okay?"

"Oh, *jah*. Your *mamm*'s wearin' one of her new aprons and dresses, and the kitchen counter's covered with perty cookies," she replied breezily. Then she sighed. "But we'll miss ya, Andy."

Impulse urged him to call his supervisor and claim an emergency at home . . . but Dr. LaFarge had chosen him over four other candidates for a position on the hospital's obstetrics staff, if his final exam scores were high enough. "I'm really disappointed, Rhoda," he murmured. "And I'm sorry this means you'll be getting home a lot later than we'd figured."

"*Jah*, well, sometimes there's nothing for that but to go with the flow, ain't so?"

Andy grimaced. Because Rhoda had gone with his flow, she'd also gone against the tenets of her faith. Yet she sounded okay. Not intimidated by whatever her bishop might require of her, and not sorry she'd come today to care for his mom and kids. "Have you told Brett and Taylor you won't be back?" he whispered.

Silence. "We're havin' us a real *gut* time this afternoon. Makin' a fine mess of the kitchen table, too," she answered, sounding a little too cheerful.

"Gotcha. They're right there in the kitchen, listening."

"For sure and for certain. Ya want to talk to them?"

Rhoda had certainly passed that off without missing a beat. "Tell them they're not to give you any flack about getting to bed on time," he instructed. "As I recall, Brett's got a math test tomorrow, and Taylor's presenting a PowerPoint report on insects."

"They're both ready for school," Rhoda assured him. "But I can't tell ya a thing about how your daughter got pictures of so many bugs on the computer, along with words and music, no less!"

It touched him, how the technology he and his kids took for granted was totally foreign to Rhoda. Once again, he saw advantages to living more simply . . . to being more tuned in to people than to computers. Andy could imagine Rhoda quizzing Brett about his math, with paper and pencil—or challenging him to work the addition and subtraction problems completely in his head. He could envision the wonderment on her face as Taylor played the PowerPoint presentation and explained what she had been studying these past few weeks.

He envied Rhoda the time she had spent with his children today. Somehow, her priorities seemed more in line than his, even though he'd been finishing his degree so he could support his family.

"Thank you again, Rhoda," he murmured. "I'll be home as soon as I can. But it'll be nine or ten at the earliest."

"We'll be here waitin' for ya."

As the phone clicked in his ear, Andy blinked rapidly. It made no practical sense, yet having Rhoda waiting for him at the end of a day, in a tidy home that smelled like chili and homemade Christmas cookies, seemed like a dream come true.

But it was an impossible dream, wasn't it?

Rhoda watched, her heart in her throat, as Taylor and Brett tore into the packages she had wrapped for them. They had plugged in the lights of their decorated tree, and had turned on the two lighted Santa Claus figures that sat on the coffee table. Betty sat on the couch with her small gift in her lap, watching her grandchildren.

"It's a baby Jesus—wrapped in a quilt!" Taylor exclaimed as she held the little carving up for everyone to see.

"And I got two sheep," her brother crowed as he grabbed another little bundle from his box.

"Mary and Joseph, too, but they're Amish people!" the little girl went on as she unwrapped her next little bundle. "Oh, Rhoda, these are so cool. Is this what everybody looks like, where you live?"

Rhoda laughed. "Well, the men have beards and wear those black hats—"

"But they've got no faces." Brett yanked the rest of the green tissue paper from the trio of male figures and studied them. "So, if these are the three wise men, how come they're holdin' an ear of corn, and a chicken, and a bucket of white stuff?"

"That's milk, on account of how the fella who carved this

set is a dairy farmer. Makes the best ice cream ya ever tasted, too," Rhoda remarked. "These wise men are bringin' their homegrown gifts to the baby Jesus as their best offering to him. We Amish don't put faces on our dolls, as we don't want to make figures of people in God's image. That's God's doin'."

"Ha! And here's the cow," Taylor announced.

"And I got a shepherd holdin' a lamb," Brett chimed in.

"But I . . . got the best pieces." Betty, who had succumbed to the children's eagerness, held up her parts of the Nativity set. "The manger . . . with an Amish angel on the roof, and . . . a star made like a quilt piece."

"We gotta set this up on the table!" Brett declared. "I want to look at it and move the pieces around."

Rhoda's heart swelled. It pleased her that Andy's kids knew the basics of the Christmas scene she'd given them, and that they were so excited about receiving Tom Hostetler's work. It pleased her, as well, that the two Santa figures got put over beside the Christmas tree so the Nativity set could occupy the table. When the kids had carefully placed the manger in the center, they began to arrange the people and the animals—and then repositioned them as they mentioned the parts of the Christmas story each figure played.

Rhoda moved up to the couch to sit beside Betty, partly because she wanted to memorize the precious expressions on Brett's and Taylor's young faces as they enjoyed the gift she'd chosen for them.

"Such a . . . wonderful present, Rhoda," Betty murmured. She smoothed the front of her white apron. "And so . . . nice that you came early today . . . to sew my aprons and that polka-dot dress for Taylor."

Rhoda swallowed a lump in her throat. Andy's mother was so grateful for every little thing. She seemed perkier day by day, too, as though she was overcoming the limitations her stroke had imposed on her body. It seemed only fair to let Betty know that she'd wanted to finish her aprons because she wouldn't be coming back . . . but the words just wouldn't come out. She couldn't bear to upset her.

And she hated to spoil the fun Taylor and Brett were having, studying the details Tom had painted on each of his Nativity figures. If she said she couldn't work here anymore, the kids would ask endless questions that would shine a dubious light on her and their *dat*, even though Rhoda felt, deep down, that the kisses she and Andy had shared were a sincere expression of their feelings. While it wasn't fair to leave all the explaining to Andy . . . maybe it was best.

As usual, Rhoda insisted the kids redd up the room and set their backpacks by the door before they went to bed. And as usual Brett groused a bit, but they picked up the torn paper from their gifts and straightened the area around their computer. Not wanting to do anything differently, Rhoda followed them upstairs, secretly savoring their bedtime rituals . . . watching Brett make faces in the bathroom mirror as he brushed his teeth . . . noting how Taylor shifted her stuffed animals as she pulled her comforter down, so she could sleep with them all cuddled around her. When the kids had chosen their clothes for Friday, she wished them good night.

"Say your prayers, don't forget," she reminded them. "And before I go to bed tonight, you'll be in my prayers, too."

Taylor gave her a quick hug, looking wistful. "It's nice to think somebody like you talks to God about us, Rhoda. I don't remember anybody ever saying that before."

Oh, but her heart clenched as she squeezed Taylor's slender shoulders and nuzzled her soft curls. When she passed by Brett's bedroom door, his lights were already out and he was settling himself beneath his covers. How she wanted to kiss him good night, but that would probably start a flood of tears and questions. So she went back downstairs.

Betty was shuffling along the hallway toward her room. She grinned around the frosted cookie she had stuck in her mouth, wiggling her fingers to reveal another cookie in each hand.

"*Gut* night, Betty. Sleep well," Rhoda murmured.

The house settled around her. The wind tapped a branch against the front window, and then, when the furnace shut off, the stillness was complete. Though Rhoda wasn't accustomed to having a Christmas tree in her home, the little white lights on this one soothed her. She turned out the table lamps and stood at the tree, noting ornaments the kids had made, and mementos of their earliest Christmases and places they had visited.

Did they miss their mother? She recalled how hollow the holidays had felt that first year after Dat had passed. She wished Brett and Taylor could know a home filled with love and happiness, the way she did.

Watch over them, Lord. Help them understand why I had to leave—and that I didn't want to.

Was it too soon for having such thoughts? Had she thrown herself into this job, this family, because her loneliness had driven her here—or because the Leitners needed her? Did she truly feel at home among them after such a short time? If she allowed such feelings to take hold of her heart, would she be tempted to leave the Amish church to become a part of this family? Rhoda didn't want to think about Mamma's disappointment and sadness if that happened.

Headlights beamed through the lace curtains and Rhoda remained beside the tree, holding her breath. When Andy opened the door he stood there watching her . . . holding her gaze without breaking the silence. As he closed out the frosty breeze coming in around him, he gazed around the front room, inhaling deeply.

"It smells *so* good in here," he finally whispered.

"*Ach*, and here I stand while I could be warmin' up your bowl of—"

"Rhoda."

The way Andy said her name stilled her heart. His weary sigh echoed in her soul and she longed to caress away the tension lines etched into his handsome face. *"Jah?"*

"I won't stand next to you, because that'll lead us into temptation," Andy said in a low voice. "So I'll eat my chili and take you home, but we must agree not to touch. Not to . . . kiss again. Understand?"

She nodded, her lips pulsing as though he were kissing her anyway. "It's best. There'd be no explainin' if one of the kids came downstairs."

"And we'll be able to honestly say—to your mother, or your preacher, or whoever—that we backed away from a relationship that would only get you in trouble."

"Jah." Not that Andy's honorable intentions satisfied her need to know more about him . . . to hear his voice and feel the warmth of his arm around her shoulders. Nor did his emotional distance make her future shine any brighter. But there wasn't much to be done about that. He was behaving as he should, and she ought to be grateful for his restraint.

As Andy ate his chili and marveled over the wonderful sugar cookies she and the kids had made, Rhoda repeatedly swallowed the lump that rose in her throat. She busied herself wiping crumbs from the countertop while he ate, so he wouldn't see her blinking back tears. She tried not to think about this being the last time she would cook in this kitchen, for this family.

"I helped deliver my first baby today," Andy remarked.

He chose a star cookie frosted in yellow, encrusted with jimmies.

Rhoda heard awe in his voice and stole a glance at him. His dark brown eyes glimmered in the low light. "Everything went all right for mother and child, I hope."

"Perfect, yes. This was the couple's second child, so the mom knew what to expect and the dad was right there coaching her," he replied quietly. "Brought back the nights I spent in the delivery room when Taylor and Brett were born."

He paused then, a mixture of joy and regret edging his expression. "I found myself wishing Megan could still feel the love she shared with us back then . . ."

"*Jah*, that would be *gut* for all of ya," Rhoda murmured. It was the right thing to say, even if she preferred to imagine herself patching this family together rather than Andy's ex-wife coming back.

Andy stood up then, as though to dispel his regrets. "No sense in wishing for what will never be, though," he remarked. "And maybe you Amish have it right. Maybe her leaving us was God's will . . . God telling us we could all do better for ourselves if we went our separate ways."

Andy held her gaze then. "After all, I would never have considered a career in nursing if I were still married to Megan. Last I heard, she married a wealthy fellow and moved to some upscale town on the California coast. I could never have given her that sort of life, and I know she's happier now."

"But what about the kids? How can she live with herself, knowing she left—" Rhoda clapped her hand over her mouth. "Sorry. That's none of my beeswax."

Andy's smile forgave her immediately. "Those are questions anyone would ask, Rhoda. But it became apparent that while Megan liked the *idea* of being a mother . . . enjoyed the attention folks showered on her while she was pregnant and tending our babies, the realities of raising kids frustrated her."

"Ah. The stinky diapers and fussy cryin' at all hours. The spit-up all over a clean dress."

"And the idea that her time—her life—wouldn't be her own again until they grew up and moved out." Andy let out a sad chuckle. "Once Taylor and Brett started walking and talking—making demands—their mom felt she was losing herself."

Rhoda's eyes widened. What on earth did that mean, *losing herself*? What woman could begrudge her children the time and love and effort it required to raise them? "Well, ya surely are talkin' about it more reasonably than I would be. Beggin' your pardon, but Megan sounds mighty self-centered."

"There's that," he agreed. Then they both laughed at how he'd picked up on Rhoda's habit of saying that phrase.

"Well, thanks for listening. And thanks for taking care of my family, Rhoda," he continued, as though he wanted to say it all in an uninterrupted rush to be sure he got it out. "Even a couple weeks of being around your simple goodness has helped me see my divorce in a different light. I believe I've honored God's plan by entering another profession . . . and doing the best I could with my family, in the meantime. That's more of a comfort than you can possibly know."

Well, at least one of us is feelin' better.

The ride home felt awkward, in a car filled with unspoken emotions, but Rhoda contented herself with gazing out the window at the snow-blanketed fields. When Andy pulled over into a driveway, before they reached the first farms of Willow Ridge, she looked across the darkness at him.

"I probably shouldn't say this, but you've already left your mark on me—on my kids and Mom," Andy said earnestly.

"I didn't want to drop you off without saying how badly we'll all miss you—how much I wish I could get to know you so much better, Rhoda."

Her breath left her in a slow sigh. "Me too, Andy," she replied with a hitch in her voice.

"Please don't cry," he murmured, closing his eyes. "It's all I can do, not to kiss away your tears."

"Sorry."

"Don't be. Please."

She reached into her coat pocket for a tissue and loudly blew her nose. Andy backed onto the blacktop and drove the short distance to the Sweet Seasons without saying anything more, but Rhoda sensed his heart was as full as hers. When he turned in at the Lantzes' lane, they saw a lamp burning in one of the upstairs apartment windows, its light muted by the closed curtains. "Mamma's waited up," she murmured. "Might as well pull up in front of the smithy."

"If it weren't past ten o'clock, I'd go in and say hi to her," he murmured.

Rhoda let out a nervous laugh, peering up through the windshield to see if her mother's form was outlined in the window. "That's not such a *gut* idea, but I appreciate ya wantin' to be polite. She's let her hair down by now and she's most likely in her nightgown. I'd best get on upstairs." When she pulled on the door handle, Andy took hold of her arm.

"Whoa there, Rhoda. I owe you some money and I won't let you refuse it."

How had he known she'd intended to do just that? As Andy took bills from his wallet, folded them, and curled her hand around them, his touch made her tremble. "Thank you from the bottom of my heart, Rhoda. I wish you all the best."

"*Jah*, you too," she rasped. "Tell the kids—your *mamm*—what a joy they've been. I'm sorry I couldn't find the right time or the words to tell them good-bye." She slipped her hand out of his and stumbled out of the car, her vision blurred with tears. Bless him, Andy didn't pull away until she'd found the handle of the smithy door in the beam of his headlights—

"Rhoda Lantz, I had figured you for an obedient, God-fearing young woman," a stern male voice challenged. "You have disappointed me greatly tonight."

Hiram! How had the bishop known when she'd be coming home? How long had he been waiting here to catch her with Andy? Rhoda gawked at him, speechless, as he stepped from the shadows at the side of the building. Did Mamma know he was here?

"When Preacher Tom told me of your sin with this *Englischer*, he and I wanted to believe you had truly repented when you confessed to him," Hiram continued, "but I see we were wrong."

Andy was getting out of his car, and Rhoda heard the rapid *clump-clump-clump* of her mother's footsteps descending the stairs from the apartment. All of the evening's best intentions, along with Preacher Tom's promise to keep her confession to himself, had apparently come to nothing. Her head began to spin.

But ya did what ya promised Tom! This is Bishop Knepp stickin' his nose into your business, even though he's under the ban . . .

Rhoda knew better than to say that to Hiram's face. As Andy stepped toward the bishop with his hand extended, her heart thudded dully in her chest. "We've not met, sir," he said, "but—"

"Andy Leitner, this is Hiram Knepp, the bishop of Willow Ridge," Rhoda blurted. Her gaze darted from one man to the other.

"I assure you that Rhoda and I have discussed this situation," Andy continued in a low, firm voice. "Because of the circumstances of her faith, today was her last day working for me. It was never my intent to cause her a problem."

Hiram kept his hands in his coat pockets. "You have no idea about the *circumstances* of her faith," he replied in a voice that was frostier than the winter night. "She will most likely be shunned—ostracized by her family and friends—well into the New Year, because of your thoughtless lusting. You have compromised Rhoda's reputation in our community, as well as her chance for salvation in our Lord Jesus."

The smithy door swung open and Mamma stepped out, clutching her coat around her and holding an oil lamp. Her hair was still wound into a bun beneath a kapp, so she'd been waiting up—but her peeved expression told Rhoda that Mamma hadn't expected to deal with Hiram. "Bishop, the minute I hear our Willow Ridge church no longer believes in forgiveness, I'll be packin' up to go elsewhere," she said in a strained voice. "And it doesn't set any too well with me that you, as our bishop under the ban, have been sneakin' around in the dark to catch my daughter at somethin', either. Rhoda's chances for the grace of Jesus are lookin' every bit as *gut* as yours do right now."

Rhoda's eyes widened. Her mother had always spoken her mind when Hiram challenged her, but this pronouncement resounded like a slap in the bishop's face—a direct defiance of his authority. Rhoda wanted to grab Mamma in a fierce hug, but this wasn't the time to show her gratitude.

"I did as Preacher Tom instructed me," Rhoda said nervously. "I quit workin' for the Leitner family—"

"But you returned for one last day, just as Lot's wife defied the angels' orders and looked back at Sodom," the bishop insisted. "You chose to turn toward your sin—"

"Sounds minor, my girl finishin' out an honest job, compared to you hidin' that fancy car in your barn and drivin' it around when nobody was lookin'," Mamma fired back.

"And I take full responsibility for giving Rhoda two rides home," Andy spoke up as he stepped toward the bishop. "And yes, I kissed her, too. If this means I should come before your church and confess, I'm ready to do that. Rhoda has done a wonderful job caring for my family. Even though she explained the problems my giving her a ride would cause, I overrode her reasoning. The blame is mine."

Rhoda's heart hammered. She'd never expected Andy to come forward this way. It embarrassed her, having their kisses discussed so openly, yet Andy's support touched her deeply.

"You have no place in our church, Mr. Leitner. Matter of fact," Hiram continued bluntly, "you have no place in Rhoda's life, or in Willow Ridge. Go home and leave us to repair the damage you've done."

Andy looked startled, but his apologetic glance told Rhoda he was departing to save her further backlash from the bishop—not because he agreed with what Hiram had said. And just maybe . . . maybe he intended to see her again? Or was such a wish her heart's way of coping with this unexpected confrontation?

As Andy's car pulled away, a gust of wind extinguished Mamma's lamp. The three of them stood in the whistling, wind-whipped darkness then. Hiram leaned closer to nail Rhoda's gaze with his own. "I expect to see you in the front pew at the next preaching service to confess your sins, Rhoda. To plead for mercy and forgiveness. Do I make myself clear?"

Could a bishop order her to appear at the next Members' Meeting while he was still shunned? Rhoda knew better than to press that question. As her mother slung an arm around her shoulders, she instinctively leaned into Mamma's strength, needing the sense of solidarity.

"*Jah*, we'll be there, Bishop," her mother stated,

"mostly to watch how folks vote for *your* reinstatement into the congregation's *gut* graces that day. Far as I can see, ya haven't picked up much in the way of humility while ya were shunned, Hiram."

When the bishop opened his mouth to reprimand her, Mamma held up her hand for silence. "I hear a lot of talk in my café," she said in an unwavering voice, "and I'll be surprised if ya get the unanimous invitation ya need to come back into the fold. I don't know what that means, as far as you resumin' your place as our bishop. But ya might want to pray on it."

"Miriam, once again your lack of respect forces me to—"

"*Gut* night," Mamma said as she opened the door to the smithy. "My Jesse would never have tolerated your behavior toward his daughter, just as Tom and Gabe have raised questions about the way you've hounded me. And if Ben were standin' here, this conversation wouldn't be takin' place," she stated sternly. "Once again you're steppin' over the lines, Hiram, and ya seem to be the only one who doesn't see it."

"I will trust in the Lord God, who chose me by the falling of the lot to be your bishop," Hiram replied tersely. "And I will abide by whatever decisions the members make a week from Sunday."

"*Jah*, we all will." With that, Mamma propelled Rhoda through the open door and locked it behind them. The two of them strode quickly across Ben's shadowy blacksmith shop, which was lit only by the pale light drifting down the stairway from their apartment. At the bottom step, her mother gripped her shoulder.

"Tell me true, Rhoda," Mamma insisted. "Did ya do anything else that needs confessin'? If you're to come out of this situation with Tom still takin' your side, he needs to know—"

"It was like Andy said, Mamma. *Jah*, he gave me another

ride home—and *jah*, I went back to spend one more day workin' with his family," Rhoda whispered, "but no more kisses. Nothin' else to confess, except that . . ."

She turned her face, knowing how her affection for the Leitners had put Mamma in a difficult position. "Well, Andy's the most wonderful-*gut* fella. And it makes me sad enough, leavin' him and his family, that I may well declare myself a *maidel* and be done with it."

"Oh, honey-bug, you're young yet! Plenty of time for—"

"None of the other fellas I know will ever measure up to Andy," Rhoda stated, her heart in her throat. "And ya know *gut* and well they wouldn't have offered to stand up with me in church, confessin' to what happened, the way he just did."

She gazed at her mother, trying in vain to hold back her tears. "It was only a *kiss*, Mamma, and two rides in Andy's car. Andy believes in God, same as we do. If he were a Plain fella, we'd be havin' no trouble with this situation. Ain't so?"

Her mother closed her eyes and sadly shook her head. "The devil's in the details, daughter. Fallin' for a man who's not one of us leaves ya only one path to follow . . . and it's not the way any of us hope you'll go."

Rhoda hung her head. Her mother was being much kinder than she had expected.

"But I still believe that all things work out for them that love the Lord," Mamma went on softly. She stroked Rhoda's cheek, lifting her chin to gaze into her eyes. "And I believe the Lord has His way of showin' us what's best, even if it's not what we've been hopin' for or expectin'. No matter what comes of this, you'll always be my daughter and I'll always love ya, Rhoda."

"Oh, Mamma." Her words came out as a sigh. She wished it were easier to walk away from her intense feelings for a man she wasn't supposed to want . . . a man she'd known for only a couple of weeks.

"Let's get our rest now. Things'll look better in the morning." Mamma gestured for Rhoda to precede her up the stairs. "And if ya still want to work someplace other than the Sweet Seasons, we can ask around. Life's too short when you're happy at what ya do—and too long when you're not."

Chapter Fifteen

Andy jammed his foot on the brake just as the traffic light turned red. When cars rushed into the intersection from both directions, he realized how close he'd come to getting crushed in the cross traffic. He was on his way to two exams he hadn't studied enough for, while his children's protests replayed in his mind . . .

"I don't believe you! Rhoda wouldn't leave us!" Brett had declared vehemently. Then he had refused to eat breakfast.

Taylor had begun crying so hard she could barely talk. "But we did our best to . . . I—I thought she loved us, Daddy."

Andy closed his eyes against the uproar in his mind, against the pain of their morning's discussion in the kitchen, until a honking horn behind him urged him to drive ahead. Rhoda *did* love his kids, and his mother, and . . . was he assuming too much, thinking she might feel a spark for him, as well? He had barely gotten Brett and Taylor out the door in time to catch their bus, and he sensed his mother had dragged herself back to bed to remain there until he roused her this evening. She had looked so disappointed. So confused and defeated.

*All because of kisses and two rides home. Rhoda warned
you about her code of conduct and you had to go and fall for
her anyway. What'll you do after the shock wears off and the
kids start asking why she had to leave?*

His exam on health-care ethics went by in a blur. An hour
later, when he sat for the final on pediatric and obstetrical nursing, Andy's eyes were skipping entire sentences of the questions
and he caught himself checking off answers before he had fully
considered all of the choices. He left the lecture hall with the
sinking feeling he had just blown his chance at that obstetrics
position Dr. LaFarge had held open for him.

All because of kisses. And two rides home.

But his state of mental chaos involved more than what
had happened on the road between New Haven and Willow
Ridge. He was in withdrawal, craving Rhoda's efficiency
and sunny sense of humor, and he knew of no cure for it.
When Hiram Knepp had told him he had no place in the
Amish church, or in Rhoda's life, something inside him had
whimpered and curled into a ball.

Now, however, Andy felt the same fiery defiance Miriam
Lantz had displayed last night. He returned home from
campus, devoured three sugar cookies from the platter on
the kitchen counter, and then plopped down on the couch.
He turned the Amish manger scene so it faced him, marveling at the intricate details of the figures' clothing and
their gifts for the Christ Child. Rhoda had paid a hefty
amount for this hand-carved set, further evidence of her
affection for his family . . .

As Andy carefully held the carved manger, where a face-
less baby lay beneath a painted patchwork quilt, it occurred
to him that Jesus had been born into a family and a situation
as conflicted as his. Had Mary and Joseph not followed an-
gelic advice, God's son would have been slain by a jealous
King Herod before He could even walk. All through His life,

Christ had faced opposition, disapproval, and rejection, yet with God's help He had triumphed over death to change the world with His message of love and hope.

It's not over until it's over! Andy's heart beat faster, yet easier. He craved absolution as much as his family demanded closure . . . and no domineering Amish bishop would stop them from getting what they needed.

Spurred on by this surge of determination, Andy buried himself in online research for the next couple of hours. Once again he followed links to articles about Old Order ways . . . *to become Amish you must live among the Amish to show that you've given up modern ways*, he read. *You must learn the Amish language, Pennsylvania Dutch, which is based on German* . . .

Andy paused. He'd done pretty well in his high school German classes, and it hadn't been all that difficult for him to pick up on the Latin he'd needed for his nursing classes. If he could find a willing tutor . . .

He resumed his reading, more intent now. *You must give away worldly possessions . . . wear Amish clothing . . . take instruction and be baptized into the faith. It may take years for the Amish to accept you so that you can become one of them.*

Andy exhaled wearily. What was he thinking? If it depended upon Bishop Knepp's acceptance, he and his family would never become members of the Willow Ridge congregation . . .

Andy shook his head, noticing it was nearly time for the kids to get home from school. It was surely another sign that his brain was fried, that he was even remotely considering joining the Amish church. What would he do for a living? From what he'd read, only unmarried girls could teach in an Amish school, and he probably wouldn't be allowed to practice nursing—if indeed he passed his exams. Where would he live if he had to give up this home in New Haven? How would he and the kids get by without their computers, the TV, and his car? He imagined himself wearing a broad-brimmed hat and a vest, like the figures in the Nativity scene—

Get real, man. This is the most harebrained scheme you've ever considered. You've only known Rhoda for a couple of weeks. You can get another housekeeper . . . get on with Real Life.

Yet when the kids came through the door a few minutes later, he held up his hands to stop the questions and the protests he saw on their long faces. "Here's the deal," he announced. "If you don't mope and whine and argue with me about Rhoda's leaving, we'll go to the Sweet Seasons for breakfast on Saturday. To celebrate me finishing my tests and getting my degree."

"And we'll see Rhoda there?" Taylor asked cautiously.

"Most likely. But she'll be working, understand," he replied. "And there'll be other people eating there, of course. Saturday is probably their busiest day." Once again Andy wondered if he'd lost his mind. Would this visit be a way to restore their sanity? Or would seeing Rhoda only make them all miss her more? At least he wouldn't have to eat cold cereal.

"Why can't we go there *now*?" Brett demanded.

He'd thought of that option himself at least a dozen times today. "Sorry, bud. They closed at two," Andy answered. "They only serve breakfast and lunch, because they believe in eating dinner at home with all the family together."

"So why don't we call and ask if we can go to Rhoda's house for supper?" The wistful twinkle in Taylor's eye said she knew the answer to that, but at least her question made them all chuckle.

Andy shrugged, wishing he could go along with their suggestions. "It's Saturday or not at all. Sorry."

"Saturday! *Yesss!*" Brett cried out. "You in, Taylor?"

"Yesss!" she echoed.

"Can we bring home a . . . pie and some fresh cinnamon . . . rolls?"

They turned to see Andy's mother leaning heavily on her walker as she reached the end of the hallway, but at least she was up and interested in their discussion. Andy smiled at her. "Mom, we can bring home whatever you want."

"Then we'll be . . . bringing Rhoda back," she replied pointedly. "She's . . . *gut* for all of us. Especially *you*, Son."

Heat crept up out of his collar as the kids' eyes widened. Maybe he'd better clarify the situation right here and now. "Unfortunately, she got into trouble because I took her home," Andy hedged. "It's against Amish religious rules for her to ride in a car with an unmarried, un-Amish guy. So it was her bishop and one of the preachers who declared she had to stop working for us."

When he saw questions dawning on Taylor's face, Andy drew upon what he'd read online. "The Lantz family is close-knit, and Rhoda's been baptized into the church, so I don't see her going against her religious beliefs to be our caretaker anymore," he explained softly. "If she leaves her Old Order Amish faith, the church members will excommunicate her. And they believe she won't go to heaven to be with Jesus when she dies. I don't want to cause her family that kind of grief."

Brett got very quiet. He went to sit on the couch beside his sister, who had picked up the carved figurine of the baby in the manger. "How could Jesus not love Rhoda? He knows how much she's helped us," Taylor murmured.

"And He knows how we behave better, because we *want* to, when Rhoda's here," Brett added somberly. "Jesus ought to give her a *lot* of points for puttin' up with the names I've called her."

"I wish it were that simple, kids." Andy was pleased that his children were considering matters of faith on such a deep level—surely another accomplishment he could credit to Rhoda. She didn't preach at them, but she spoke openly about her beliefs, a topic Andy hadn't gotten around to often enough. *Just one more reason Rhoda's good for all of us.*

"Well, then," he said with pointed cheerfulness, "we'll go to the Sweet Seasons on Saturday morning. We'll be on our best behavior, too, so Rhoda and her mom will be glad we came. Meanwhile, I could use some help getting supper on the table."

Miriam saw them come in—two inquisitive children followed by a stooped woman clinging to Andy Leitner as she shuffled through the door. Four sets of eyes eagerly scanned the crowd in the Sweet Seasons dining room, looking for Rhoda, no doubt.

Miriam stopped rolling her pie crusts to observe them from the kitchen. She reminded herself to remain open-minded and objective, for her daughter's sake, because once Hiram spotted them from his table on the far right, the situation might boil over faster than an unwatched pot. The two preachers, Tom and Gabe, sat at a table catty-corner to the bishop's, observing Hiram's ban by not eating with him. But they would certainly join in on whatever discussion he started about Rhoda and her involvement with Andy. In their usual center spot, the three Brenneman brothers, the two Kanagy boys, and the three Hooleys chatted noisily as they ate their breakfast.

Rebecca, bless her, seated the Leitners at a table on the left side of the café. Miriam's heart quivered when she saw that Andy and his kids immediately noticed Rebecca's resemblance to Rhoda and Rachel even though she wore jeans and a T-shirt with a canary-yellow sweatshirt she'd called a *hoodie*. Rachel was ringing folks up at the cash register, unaware that anyone of special interest had arrived.

Rhoda was at the big stove, holding a metal bin from the buffet table as Naomi filled it with steaming hash browns cooked with onions and bell peppers. As the two of them then topped the potatoes with a layer of crumbled cooked sausage, an excited voice rang out in the dining room.

"Rhoda the 'Ranga-tang! We came to see ya!"

Rhoda's head popped up and the look on her face said it all: not only did she recognize that little-boy voice, but she lit up brighter than the star of Bethlehem at the sound of it. "Brett!" she called out, oblivious to the way the folks out front were watching this exchange. "Brett the Baboon, is that you?"

Miriam then witnessed Rhoda's true feelings for this family and saw that those emotions were mutual: the Leitner children rushed between the tables to hug Rhoda as she came out of the kitchen, while Andy . . . Andy stood watching his children lavish their affection on Rhoda, with a wistfulness that touched Miriam's soul. He might be English, but he was sincere—and he was as crazy about Rhoda as she was about him. Ben Hooley had the same devotion and desire written all over his face every time he looked at *her*.

"Well, now. That has to be the family your girl was helpin' these past couple weeks," Naomi remarked as she came to Miriam's counter to watch the reunion. "Nice lookin' fella, that dad is. And what do ya make of that? His *mamm*'s wearin' a Plain-style outfit, apron and all, except the dress is a perty print like you'd see our Mennonite friends wearin'."

"*Jah*, Rhoda drew up the pattern and sewed it for her."

"Ya don't say." Naomi's expression registered her recognition of the depth of Rhoda's involvement with the Leitners. "I get the feelin' Hiram's not gonna sit still much longer."

"The bishop's already gotten his two-cents'-worth in," Miriam murmured. She ran water on a tea towel, rung it dry, and then spread it over her pie crusts and dough to keep them from drying out. "Ya might as well know, Naomi. Rhoda's in hot water—already confessed to Preacher Tom— about ridin' home in Andy's car because it was too late to call Sheila Dougherty when he got off an emergency shift at the hospital. Hiram's ordered her to sit up front next preachin' Sunday, to confess. No doubt he'll recommend we shun her."

"Oh no." Naomi squeezed Miriam's wrist. "What a shame that you and I understand how ridin' with Andy was proba- bly the only practical way for Rhoda to get home, while the preachers'll see that she pays the full penalty for—"

"Seems Ira Hooley and Millie Glick saw Rhoda and Andy kissin' in his car, too." There. Miriam could finally spell out what had lain so heavily on her heart. It didn't right her daughter's wrong behavior, but she felt better for shar- ing such a burden with her best friend before it became common gossip.

"Oh, Miriam, I'm so sorry you've had to—"

"Don't be sorry for me, Naomi," she murmured. "Send up some prayers instead. We're gonna need them." She caught a movement in the opposite corner of the crowded dining room. "I'd best get out there. Hiram and I have al- ready clashed about Rhoda's situation, and the last thing we need is a confrontation in front of our customers."

Miriam rinsed her floury hands and then stepped out into the busy dining room, where Naomi's daughter, Hannah, was seating four English folks who had become Saturday breakfast regulars. Rhoda was chatting with the Leitners, her arm slung around Rebecca's shoulders—probably telling the story of how this triplet had unexpectedly returned to them last summer. Curiosity was compelling Rachel to join her sisters and to take menus to the table for these folks she'd never seen eating here.

Rebecca's return was yet another thorny situation, when Hiram had tried to call the Lantz family on the carpet for what he perceived as a sin. But here's our happy ending, for all to see, she reminded herself as her three daughters stood together. *Lord Jesus, I'm askin' Ya to please show us all the right way to love one another as Your children . . . Amish and English alike.*

Miriam grabbed a carafe of fresh coffee on her way to speak with Hiram, hoping to distract him before he left his table. When Tom Hostetler, Gabe Glick, and Hiram rose, however, and the three of them put on their black hats, it appeared they had already decided on a unified course of action. She refilled coffee mugs for English folks at the nearest table, watching the men from the corner of her eye as she chatted with her customers. At this point, she'd best leave the situation to God—

But lo and behold, Andy Leitner stood up and stepped toward Hiram, smiling politely and extending his hand. "Good morning, Bishop," he said. "Looks like we all know the best place to enjoy a fine Saturday breakfast. I'd like you to meet my mother, Betty Leitner, and my children, Taylor and Brett."

"And these are our preachers, Tom Hostetler and Gabe Glick," Rhoda chimed in. "This is Andy Leitner, the fella I was workin' for earlier."

Rhoda looked like a scared rabbit as the three church leaders approached, but she'd faced the situation straight on, and for that Miriam was grateful. And bless them, Tom and Gabe reached out to shake Andy's hand, which forced Hiram to do the same.

Was it her imagination, or had the café gotten quieter?

Miriam noticed Ira Hooley gazing intently at the Leitners, as though to get a good look at the man Rhoda had ridden off the straight and narrow with. Ben turned to see what was going on, gauging the scene that involved all the folks standing around Andy and his family. When his younger brother rose, Ben clapped Ira on the back and steered him toward the buffet table to keep him from getting Rhoda more flustered. So far, the situation was nice and polite—

"Hey, you fellows have hats and beards just like the three wise guys in the manger scene Rhoda gave us!" Andy's little boy piped up.

A startled silence filled the dining room, and then chuckles rose from some of the tables.

"Brett, they're the three wise *men*," his sister corrected in a loud whisper. Her face turned bright pink as she looked toward Hiram and the preachers. "You've gotta excuse my little brother," she pleaded. "He's only seven. But he's been so wrapped up in that Nativity scene, he's not played any computer games since Rhoda gave it to us."

Miriam smiled. Some good was coming from Rhoda's being with these children, if they were that excited about the birth of Jesus.

"And this man, Preacher Tom, is the fella who carved and painted your Nativity set," Rhoda spoke up, gesturing toward the youngest of their church leaders. "He's the one who makes the *gut* ice cream I was tellin' ya about, too."

Brett brightened and hopped down from his chair. He walked around the table to stand before Tom Hostetler, gazing up with a wide-eyed smile. "So . . . you preach sermons at church, and you run a farm with lots of cows to milk, and you carve cool manger scenes, *and* you know how to make ice cream?"

Tom placed his hands on his knees so he was looking

directly at young Brett. "*Jah*, I do. Workin' with my hands keeps me out of trouble, ya see."

"Wowwww," the boy replied as he met Tom's gaze. "That is so *awesome*."

Miriam got caught between a giggle and a sob. No wonder Rhoda was so taken with these two kids. Who wouldn't love a girl who faced three strangers to stand up for her well-meaning little brother? And wasn't the Leitner boy a dear for pointing up Tom Hostetler's many fine talents? He was small for his age—the same size as Hiram's twins—but Josh and Joey Knepp were usually too busy raising a ruckus to speak with an adult the way Brett had.

"Thank you," Tom murmured. He straightened to his full height. "I'm glad you and your sister like that Nativity set. Merry Christmas to ya."

Brett grinned. "Merry Christmas back atcha, Preacher Tom. You rock!"

Miriam chuckled. Tom seemed flummoxed yet pleased. And when Hiram looked ready to bring the conversation around to a more somber subject, Gabe nodded at the Leitners. "Nice to meet you folks," he said. "We'll get ourselves along now, so you can enjoy Miriam's fine breakfast."

Hiram flashed the two preachers a look of irritation, and Miriam thought he might linger to reprimand Andy again for leading Rhoda astray. Indeed, Andy stood patiently, watching Hiram's face. Then his expression lightened. "Nice to meet you fellows, as well," he said to the other two preachers. "Have a wonderful Christmas with your families. You too, Bishop Knepp."

Miriam relaxed as Tom, Gabe, and Hiram slipped into their heavy coats at the coatrack and then headed out the door. Conversations started up again in the dining room. After Miriam refilled the mugs for the younger fellows at the center table, she started over to meet the rest of Andy's family.

The bell above the door jangled and Tom stepped back inside, smiling sheepishly. "Forgot about this," he murmured as he slipped some folded bills to Miriam. "No need for change. Have a *gut* rest of your day, Miriam."

She flashed him a grateful smile, more for the favor he'd done Rhoda than for paying his tab. "*Denki*, Tom. Have a fine day yourself."

As Andy watched the café's door close behind the three men wearing black overcoats and hats, something propelled him away from his table. Coatless, heart pounding, he stepped out into the blustery morning. One of the preachers was walking slowly toward the road, bent against the wind, while the other two headed toward their separate horse-drawn rigs—but who was who? To his unaccustomed eye they looked identical from behind, and it wasn't Hiram or the ancient Gabe Glick he wished to speak with. On instinct, he loped to catch up with the man who had parked near the smithy. "Preacher Tom?" he called out.

"*Jah?*" The man who had so patiently engaged his son turned around.

Andy felt a rush of relief. "Do you have a moment? Can we talk?" Hoping he would listen without lecturing, Andy approached Tom Hostetler, who stood beside an enclosed black buggy that was hitched to a fine-looking horse. "I—I've been doing some research, but personal questions demand personal answers. How can I become Amish?"

He'd blurted out his question on the spur of an opportune moment, and he hoped Preacher Tom wouldn't interpret his tone—his inquiry—as impertinent or even insulting. True, he knew very little about Rhoda Lantz, to be considering such a major life change. But didn't he know the *right* details about her personality? The important qualities he wanted in a wife? Wouldn't it be the intelligent thing to fully understand what he was getting himself into *before* he lost his heart to Rhoda?

Too late, his heart mocked, even as his mind pursued the truth.

"Well, now. For that, we might want to step inside, out of the wind." Tom nodded toward the smithy door. "Ben Hooley, the blacksmith, is still eatin' his breakfast, so we've got a few."

Nodding gratefully, Andy stepped into the farrier's shop. None of the gaslights in the ceiling were on, but the forge fire had been lit and the shop welcomed them with its warmth. "Thank you so much for your time—"

"I hope your interest in Rhoda, and in our ways, is sincere, Mr. Leitner. But don't expect me to encourage ya. She and her *mamm* have already endured their share of trouble after ya drove Rhoda home. And kissed her." The bearded preacher studied him with an unwavering gaze. "To become Amish, ya must accept the Lord as the one true guide in your life. Ya must focus on servin' Him first, while severing your connections to worldly concerns and conveniences. Even your family and their needs must take a backseat to your devotion to God. Most English who want to become Amish have *gut* intentions, yet very few can make the change."

Andy jammed his hands in his jeans pockets. "When your bishop confronted us the other night, I offered to confess before your congregation, alongside Rhoda. I—I understand now how you would never allow such a confession, but . . . but what if I learn your language, and sell my house to move here, and take up your ways—do my very best to assimilate your faith—and Hiram still won't allow me to become a member of your church?"

"That's a chance you'll have to take." Preacher Tom seemed to be processing his thoughts, taking his time with his response. Up close, the lines in his face and the silvery spangles in his hair made him look older than Andy had figured him. He seemed a pleasant enough fellow, but not one to suffer fools or bend the rules.

Tom focused intently on him. "We are who we are. *You* must make the changes in your lifestyle, and take the instruction that leads to baptism into our church. Ya must become like us in thought, word, and deed, because we will not change our ways to accommodate ya."

Preacher Tom glanced away, as though gathering more verbal discouragement. "Becomin' Amish is an all-or-nothin' decision that will affect your children and your mother, as well. For the rest of your lives," he added firmly. "For one thing, it'll mean your kids will be educated in a one-room schoolhouse, only through the eighth grade. To a professional man like yourself, that probably seems backward or uncivilized—especially because your two kids are obviously bright."

Andy let out a long sigh. The preacher's honesty was taking a toll on his exuberant affection for Rhoda. "And what about my own profession?" he asked quietly. "I completed my nursing degree yesterday. Took out loans to pay for it, and with two kids to raise I have to generate some income pretty quickly."

Tom Hostetler's eyes widened at the mention of Andy's new career, yet he seemed intrigued rather than put off by his traditionally female occupation. "Folks of our faith believe in trustin' God to provide our ways and means, but that much aside, I don't know the answer to your question," the preacher murmured. "Truth be told, we've never had an *Englischer* join our district. We live on farms because we raise the crops to feed our horses and other livestock . . . but beyond that, I can only say that your question about your career will be answered once you've satisfied our other requirements. From our standpoint, there's no need to concern ourselves with how you'll earn your livelihood until you're actually one of us, ain't so?"

Andy sighed, but he could see Tom's point. He felt encouraged yet overwhelmed by the answers he'd received—and compelled to test a sentiment that Bishop Knepp had rejected. "I hope you'll believe it was never my intention to compromise Rhoda's reputation or her faith."

The preacher's expression didn't soften. "No matter what your intention was, she's bein' held accountable for her sin, because she fell prey to temptation . . . as we all have at some time or another." Tom sighed as though he had borne a lot of burdens during his time as a minister in Willow Ridge. "Rhoda's a strong girl, and I believe she'll do the right thing. I hope you will, as well, Mr. Leitner. Her entire family has a stake in your behavior, ya see. None of us lives unto ourselves. We're each a part of the whole, a member of our community and of God's world."

Andy nodded ruefully. "You've given me a lot to think about," he murmured. "Thanks again for talking with me."

The minister opened the smithy door, letting in a shaft of bright sunlight where tiny snowflakes danced like diamonds. "Never forget that when the world pushes ya to your knees, you're in the perfect position to pray," he said as he turned toward Andy again. "Works wonders, whenever it seems there's no easy answer to the predicament you're in."

From the doorway, Andy watched Preacher Tom unhitch the reins from the post, step up into his buggy, and then back his horse a few yards so they could head toward the road. It was a simple, everyday maneuver for an Amish person, yet he didn't have the slightest idea about driving a horse-drawn vehicle . . . one of a million things he would have to learn if he followed through on the idea of becoming Plain.

Had he been a fool to admit this aspiration to Rhoda's preacher? What if Tom talked her out of any interest she might have in becoming a member of his family . . . becoming his wife?

When the preacher gave him a quick wave, Andy's heart fluttered with hope. He waved back, certain Hiram Knepp wouldn't have shared such a gesture. He hurried across the snowy parking lot and back into the Sweet Seasons, gladdened by the smiles on his kids' faces as they returned from the buffet table with loaded plates.

"Where'd you go, Daddy?" Taylor asked brightly. "We decided to help ourselves—"

And wasn't that exactly what all of them would have to do, if his crazy scheme to connect with Rhoda was to work out?

"—so I took some of the breakfast casserole. It smells so yummy, with all that bacon and cheese."

"Lookit what I got, Dad!" Brett piped up behind her. "That fellow over there helped me load up with biscuits and gravy, and these fried apples, and a big ole cinnamon roll!"

His son pointed toward a man who was leaving the buffet table. He didn't wear a beard, but his suspenders and collar-length sandy hair announced he was Amish. Andy mouthed a thank-you and pointed toward Brett. He got a thumbs-up in return . . . yet another sign that these folks in Willow Ridge were friendly despite the way they preferred to keep to themselves, sequestered in their faith. And when he saw the way his mom beamed as Rhoda came to the table with her order of fried eggs, sausage patties, and another huge cinnamon roll, he again felt that sense of rightness that settled over him whenever he was in Rhoda's presence.

She looked up at him, her smile hopeful. "I'm ready for

a late breakfast, Andy, if ya don't mind me joinin' ya. What would ya like?"

Oh, but his imagination came to life at the playful shine in her eyes. He reminded himself not to say or do anything these Amish folks might hold against her when she confessed, even though most of the fellows who'd been watching them from the center table had left while he was in the smithy. "Surprise me. Whatever you bring will be wonderful-*gut*. Ain't so?"

When Rhoda laughed, Andy wondered if she was happy to see him or making fun of his attempt at talking Amish English. Not that it really mattered: when she came from the kitchen a few minutes later with two plates of breakfast casserole, fried apples, and strips of bacon that still sizzled, Andy sighed with contentment. His kids and his mom all seemed happier than they'd been for days. For now, it was enough to watch Rhoda as she sat across the table, between Taylor and Brett . . . everyone eating together, catching up on everyday events since Rhoda's last day of working for them. Even though they weren't sitting in their own kitchen, Andy felt so at home.

Thank You for this moment of joy, Lord, he prayed. *No matter what happens from here on out, I want to remember this special morning.*

Chapter Sixteen

Lord, I wish this dinner was already over.

As Rhoda looked at the many folks seated around their extended table for Sunday dinner, her heart beat painfully fast. The women sat on one side—except for Annie Mae, who was on the men's side between Joey and Josh, so they would behave—while Preacher Tom and Ben sat on the ends. Little Sara and Timmy Knepp sat in high chairs alongside Nazareth and her sister. Jerusalem Hooley had insisted on following the rules for Hiram's shunning, so the bishop sat at a small table behind Rhoda. What with the five Hooleys, the Knepps, Tom Hostetler, and Rebecca joining them today, seventeen people filled the Lantz kitchen.

Please, Lord, I just want to get through this meal without Ira or Hiram or Jerusalem or Preacher Tom lecturing me about Andy or what we did in his car—or what might come of it after I confess next Sunday.

Rhoda sighed. God deserved a better prayer from her. Yet, as much as it had thrilled her when Andy and his family came to the café yesterday, his visit only added fuel to the fire: even a blind man could have seen the way the Leitners welcomed her into their company and the way she wanted to be with them. The Christmas season would shine so much brighter if only she could be eating dinner with Taylor and Brett teasing her right now, or with Andy making much of the seasonal foods she wanted to cook for them.

But that's not going to happen. Better get on with your Plain life . . . if only ya could figure out what to do with yourself.

"We'll bow for a word of thanks now," Preacher Tom intoned from his end of the long table.

As they bowed their heads for a silent grace, Rhoda swore she felt Ira Hooley gazing across the table at her. And was Hiram glaring at her from behind? He had balked at the small table Mamma had set for him, but the alternative would've been for him to leave and fix his own food. Patience had never been Bishop Knepp's strength, and a week remained before he knelt in front of the congregation to implore their forgiveness.

Would Hiram order her to her knees the minute his confession was accepted, to interrogate her about her involvement with Andy? Or would Bishop Shetler and Bishop Mullet, assisting their church from Morning Star and New Haven, allow her to confess first, before they took up the matter of Hiram's reinstatement? Rhoda's stomach twisted. She'd never had to endure a kneeling confession, and this final week of waiting would be the most difficult yet . . .

"Seems Rhoda has a lot to pray on," Ira teased from across the table. "Or maybe she's really daydreamin' about that Leitner fella."

Heat flared in Rhoda's face. She glared at Ira as she accepted the bowl of broccoli from Rachel, but before she could reply to his remark, Jerusalem Hooley smacked the tabletop loudly enough to make them all jump.

"That'll be enough of your smart remarks, Nephew," the middle-aged *maidel* warned as she glared at him from the opposite end of the table. "Frankly, I wonder why your parents didn't steer ya into joinin' the church. You're twenty-eight, Ira. Long past the time where ya can point a finger at Rhoda, who became a member years ago."

The kitchen got quiet. Both Ira and Luke knew better than to sass their aunt, so they focused on passing food: a bowl of bright red apples cooked with cinnamon imperials . . . a basket of Mamma's oatmeal rolls . . . the pan of scalloped potatoes . . .

"We'll most likely start up an instruction class after the holidays, for young folks wanting to join in the spring," Tom remarked. His tone was matter-of-fact, not pressuring the Hooley brothers or Annie Mae, but the three of them began to eat as though they wanted to keep their mouths too full to respond.

"And what do you have to learn to become a member?" Rebecca asked. Her face, framed by chestnut hair that had grown enough since summer to reach her collar, shone with sincere interest. "It seems, from what I've seen, that you Amish are trained in the ways of your faith from the cradle."

Preacher Tom smiled at her. "*Jah*, that's right. But once our young folks have had a chance to explore the English world during their *rumspringa*, they concentrate on becomin' committed members of the faith—members of the community who see to each other's needs, ready to follow God's will for their lives. Most take their instruction when they've picked out somebody to marry."

"So . . . are ya thinkin' about joinin' us, Rebecca?" Mamma asked. Her voice vibrated with hope, and as she slipped her hand into the crook of Rhoda's arm, Rhoda felt her mother's pulse thrum. "I'm not expectin' ya to, understand. I know ya have your own life and plans for your computer business—"

"As it says in the Scriptural story about the rich young

ruler," Hiram chimed in when he rose to fill his plate, "it's easier for a camel to get through the eye of a needle than for a wealthy man to enter the Kingdom of God. The same could be said for English thinking they want to be Amish. It's too difficult for them to give up their worldly possessions and habits to follow the narrow road to salvation."

"Ah, but in the next verses Jesus's disciples ask Him who could possibly be saved, if not that wealthy fella who'd kept all the commandments," Ben said, continuing the familiar story. "And Jesus said that for people it was impossible, but that all things are possible with God. So, *jah*, Rebecca, while we've been raised up with our Plain values all along, we still rely on the Lord to accept us into His Kingdom. And I believe that applies to English wantin' to become Amish," he went on with a glance toward Rhoda. "It's not an easy road, but with God's help it's possible."

Rhoda's cheeks prickled. Mamma had apparently filled him in on her situation. Was Ben telling her not to give up on Andy? Or was he merely deflecting some of Hiram's harshness?

"Well, it's not like I'm wealthy enough to worry about that part," Rebecca said with a laugh. "And, like Mamma said, I'm not ready to give up my computer business, either. I was just curious. Interested."

Ah, but the bishop's the wealthiest fella in Willow Ridge, Rhoda pondered. *I wonder if he would give up those magnificent Belgians he raises, and the modern barn he keeps them in, to enter the Kingdom?* She watched as Hiram stood at Tom's side, dishing up potatoes and cinnamon apples. Something about the bishop's expression hinted that he wasn't finished with this lesson yet, and that he was about to use her as a main point.

"As Jerusalem has said," Hiram remarked, his gaze sweeping the side of the table where his daughter Annie Mae and Ben's brothers sat, "it's past time for some of our young people to get off the fence and come into the fold. Perhaps taking instruction would be more *meaningful* if the three of you attended together—and invited Millie Glick to make it a foursome. There comes a time to be fruitful and multiply, to become productive families in our community."

Annie Mae's face turned the color of the cinnamon apples, while Ira nearly choked on his food. Luke, however, was studying Rebecca's face with an expression Rhoda found . . . interesting. It was a good thing Annie Mae couldn't see him, as she'd confided to Rhoda that she'd stopped dating Yonnie Stoltzfus and other fellows to concentrate on this handsome, adventurous newcomer. Rhoda felt bad for the slender girl across the table: what fellow would court Hiram Knepp's daughter, knowing he'd have to toe a stricter line while all of Willow Ridge speculated about them?

When Hiram came around to stand behind her and Mamma, Rhoda sat absolutely still. He reached between them to stab a few slices of pork roast. "And just as there is a time to embrace our faith and marry, there is a time to refrain from embracing," he paraphrased pointedly.

Beside Rhoda, Mamma stiffened. Bad enough that they all felt a lecture coming on, but Hiram also dripped meat juice on Mamma's shoulder—not once but twice—as he brought the pork roast to his plate.

"Must we discuss this at the table, Hiram?" Mamma demanded in a strained voice. "It's common knowledge what Rhoda has done. Nothing's to be gained by goin' over it again."

"No point in ruinin' this fine meal, either," Nazareth Hooley added. "Miriam was nice enough to ask us all over to celebrate the birth of Jesus—"

"Who died for our sins," Hiram pointed out. He stood so

close behind Rhoda, she wondered if he might rest his plate on her head to humiliate her further. "And the part of our faith most English and our Mennonite friends find impossible to accept is our belief in shunning, Rebecca. Has your sister told you about how she might be forced to eat at a table alone and avoided by her friends in public—the humiliations I have endured these past five weeks—if the members vote to put her under the ban? And has she told you about the sins she committed with Andy Leitner?"

Rhoda wanted the floor to open up and swallow her. Beside her, Mamma felt so tightly wound she might just spring up like a jack-in-the-box—except that Hiram still stood close enough that she would send his plate flying if she did that. Rachel, on Rhoda's other side, reached for her hand under the table.

Poor Rebecca looked sorry she'd asked her innocent question. "No, sir," she murmured, sending Rhoda an apologetic, flummoxed look. "And it's really none of my business."

"Ah, but the Amish consider a member's sin everyone's business," the bishop replied. He chuckled, as though Rebecca had played right into his little drama. "That's why she'll kneel before us next Sunday and confess the evil of her ways, and then she'll leave the room while the rest of us vote on her punishment. Were you there to witness that event, Rebecca, you would think very, very hard about becoming one of us. The Plain life's not for the faint of heart."

Rhoda could barely breathe. Every face around the table looked tight with sympathy for her and aversion to the bishop's tactics. She dared not move or speak. She sat looking down at her dinner, which was growing cold along with everyone else's.

"And because I take my duty as the spiritual leader of Willow Ridge very seriously," Hiram continued, "I must insist that Rhoda have no further contact with Mr. Leitner. And if he expresses an interest in becoming Amish, I will refuse to let him take instruction or to join our community of faith. His professional training will only provoke the brightest of our youth to jump the fence and pursue more education. And his presence will lead Rhoda into further temptation. Perdition rather than redemption."

Hot tears stung Rhoda's eyes. She looked at Preacher Tom, wondering how much he had influenced the bishop's edict, but Tom's startled scowl suggested he'd had nothing to do with it. Again the kitchen went silent. Her mother's eyes took on a defiant shine. The others around the table masked their initial shock by resuming their eating—except for Ben, who held his fork like a pointer.

"You're assumin', Bishop, that at the preachin' service this Sunday you'll be voted back into your duties," he said in a low voice.

"Once the lot falls to a preacher or a bishop, he retains that position for life," Hiram shot back. "The moment I chose the hymnal with the slip of paper in it, God's choice became clear. And irrefutable."

Oh, how Rhoda wanted to lash out. Instead, Rachel squeezed her right hand and Mamma gripped her left, the sign of solidarity that had gotten them through many a trial these past couple of years since Dat had died. Never had she felt so humiliated . . . so angry and frustrated. Here she sat, in front of Ira, who had initially reported her and Andy . . . and across from Annie Mae, whose whispering in the pantry had led to Jerusalem's hearing the story, as well . . . and with Tom, to whom she had confessed. With Hiram standing behind her chair, there was no escaping those who already knew firsthand of her activities, yet she would have to endure this sort of scrutiny all over again when she confessed on Sunday before the entire district.

Now Rhoda fully understood what Mamma, Naomi, and Micah had endured when Hiram had insisted they confess last summer, when Rebecca's return had sparked such controversy. For the first time ever, she questioned the faith she'd been baptized into: If she obeyed the bishop—never saw Andy again—would she regret remaining Amish? Would she live out the rest of her life in mourning for the family, the love, she'd given up?

Or is it time for ya to leave? Hot tears rolled down her cheeks as she hung her head. How she hated this tug-of-war going on in her heart right now.

"You've made your point, Hiram," Jerusalem remarked tersely. "Please sit down and eat so the rest of us—"

"*Jah,* Pop, we wanna be gettin' out of here!" Joey piped up.

"Wanna go sleigh ridin' this afternoon!" Josh added gleefully.

Between them, Annie Mae dropped her fork to hook an arm around each twin. "That'll be enough out of you two—"

"For interruptin' me, and for sassin' your father," Jerusalem continued as she rose to her feet, "you'll be standin' with your noses in the corner while the rest of us finish our meal and dessert." Her expression grew ominous as she pointed toward two corners of the kitchen. "Nazareth brought that strawberry rhubarb crisp ya like so well, too, but you'll be havin' none of it, boys. Move along now."

"There'll be no sleigh riding, either," Hiram added sternly. "You boys are not to take the sleigh out by yourselves— ever—and nobody else will be going with you today, either. Understand me?"

"*Jah,* Pop," the boys murmured in unison.

As Joey and Josh went to stand in their corners, Rhoda felt

secretly relieved that they had misbehaved, distracting their *dat* from his lecture. This discussion had embarrassed their guests and spoiled the visiting Mamma had been looking forward to—especially since Rebecca had joined them for this holiday dinner. The pork roast was especially tender and tasty, seasoned with garlic powder and dill, the way Mamma baked it in the café. Jerusalem had brought the pretty cinnamon apples and the fresh broccoli, while Nazareth had provided dessert and their relish tray, all prepared yesterday so they would do minimal work on the Sabbath.

But Rhoda had lost her appetite. She laid her fork on her plate and sat with her hands in her lap. Now that Hiram was returning to his table, however, everyone else seemed to be eating faster, the sooner to be finished so they could escape the table and the unpleasantness he had created.

Bless her, Rebecca broke the uncomfortable silence while she spooned up some of Mamma's strawberry jam to spread on her oatmeal roll. "This food is *so* good, and I think it's so cool the way you aunts brought some of these dishes with you," she said with a grin for the Hooley sisters. Then she took a huge bite of her soft, warm roll, closing her eyes as though she'd never tasted anything as delicious. "I can't wait to move into the apartment with Rhoda, and I'm hoping all of you wonderful-*gut* cooks will share your know-how with me."

"And I can't wait to have ya close by, honey-bug," Mamma replied softly.

Seeing how she'd made everyone smile again, Rebecca continued in a rising voice. "We could put recipes from local ladies on the Sweet Seasons website. And any dishes that use the specialty grains Ira and Luke will process in their mill could be put up on the site, too—with photos, so folks will taste how good your food is just from looking at it. They'll *have* to come here to enjoy some or to get the ingredients from the Mill at Willow Ridge!"

"I like the sound of that," Luke said with a nod.

"Jah," Ira agreed, "folks who've never cooked with quinoa or millet are more likely to try those grains if they have recipes—especially if they can sample them when they come to check us out."

"We could host a grand opening, with a tasting table," his brother chimed in. "We were going to try that in Lancaster, but we never got around to finding gals who would bake up what we needed."

"What a *gut* idea!" Nellie Knepp exclaimed. "I could do that bakin' for ya! And if ya need somebody to work in your shop, I'd be able to help out most any day, after school."

Behind them, Hiram loudly cleared his throat. "Are you not listening to yourselves, my friends? And have you not heard my warning to Rhoda?" he demanded in the voice he used when he was preaching. "Sounds to me like Willow Ridge will soon be on the level of Bird-in-Hand or Paradise, in Lancaster County, where the traffic is bumper-to-bumper and the shops teem with people. It's not our mission to create such a tourist trap. We would become far too worldly with so many English traipsing through our shops."

Once again Rhoda bit back a retort. Hadn't the Hooley brothers built their mill with just such a shop in mind? And wouldn't every business in Willow Ridge benefit from the attention the new websites would generate? As she noticed how Mamma's eyebrows rose and Ben pressed his lips into a tight line, Rhoda wondered how the folks around this table would vote, come time to accept Hiram back into good standing.

What happens when a bishop loses the approval and trust of his flock, Lord? Seems Hiram has peeved several members today—and this after he shocked us all by ownin' a car. Yet Ya chose him to serve us for the rest of his life.

These were issues few Plain communities ever faced, because following the leadership of the bishop and the other preachers was a basic tenet of their faith. Yet as serious as this issue was, it gave Rhoda a moment of hope. *Maybe folks'll be so concerned about him that my confession will seem like small potatoes next Sunday.*

Chapter Seventeen

On Friday afternoon, Rhoda lettered and hung the sign Mamma had asked her to put on the door:

MERRY CHRISTMAS!
CLOSED DECEMBER 20TH–JANUARY 11TH
FOR MIRIAM AND BEN'S WEDDING

She finished wiping down the tables and then gazed out the café's front window. It was blessedly quiet in the Sweet Seasons after a mighty busy day. It seemed as though all the locals were getting in a few last meals today and tomorrow before the place closed on Monday for a couple of weeks. The morning snowfall had wrapped Willow Springs in a fresh white blanket, adding to the hush . . . a sense that once she wasn't waiting tables, her life would be very, very quiet even with the excitement of Mamma's wedding preparations.

Naomi and Hannah had headed home. Rachel had left with Micah for another weekend of collecting wedding gifts, this time visiting kin near Richmond and Carrollton. Mamma

was in the kitchen baking a special order of pies and treats
for an employee Christmas party at the regional hospital.

Rhoda desperately wanted to help deliver those goodies
tomorrow afternoon, imagining she'd have a chance of seeing
Andy. It was silly, of course, to believe he'd be working that
particular shift or that she'd catch sight of him among all the
other folks there, but it gave her something pleasant to think
about . . . instead of fretting over her confession this Sunday.

"You okay, Rhoda?" Rebecca had cleaned the big coffeemaker and was preparing the first batch of tomorrow's
water and coffee. "You haven't seemed like your usual perky
self today, Sister."

Rhoda shrugged. How did she describe her feelings, her
fears, to someone who hadn't grown up in the Amish church?
"Just wishin' my ordeal with Hiram was behind me," she
murmured. "What with the bishops from New Haven and
Morning Star bein' in charge, there's no tellin' how things
might go."

Rebecca came to stand beside her at the window, sling-
ing an arm around her shoulders. "I bet you're missing those
two kids and Andy, too," she said in a low voice. "I can certainly see why. What a nice family they are—and as crazy
for you as you are for them. Not to criticize your Plain ways,
but it seems awfully . . . *harsh* for Hiram to forbid you to see
them again, and to declare he won't allow Andy to join your
church, either."

"*Jah*, I've been turnin' that over and over in my mind,"
Rhoda murmured. "The Old Ways have been followed for
centuries, yet now that it's *me* goin' to my knees, it all seems
unfair." She sighed. "I guess that's the way of it. So—when're
ya movin' in with me, Sister? I'm lookin' forward to your
company."

Rebecca chuckled at the abrupt change in topic. "I think
we should allow Mamma and Ben to enjoy all their wedding

excitement before I start hauling my stuff here. But, gee—that's only two weeks away!"

"*Jah*, and I've told her I'll do the bakin' for the feast," Rhoda replied. "Figured it'd be a real *gut* afternoon to bake her coconut cake layers and the sheet cakes, too. I'll put them in the freezer so Rachel can decorate them when she gets back. She's steadier with a pastry tube than I am, ya see."

"*Puh!* I can't think of a thing you're not really good at, Rhoda," her sister insisted. "And I hope you'll let me help with—oh my, here comes a sleigh! No, two of them!"

They hurried to the front window to watch. Rhoda shielded her eyes with her hand, squinting into the sun's glare. "*Jah*, and they've got those horses runnin' awful fast in that fresh snow, too." Rhoda squinted into the sun's glare. "Why, that's Levi and Cyrus Zook in the green sleigh."

"The boys in the black sleigh are so short, I can hardly see that anybody's driving it." Rebecca cupped her hands against the glass to shade her eyes.

"Ohhh, that's because it's the Knepp twins," Rhoda murmured, shaking her head. "Hiram and Jerusalem are gonna pitch a fit when they find out—oh my stars, they're headin' onto the blacktop. We've gotta stop this."

Rhoda rushed out the front door, hollering as loudly as she could. "Get outta the road! If a car comes, it's too slick to—"

Wild, childish laughter rang out in the crisp air as reins clapped on the horses' backs. One of the horses whinnied and their hoofbeats sped faster as the two sleighs approached the Sweet Seasons. Rhoda kept running at them, waving her arms above her head even as her shoes slipped on the packed snow in the parking lot. "Pull in here, outta the—Joey, a car's comin'!" she shrieked when a vehicle topped the hill, approaching the two sleighs from behind.

"Car's coming!" Rebecca echoed behind her, pointing frantically toward the car.

Levi Zook motioned for Cyrus to pull into the Lantzes' lane. The Knepp boys, however, were caught up in being ahead in the race and they had far less driving experience. As they flew past her, Rhoda again yelled at them. "Joey! Josh! Pull over! Car coming!"

"Boys, get outta the road!" Ben hollered. He had no doubt heard Rhoda screaming as he worked in his farrier shop. He rushed around her and Rebecca, jogging as fast as the slick pavement allowed.

Rhoda's heart flew up into her throat. The driver of the car had finally spotted the sleigh, but when he jammed on the brakes, the car fishtailed crazily. The horn honked again and again until the car went into a full spin.

The next few moments took on a sense of slow-motion unreality as Rhoda watched in horror, gripping her sister's hand: the Knepp's Belgian, spooked by the blaring horn, swung around in the middle of the road. The sleigh whipped across the slick surface in an arc, tossing the twins out of the seat. A deafening whinny blended with the boys' cries, and when the spinning car's back end struck the terrified horse, Rhoda knew that sickening *thud* would live on in her memory. The Belgian kept screaming as it fell to the pavement, held captive by the sleigh's metal shafts. The sleigh continued to slide until the weight of the horse stopped it. The car careened into the ditch.

Then, silence.

Rhoda stood frozen, with Rebecca's hand her only grip on reality. Ben resumed his running. "Josh! Joey!" he called out hoarsely. The Zook boys, their faces as pale as the snow, had hitched their horse to the rail by the café. As they, too, made their way across the parking lot, Rhoda came out of her shock.

"Get Mamma," she told Rebecca. "We've got to call Hiram—I'm callin' Andy first, though."

"And call 9-1-1," Rebecca added.

Rhoda hurried to the phone shanty out back, aware now that she hadn't grabbed her coat, but there was no time for that. Thank goodness she'd tucked the little ad with Andy's number on it into the drawer of the phone table. As she punched the numbers, she tried to focus her thoughts. *Dear Lord, please be with Josh and Joey and all of us who're scramblin' to get help over here—and please let Andy be at—*

"Hello?" came a voice through the receiver.

"Andy! Ya gotta come, quick! There's been a sleigh wreck, right here at the café. Hiram's little boys got thrown out onto the road, and—"

"I'm on my way. Cover them, and don't move them or let them get up." *Click.*

Rhoda tried to catch her breath and slow her runaway heartbeat. Cold wind blew into the shanty with Mamma, who shut the door behind her as Rhoda was hanging up. The heavy coat she'd brought felt awfully good as her mother held it so Rhoda could put her arms into its sleeves.

"Mamma, Andy's comin', but Rebecca thinks we should call the ambulance, too," Rhoda said as she tied on her bonnet. "Ya know how Hiram feels about gettin' doctors involved. He wouldn't take Linda—his own wife—to the hospital when she was havin' trouble deliverin' that last poor baby, so the both of them died."

"We're callin' 9-1-1," Mamma declared quietly. "We've got English folks in that car to consider, and I'll not have it on my conscience that we didn't do everything possible for the twins. If the bishop doesn't like my decision, well, it won't be the first time."

Nodding, Rhoda punched 9-1-1 and gave the operator the information she asked for. The regional hospital was on the far side of Morning Star, so it might be several minutes before the ambulance arrived . . . yet another reason Rhoda was thankful she had gotten to know Andy Leitner. She would probably be in deeper trouble, come Sunday, for defying the bishop's order not to see Andy again, but what if Josh and Joey had serious internal injuries? What if they didn't regain consciousness, or—heaven forbid—what if one or both of them died? She would never forgive herself if they passed on for lack of proper care . . .

"We need to call Hiram now, although I sent the Zook boys over there in case nobody hears the phone," Mamma said. "Rebecca has run to the quilt shop for blankets and the Schrocks' help—"

"I—I've never been so scared in my life, Mamma," Rhoda rasped as she dialed the bishop's number. She didn't realize she'd started crying, but fat tears were plopping onto the tabletop. "Both boys got thrown from the sleigh. Rebecca and I saw the whole—*jah*, Jerusalem?" she said into the phone. "We've had a horrible accident here by the Sweet Seasons. Hiram needs to come right away. Josh and Joey got thrown out of the sleigh when a car spooked their horse, and—"

"Oh, my Lord! Hiram's off visitin' an English client. If they don't answer their phone I'll send Annie Mae to get him," the *maidel* gasped. "I'll be right there. Don't let anything bad happen to my little boys!"

As Rhoda and Mamma came around to the front of the café, Rebecca had reached the road with Mary and Eva Schrock close behind her, all of them carrying quilts. Seth and Aaron Brenneman, who were working on the new house, had come out to see what all the honking was about. The two young men joined Ben at the ditch, their faces grim as they approached the two little boys, who had landed about ten feet apart. Joey and Josh were too still, sprawled on the snowy ground with their arms and legs spread in unnatural positions.

Rebecca dropped her quilts and turned away suddenly, her face pale. "Oh, this doesn't look good. I'm going over to see about the car's driver."

Mamma nodded and grabbed Rhoda's hand as they carefully walked closer. The horse let out an agonized cry, flailing as it lifted its head. Its hind legs were bent the wrong direction, and as Aaron brought a blanket to cover it, he was shaking his head. "Gonna have to put this poor fella down," he murmured. "I've got to wonder what those boys were doin'—how they came to be out racin' around with the sleigh and one of their *dat*'s Belgians."

"We've got a lot of explainin' to hear," Mamma agreed in a tight voice. "It's a *gut* thing the Zook boys pulled over. Except that leaves them to do the explainin'."

Ben looked up from tucking a quilt around one of the twins. "Aaron, I keep a pistol in my farrier trailer for times like this. Look in the drawer of the nightstand up at the front end."

As the youngest Brenneman brother took off across the road, Rhoda tried not to think about a beautiful animal losing its life, or the boys' frightening stillness. She moved in beside Ben with another quilt. "Andy Leitner's on his way. Says to cover them and not to move them. I think this is Joey, but I can't always tell them apart unless they're talkin'," she murmured. She glanced over to the other twin, shaking her head. "They were ridin' high, racin' the Zooks without payin' one bit of attention to traffic . . ."

Ben lifted his head from Joey's chest. "Thank the *gut* Lord he's breathin', but it's awful shallow. He won't be sneakin' out with one of his *dat*'s horses again anytime soon." He glanced toward Seth, who was wrapping a quilt around the other twin. "How's he doin'? Got a pulse?"

"*Jah*, and he's startin' to moan. Gonna be in perty fierce pain, what with this arm broke and maybe a leg."

A single shot rang out. Rhoda clenched her teeth to keep from crying. At least Hiram's poor horse was out of its misery, while the bishop's boys might suffer a long while yet.

The sound of an approaching car made them all look up. Ben sprang to the edge of the road, waving his arms to warn the driver away from the horse and Aaron, who still knelt beside its body.

At the sight of the familiar vehicle, Rhoda's shoulders relaxed a bit: Andy had arrived, so surely this heart-wrenching situation would improve. He quickly surveyed the scene and moved toward them, gripping his medical bag. "What happened?" he asked in a low, no-nonsense voice.

As Rhoda recounted the way the twins had been thrown from the sleigh, Andy did a fast once-over on each boy before beginning a more thorough examination on the one she was kneeling beside. "I hear sirens," he murmured gratefully. "Wasn't sure you'd call for help."

"Hiram'll no doubt give us a piece of his mind for that," Mamma replied, "but I thought it best, partly because of whoever was drivin' that car."

Rhoda looked down the road, relieved to see her sister talking with that driver as he leaned against the car, which was nose down in the snow-filled ditch. "Well, that fella's up walkin' around, anyway. Probably more scared than hurt, if he was wearin' his seat belt."

Andy was gently rolling Joey onto his back, checking for broken bones and whatever else his skilled hands might detect. When he placed his stethoscope to the boy's chest, however, his expression tightened. He checked inside Joey's mouth, pinched his nostrils shut, and then breathed down his throat . . . inhaled deeply and breathed into him again.

Rhoda clapped her hand over her mouth, refusing to

believe this lively little boy might die. Watching Andy she wondered, was this how God had breathed life into Adam all those centuries ago? While that thought startled her, she was filled with gratitude and relief that Andy had arrived when he did. Joey coughed, thank goodness, and gasped for the next breath on his own.

"This little guy's on his way to surgery," Andy said. "Is Bishop Knepp around? He'll need to sign admitting papers and—"

"Somebody's fetchin' him, *jah*," Rhoda said, "but we don't know how long he'll be. And he might not agree to that, ya know. He'll say it was the will of God that his boys got hit after they disobeyed him by sneakin' out in the sleigh."

Andy's eyes widened in disbelief, but he saw that Ben, Miriam, the Schrocks, and the Brenneman brothers were nodding their agreement. "No disrespect intended, but those emergency vehicles are nearly here, and I'm going to let the members of the EMS team do their jobs. We'll handle Hiram later."

Rhoda's eyes widened at the prospect that both Josh and Joey might need to be hospitalized, yet she trusted in Andy's judgment. He had a son not much older than the twins, and he was caring for these boys in the same way he would his own children.

As a police cruiser pulled around to the car that had gone off the road, followed closely by a wailing fire engine and then the ambulance, Rhoda wondered just how serious the boys' condition might be. She and Mamma and the men stepped away to allow the ambulance crew more room to work as Andy waved them over to where the bundled boys lay. He was talking in low tones, using big medical terms as he indicated that Joey needed immediate attention, most likely. Rhoda didn't dare interrupt him to find out.

Mary and Eva Schrock huddled with them, shivering in

the wind. "I had no idea all these folks would be comin'," Mary murmured to Mamma beneath the scream of the three sirens. "If Hiram sees what-all commotion they're stirrin' up, with the police gettin' in on it, he'll be mighty peeved."

Rebecca joined them then, while the policeman questioned the driver of the car. "It's standard procedure to have all these vehicles come with the paramedics when you call 9-1-1," she said. "That happened every time we called the ambulance to take Mom to the hospital when her cancer pain got bad."

Rhoda and Mamma grabbed Rebecca's hands, sorry to recall that such sorrow had touched her English life. It was a sobering sight when two of the ambulance men deftly shifted each Knepp boy onto a stretcher to carry them one by one inside the vehicle as a third fellow took down information from Ben. The men from the fire truck talked briefly to Seth and Aaron, and then they pulled away down the blacktop. As one of the paramedics was closing the ambulance doors, Rhoda caught sight of an approaching buggy.

"Wait!" she called out to them. "Here come a couple gals who should be there at the hospital with Josh and Joey. Can ya give them a ride?"

"I'll take them," Rebecca offered quietly. "Might be helpful if somebody who's had some experience with hospital procedure goes along, and that way they'll have a way home when they're ready. I'll get my keys."

Rhoda squeezed her sister's hand and hurried toward the approaching buggy to tell the Hooley sisters what was going on. After Jerusalem pulled into the café's parking lot and hitched the horse, she asked, "How bad is it?"

At the sight of the Hooley sisters' frightened faces, Rhoda blinked back fresh tears. "We're not sure. Josh has been moanin', but Joey quit breathin' for a bit and Andy had to bring him around. They've got broken bones, for sure, and Andy was sayin' they'll need some surgery."

"Should've seen this comin'," Jerusalem murmured. Her brow furrowed as the ambulance pulled away, and beside her, Nazareth pulled out a handkerchief and blew her nose loudly. "The Zook boys went flyin' by in their sleigh after school let out, wavin' and hollerin'. Then Joey got the idea that the goats needed more straw and feed, cold as it is today."

"*Jah*, and quicker than a lizard darts behind a rock, they must've hitched up and raced outta the yard," Nazareth joined in. "We can't see that side of the barn from the house, so we hadn't yet realized they'd slipped out on us. They knew their *dat* was over to Warrensburg, and probably figured to be back before anyone was the wiser."

"Well, our prayers go with ya," Mamma said as she approached. "Our Rebecca's *gut* help, so don't hesitate to ask for her cell phone or whatever else she can do for ya. If Hiram stops by, we'll send him to the hospital."

"Or if ya know the number where he is, Rebecca can call and tell him you're on your way there," Rhoda suggested as her sister's red car purred to a stop beside them. "Maybe that English client-fella will give him a ride."

"Lord love us all, once the bishop hears about this," Nazareth murmured, opening the car door. "No doubt he'll blame the two of us for not watchin' the boys close enough, and then he'll be pointin' a finger at you folks for gettin' medical attention that also brought the police into it."

"God'll get us through it, Sister. *Denki*, Miriam and Rhoda, for seein' to things on this end." Jerusalem ducked through the sportscar's door and squeezed behind the front seat to sit in the back with her sister.

As they pulled onto the blacktop, Rhoda waved good-bye. *Lord, I'm hopin' You'll be with us all as we do what needs*

*doin'. Watch over Josh and Joey while they're hurtin' and
scared. They're just ornery, Lord, and too young to think
about what they were gettin' into . . .*

The policeman was walking their way, with the car's
driver alongside him, and Rhoda's stomach tightened.
What with the other emergency vehicles gone—and Rebecca, as well—she supposed the officer needed to talk with
her next . . . not that she really wanted to think about the horrible accident she'd witnessed. The sense of unreality, the
shock, was wearing off now. Even though the Knepp twins
were on their way to being cared for, Rhoda was worried.
Drained. So much had happened in such a short time, and
she was now caught up in a chain of events toppling like a
line of standing dominoes.

The driver of the ditched car was a tall fellow about
Mamma's age with a bristly air about him. His dark hair
was cut short and he wore a suit and tie beneath his camel-
colored overcoat. "Please believe how sorry I am that those
young boys were injured," he said as his gaze lingered on
their black coats and bonnets. He handed Mamma a business
card. "I'm not at liberty to discuss details of the accident
until I've consulted with my attorney, but here's my contact
information. I hope you'll pass this along to the boys' father,
with my belief that it's in everyone's best interest to settle
this out of court."

Rhoda frowned, baffled. How was it that this man was
already concerned about legal matters, when two little boys
might be fighting for their lives?

"*Jah*, I'll see that their *dat* gets this," Mamma replied
cautiously. She glanced at the card and passed it to Rhoda.
In fancy script, it said he was Conrad Hammond, CEO of
Hammond Realty, and he had a bunch of letters after his
name. Rhoda had no idea what those initials meant, except

that he had probably become very wealthy in his real estate dealings.

"That'll be all for now, Mr. Hammond. We'll be in touch—and it looks like your tow truck is here," the officer said, nodding in the direction of his car.

Mr. Hammond strode off, obviously glad to see the truck, and to be free of further questions. Ben and Andy, who had carried armloads of quilts back to the Schrocks' shop, came up to join them. "We could've hauled that Hammond fella out of the ditch just fine with Pharaoh and another horse or two, if he'd waited," Ben remarked. "But we've been busy tendin' those boys."

The policeman's smile only curved on one side. "Something tells me he wouldn't want to risk more damage to his Jaguar," he remarked. He looked at Rhoda then, with eyes that seemed to take in every detail of her face. "I'm Officer McClatchey, and I understand you were another witness to what happened in front of your restaurant. The young lady I spoke with earlier said you are her . . . sister?"

Rhoda had to smile at that one. "*Jah*, that's a long story, as our Rebecca didn't grow up Amish. Can—can we go inside, where it's warmer? I've been out here a *gut* long spell in this wind."

"Fine idea," Mamma said. "I'll put coffee on, and we've got sticky buns or pie or what-not, too."

Rhoda had no appetite, but she was pleased that Ben and Andy were coming inside with them. Though Officer McClatchey didn't seem mean or threatening, it eased her mind to have her mother and two familiar men present while he was talking with her.

Within minutes, Mamma was pouring coffee and had a plate of goodies on the table where the three men and Rhoda had settled. The policeman passed on the food, but after a long sip of coffee he opened his notebook. "For the record, your name is Rhoda Lantz, correct?"

She nodded, wondering how much she was expected to reveal . . . how much Rebecca might have said already. "*Jah*, I'm Rhoda."

"So what happened? Tell me what you saw after you first noticed that horse-drawn sleigh going toward the road."

Rhoda's throat went dry despite the coffee she'd sipped. Was she supposed to include what Jerusalem had said, about the twins slipping away when they'd seen the Zook boys go by? What if her account didn't match up with the story Rebecca had told him?

"Understand that you're puttin' Rhoda in a spot," Ben explained quietly. "We Amish don't cotton to gettin' involved with the law. Our bishop insists we settle our problems amongst ourselves, and since those two boys in the ambulance are the bishop's sons—and he doesn't much like doctors or hospitals, either—we're already stretchin' a lot of limits here."

"I've heard that about Plain people, yes," the policeman said, "but Mr. Hammond isn't Amish. It's my job to report what happened, to ensure that the insurance companies have the information they need to settle claims, and to be sure everyone gets a fair shake."

"We Amish don't believe in insurance," Mamma pointed out. "We pay our way, and we take care of our own."

Officer McClatchey leaned forward, a wry expression on his weathered face. "According to Rebecca, the bishop's boys weren't watching for traffic when they started across the road—dangerous, but understandable," he remarked. "Mr. Hammond wasn't watching for traffic, either, and when I quizzed him several times about it, he finally admitted he was talking on his cell phone when he lost control of his car."

Andy cleared his throat, gazing at Rhoda. "That explains

why Mr. Hammond is so interested in settling out of court. He doesn't want Hiram to sue him—"

"What does that mean, to sue?" Rhoda interrupted. This was getting very complicated, and her head was starting to pound.

Andy smiled kindly. "It means Hiram would demand a large sum of money to cover any medical expenses and whatever else Hammond's insurance company might pay him to compensate for the harm done to his boys," he explained. "And if one or both of the twins dies, Mr. Hammond could be found guilty of involuntary manslaughter—which means he killed someone, even if he didn't intend to."

Rhoda grabbed Mamma's hand, wishing Andy hadn't mentioned the possibility that Josh or Joey might die. Even though this information was spinning in her head, sounding very ominous, it suddenly seemed important to report what she had seen, no matter what Hiram might think about it. After all, Rebecca had already given her account of the accident. And Rhoda certainly wanted to help Josh and Joey any way she could.

"When we saw the Knepp sleigh comin', racin' with the Zook boys in their sleigh, Rebecca and I ran outside, hollerin' at them to get off the road," Rhoda began. "But Josh and Joey weren't listenin'. And when Mr. Hammond's car started spinnin', his horn started honkin' and that spooked the Knepps' horse."

Rhoda paused, wishing these frightening images weren't running through her mind again. "The horse whipped around, so the sleigh slid on the ice and threw the boys out," she continued in a low voice. "And then the car hit the Belgian before it spun into the ditch. It all happened so fast . . ." Her voice died away. She'd told the truth, but she didn't feel any better for it. Actually, she felt even worse about what those little boys had gone through in the blink of an eye.

The policeman smiled. "That's amazing. Your sister told the story in almost exactly those same words, with the same details, while Mr. Hammond couldn't seem to repeat his own story accurately." He drained his coffee mug and closed his notebook. "Thanks for giving me your account, Rhoda. I know this has been a difficult day for you, and I'm sorry— for all of you folks—that this accident happened right in front of your place, and so close to Christmas."

After Officer McClatchey took down the Sweet Seasons phone number and address, he went off to file his report. Ben, Mamma, and Andy remained at the table with Rhoda to finish their coffee, but they had little to say. It seemed everyone was still stunned about what had happened to the Knepp twins.

Finally Andy took the last cookie from the plate. A dove it was, frosted in white with sparkly white sugar accenting its edges. "The Holy Spirit, who came to live among us at Christmas," he murmured. "Almost a shame to eat this cookie, pretty as it is." He flashed Rhoda a lopsided smile that made her heart skitter. "The Christmas cookies you made us are long gone. I've got a high school girl from down the street coming to look after the kids when they get home from school, but it's not the same as having you there, Rhoda."

"*Jah*, well . . ." What else could she say? Mamma and Ben were watching her closely, and she didn't have the heart to tell Andy that she'd been ordered not to see him anymore. "And how's your *mamm* doin'?"

He shrugged. "Not as well, but she gets from one day to the next. She wears those two dresses you made her all the time now." He closed his eyes over the first bite of his cookie and then scooted his chair away from the table. "Well, I'll swing by the hospital to see how the boys are doing, and then—"

The loud jangling of the bell above the door made them all look up. Rhoda's breath caught: Hiram stood there in his black hat and overcoat, glaring at their little group as though he intended to clear them out the way Jesus had overturned the tables of the Temple moneychangers.

Then he focused on Rhoda. "One of my Belgian geldings is dead out there at the side of the road," he said in a terse voice. "I've heard that Joseph and Joshua disobeyed me by joyriding in the sleigh, and that they were injured. And you've sent them to the hospital without my permission. And you have invited this *Englischer* into your midst yet again when I've specifically ordered you not to. The wages of sin is death, Rhoda. Can you not see how God punishes those who defy my commands?"

Chapter Eighteen

Andy remained in his chair. This was no time to leave the Lantz family to answer for the care he had given Hiram's sons, and he sensed it was a good opportunity to figure out what made the bishop tick. While he understood that Amish folks believed everything that happened was the will of God, it was another thing altogether for this man to claim that God was punishing his boys for misbehaving—and that Rhoda and her family would be next on the hit list. Where did this guy get off, thinking he had such complete knowledge of heaven and hell and all things in between?

"With all due respect, Bishop," Andy began, "it was *my* opinion that your sons would need more treatment than I could give them. They have broken bones, not to mention internal injuries we can't detect without—"

"I'll deal with you later," Hiram interrupted curtly. "My immediate concern is that Rhoda has once again jeopardized her salvation by continuing in her sin with you, when she assured me she wouldn't see you again. Her duplicity sickens me."

Miriam smacked the tabletop and stood to face the man in the doorway. "Your immediate concern should be your sons, Bishop," she stated. "And maybe ya could see your way clear to thank Andy for the way he got your Joey to breathin' again. Had he not come to help, we'd be weepin' and wailin' over your dead boy instead of sippin' coffee right now."

Hiram's eyes widened, but before he could reply, Miriam jumped in again.

"And I refuse to believe that the God I love and trust is usin' your sufferin' little boys as an example for folks who ignore your authority," she continued in a low, unwavering voice. "Could be He's tryin' to get *your* attention, Hiram. Ever thought of that?"

Andy sat up straighter, amazed at Miriam's challenge— just as Ben and Rhoda were, judging from their expressions. How he admired this courageous woman of faith! For her, and for Rhoda and Ben and those two older ladies he'd seen riding off with Rebecca, he vowed to do everything in his power to ensure Josh and Joey Knepp's recovery.

"Here." Rhoda stood up then, holding out a business card. "The English fella whose car hit your horse asked us to give ya this. He was another reason we called the ambulance, ya know—the policeman said they needed all the details to keep this fella's insurance company informed."

"Mr. Hammond said he wanted to keep this outta court," Ben chimed in. "You'll want to talk to him sooner rather than later, I'm guessin'."

Hiram held firm in his spot by the door, until Rhoda finally approached him with the card. Andy watched the bishop's face as he read it . . . suspected that Rhoda had played this card to divert his attention away from her, and Ben had gone along. Sure enough, Knepp's brows rose. He tucked the card into his pocket as though he didn't have to see Conrad Hammond to believe this catastrophe might have a silver—or green—lining to it. "Well, Hooley, if you'll take care of my dead horse—"

"*Jah*, I can do that, Bishop."

"—I'll get to the hospital to be sure the doctors haven't overstepped," Hiram went on. "It's up to God to heal my sons."

As Hiram gripped the doorknob, Andy rose from his chair. "I'd be happy to give you a ride, sir. I'm going there to—"

"My driver's waiting. And you, Mr. Leitner, have done enough meddling in our Plain affairs," he replied stiffly. "If Rhoda hasn't told you this part, along with forbidding her to see you again, I informed her that if you had any inkling of becoming Amish so you could be with her, I would refuse to baptize you."

Andy felt as though the bishop's Belgian had come back to life to kick him in the gut. Apparently Preacher Tom had mentioned his inquiry about the Amish faith . . . or had Rhoda guessed that part? Wished for it? While he was taken aback by Hiram Knepp's vengeful, ungracious attitude, he was sorrier that he'd gotten Rhoda into even more trouble with the leaders of her church. Nothing he could say or do would improve this tense situation, so he remained silent. He held Hiram's gaze until the man in black turned and left, letting the door bang behind him.

Andy exhaled. "It was never my intention to cause any of you such trouble—"

"Trouble? Puh!" Miriam came over to him and took his hand between hers. "Seems trouble with the bishop has been our lot since my Jesse died, and it's taught me to be a stronger woman," she insisted. "Andy, please don't believe the rest of us resent you one little bit. *Jah*, it's a tough subject, knowin' how you and Rhoda care for each other, but there's no such thing as too much love in this world. We thank ya from the bottom of our hearts for lookin' after Josh and Joey. When God gives somebody the gift of healin', we should all be grateful to be on the receivin' end of it."

"For sure and for certain," Ben agreed as he reached over to shake hands. "We'd have been a lot worse off had ya not been here explainin' the law and that Hammond fella's insurance, helpin' Rhoda when she was givin' the policeman her story. I'm real sorry about the way Hiram just talked to ya, Andy. He might be our bishop, but he doesn't speak for all of us, understand."

"Thanks. I appreciate that." Andy sighed and looked at the cookie he'd laid on the table . . . that dove of peace had lost its head, and indeed that's how this situation felt to him right now. "I'll go on to the hospital, because my shift starts in half an hour. While I'm there I'll see how things are progressing with the boys. Hiram's their father, and legally he calls the shots about their care. Could be, once he sees them, he'll adjust his attitude when he realizes how close to the edge they were."

"*Jah*, and what with my aunts already bein' there, Hiram might catch an earful if he tells the doctors he's takin' them home." Ben clapped him on the back. "You've done all the right things, Andy. Sorry ya got crossways with the bishop."

Nodding, Andy went to the coat tree and slipped into his parka. He heard someone behind him and smiled at Rhoda as she, too, put on her coat. "Will you be all right?" he asked quietly. "That was a nasty accident you saw, and it might haunt you for a while."

She smiled glumly. "I'm thinkin' Rebecca and I might be talkin' things over. We've all found out that her bein' English isn't such a bad thing, far as understandin' the way things happen in the outside world."

"You'll have to tell me more of her story sometime."

Rhoda smiled up at him as he opened the door. "*Jah*, I'd like to do that. She's a real special sister. But for a while, I'd best stay outta trouble, what with confessin' before the membership on Sunday—which is when Hiram's ban is to be lifted, too."

Andy's eyebrows rose. He didn't understand all the details of Amish confession or shunning, but he sensed Sunday would be a pivotal day for the Lantz family—and for the Willow Ridge community, as well. "I hope everything goes all right for you, Rhoda. I'll send up some prayers for you."

"*Denki*, Andy. That would be wonderful-*gut*."

The café door closed behind them, and Andy's breath caught at the expression on Rhoda's face as she gazed up at him. He saw fear and yearning, an affection that hadn't been dampened by the bishop's harsh decrees. Her arms flew around him and he held her close, resting his head on hers. "Rhoda, I'm sorry—"

"Don't be," she pleaded.

"—I've caused you so much pain and heartbreak."

"Wasn't you doin' that, Andy. It was your world crashin' into mine," Rhoda insisted. "It's been so *gut* to see ya today even if the circumstances were horrible-hard."

Andy closed his eyes, savoring the warmth of her slender body and the strength of her hug. Did he dare admit his feelings? His intentions? Would that make Rhoda feel better or only cause her more pain? "I . . . Rhoda, I've asked Preacher Tom how to become Amish—"

Her eyes glittered with unshed tears. "You'd do that for *me*?"

Oh, but her blue eyes and sincerity tugged at him. He could only nod, trying to find his voice again. "I can't expect you to leave your faith," he explained. "But this decision would affect my whole family, and possibly my ability to earn a living as a nurse. And it would mean learning your language, and selling my home and car and most of my possessions. So it's a huge gamble—especially considering what Hiram Knepp has said about allowing me to join."

Rhoda swiped at tears. Then her lips twitched in a mischievous grin. "Well, now. It's not like Willow Ridge is the only Amish colony hereabouts, ya know. New Haven and Morning Star have different bishops, but the faith is the same."

He let out a laugh and kissed her before he caught himself. Wasn't it just like Rhoda to see her way around the obstacles life put in her way? And wasn't that just one of the reasons he'd came to care for her so quickly?

"Rhoda, you're a gem. Never forget that."

She chuckled. "Tell your *mamm* and the kids hullo for me. I miss them."

"I'll do that." He jogged across the road to his car. Hard to believe the cookie in his hand had remained intact during their hug. He had to smile. The dove might've lost its head, but its beautiful, sparkly body was still intact, a reminder of how God had sent the dove to Noah after the flood, as a sign that all was not lost. His love remained and a whole new world—a whole new life—lay ahead.

And wasn't that a thought worth holding on to?

"Mr. Knepp?"

Rebecca glanced up from her magazine as a surgeon in turquoise scrubs came out the swinging doors of the operating room. *Thank you, God*, she thought as Jerusalem, Nazareth, and Hiram eagerly stood up to meet him. The afternoon vigil had gone fairly well, with the Hooley sisters reassuring each other and chatting with her to pass the time—until Hiram had blown in like a thunderstorm.

The bishop had demanded to see the hospital's chief of staff as well as the director of the emergency unit, and the fact that they were both women infuriated him more. He had complained vehemently about the fact that his sons had been transported here without his knowledge or permission—that the ambulance crew had gone against his religious principles. He had been ready to barge into the operating room to fetch the twins until the chief of staff had threatened to call security. She'd reminded him repeatedly that the boys were still in surgery and could not be wheeled out until they were sewn up.

"Hiram, they were so badly injured, you would've brought them here yourself to be patched up," Jerusalem had insisted tearfully. "I assume full responsibility for your sons' bein'—"

"And where were you when they took the sleigh from the barn?" he had shot back. "Had you truly been *responsible*, Joey and Josh wouldn't be in this condition."

Rebecca had nearly bitten her tongue in half to remain quiet. Nazareth had crumpled, sobbing. Jerusalem had backed down, but her stricken expression was a mixture of exasperation and resentment that was sure to explode later, after this crisis had passed.

Now, as the surgeon extended his hand and Hiram didn't shake it, the Hooley sisters remained a few feet behind him. Nazareth gripped Jerusalem's elbow.

"Mr. Knepp, I'm Dr. LaFarge, and I've overseen your sons' procedures," he said in a low voice. "I'm pleased to report that their broken bones have been set, we've repaired several torn ligaments, and we've stopped some internal bleeding. After a day or two of observation and follow-up testing, your twins will be on the road to recovery."

"Glory be!" Nazareth murmured.

"Our prayers have been answered," Jerusalem agreed as she wiped her eyes.

Hiram, however, stood ramrod straight. Even without his hat he cut an imposing figure, and his displeasure seemed to suck the air from the waiting room. "I'm taking them home with me. *Now*. With God's care, they will heal."

"You don't understand, sir," Dr. LaFarge stated. "When we learned that Joey had stopped breathing at the accident site, we ran tests that revealed a pulmonary weakness, which might well be hereditary. Though his lungs are functioning again, both boys should remain under observation—"

"That, too, is the way God made them," the bishop interrupted. "I have already expressed my chagrin to your chief of staff. I have signed the necessary waivers to take them home. I'm their father, and I have that right."

The surgeon crossed his arms, remaining deadly calm. "All right, then. But they can't leave until they've regained consciousness and we've detached their monitors and IVs. They will remain in my care until I see that they are awake and mentally alert. We're concerned about the possibility of concussions."

Rebecca wanted to cry for the Hooley sisters. They felt bad enough that the twins had sneaked out with a horse and sleigh, and now they worried that the boys might not recover completely from an accident caused by a careless driver. She, too, was haunted by the images still flashing through her mind after witnessing that heart-wrenching wreck.

At the sound of Nazareth blowing her nose, Hiram turned to the two sisters. "It's best that you go back," he stated. "Your time would be better spent preparing the downstairs room beside my office to be the boys' sickroom. I'll see that they get home."

Just that curtly, he dismissed them.

Seething, Rebecca fetched her parka. She waited patiently as the Hooley sisters helped each other with their heavy black coats and then tied on their black bonnets. Why did she suspect Hiram had something up his sleeve? His lack of compassion—his blatant arrogance—made her wonder yet again why her mother and the other good-hearted people of Willow Ridge tolerated this man. Did they consider it God's will that such a tyrant was in charge of their earthly lives and their souls' salvation?

Once out the doors, both women sighed loudly. "There was a time I thought Hiram was maybe worth my efforts," Jerusalem muttered, "and I was happy to help with the kids while he was under the ban, but this is the last straw, Sister. I believe the Lord's tellin' me to move along. Maybe back home to Lancaster County."

"*Jah*, I'm with ya, far as not puttin' up with that pig-headed bishop any longer," Nazareth replied in a wavery voice. "But what about the children? And what about . . . well, maybe I'm bein' a silly old fool, but I'd like to keep company with Preacher Tom awhile longer, to see what comes of it."

Rebecca clicked her key fob to unlock the car doors. "Forgive me if I'm speaking out of turn," she said, "but I don't see how you two have tolerated that man as long as you have. I think those kids—and your nephews—would miss you a lot, Jerusalem—"

"Not to mention *me* missin' ya, Sister! We've done everything together, all our lives," Nazareth pointed out.

"—but I bet other folks would offer you a place to stay," Rebecca continued. "Mamma and my sisters love having you around. You fit in at Willow Ridge as though you've always been there."

As Nazareth squeezed behind the front passenger seat to get

into the back, Jerusalem smiled ruefully. The poor woman's exhaustion was etched around her eyes and she seemed to have aged twenty years since the accident. "*Jah*, but there would be no stayin' away from Hiram, no matter who we lived with," she pointed out. "And then there's the matter of my four goats and the wee ones that're on the way. With the twins laid up, there'll be no one I could trust to tend them."

Rebecca smiled tiredly. "Mamma would probably say that things will look better come tomorrow."

"*Jah*, that's a *gut* way to look at it. The Lord'll provide." Jerusalem climbed into the back, and once they got on the road, it was a quiet ride to the Knepp house.

After Rebecca parked, she opened the door to assist the sisters out of the car, gripping their hands until they had a solid foothold on the snow-packed driveway. "Be careful, now," she said. "It's dark and slick out here."

Jerusalem let out a little laugh. "*Jah*, that's the way of it a lot of times in this life—dark and slick, with plenty of chances to land on your backside. *Denki* for lookin' after us today, child. You've got your mother's *gut* heart."

As the two older ladies grabbed hands and made their way toward the squares of light coming from the front windows, Rebecca felt a glow inside. That felt like the nicest thing anyone had ever said to her. She was cautiously walking around to the driver's side when the front door of the house flew open and out rushed Cyrus and Levi Zook. They stopped a few feet in front of the Hooley sisters, shivering without their coats.

"We—we come over to ask how the twins're doin'," Cyrus stammered. "And we're mighty sorry we double-dog dared them to race us in the sleigh, too. We helped them hitch it up, ya know. Didn't mean for nobody to get hurt."

"*Jah*, Mamm told us to sit tight until ya got back," Levi

joined in. "She sent some supper and says we're to ask about any chorin' we can do for ya, too, on account of how Joey and Josh'll be laid up."

"*Jah*, and it's gonna be a *gut* long while before we're allowed to drive the sleigh again, too," Cyrus added with a forlorn sigh.

"Well, now." Jerusalem studied them in the light coming from the window. "I'm glad to see you boys ownin' up to the trouble you caused today. Let's go inside where it's warm and talk about this, shall we? Mighty nice of your *mamm* to see to our supper, too."

As Rebecca pulled out onto the blacktop, she smiled at the way the Hooley sisters had indeed woven themselves into the fabric of this community. How would it be when she moved into the apartment with Rhoda, though? Was she heaping more trouble on her sister and Mamma by bringing her technology and her English lifestyle into the Lantz household?

Show me what You'd have me do, Lord, she prayed as she drove down the dark county road. *Things are getting tricky in Willow Ridge.*

The obstetrics wing was very quiet on this Friday evening, so Andy slipped downstairs. When he saw that Hiram wasn't in the recovery room with his boys, he went over to check on them. Josh was just waking up and had a disoriented expression on his bruised, scraped face, while Joey—who had undergone more extensive surgery—was still sleeping off his anesthesia. Both boys sported casts and bandages, and with IV tubes and monitors all around them, they looked frail and vulnerable. After a glance at Josh's chart, he went to the boy's bedside. "Hey there, Josh," he murmured. "Do you know where you are? Do you remember what happened to you?"

The boy blinked and turned away, as though he wanted to be left alone.

"Your dad'll be here any minute," Andy assured him. "Joey's right here in the bed beside yours. Just rest now, okay? I'll get your nurse."

Andy felt a tug on his heartstrings when he imagined his own son in such a painful predicament. From the talk around the nurses' station, Hiram had made quite a scene and might well be taking his twins home tonight, against the advice of every medical professional here. Dr. LaFarge had instructed everyone on duty to tread lightly: despite the fact that the Amish preached forgiveness and peacemaking, Knepp was a textbook example of a man most likely to file a lawsuit.

Andy paused at the nurses' station to smile at Kayla Burke, who had attended nursing school with him. "The Knepp twins are coming around," he said in a low voice. "Has their father seen them yet?"

"No, and I've heard he's a handful," she replied. "I'll check on them and let Dr. LaFarge know how they're progressing."

Andy headed for the elevator to return to Obstetrics, but when he heard a familiar voice coming from the waiting room, he paused.

"Yes, Mr. Hammond, we Amish believe that God directs us to forgive and submit to His will," Hiram was saying in a low, purposeful voice. "But God also holds us accountable for our misdeeds. I lost a fine horse today—a Belgian I was ready to sell for around four thousand dollars, as that's how I make my living. And my sons have undergone hours of extensive surgery because of your careless driving. Your *negligence*."

Andy peered quickly into the waiting area. The bishop was using the courtesy phone, his back to the door as he gave Conrad Hammond an earful. Curiosity made Andy wait on the other side of the wall to get a sense of how high Hiram might be hanging this verbal noose.

"Yes, we Plain people prefer to stay out of court and to not get involved with the police," Hiram continued archly. "And indeed, Mr. Hammond, once you've paid the bill for today's ambulance fee and my sons' extensive hospital procedures, plus any physical therapy they might require, you'll be finding other ways to compensate what I've endured today. As a Realtor and a representative of your political district, you'll be in quite a predicament if it gets out that two young boys were maimed—or died—because you lost control of your car while talking on your cell phone."

Andy blinked. The bishop was certainly using the details from Officer McClatchey's accident report to his advantage.

"I'll be in touch with you after I ascertain the extent of my twins' injuries. They should be in the recovery room by now."

The next part of the conversation was drowned out by a page requesting Dr. LaFarge to come to the emergency room. Instinct prodded Andy to return to the nurses' station rather than go upstairs. His head was spinning as he tried to wrap his mind around the bishop's strategy—he was going for Hammond's financial jugular, after protesting that the emergency crew and the hospital staff had ignored his rights. Andy was surprised at how knowledgeable Hiram Knepp seemed when it came to legal affairs and worldly procedures.

"You're back?" Kayla asked as he slipped behind the counter of the nurses' station. "I'm taking ice chips and teddy bears to the Knepp boys. They're a little scared, waking up in a strange place, but I wheeled their beds closer together so they can talk."

"Their father's headed this way. After the conversation I had with him at the scene of the accident, I'd like to be here, uh—in case he has any questions," Andy added quickly. He was reviewing the details of the boys' surgery on the computer . . . checking their vital signs on the monitors, in case Hiram made good on his threat to take the twins home tonight. "Come and get me if he becomes testy."

Kayla selected the two biggest bears from the toy basket and went on her way, while Andy went down the long list of injuries and conditions the surgical team had documented. The boys were stabilizing well, considering the body trauma they'd sustained, but another day—even spending the night here—would greatly increase their chances for a full recovery. As he heard the quick, purposeful tread of boots coming down the hallway, he prepared himself for whatever Hiram might do.

Help me stay calm, Lord, and say the right things.

As the bishop stopped beside the counter, Andy had the satisfaction of watching his startled reaction.

"Leitner. You work *here*?" Knepp masked his surprise by glancing toward the recovery room. "I looked in on the twins about an hour ago, but they were still unconscious. May I go in now?"

"I'm sure they'd love to see you. I was with them as they were coming around," Andy replied. He noted the discrepancy between Hiram's statement and Kayla's, but kept a benign smile on his face.

"After assessing their condition, I've decided they should remain here until Dr. LaFarge releases them." Hiram sighed as though he carried the weight of the world on his shoulders. "Perhaps it was God's will that they come here, after all."

"You've made a wise decision, Mr. Knepp. We'll wheel them to a room after the doctor looks in on them. We can roll in a bed for you, if you'd like."

"That won't be necessary."

As Hiram headed toward the curtained room where Kayla was tending the twins, Andy bit back a smile. Oh, but this change of heart suggested some interesting scenarios, considering what he'd overheard in the waiting room. The bishop was now thanking Kayla for her attention, and then he talked briefly with his sons, who answered in hoarse but eager voices. After he assured them he would be back tomorrow, Hiram emerged from behind the curtains. With a nod at Andy, he put on his black broad-brimmed hat and then swung his long black coat over his shoulders as he strode toward the exit.

Andy signed off from the computer, almost wishing he worked tomorrow morning. The rest of his shift in the obstetrics wing went quickly, as he had patients to check on and plenty to think about.

As he climbed into his cold car, Andy realized how tired he was, yet how satisfied he felt. He'd answered Rhoda's frantic call and saved Joey Knepp's life. He'd been invited into the Sweet Seasons as though he were one of the family, to lend support as Rhoda talked with the police officer. He'd immersed himself in Rhoda's compassion again . . . had hugged and kissed her and admitted he was considering a change of faith.

You'd do that for me?

Her sweet, unassuming smile warmed him all over again.

And she hadn't missed a beat when it came to responding, either. *New Haven and Morning Star have different bishops, but the faith is the same.*

He would have to approach this very carefully . . . couldn't misrepresent the life-altering consequences for his kids and his mom, if he talked to them about this idea.

When *I talk to them*, he corrected. *That's got to happen. Soon.*

Chapter Nineteen

I wish this preachin' service could be over soon, Rhoda thought. She sat on the front pew bench of the women's side with her head bowed, as folks needing to confess were supposed to do. It didn't help that church would take about three hours before the Members' Meeting convened, when she could at last admit her sin and await her punishment for kissing Andy and riding in his car.

It didn't help that Hiram sat directly across from her, either. He rested his elbows on his knees, his gaze fixed on the Riehls' plank floor, awaiting the members' decision about reinstating him, fully forgiven. It was a highly unusual fix for a bishop to be in, yet he seemed unconcerned. Had he made some kind of a deal with Enos Mullet and Jeremiah Shetler, the bishops who had assisted their congregation during his ban?

Who gets to go first, Lord? If Hiram is welcomed back into the fold before I make my confession, will he insist that I be shunned? After all the hurtful things he's done to us, it hardly seems fair—

Rhoda stopped that thought before she finished it. God

alone was the judge of human behavior and He decided what was right and wrong. It was best to set aside her worries and focus on what the preachers said today, because this was one of the most important mornings in the history of Willow Ridge. Plenty of folks had spoken out against Hiram's attitude, and his owning a fancy car. The tension in Reuben and Esther Riehl's crowded home was so thick, she felt it pressing her nearly to her knees.

Preacher Tom's sermon on the angel Gabriel's visit to Mary, announcing she was to be the mother of a Savior, lifted Rhoda's heart. Such courage Jesus's mother had shown when she had praised God for the huge responsibility He had placed upon her. Tom spoke more eloquently than usual, carried away by the miraculous event of Jesus's birth. He reminded them that no matter what trials and tribulations they had encountered in this season, the Christ Child was to be loved and celebrated. Jesus, too, had endured great pain in His brief lifetime, to better understand human suffering . . . *her* suffering, Rhoda realized.

Then came the silent kneeling prayer, followed by Deacon Reuben's reading of the first two chapters of Luke. Bishop Shetler preached on the miracle of Christmas and the salvation it still offered them centuries later. What with Hiram decreeing that she should never again see Andy, and bearing up under the guilt of showing her affections for an English fellow, the season's joy had nearly passed her by this year. Next Thursday was Christmas, and the Thursday after that Mamma would marry Ben. Oh, how she hoped her family's happiness wouldn't be spoiled by whatever punishment she received today.

As they stood for the benediction and the closing hymn, Rhoda's throat was so parched she couldn't sing. But Hiram sang out with his customary gusto. Only a few moments more . . .

"We shall now begin our meeting," Enos Mullet announced in his reedy voice. "All who are not baptized into the fellowship are excused."

Older children led their young siblings toward the room with the coats, so they could play outside. Rhoda recalled such outings when she and Rachel were small, when Matthias Wagler's older sister Ruth had taken charge of them so Mamma could attend the meetings. Such a sense of belonging had surrounded her all her life, and now she faced the possibility of separation during a shunning—

"Rhoda, we shall begin with the matter of your riding in a car with an Englishman and being seen kissing him," Jeremiah Shetler announced. "Have you come to confess?"

"*Jah. Jah*, I have," she murmured. Oh, what a blessing to have this matter handled by the bishop from Morning Star! Rhoda went to her knees before him and Enos Mullet, Preacher Tom, and Preacher Gabe, overcome by relief and remorse all at once. "I knew I was goin' against my vows, puttin' myself in temptation's way," she continued contritely. "So I spoke with Preacher Tom about it, and I stopped workin' for that family."

While she confessed to behavior that went against the *Ordnung*, and said she regretted bringing shame to her family, Rhoda did not say she was sorry for the affection she felt for Andy and his family. That would be a lie, and God would hold that against her. As tears streamed down her face, her words came out in such a rush she wasn't certain what-all she said. But when she finished, Rhoda looked up to see quiet compassion on the four preachers' faces. She felt the freedom of releasing her burden, even if she didn't yet know what penance the members might require of her.

"If you'll step outside, Rhoda, we'll call you in when we've reached our decision."

She walked quickly down the aisle between the closely packed pew benches, meeting no one's eye. Grabbing Esther Riehl's coat from a peg by the kitchen door, she stepped outside into the bright sunshine. *I did my best, Andy,* she thought. *Maybe someday, if ya really do take your instruction, we'll look back on all this troublesome stuff as God's way of makin' us strong enough to mesh together as a family.*

Whoops went up on the other side of the buggy-lined driveway, where two teams were running a relay race carrying huge snowballs back and forth. Rhoda watched the children's pink-cheeked exuberance, too caught up in her own concerns to step off the porch and cheer them on.

Behind her, the door opened. Annie Mae grabbed her in a fierce hug. "C'mon in, Rhoda! You're home free!"

Could it be? And so fast? Rhoda rushed back inside, pausing only to hang up Esther's coat. Back down the aisle she walked, daring to believe the smiles she saw on everyone's faces . . . the quick clasp of a hand as she passed the pew where Mamma sat. She knelt before the four preachers to hear their verdict.

"Rhoda, we believe your confession was heartfelt and sincere. The members have voted unanimously to accept it without need for further repentance," Bishop Mullet announced. "You may resume your place amongst the members while we take up the other matter before us this morning."

Rhoda's hand went to her mouth to keep a loud *whoop!* inside. She found Rachel's radiant face several rows back and then squeezed onto the end of that pew after the other girls made room for her. Her twin reached across Annie Mae to grab her hand, and from all around her came pats on the back and a silent grasping of hands while the bishops proceeded with the meeting.

"Six weeks ago we placed your bishop under the ban for his ownership of a car and his possession of a driver's license—a highly unusual and unfortunate event," Jeremiah Shetler said solemnly. "I remind all of you to prayerfully consider what you hear now, and how you respond with your comments and your votes. While a bishop is human—as prone to falling short of God's expectations as the members of his flock—it's a matter of great concern when his sins come between him and the people God has chosen him to lead."

Hiram came forward to kneel. "I again admit the error of my ways when I accepted a car as payment for a debt and then procured a license," he stated. "It was wrong of me to hide that car and to drive it, as well. And for those times these past six weeks when I appeared to forget the separation I was to maintain as part of my shunning, I am also sincerely sorry."

Folks mumbled, shifting on their pew benches. Was that all Hiram was going to say? The two bishops and the preachers gazed at him as though they, too, had expected more.

"All right, Hiram, if you'll step outside," Jeremiah said, "we'll call for discussion and the vote on—"

"I have something else of great urgency to say," Hiram interrupted as he rose from his knees. He looked out over both sides of the whispering crowd, waiting for the chatter to stop. "First, I wish to thank you for your prayers when my sons were rushed to the hospital Friday after their sleighing accident. I was determined to bring them home that evening to allow God's healing to take place, but as I sat between their hospital beds, entreating our Lord's guidance, He came to me with a revelation so amazing I could scarcely take it all in."

Rhoda gazed at her sister and then at Annie Mae. The bishop's daughter seemed as surprised as everyone else to hear about this. They all gazed intently over the rows of kapps in front of them.

Hiram cleared his throat. "God has instructed me to start a new colony, saying that my mission here in Willow Ridge is finished."

Gasps rang out among the women. The men looked at each other in disbelief.

"Again, I was stunned to hear this, but in the stillness of that hospital room where my sons lay sleeping, there was no mistaking the Lord's voice." Hiram clasped his hands in front of him, somber yet visibly excited. "When I asked how this was to be accomplished, the Lord pointed out that our district has grown to about twenty-five families, which is the upper limit of what a bishop and two preachers can attend to."

He paused, raising his arms as though invoking the Holy Spirit. "And when I asked Him where I was to go and what I was to do next, the Lord promised to lead me along the path He had mapped out. And by Saturday afternoon—just yesterday," Hiram proclaimed, "He showed me a large tract of land coming up for sale. And God told me how I was to go about procuring it for His Plain people."

Oh, but heads where swiveling and whispers filled the air! Annie Mae grabbed Rhoda's hand as her father's announcement shook her to the core. "Of all the—oh, but I'm not even believin' this," she muttered. She gawked at her sister, a couple of pews behind.

Nellie, too, looked pale. As stunned and scared as Annie Mae.

"I will have more details when we meet again in two

weeks," Hiram went on in a rising voice. "For now, I have been instructed to place an ad in *The Budget*, calling for families to join me in this holy venture. I invite any of you to assist me, as well. A fledgling community requires committed families willing to reestablish themselves in occupations that will support a colony and foster its growth."

"And just where is this acreage you're talkin' about?" one of the men demanded. "Seems to me—"

"I will disclose its location at our next meeting, when the details are firmly in place," Hiram replied. "This is an undertaking of a magnitude none of us has ever known—or funded," he added pointedly. "But the Lord has spoken. The way so many details have fallen into place in such a short time compels me to believe that this is indeed our God at work.

"And now, if you'll excuse me, I must visit my sons," Hiram continued before anyone could interrupt him. "I'm eager to assess their healing. Excited about the possibility that more heavenly messages will be revealed."

Hiram left from the front entrance rather than through the kitchen, probably so folks couldn't pester him with questions. The *bang!* of the door reverberated in the crowded room, and then pandemonium broke loose.

"Do ya suppose God Almighty honestly spoke to Hiram?"

"Ya can't tell me he's playin' us straight, comin' up with this cockeyed—"

"Well, if that don't beat all!"

"Let's come back to order, please," Bishop Shetler called out above the noisy crowd. "Please, folks. Quiet yourselves. Plenty of time to visit over the meal, after we adjourn our meeting now with a prayer."

Rhoda's head was spinning as she bowed it. Who could have guessed at *this* development? Was it a coincidence that their bishop, often the subject of criticism these past weeks, had received such divine guidance *now*, when it seemed he might not be voted back into the fold?

Silence reigned for longer than usual, which was probably Bishop Shetler's way of allowing folks to pray earnestly about Hiram's unexpected revelation. "Amen," he murmured.

Everyone stood at once, talking in a frenzy that filled the room. The women rushed toward the kitchen, all chattering, as the men began arranging the pew benches for the common meal.

Rhoda stood up, dazed. She was still holding Annie Mae's hand, which was shaking. What must the poor girl be thinking of her father's announcement? Bad enough that their family had been shaken by Josh and Joey's accident. As Nellie joined them, both Knepp girls looked as pale as the snow that had fallen in the night.

Annie Mae exhaled sharply. "I'm not goin' with him. That's all there is to that, and I don't care what Dat or anybody else says," she declared in a vehement whisper.

"I'm stayin' with you, Annie Mae." Frightened tears splashed down Nellie's face.

"Will ya help us, Rhoda? Don't ya see how it is?" her friend entreated. "He's up to somethin' and I want no part of it. Please promise you'll keep this under your kapp, though."

What could she say? Rhoda understood perfectly why the girls didn't want to follow their father. But families were meant to stay together, just as daughters were to obey their *dats*. And what might Hiram do if he learned she had gone against the Old Ways—and him—to shelter Annie Mae and Nellie?

"*Jah*, we'll figure out something," Rhoda heard herself reply as she gripped their hands. "Mamma will see your side of it. Don't you worry about a thing."

* * *

The women streamed toward the kitchen to set out the meal, but Miriam made her way against the current. When she reached Ben, she pulled him close so he could hear her as the men talked of Hiram's announcement.

"Better ask Jeremiah if he'll marry us," she suggested. "I'm not likin' the way Hiram's betwixt and between—not voted back into the membership. Who knows if he'll even stick around Willow Ridge for the wedding?"

"*Jah*, you've got that right, perty girl." Ben's eyes glimmered as he stole a kiss. "Truth be told, I was wonderin' how things might go if Hiram was still ridin' his high horse when he married us, anyway."

Hearing the snatches of the men's conversations as they shifted tables into place, Miriam sighed. "What on earth do ya think Hiram's got up his sleeve? And where's he comin' up with a tract of land big enough to start a new community?"

"Time'll tell. I'm sure the folks here have their own ideas about all that." He flashed her a grin that made her shimmer all over. "Don't worry, we'll have the best wedding ever, Miriam. I'll see to it."

Wasn't that Ben's way, to smooth out the rough places in her life? With a satisfied sigh, Miriam headed back toward the kitchen. Reuben's wife, Esther, their hostess, had butchered several of the chickens she raised and then baked the pieces in seasoned broth. She had also made up platters of deviled eggs sprinkled with paprika and parsley, the red and green of Christmas.

"Esther, the smell of this chicken bakin' made me want to get up during the sermon to be sure it was cookin' just right!" Nazareth teased as she handed the metal pans out of the oven to her sister. "Back in Lancaster, our district had cold cuts or sandwiches, mostly, so it's been a real treat to join you folks for your common meals."

"Oh, and would ya look at this perty pink stuff Hannah and Naomi brought," Jerusalem said. "I haven't yet tasted it, but I can already tell ya I'm gonna have seconds."

Hannah Brenneman grinned as she handed big glass bowls out of the fridge. "*Jah*, this is one of those fruit salads ya could just as well eat for dessert. Made it with cherry pie filling, cream cheese, pineapple, and—"

"*Ach*, I've gotta have that recipe! Something different to serve for Christmas dinner," Lydia Zook remarked. "And would ya look at these wonderful-*gut* cookies Rhoda made for us today? I'd think you'd be so busy bakin' for your *mamm*'s wedding, the cookies would've gone by the wayside this year."

Rhoda looked ever so relieved after her confession, and it lifted Miriam's spirits. These women had welcomed her daughter back, had understood how a girl's heart could sometimes lead her off the narrow path of the Old Ways. It was a blessing to be among these longtime friends, knowing everything had been set to rights again.

"Mamma's cakes are in the deep freeze, waitin' for Rachel to decorate them," Rhoda replied. "And it wouldn't be Christmas without cookies, ain't so? My favorites on those trays are the brownies with a layer of raspberry jelly under the frosting."

"And aren't we mighty glad that Jeremiah Shetler didn't press for a ban like Hiram probably would've done?" Miriam's sister Leah slung her arm around Rhoda's shoulders. "Would've dropped a wet blanket on Christmas Day and your mamma's wedding, I can tell ya."

"So what do ya suppose put the bee in Hiram's hat about startin' up a new colony? I sure didn't see *that* comin'."

Jerusalem Hooley's remark brought the conversation back to the topic they had been discussing at the service's end. Miriam noticed how Annie Mae and Nellie Knepp kept quiet as they unwrapped the relish trays they had made.

"I was thinkin' you might have the inside story on that, Jerusalem," Naomi remarked. "Hiram was dead set against keepin' the boys in the hospital, and now it seems he was there gettin' messages from God. He made it sound like when the Lord was talkin' to the prophets in the Old Testament, where everything was spelled out just so."

"Ya could've knocked me off the pew bench with a feather," Jerusalem said in a low voice. "Ever since he came home Friday night, declarin' he'd leave the twins there until at least tomorrow, things have smelled . . . fishy, if ya ask me."

"He's spent a *gut* deal of time at the hospital, too," Nazareth added. "Yet when we ask how our boys're doin', he has to think about it before he answers. He's told us to stay at the house with Timmy and Sara."

Miriam's eyebrows rose. While everyone here believed that God had spoken directly to the prophets in the Bible—and that there was no reason He wouldn't still be directing His people that way—the whole situation was taking an odd turn.

But there had never been any predicting what Hiram might do, or what he might choose to reveal. She could see how the Hooley sisters would be especially concerned about what the bishop—or was he still their bishop?—might be cogitating. After watching over his family these past six weeks of Hiram's ban, these dedicated women probably wondered if they should find a different place to live.

Or would they head back to Lancaster County? Originally, they had come to help Ira and Luke settle in, saying it was only a temporary stay. As Miriam carried a big platter of baked chicken out to the waiting tables, it seemed Ben had answered a lot of questions with his observation: time will tell.

And between now and then, Lord, I ask Ya to keep our hearts and minds open so we don't miss whatever messages You're sendin' us. Willow Ridge is all ears, waitin' for Your guidance.

Chapter Twenty

When they returned home from the meal at the Riehls', something compelled Rhoda to call Andy. Maybe it was the news about Hiram, or maybe she just needed to hear his voice—and when she entered the phone shanty and found a voice message from him, her heart fluttered. He had been thinking of her, just as she had been wanting to contact him!

"Rhoda, I hope you're okay after witnessing the twins' accident," his mellow voice came through the message machine, "and I hope your confession went well today. You've been in my prayers. I want to talk to you about an idea I have, whenever you find time to call."

Her fingers danced over the numbered buttons on the phone. She held her breath as it rang. "*Jah*—Andy?"

"Rhoda! I wasn't sure when you'd be back from church. How did everything go?"

"Oh, it was a lot more than preachin' we got today," she exclaimed. "My confessin' went quick and easy—"

"Glad to hear it. If you'd been shunned—"

"—but Hiram didn't even wait for the members to vote about lettin' him back into membership," she continued in a rush. "He said God sent him a revelation while he was at the hospital, about how he was to find a tract of land big enough to start a new Amish colony! Now *that* got everybody talkin', I can tell ya!"

There was a pause before Andy said, "Is that the way new colonies are started? Somebody finds land and declares he's leaving the community?"

"Well, we split off to form new groups when we reach about twenty families, because that's about all a preacher or two and a bishop can handle," she replied. "So if Hiram moves away, that means we'll have a drawin' of the lot between our preachers, and one of them'll be the new bishop. I thought ya might want to know about that, if . . . if you're still thinkin' to become Amish."

He chuckled. "That's about the best Christmas present I could ever hope to receive, Rhoda. So how are your mom and Ben and the others reacting to Hiram saying God was telling him to do all this?"

Did Andy know something he wasn't saying just yet? Rhoda cleared her throat. "Well, we wonder about it, *jah*. But nobody was tellin' Hiram they didn't believe him. He invited families to join him, to get the new town started up, but so far I haven't seen anybody jumpin' in with him."

Once again there was a short pause. Rhoda shifted with the excitement of talking to Andy again, and her curiosity was bubbling like soda pop. "So what was that idea ya wanted to talk to me about?"

He chuckled. "It's so good to hear you sounding happy again, Rhoda. I was wondering, though," he said in a more pensive tone. "If you've been forgiven and taken back into the membership, does this mean you're still forbidden to see me?"

"If ya really, for sure and for certain want to join us, I can't see where that's a problem anymore," she replied pertly. "As long as folks here understand your intentions, why—I could even help ya with learnin' our language and doin' things the Amish way, and—"

"What's your schedule like this week, with Christmas coming up? I'd like to meet with Preacher Tom, and you, and if your mother or Ben or anyone else would care to join us, we can talk about exactly what I need to do," he continued with quiet excitement. "I want Taylor and Brett and Mom to be in on this, as well, so they understand the big picture."

Rhoda sucked in her breath. Andy was sounding very serious about changing his faith—for *her*. "But I want ya to know something," she said in a somber voice. "If we tell ya things that don't sound like a *gut* fit for ya, or if your family thinks it's not gonna work . . . I'll understand."

She closed her eyes, choosing her next words carefully. "And if that's the way of it, I won't hold ya to joinin' us. Even Rebecca, sister that she is, knows that bein' Amish just isn't the right thing for her. And that's okay. I still love her."

"Wow," he said with a sigh. "You're the best, Rhoda."

She got all tingly inside, but then recalled the rest of his question. "Christmas Eve we'll all go to the schoolhouse for the program the kids put on each year. We'll spend Christmas Day at home with our families, ponderin' on the miracle of Jesus's birth," she began. "But then the next day is our Second Christmas, and that's when all the fun happens! Jerusalem wants us to come to Hiram's house on account of the twins needin' to stay put once they get home—"

"Will that change, now that Hiram's revealed his new plans?"

Rhoda thought for a moment. "I'm thinkin' Jerusalem and Nazareth might spend Christmas Day with Ben and his brothers, so the Knepp family can have their own day together. Which means Second Christmas will be Hiram's only chance for a big dinner—and no doubt he'll be talkin' up his new colony while the rest of us are there."

"What if I ask Preacher Tom to meet with us on Saturday, then? He's probably spending those two Christmas days with his own family—"

"*Jah*, he'll visit his married daughters, most likely."

"Ah, good. Now tell me the truth, Rhoda," Andy went on in his low voice. "If you girls and your mom will be smack in the middle of wedding preparations on Saturday—"

"We've got time for *you*, Andy," Rhoda chirped. "Naomi and the Hooley sisters are headin' up the wedding feast, and they're helpin' us redd up the house for the ceremony, too. The dinner's to be held in the Brennemans' shop again. We got lots of practice at this when Rachel and Micah got hitched in October, ya see."

Andy let out a low laugh. "This all sounds so delightful," he remarked. "So *together*, with all your family and friends doing everything for each other, I . . . I yearn to feel such close connections, Rhoda."

"Well," she replied quietly, "we can show ya how that's done. I'll tell Mamma and Ben about Saturday, then. Just let us know the time and where we're to show up."

After immersing herself in the music of Andy's voice as he told her how his family would spend Christmas, she hung up with a happy sigh. This had been quite a day of revelations.

Miriam gazed out the window in the loft apartment's kitchen. The fresh snow sparkled like a million little diamonds as the sun rose over Willow Ridge, and the rolling hills and pastures around them shimmered in their Christmas morning finery. A brilliant red cardinal perched on a bare branch of the sweet gum tree as though he were gazing at her. Her heart felt happy yet subdued as she turned toward Rhoda, who was setting the table for their simple breakfast.

"This is the first time in my life I've spent Jesus's birthday with just one other person to help me celebrate," she remarked quietly. "But I'm glad that one other person is you, Rhoda. A blessed Christmas to ya."

"And back to you, Mamma." Rhoda wore a deep red dress and a smile that held secrets, yet she looked radiant. Truly happy. "What with Rachel spendin' her day with Micah's family, and Rebecca bein' with her *dat*, and the Hooley bunch all gettin' together in the apartment above the mill, it seems we all have our places. And we're all with the folks we love best, ain't so?"

"Ya said that just right, honey-bug. And that breakfast casserole's smellin' mighty *gut* while it bakes." Miriam chuckled as she stirred the apples that were simmering in the skillet with butter and cinnamon. "Never thought I'd say this, but it's nice to have some of our favorite leftovers from the café's freezer for our dinner. And while it's felt mighty different, not gettin' up in the middle of the night to bake this week, it's gotten me into the right frame of mind for thinkin' about the Christ Child . . . and contemplatin' how different things'll be after I marry Ben next week."

Rhoda bussed her on the cheek. "You'll adjust fast, Mamma. Seems like Ben's been one of us for a long time."

"*Jah*, he blew in with a storm and just that quick I fell for him."

Her daughter's eyebrows rose as she pulled their casserole from the oven. "You understand how it's been for Andy and me then, ain't so? I know ya think we've not known each other long enough to be gettin' serious, but I've told him he can back out of becomin' Amish, if somethin' doesn't sit right."

Miriam's lips twitched. She'd left herself wide-open for

that, hadn't she? They sat down, bowed their heads briefly, and then smiled across the little table at each other. "It made me feel better, hearin' Andy wanted to meet with Tom and the rest of us. Nothin' to hide that way. I've always told ya to go after what makes ya happy, honey-bug, and I'm not all that surprised that ya chose an uphill road. Ya never were one to accept the easy, fast way. And I'm proud of ya for that."

"Oh, Mamma." Rhoda blinked back tears. "It means ever so much to hear ya say that."

"Faith and love can weather any storm. I'm willin' to help you and Andy, long as ya follow the path Preacher Tom sets out as the proper way to do this." As Miriam stepped into her open blue bedroom to fetch a gift she'd been keeping in her nightstand, her heart overflowed with so many feelings. Her three daughters were so much alike, yet each had grown up her own way with such confidence and grace. Miriam handed the wrapped gift to Rhoda and then sat down again. "I'm hopin' you'll use this as your guidin' light when it seems your biggest questions don't have any easy answers."

Rhoda slipped her finger beneath the tape, saving the wrapping paper as they did whenever it was possible. "Oh, Mamma," she murmured again. "A New Testament—"

"The one my folks gave me on my baptism into the church. I wanted ya to have it." She paused, as a lump had risen into her throat. "When your *dat* and I published our intent to marry, Mamm and Dat were none too happy. Oh, they thought Jesse Lantz was a nice enough fella, but they'd had their hopes set on a boy my age from down the road, because his *mamm* was best friends with mine."

She smiled as she recalled that time, so many years ago. "Jesse grew up in a different community. He'd set his sights on comin' to Willow Ridge because they were in need of a farrier, and he'd found this piece of ground he liked. Had the

house built as my wedding present . . . even if I had nothin'
to say about how it all came together," she added with a wry
smile.

Rhoda smiled sweetly. "So ya broke your parents' hearts
and hitched up with him anyway."

"That was the way of it, *jah*. And I never looked back. It
was the right thing for me to do, and they eventually accepted him."

Rhoda ran her hand reverently over the old Bible's cover
and then set it on the kitchen counter to keep it clean.
"*Denki*, Mamma. I'll treasure it always." Then she flashed a
kitty-cat grin and walked over to pull her Murphy bed down
from the wall of the pale green bedroom . . . took something
from between its mattress and the frame. In this tiny apartment with its rolling walls and open rooms, hiding Christmas gifts was a challenge. "Haven't quite finished your
present, Mamma, but here's what I've been doin' while ya
were up so early bakin' that last week before we closed up
the café."

At the sight of so many fabric colors, Miriam stood up to
finger them. "My word, child, what on earth—?"

"New dresses, Mamma! You've been too busy to sew,
what with Rachel's wedding and runnin' the café," Rhoda
said as she laid the stack of cut-out pieces on the loveseat.
"So I thought ya might like some perty new colors for your
perty new life with Ben. Some are for winter, and some for
spring."

Oh, but her eyes feasted on the bright apple green . . . the
deep pink of the fuchsias that hung in baskets on the porch . . .
a blue like robins' eggs . . . the yellow of the tulips in her
spring garden. "My word, Rhoda, I'd have chosen these colors
as a younger woman—if the bishop back then would've allowed us such bright dresses—"

"Puh! Ben thinks you're plenty young enough. And as for

what the bishop thinks, well—" Rhoda shrugged. "It won't be Hiram tellin' ya these colors are unfit for Plain women, ain't so? It's all worked out to the *gut*, for those who love the Lord."

"*Jah*, there's that." Miriam's eyebrows rose as Rhoda returned to her bedroom and shifted some of the dresses in her small closet. What could she be up to now? To think this daughter had slipped up to the house to use the sewing machine on those cold, dark mornings . . . well, it was a gift such as Miriam had never expected. And it meant Rachel was in on the surprise, too, yet she hadn't given the least hint!

When Rhoda pulled out a brilliant royal-blue dress, along with a glimmering white voile apron, Miriam's hand fluttered to her mouth. "Oh, honey-bug—"

"*Jah*, it's your wedding dress, Mamma. Rachel and I made it, and a new kapp for ya," she said with a quiver in her voice. "Not many daughters get to do that for their *mamms*. It was a special treat to sew it for ya, because you're a truly special woman, Mamma."

Miriam grabbed her daughter in a hug, laughing and crying all at once. "You girls and your secrets! I was thinkin' I needed to stitch up a new dress, but ya beat me to it."

"We've been keepin' each other's secrets since we were born, Mamma." Rhoda eased away to gaze into Miriam's eyes. "There's more to that, but let's eat our breakfast before it gets cold."

And what did *that* mean? Miriam savored each bite of the cheesy bread casserole studded with sausage chunks, onions, and bits of bacon. It was best to let her girls carry this through rather than spoil the morning's fine mood with too many questions. She and Rhoda were sharing the last sweet spoonfuls of their fried apples when Miriam heard the smithy's outside door open and bang shut. Sure enough, a familiar pattern of footsteps ascended the stairs and their visitor knocked before she entered.

"*Jah*, Sister, come on in," Rhoda called out. "Sorry we didn't save ya any of our breakfast. We can scrape ya up something if ya want."

Rachel waved her off and came over to hug Miriam. "Merry Christmas to ya, Mamma," she said. "Might be my first Christmas as a Brenneman, but some things still have to happen a certain way, ya know?"

Another little mystery. Miriam pondered this as Rachel slipped out of her coat and bonnet, for she'd already made her peace with her married daughter spending the day with her new family.

"So what do ya think of these bright colors Rhoda's been sewin' up for ya?" Rachel asked, gesturing toward the partly completed dresses and capes. "Mary Schrock teased us about you switchin' over to the Mennonite side when Rhoda picked out that fabric in her shop. But we thought ya could at least wear them for chorin' if they didn't suit ya for—"

"Those will *not* be my chorin' dresses, silly goose!" Miriam shot back. "And I thank ya for that wedding dress, too. Mighty thoughtful of the both of ya, to see that your *mamm*'s got herself covered."

"At least until Bennie-boy gets ahold of ya," Rhoda teased.

"*Jah*, well, we know what comes of that sort of shenanigans, ain't so?" Rachel chimed in. Then she focused her shining blue eyes—Jesse's dear eyes—on Miriam. "I wanted to tell ya this before I broke it to the Brennemans, Mamma. I'm perty sure we've got a baby on the way."

A little yelp escaped Miriam as she stood up to throw her arms around Rachel. "Oh, honey-bug, that's just the *best* news! I've heard ya upchuckin' a few times and I was wonderin'—"

"*Jah*, Rhoda guessed before I did. I was thinkin' it might be a flu bug—"

"Puh! When have ya ever gotten the flu, Sister?" Rhoda shot back.

At the same moment Miriam opened an arm, Rhoda stepped into their huddle . . . the wonderful, warm circle of love they'd shared many times since Jesse's passing. This blessed news was one more thing she wished she could have shared with him. But then, he already knew, because he was watching over them from heaven.

And wasn't that the perfect sentiment for this Christmas Day? Miriam sighed happily as she held her daughters close. "Well, now. This'll go down in my memory as the nicest Christmas Day of all, girls. Everything I need to feel joyful and at peace is right here in this room."

Rhoda chuckled. "At least until the wedding next Thursday, *jah*?"

Chapter Twenty-One

On Friday, Second Christmas, the Knepp kitchen bustled with the usual preparations for a big holiday meal. Rhoda felt the undercurrent of nerves . . . saw the strain in Annie Mae and Nellie's eyes, and detected a tightness around the Hooley sisters' mouths, as well. What with having the twins to care for, Jerusalem had asked Mamma to roast the chickens and bring the stuffing and gravy for the traditional Christmas meal, while she, Nazareth, and Hiram's girls had cooked up an array of side dishes. Rachel had baked bread and Rhoda had brought a box of her cookies.

"Well, if anybody goes away hungry today, it's their own fault," Mamma said cheerfully. She lifted the lid from one of the big pots on the stove. "Oh, green beans with tomatoes! I've always liked the red and green together, and it's a nice change from the casserole with the mushroom soup, ain't so?"

While Jerusalem and Nazareth joined in with Mamma's happy chatter, Rhoda and Rachel clustered near the Knepp girls to slice the bread and arrange cookies on a platter. "So how's it goin' with your *dat*?" Rhoda asked quietly.

Annie Mae glanced around to be sure none of the little ones were listening to them. Timmy and Sara were playing

with their new Lincoln Logs near the kitchen doorway, while
Josh and Joey played Chutes and Ladders in the front room
where the men were visiting. "We're not sure," she murmured. "Dat stayed at the hospital most of the time the twins
were there. He's been tendin' to a lot of business away from
home ever since."

"Which has made it easier," Nellie remarked quietly. "But
he surely must be gettin' his ducks in a row for whatever
God told him to do about that new colony."

"Rhoda and Rachel!" Jerusalem called from the other
side of the kitchen. "Try this goat cheese on a sliver of that
fresh bread! Tell me what ya think of it."

Rhoda glanced over to see the older Hooley sister holding up a lidded container she'd taken from the fridge. "Now
that's something I've never tried. But if you made it, Jerusalem, it's got to be *gut*."

"*Ach*, but the twins just gobble it down. It's more fun for
them to milk the goats when they see somethin' tasty comin'
out of their efforts."

"They won't be goin' out to the barn for a while yet,"
Nazareth remarked. "But it's mighty fine to have them home
and doin' so well, even with those casts on their arms and
legs. Worried us, while they were havin' so many tests to see
how their insides were doin'."

"*Jah*, the *gut* Lord was watchin' out for them when they
went flyin' out of that sleigh," Mamma agreed.

Rhoda took the spoonful of cheese Jerusalem offered her,
and she spread some of it on a slice of bread, breaking it in
half to share with her sister. They took their first bite together, and Rachel's eyes lit up just as hers did.

"Mmm! Creamier than cream cheese," Rachel said with
her mouth full.

"This would taste *gut* on a lot of things," Rhoda said.
"Maybe stuffed in celery, instead of peanut butter."

"Oh, back home in Lancaster, we made macaroni and cheese and pizza and all manner of things with our goats' cheese," Jerusalem replied with a chuckle. "Even used it as the cheese layer in lasagne casseroles—"

"And it makes real different grilled cheese sandwiches, too," Nazareth remarked. "What with some baby goats on the way, we'll have more milk than we can use up once the new ones are weaned. Then they'll start producin', too."

Rachel polished off her sample, considering this. "Why not sell it, then? Nobody else around here has goats, so your cheese would be a real popular thing—maybe with those grains the boys'll be sellin' at the mill."

"That's what I said, too." Glancing toward the front room, Annie Mae lowered her voice. "And who knows? If Luke and Ira take up my offer to bake for them, that and sellin' goat cheese may be how I get by after . . . Dat spells out his new plan."

The three older women were taking the baked hens from the oven, all sizzling and golden brown. "Time to be gettin' everything on the table, looks like," Rhoda said in a louder voice. "I'll put this cookie plate over by the cherry cobbler and that cranberry upside-down cake. I can see what I'm havin' for my first dessert!"

"*Jah*, I made that," Nellie said as they carried food to the table. "With the cornmeal texture, it's somethin' different from your usual pie or cake. Looks perty for Christmas, too."

After the steaming platters and bowls of food covered the center of the table, plus a card table beside Jerusalem's place, everyone sat down. Joey and Josh perched on pillows in their seats, while Timmy and Sara grinned from wooden high chairs that had been carved by a family member generations ago. What with the Hooleys, the Knepps, and the Lantzes, seventeen people lined the sides of the long kitchen table, and for that Rhoda was thankful as they bowed in silent prayer. *Whatever's cookin' beneath the surface today, Lord Jesus, I'm askin' Ya to guide our thoughts and our words if things get touchy.*

Everyone passed the roasted chicken, mashed potatoes, and hot vegetables. A big glass bowl of fresh cranberry sauce gleamed like a ruby, and Nazareth had made a green gelatin salad with fruit and marshmallows for the kids. Soon Rhoda's plate didn't have any space to spare. Oh, but Mamma's chicken with stuffing smelled heavenly, while Nazareth's creamed corn enticed her, too. Luke and Ira had small mountains of mashed potatoes on their plates. With their other food piled so deep, she wondered why everything didn't ooze off onto the tablecloth.

"So how's it feel to be home from the hospital, eatin' home-cooked food?" Ben asked the twins.

Joey held up a chicken leg with a grin that looked lop-sided on his bandaged face. "It's *gut*," he declared. "And Monday we go back to play games with a special nurse!"

"*Jah*, it's *thare*-pee," Josh confirmed as he scooped potatoes with his spoon.

"Physical therapy," Jerusalem clarified. "That's to make sure your arms and legs heal right, so all your parts'll be movin' the way they're supposed to."

And isn't that interesting, after the way Hiram called us on the carpet for sendin' his boys off in the ambulance? Rhoda tucked a forkful of green beans into her mouth as she stole a quick glance at him. He had remained uncommonly quiet during the meal. The other adults' faces showed surprise and curiosity as they wondered about Hiram's change of heart—not to mention how much the twins' treatment was costing him.

From the head of the table—for he refused to eat at a separate one in his own home—Hiram noted the reactions around him. He laid down his fork with a purposeful sigh. "After I considered how Joey almost died on the side of the road," he said somberly, "I realized that the medical attention they received was the will of God—a gift from our Lord, come down at Christmas. So today we're feasting rather than mourning a lost child. My sons will be strong and healthy come time to begin our monumental task of organizing the new colony God has decreed as my mission."

There it was, conversational bait tossed out for someone to snap up. Hiram was testing to see who would go with him, like sheep faithfully following their shepherd.

Annie Mae and Nellie reached for the bowls in front of them to pass them again, but Hiram held up his hand to halt them.

"I see today's dinner, which was Jerusalem's idea," he said as he grasped the *maidel*'s wrist, "as a providential gathering of some key citizens of Willow Ridge. Every one of you has important skills to offer a new colony. I value your commitment to Plain principles, so I'm offering you choice tracts of land at half their market value."

Rhoda's mouthful of food went down before she was ready and she had to gulp water to keep from choking. This was getting interesting! And Hiram knew just when to pause . . . how to make folks squirm in the silence they weren't filling with their responses.

"Micah, we'll certainly need your carpentry skills early on, for building the first homes, businesses, and the schoolhouse," their host continued. "I've run the first in a series of ads in *The Budget*, inviting folks from all over to join us here in Missouri, where good farmland is still affordable. The sooner a core group of settlers is established, the more desirable our new colony will appear."

Micah's beard, now long enough to frame his face in blond waves, rippled as he wiped his mouth. He glanced across the table at Rachel. "I see your point, Hiram, but my brothers and

I are supportin' our *dat* and *mamm*. Couldn't even consider movin'—"

"And Ben, every settlement needs a farrier. A restaurant is a must, as well, for those who will be laying pipe for the water system and other infrastructure for our business district." Hiram gazed directly at Mamma. "We've had our differences, it's true. But that's how God refines us in His fire to make us stronger for the challenges ahead."

Ben was shaking his head, opening his mouth to respond, when Annie Mae tossed down her napkin. "I'm not goin' with ya." She stood up and left the table.

"Me neither," Nellie chimed in as she followed her sister through the front room.

A stunned silence rang in the kitchen as Hiram glared after his two errant daughters. Wide-eyed, the four younger children stopped eating to watch their father's reaction. Rhoda's pulse raced, knowing that her friends had just invited all manner of chastisement.

"Come back here. Face up to the consequences of your disobedience," Hiram called after them. "You know I'll deal with you more harshly later if you don't."

Footsteps clattered up the oak stairs at the far end of the house. Rhoda suspected the Knepp sisters would be packing up their belongings. How could they possibly stay here, after defying their father in front of folks who weren't family?

Jerusalem removed her hand from under Hiram's. "I'll not be joinin' ya, either. May God strike me down if I'm defyin' His will, but this scheme of yours sounds like something hatched in the Devil's own den. I want no part of it."

"My feelings exactly," Nazareth declared. "I'm stayin' here in Willow Ridge with my nephews."

"*Jah*, even if I weren't finishin' a new house for Miriam," Ben chimed in, "I wouldn't have the least inclination to start fresh again, someplace else."

"Glad you said so, Ben," Mamma remarked pertly, "because for sure and for certain I'm not leavin' my bakery—or my new home—if ya take up with Hiram."

Rhoda stifled a chuckle as Rachel covered her grin with her hand. Oh, but the look on Hiram's face could've curdled milk.

"Don't bother askin' us to leave, either, what with our mill just openin'," Luke Hooley said. "My family's stickin' together in Willow Ridge, and their decision feels right to me."

Ira crossed his arms at his chest, nodding.

Hiram's eyebrows rose slowly as he focused on each one of them in turn. "It saddens me that I've offered you a golden opportunity, a ticket to the promised land, and you won't look beyond your immediate plans—your *convenience*—to answer the Lord's call," he said in a low voice. "You're like the servant in the parable of the talents, who buried his master's money in the ground and had nothing to show for it on the day of reckoning."

Another silence filled the kitchen, but this time it felt different. Rhoda noted a resolute set to the Hooley brothers' faces, and as Mamma scooted her chair back, she and Rachel stood up, too.

"Jerusalem, Nazareth," her mother said quietly, "it was mighty nice of ya to include us in your plans today, but I'd be imposin' on Hiram if I stayed any longer."

"*Jah*, it's not like any of us has much appetite left." Jerusalem rose, as well, while Nazareth knocked the spoon against the green-bean bowl as though she was ready to clear the table.

"I'm not finished eating," Hiram said. "Sit down. All of you."

"I agree with Aunt Jerusalem," Ben replied. "Had ya confessed and been voted back into *gut* standing with the membership, Hiram, this new colony might feel more like an opportunity than another one of your escapades."

"That's not a wise thing to say, considering you and Miriam are to be married on Thursday," Hiram pointed out.

Ben smiled, the picture of confidence. "Jeremiah Shetler's comin' to do the honors," he replied. "What with your position as our bishop lookin' hazy, I wanted to be sure Miriam and I would be legal when we tied the knot. Stickler for followin' the rules that ya are, I think ya see my point, ain't so?"

Hiram gripped the edge of the table, his dark eyes flashing. "You'll be sorry you said that, Hooley," he stated as Ben went for their coats.

"Ben's as honest as the day is long." Jerusalem shoved her chair under the table with a loud *whack*. "You go right ahead and finish your dinner, Hiram. And then ya can clean it up, too. I've had enough."

Chapter Twenty-Two

Saturday morning Andy slowed down to peer out the car window at a two-story building on the outskirts of Willow Ridge. It had housed a hair salon years ago, and most recently had been a floral and gift shop, but neither business had done well in a predominantly Plain area. So now it stood empty, beckoning him.

On impulse he pulled into the lot and jotted down the number on the faded for-sale sign propped in its big window. He'd been thrumming with a sense of hopeful anticipation all week—the feeling that his meeting with Rhoda, Tom Hostetler, Miriam, and Ben would open the portal to the major life change he'd been searching for. This vacant store-front would require a lot of renovation, but he didn't want to overlook any potential piece of the puzzle he sensed was his future.

With God, all things are possible. Jesus's words from the story of the rich young ruler had become his mantra lately, and as the Sweet Seasons Bakery Café came into sight, Andy's pulse accelerated. The thought of seeing Rhoda again made him happy. The sparkling winter sky reminded him of her eyes. As he pulled into the parking lot, he grinned at the horse-drawn buggy tied to the café's railing. If all went well today, that would soon be *his* mode of transportation . . . even if he had no idea how to hitch up a horse.

When the door burst open and Rhoda rushed out, coatless, her excitement swept him away. "Andy, it's so *gut* to see ya!" she exclaimed as she grabbed him in a tight hug. "I sweetened everybody up with a pan of rhubarb cobbler to go with our coffee."

Andy's breath caught in his throat as she kissed his cheek, his lips—right there in the parking lot, where her mother and Preacher Tom could see them through the window. He savored the clean scent of her . . . the open affection he had craved for so long. "*Denki*, Rhoda," he murmured. "Let's get you inside before you freeze."

"Puh! You're my sunshine, Andy. I've been waitin' ever so long for this day." She glanced toward the car then. "Didn't you bring your *mamm* and the kids?"

"Mom's under the weather with a cold. And while Taylor, Brett, and I have talked about what it would mean to become Amish," he replied quietly, "the decision is mine to make. Once God and I are on board with this commitment, they'll be quick to adjust—and Mom will stay with her own Methodist beliefs."

Rhoda's smile softened. "I'm thinkin' your priorities are in the right order, talkin' things out with adults today."

As she led him inside, Andy again prayed that he was doing the right thing. What if he couldn't hack being Amish? What if he was too dependent upon the conveniences and gadgets he'd used all his life? And if he jumped through all the hoops toward membership, for the months—maybe years—that might require, and these Plain folks found him unworthy . . . what would he do then?

And yet, as he saw the friendly, familiar people around Miriam's table with their mugs of coffee, and that pan of crisp that made the room smell sweetly divine, Andy dared to believe that the life he'd dreamed of would fall into place.

"*Gut* mornin' to ya, Andy," Miriam chirped. She began to spoon large portions of the cobbler into bowls. "And *denki* for bein' yet another excuse to celebrate the holidays with Rhoda's bakin' and Preacher Tom's homemade ice cream."

"*Denki* for talking with me today," Andy replied as he nodded to Ben and Tom. "With your wedding coming up next week—"

"And we hope ya can join us for that," Ben insisted as he stood to shake Andy's hand.

"Won't be like you're the only English person there, either," Rhoda chimed in. "My sister Rebecca's comin'; and her *dat*; and Derek Shotwell, the banker; and Sheila, our driver. You and the kids and your *mamm* could see how we do things then, ain't so?"

Not even here for a minute, and he'd been invited to Miriam and Ben's wedding. Andy sat down in the chair beside Rhoda's. "I'm flabbergasted that you would include us, and—and I thank you from the bottom of my heart."

"*Gut* way to meet a lot of the locals, too," Preacher Tom remarked as he placed generous scoops of vanilla ice cream on the warm cobbler. "And an introduction to sittin' through our church services, gettin' your backside accustomed to a hard wooden bench."

As he accepted the first bowl of cobbler from the minister, Andy chuckled. "*Jah*, I have a lot to learn. If I offend you by trying out the little phrases I've heard Rhoda say, that's not my intent."

"Rhoda's a fine teacher. After the way ya talked to me about becomin' one of us," Tom said in a rolling German accent, "I want to give ya every chance to succeed at it. We're feelin' a lot freer about this because Hiram's taken himself out of the picture, ya see. He's sayin' God commanded him to start up a new colony. And nobody at this table's inclined to go with him."

Andy paused with a spoonful of cobbler halfway to his mouth. Was it his place to reveal what he'd overheard in the hospital? Or were these folks, in their subtle way, inquiring if he had more information? "How are the twins doing?" he asked cautiously.

"Oh, Joey and Josh were holdin' up chicken drumsticks at dinner yesterday, talkin' about physical therapy," Miriam said. She looked him directly in the eye, her expression intense. "Myself, I'm havin' a hard time swallowin' Hiram's change of heart. How on God's *gut* earth did an English doctor talk him into lettin' the boys stay in the hospital all those days and then get therapy, too?"

Andy admired Miriam's direct question. He set down his spoon. "I overheard an interesting phone call at the hospital that Friday night after the wreck, when I was working my shift," he began quietly. "Your bishop—"

"Not anymore," Tom murmured.

"—was on the phone with the real estate agent who ran into the boys' horse. Hiram insisted that Mr. Hammond would pay all of the twins' medical expenses—"

"There ya have it," Miriam muttered.

"—and that he would also compensate for the dead horse and whatever else Hiram demanded, in exchange for not pressing charges," Andy continued. "Hammond is a representative in the state legislature. He doesn't want it to get out that two boys nearly died because he lost control of his car while talking on his cell phone."

Tom's face fell. "This sounds even worse than I'd imagined."

The preacher looked at Miriam and Ben. "Yesterday when Hiram was offerin' ya tickets to this new promised land, did he let on where it was?"

"Nope. He said he'd give all the details at the next preachin' service," Rhoda replied soberly.

"Oh, no he's not." Tom shook his head slowly, disbelief mingling with a sad understanding. "There's but one thing to do now. Andy, correct me if I'm jumpin' to the wrong conclusion. Do ya suppose Hiram's gettin' his tract of land from this Realtor fella as part of the deal?"

Andy smiled ruefully. "That was my first thought. If you'd like me to find out more—"

"I don't wanna hear another thing," the preacher declared as he held up his hands. "I'm sorry this has got in the way of our real topic for this morning's meeting, but I appreciate your bein' up-front with us, Andy. I believe you've entered our lives for a *gut* purpose—not that our Rhoda isn't a fine reason to come to Willow Ridge, of course."

The faces around the table relaxed. Rhoda nudged him with her elbow. "See there, Andy? They're comin' around to our way of thinkin'."

As she took a huge bite of her cobbler, which oozed with melted ice cream, her girlish grin tickled something inside him. But there was no getting around the realities he faced. "I hope you'll all be willing to help me with the requirements Preacher Tom has told me about. I understand it might take a couple years—or even more—to be accepted by your members. I have a lot to learn . . . a lifetime of English thinking to overcome," he said quietly. "I've put my house up for sale, because after some serious talks with my kids, they're willing to give this a shot. They love you that much, Rhoda."

Her cheeks turned as pink as her cobbler. "They're mighty

special. And ya know I'll help them—and you—with learnin' the *Dietsch* language or anything else ya need."

"We'll all give ya a hand, Andy," Ben reassured him. "Once folks get to know ya, and understand that you're sincere about changin' your life for Rhoda, you'll find out how we Amish go out of our way to help each other."

"Which brings up the other major question I have." Andy's thoughts were racing as fast as his pulse. This conversation affirmed all the hopes and dreams he'd known these past several weeks, with the exception of one. "I believe my nursing skills are a valuable asset to this community, and a gift from God—"

"*Jah*, I've always thought so, too," Miriam said, nodding.

"—so I'm wondering how I can set myself up to make a living . . ." Another idea popped into his mind out of nowhere—or had it been waiting for him at the side of the road all along? He paused to consider it. "What if I were to set up a small clinic? I haven't looked inside, but that building a few blocks down the blacktop might work—"

The door in the kitchen swung open and Rebecca burst in with snowflakes shimmering in her wake. "Mamma, I just got your phone message, so—oops, sorry!" she added as she came into the dining area. "I'm interrupting something."

"Nah, honey-bug, you're just in time for some of your sister's warm cobbler with Tom's ice cream," Miriam replied as she jumped up to hug her daughter. "Always *gut* to see ya, Rebecca. Mercy, but your cheeks have the pertiest roses in them today."

Andy smiled at the way this daughter in tight jeans and a red plaid jacket seemed so at home here among these Plain folks. It was another testimony to the Lantz family's unlimited love that they had accepted Rebecca, knowing she had no inclination to become Amish.

"I wanted to tell ya that the Knepp girls are stayin' in the apartment with Rhoda until they figure out where else to land," Miriam continued in a more serious voice. "Ira and Luke are over at Hiram's now, loadin' up the last of their clothes and what-not, along with Jerusalem's goats."

Rebecca's jaw dropped. "Holy cow, what did I miss at dinner yesterday? You can't tell me Hiram's letting all four of them move out."

Ben laughed. "If you'd seen Aunt Jerusalem walkin' away from that table, tellin' Hiram he could clean it all up after he finished eatin', you'd see why he's not likely to give those gals much trouble. It's a long, complicated story and we'll tell ya the rest later," he added as he pulled a chair out for her.

"*Jah*, Hiram's probably sweet talkin' them today, askin' them to stay and take care of his kids," Miriam added with a wry smile.

Rebecca's eyes were wide as she took this in. "So where are *you* living now, Mamma?"

"Thanks to this fine fella," Miriam said as she grabbed Ben's hand, "there's a perty new bedroom set already moved into our new house. The Brenneman boys finished it a few days ago, ya know. Got it all swept up and ready, so I'm bunkin' there."

Andy watched Rhoda go to the kitchen for another bowl and spoon. Despite all the shifting around that must have happened on very short notice, her eyes were twinkling and she didn't seem the least bit put out about having two unexpected roommates. This was something like the TV soap operas his mom watched, and he felt honored that these folks would discuss their crisis with him in their midst.

A grin twitched on Rebecca's lips as she sat down. "Bunkin' there by yourself, Mamma?"

Her mother blushed and waved her off while Ben laughed

out loud. "*Jah*, she is, for a few days, anyway. I'm stayin' out of her way while she decides where-all she wants to put everything," he replied. "Then, when my family shows up for the wedding, the place'll be packed—like a Hooley hotel! But the bottom line is, ya have a place to stay with us, Rebecca. Whenever ya want to move in."

"Oh, but I couldn't—you'll be newlyweds! You'll want your privacy and—"

Ben gazed directly at Rebecca while Rhoda stood beside her, spooning up a huge bowl of dessert. Andy went warm inside. This was how the Lantzes and the Hooleys worked things out. Always room for one more . . . or a whole family.

"Trust me, Rebecca. Your *mamm* and I had Micah and his brothers build the *dawdi haus* on the farthest end away from our bedroom," Ben assured her with a wink. "Ya have your own outside door, too, so ya can come and go as ya please. It's got a bedroom, a bath, a sittin' room, and a little kitchen. We're tickled ya want to be here in Willow Ridge with us, honey-girl. After the wedding, it's not like anybody else will be stayin' there anytime soon."

The expression on Rebecca's face mirrored the way Andy was feeling as he watched these family dynamics in action. What wondrous love was this, that everyone accommodated each other's needs? He knew that Amish families often had three generations under one roof, and this conversation was another reason for him to hope that these generous, compassionate people would consider him worthy of Rhoda.

"Well, I can't thank you enough," Rebecca murmured. Then she turned to smile at Andy. "But I butted right in to whatever you were talking about. I'll feed my face now and be quiet!"

Rhoda giggled on the other side of him, scraping her bowl with her spoon. "Andy was just sayin' how, with his new nursin' degree, he might wanna open a clinic here in Willow Ridge."

Andy nodded, grasping the slender hand that slipped into his under the table. "I'm not cut out to be a farmer—"

"We've got plenty of that type around here already," Preacher Tom pointed out. "Truth be told, long as you've got a stable for your horses, it's not like ya have to have a lot of acreage. Some families keep enough land to raise hay and grain for their livestock, but anymore, with risin' property prices, that's gettin' less common. A lot of Plain folks have to find work away from home to support themselves these days."

"Long as we've got a big garden spot, I'm *gut* with that," Rhoda said. Then she squeezed his hand. "But we're all peckin' at ya like biddy hens instead of lettin' ya have your say, Andy. We carry on this way sometimes."

Andy chuckled. "I don't know how much land goes with that vacant building," he said, "and maybe it's not even a good investment. But from the outside, it seems feasible to have a small clinic in the downstairs and maybe use the upstairs for living quarters. I jotted down the phone number—"

"So give them a call and we'll ride down there!" The color in Rhoda's cheeks suggested she had more on her mind than poking around in a vacant building. "We could hitch up the sleigh. It could be your first drivin' lesson with a horse, Andy."

"And if that building doesn't work out," Ben said, "ya might get the Brenneman boys to build ya just the right kind of place. Maybe a home with a clinic on the side."

As Preacher Tom caught Andy's gaze, he tented his hands beneath his chin. "I'm gonna toss a wet blanket on this talk for a minute, so you'll understand this issue better from the

Old Order viewpoint before ya invest your money in that building," he said in a low voice.

"I appreciate that," Andy replied. "And I'll respect whatever you have to say."

Tom nodded, taking the time to compose his thoughts. "I've known girls who took some nurse's training during their *rumspringa*, and when they became midwives after joinin' the church, we welcomed their skills. Likewise, the church elders have no say about you settin' up a practice now, as an English fella. And everyone here understands your need to support your family."

Andy gripped Rhoda's hand, waiting for the other shoe to drop. This idea for starting a clinic seemed so right, even though it had just popped into his mind—and everyone here seemed so enthused about it—that he hoped the minister wasn't going to close his practice before it even opened.

"The final decision about your clinic will be the bishop's," Preacher Tom continued. "While all Old Order districts follow the *Ordnung*, these unwritten rules vary from one community to the next depending on the bishop's interpretation of them . . . and his personality, as well, for some are more lenient than others. I don't know who our next bishop'll be, but he may well deny ya membership in the church if you're runnin' a clinic. Or ya might have to close it down before ya can join. Just keep that in mind as ya make your plans."

Andy sighed. Everyone around the table was nodding, their initial excitement subdued. But the minister's reality check brought up another concern he had about his potential new career, so maybe he'd better spell it out before he committed to the Plain lifestyle.

"I'm wondering how I'll be able to practice without the medical technology I've come to depend on." He let this idea settle in for a moment. These folks had no idea about the amount of information he could obtain online for treating patients, not to mention how a computer would help him with the recordkeeping and accessing of patient data. "And I'll need electricity to operate the most basic computer equipment. I suppose I could adjust to keeping handwritten records and consulting big medical books, but I'm concerned that my skills will become outdated very quickly without the Internet."

Preacher Tom pondered this for a moment. "Keep in mind that your medical expertise will be years ahead of what we've got now," he said. "We Amish depend on God's power to heal, or to determine we're not strong enough to survive. That's just the way of it."

"Yes, I certainly heard about that from Hiram." Andy folded his hands on the table. He wanted to show his willingness to adapt, for as this minister had told him earlier, the changes made would all be on his side of this journey. "Anyway, we might look at this building and see right off that it won't work."

"God'll find a way for ya to have what ya really need," Miriam pointed out. She gestured around her café, her arms open. "Missouri law required me to have electricity to run this place, so I partnered with three Mennonite gals who were allowed to be on the grid."

"And now that Dad owns the building—and has a daughter with a degree in graphic design," Rebecca said, "Mamma even has a website. And so does the new gristmill. Sometimes it's not what you know, it's who," she added with a purposeful smile.

Andy could see the cogs turning in Rebecca's mind. It was amazing, as the two sisters sat side by side, how alike they were even though they had grown up in cultures that were worlds apart. *Nature versus nurture*, he thought. It would make for an interesting study as he got to know Rebecca better . . . not to mention spending more time with Rhoda, now that everyone here seemed comfortable with him.

"Why not call that real estate agency to see if someone can show it to you today?" Rebecca suggested. "And if you don't mind me tagging along on your sleigh ride, I might look the place over, too. We just never know how God may make our hopes and dreams come true."

Chapter Twenty-Three

"Now that we've got Jack hitched to the sleigh, we'll back out of the shed and into the lane," Rhoda said as she took the front seat beside Andy. "And you'll have a little time for drivin' before that agent's to meet us. Are ya ready?"

Andy's heart was racing as she handed him the reins. When Rhoda had introduced him to the tall, sturdy draft horse, letting him stroke its straw-colored mane, she had told him that horses responded to the confident tone of a driver's voice—or they would hear his fear. So he was being very careful about what he said. Rebecca sat in the seat behind them, ready for a picture-postcard ride in a one-horse open sleigh. Yet he couldn't forget how he'd come here a week ago to find a horse lying in agony, still hitched to the Knepp sleigh as the twins lay motionless on the roadside.

He whispered in Rhoda's ear. "What if he won't do as I tell him? What if we run into—"

Rhoda took the leather traces. "Jack, back!" she said as she tugged until the reins went tight.

The tawny Belgian pushed the sleigh toward the open

doorway without even looking behind them. Andy's jaw dropped.

"*Gut* boy, Jack. Back . . . back. *Jah*, now here we go, fella!" Rhoda sang out.

And indeed, the horse trotted down the Lantzes' long lane as though he was eager to take them wherever they wanted to be. Rhoda showed no hesitation whatsoever even though the gelding stood much taller than she and weighed more than two thousand pounds.

"This is so cool!" Rebecca murmured.

Yes, it was! This time when Rhoda handed him the reins, Andy took them, mesmerized by the muted *clip-clop! clip-clop!* of the horse's hooves on the snow and the merry jingle of the harness bells. "Now what?" he asked quietly.

"When we get as far as the smithy, you'll want to slow him down. Then ya check for traffic and say *gee*," she instructed. "That's horse talk for turnin' right."

What would he do if that behemoth of a Belgian bolted into the roadway? Andy didn't have a clue, but this leap of faith was only the first of many he'd have to take . . . so he relaxed with it. He trusted that Rhoda, an excellent, patient teacher, was at his side to correct any mistakes he made.

As they got to the smithy, Ben waved at them from the back of his red farrier wagon. The girls waved back. Andy concentrated on pulling the reins with just the right amount of tension so the horse slowed as they approached the road. "*Gut* boy, Jack," he called out as he looked both ways. "Gee!"

The horse whickered and shook his head, making the bells jangle happily. He turned onto the blacktop, easily negotiating the curve so the sleigh missed the ditch.

"*Jah*, here we go, fella!" Andy said. He grinned at Rhoda. "Maybe this isn't so hard, after all."

"Oh, ya gotta watch for cars and always be aware of the

surface your horse is trottin' on," Rhoda replied. "But Jack's been pullin' our buggies and sleighs for a lot of years now. He's a fine drivin' horse—aren't ya, fella?"

Again the Belgian shook his mane, as though he loved to make the bells jingle in response.

"Jack was a colt that didn't live up to the bishop's standards. Has one sock that's not white, so my *dat* got him for a *gut* price," Rhoda remarked. "Makes me wonder what-all's gonna happen with Hiram's Belgian business when he starts that new colony."

"Yeah, that's an awfully fancy barn he has at Bishop's Ridge," Rebecca replied from the back. "But he's making all his plans very carefully. You can be sure of that."

"Taking full advantage of whatever he can squeeze out of that Hammond fellow, too," Andy added. They were passing in front of the Sweet Seasons, moving smoothly along. "Now what, Miss Instructor?"

"Let's turn right here, down the Brennemans' lane. We can follow it past their house and across the Riehls' back cornfield, and we'll come out on this side of Preacher Tom's place."

Andy tugged slightly on the reins. "Easy, Jack," he sang out. "Gee here, fella."

As though he knew the route by heart, the Belgian curved toward the next driveway. Andy breathed easier. Rhoda sat close beside him, smiling proudly.

"This is where Rachel's Micah grew up—where Mamma's cookin' partner, Naomi, lives," she explained. "And that big metal building is their cabinetmakin' shop, where we'll serve the wedding feast after Mamma and Ben tie the knot next Thursday."

"This is all so fascinating, how you hold the ceremony

in your home. And then you feed all those people," Andy remarked.

"It's quite an experience," Rebecca agreed. "I was in awe the entire day of Rachel's wedding, watching everything go like clockwork with everyone helping cook and set tables and then clear them. Met a lot of people—my own family members, most of them—and I'm still figuring out which faces go with what names," she said with a chuckle. "So don't feel like the odd man out, Andy. Everyone's really friendly."

He smiled over his shoulder at her, grateful for such encouragement. And wasn't it the most glorious sensation to be gliding along in this winter wonderland of snow-covered fields, where crystal-covered trees glimmered in the sunlight? "The kids are going to wish they could've come for this ride."

"We'll bring them along real soon." Rhoda slipped her hand into the crook of his elbow. "Taylor and Brett'll be amazed to see how their *dat*'s catchin' on to so many new things. And that," she said, pointing toward a barn flanked by two silos and a two-story white house, "is Preacher Tom's dairy farm. We'd best be headin' toward your appointment now. You'll want to say *haw* as we get closer to the road."

He was getting the hang of this! As they passed the minister's side yard, Andy called out the turning command and thanked God for a well-trained horse and a loving teacher. Within a few minutes they had reached the county blacktop again, and he directed Jack toward the vacant building. A tan SUV was parked alongside it, and with Rhoda's help he pulled into the small lot and parked the sleigh.

"*Gut* boy, Jack." Andy slid to the ground, helped Rhoda out, and then took a moment to stroke the Belgian's muscular neck. He was a handsome horse, even if he hadn't made the grade as one of Hiram's show-quality stars.

A stylish woman emerged from the car and extended her hand. "Andy? I'm Jennifer Bradley. I brought along some information sheets about this property," she said in a well-modulated voice, "and I'm happy to answer any questions you might have. The owner passed away a few months ago, so it could be to your advantage that his kids want to settle the estate as soon as possible."

"May I have copies of those sheets, as well?" Rebecca asked.

Andy was curious about her interest in the place, but a tingle of anticipation kept him from doubting. As they stepped inside, a stale, closed-up odor hit them, but the rooms looked clean, overall.

Jennifer gave them a rundown of utility rates and other business information, but he was mostly tuned in to how the space flowed . . . where he might have a reception area and examination rooms, and how accessible it would be for disabled patients. A public restroom was in place, but the whole interior needed paint and carpet, plus another wall or two to separate the waiting area from the treatment rooms. There was no way of telling whether the electrical wiring and plumbing needed an overhaul until contractors looked things over. Rhoda's gaze swept the entire area as she walked quietly beside him.

"And here's the stairway," Jennifer said as she opened the door to a back hall. "Shall we go on up?"

As they ascended, Andy knew his mom would never be able to handle these stairs. However, the rooms on the top floor seemed very well suited for an apartment. A small kitchen was already here, as well as a full bathroom.

"I believe the previous owners used this area for their break room and administrative space. What sort of business do you want to run here, Mr. Leitner?" If Jennifer thought it odd that he had an Amish woman with him and another girl who looked just like her but wore English clothing, she didn't let on.

Despite Preacher Tom's warning, it was exciting to say his answer aloud because it made his dream more real. "I intend to open a small clinic," Andy answered, "and I need living space for my family, as well. Can you give us some time to look around?"

"Absolutely. Take as long as you need," the agent assured him. "I've got some calls to answer, so I'll be out in my car."

When Jennifer's footsteps had descended the stairs, Andy cleared his throat. "Rhoda, I'm guessing this is nothing like what you've been hoping for in a home—"

"But what an idea, havin' a place to do your nursin' right here in town," she said eagerly. "Rachel's Micah could give ya a rough idea what the remodelin' would cost. He built us the apartment above the smithy, ya know. Now that the mill and Mamma's new house are finished, he and his brothers could do ya a real *gut* job, and fast, because it's all indoor work."

Andy slung his arm around Rhoda's shoulders, so grateful for her open mind. Rebecca was wandering around, opening doors and studying the information sheet. "I'm going to look around downstairs some more. Give you two a chance to chat."

"*Denki*, Sister," Rhoda replied. When Rebecca had started down the stairs, she murmured, "Don't know what she's cookin' up, but she's workin' things out in her mind. She's startin' up her computer design business, ya see. Meanwhile she'll be helpin' in the café, stayin' at Mamma and Ben's new house until her work makes enough money to keep her goin'."

Andy considered that, but this rare time alone with Rhoda was too valuable to spend talking about other people's aspirations. He pulled her close and kissed her. Then he stepped away, holding her hands in his. "Rhoda, this idea will mean I have to borrow a *lot* of money," he said quietly. "Not only for my clinic and equipment but for the real estate loan and the remodeling costs. I'll have a good down payment when my house sells, but who knows when that will happen? Meanwhile, I have a family to support."

"*Jah*, the same holds true for any Amish couple gettin' hitched," she replied. "Fellas have to lay out a lot of cash once they move away from their folks. Not everybody's as lucky as Micah, movin' into a paid-for house and workin' in a business his *dat* established."

Andy smiled down at her, wishing he could present his case in a more positive light. "I don't want money issues to come between us, Rhoda. That happened with Megan and it was . . . devastating. But teaching school was what I was called to do at that time—"

"And ya were made for healin' people, too, Andy," she murmured. "This is God's own will, comin' to fruition in your life."

"Yeah, well . . ." He prayed the rest of what he wanted to say would come out right. His heart was riding on the line, and so was their future together. "It might be *years* before I earn enough to keep us going, and to pay off this debt. And . . . and maybe you'd rather take your chances with other guys while I establish my practice and meet all the requirements for becoming Amish. I'll understand if you'd rather start your family instead of waiting until I can support you, Rhoda."

Lord, but it had been hard to get that off his chest. If Rhoda wanted to marry sooner, or if she expected a more substantial basis for a fledgling marriage, he was up another creek without a paddle. The whole point of becoming Plain was to have this loving young woman by his side.

Her smile never wavered. "One of the things ya figure out

when ya live amongst Amish," she replied quietly, "is that we throw ourselves into our families and our work, trustin' God to figure out the details. When we need money or help, our families and *gut* friends are there for us every step of the way, Andy. When you're Plain, ya never walk alone."

His breath left him. Rhoda's expression inspired him to trust in God and the Amish beliefs as completely as she had all her life. She knew no other way. And she had no previous experience with a spouse's expectations not being met, so she truly believed he was capable of becoming her husband . . . her provider. Her breathtaking gaze told him she wanted him to be the father of her children and that he would indeed evolve into a beloved member of her extensive family.

"I want you to be happy, Rhoda. If you change your mind about me during this long process, let me know," he breathed.

"Too late!" she replied with a laugh. She kept hold of one of his hands, gesturing around the upstairs space. "So what're ya thinkin'? This place is a lot bigger than it looks from the outside. Long as your *mamm* could have a room downstairs, and we could have a bigger kitchen down there where it's cooler . . . maybe all the bedrooms up here—"

"Divide the building vertically? Have the exam and patient areas downstairs and the business area upstairs? That hadn't occurred to me," Andy mused. "Although maybe . . . maybe I should think more in terms of the old country doctors who made house calls. With so many Plain women still having their babies at home, and farm accidents to tend, I might be putting too much emphasis on office space. Maybe I need to be more portable."

He smiled at this idea. After all, weren't many Amish ways reminiscent of how most folks had lived a century or more ago? Maybe he'd be smarter to invest in an enclosed horse-drawn carriage that could carry basic equipment and provide treatment space . . . an Amish ambulance of sorts. Folks here would be more receptive to a nurse who came to them, because it was almost against their religion to seek out medical care. *So many ideas . . . so little money.*

Andy smiled at Rhoda. "You're making me think outside my medical-school box, and that's a *gut* thing. Shall we go downstairs and see what Rebecca's up to? I suspect she'll have other angles to consider, and she's too sharp a young woman to ignore."

"Ya got that right. We Lantz girls insist on bein' heard," Rhoda joked. "Got it honest, from our *mamm*, ya know."

Andy's laughter rang in the stairwell as they descended. When they reached the landing, Rebecca's voice carried over to them as she spoke into her cell phone.

". . . yeah, I think you'll want to look this place over . . . I can bring you the spec sheet," she was saying in an excited voice.

And what did that mean? Surely Rebecca wasn't giving someone else a heads-up on this building when she knew he was pinning a lot of his future on finding workable, livable space. Andy let Rhoda step into the main room ahead of him, reminding himself to keep the faith . . . to believe that the best was yet to be, and that everything would come together exactly as it was supposed to, if he kept God in on the process.

When Rebecca clicked off her phone, she turned toward them with an adorable grin. "Andyyyy," she teased, "what would you think of partnering with a tech-savvy, very personable, extremely astute and sensitive—"

"That would be you, right?" Andy's heart skipped a beat as he looked at Rhoda's sister.

"Yup. And in addition to designing and maintaining your

website for the local English folks who will also welcome your nursing services," she continued in a rising voice, "I could manage your computer filing and whatever else your practice requires. Could even sit at the desk as your receptionist, if you don't need somebody with medical expertise."

"And?" He loved her enthusiasm, so similar to Rhoda's.

Rebecca's laughter echoed in the big empty space. "I'd like an office upstairs—or wherever it's best for you—to run my new design business. Most of my work's online, so I'll be in the building whenever you need me." She drew a line in the air with her finger, over toward the center of the big room. "I'm seeing this as a natural dividing point between your business area and your home, because a wall here would leave the upstairs plumbing in a reasonable place for you to have a kitchen and bath on the back wall, and your family room over here, and your bedrooms upstairs. But then, what do I know?"

Andy looked at Rhoda and they both burst out laughing. "You girls are unreal, the way you think alike. But as I was telling your sister, it might be a long while before my home in New Haven sells. Meanwhile I'll need to borrow a large amount of money to float this whole idea, so you can't be in a hurry to—"

"Give me a day or two, Andy," she said with a big wink. "I'm working on that part, too."

His jaw dropped, and Rhoda hurried over to throw her arms around Rebecca's neck. "You kitty-cat! I know what you're up to," she teased. "But we'll keep that as our little secret."

Once again Andy could only gaze at the Lantz sisters. Wasn't it wonderful to think that the two of them were conspiring to answer his prayers? They would enlist the efforts of their mother and Rachel, no doubt, to create a synergy he'd not witnessed before.

Lord, I had no idea what I was walking into this morning, except that I was meeting with some of Your finest people. How far I've come today! Closer to my goals, and closer to You. And for that I'm very, very grateful.

After he told the Realtor they'd be in touch, Rhoda pointed out each place to turn as they toured the Willow Ridge countryside in the sleigh. Out past the Riehl place they went, beyond the Kanagy farm where the girls' Aunt Leah raised produce and kept bees. At Rhoda's direction, Andy drove the sleigh through open pastures and along back roads he'd had no idea existed, getting the lowdown on each of the families whose homes they passed. Neat, well-maintained places they were, too, where families took pride in the appearance of their outbuildings and yards. As they passed the Waglers' farm, two young men waved enthusiastically and the three of them returned their greeting.

"Matthias and Adam eat at the café quite a lot," Rhoda remarked. "Matthias is our local harness maker, and his brother does remodeling work."

"Fine, *fine*-looking fellows, too," Rebecca added with a laugh. "Seem to be a lot of handsome, unattached men in this neck of the woods."

"*Jah*, and they're eyein' you, too, Sister!" Rhoda shot back.

"Now this is quite a spread," Andy remarked as they approached a tall white house on top of a rise. A remarkably large barn sat behind the home, and the property was set off by white plank livestock fencing that stretched for as far as he could see.

"That would be Hiram's place," Rebecca remarked from her seat in back. "Home of Bishop's Ridge Belgians. I still can't believe he's leaving this impressive property behind to start from scratch at a new colony."

"*Jah*, well, we'll hear lots of surprisin' details in the next couple of weeks," Rhoda said, shaking her head. "And if ya think Hiram's finished chastisin' Annie Mae and Nellie for leavin' him with the four littlest kids—"

"I don't think he's done with Mamma or Ben or the other Hooleys, either," Rebecca stated. "And you're probably near the top of his hit list for sheltering his daughters. Things are going to get very *interesting* in Willow Ridge, Sister."

Andy listened to this banter, believing it. From the way Preacher Tom had reacted to Hiram's method of obtaining the land and money for his new venture, he sensed Knepp might be in for a few surprises, as well. It was indeed a fascinating time to weave himself into the fabric of this little community, for the Amish who lived around New Haven weren't nearly so . . . feisty. It made him admire Rhoda all the more because she had fearlessly given her friends a place to stay, despite the probable consequences.

As they pulled into the Sweet Seasons parking lot, Andy breathed deeply of the wintry air, feeling more than satisfied with the way this day had gone. "Do I just show up for the wedding on Thursday?" he asked as he helped the girls out of the sleigh.

"*Jah*, and we start the church service bright and early, too. Eight o'clock sharp." Rhoda's cheeks bloomed with the cold and her good health as she gazed up at him. "Then follows the wedding ceremony and the feast, and a lot of visitin' for the rest of the day, includin' a supper. If ya can't stay for the whole thing, we'll be glad to see all of ya for as long as we can have ya."

"And since Rhoda will be up front as one of the side sitters—"

"*Jah*, a *newehocker*, alongside Luke Hooley," Rhoda clarified.

"—I'll be happy to sit with your mom and your daughter, if you'd like," Rebecca offered. "You and Brett will sit on the guys' side. Would you like to hook up with my dad? He'll be looking for other English guests so he won't feel so strange wearing a suit and tie among all those black trousers, vests, and white shirts."

"That's very thoughtful of you, Rebecca." Andy's brain already buzzed at the prospect of all the details he'd be absorbing . . .

But the detail that intrigued him most was the smile the two sisters shared, as though they passed information between them with that secret code twins and triplets were wired with before they were even born. Thursday would be quite a day, for sure and for certain!

Chapter Twenty-Four

As Rebecca pulled into the Sweet Seasons lot on Thursday morning, she chuckled. What a crazy combination she was, wearing a royal-blue Plain dress and a white kapp while driving a red sports car. But wasn't that the picture of her life lately? The best parts of both her worlds seemed to be coming together very quickly, thanks to the unconditional love of the Lantz family and the way her dad understood her need to reunite with her Amish *mamm* and sisters.

When she walked into the café's kitchen, heavenly aromas enveloped her: baking chicken . . . the savory spices and butter in the dressing . . . the sweet scent of boiling celery.

"Happy New Year to ya, Rebecca!" Naomi called out from where she, Hannah, and Priscilla Schrock were peeling a mountain of potatoes. "And don't ya look perty in that blue dress? Your *mamm*'s gone up to Rachel's already. She's a happy woman this mornin', and you're one of the reasons why."

Rebecca's breath caught in her throat. All the women bustling around in the café's kitchen smiled as they greeted her. Mary and Eva Schrock waved from the dining room, where they were cutting dozens of pies. Her aunt, Leah Kanagy, looked up from the tubs of fresh vegetables she was arranging on relish trays. "Hullo, Rebecca! *Gut* to see ya!"

When Rebecca saw the Knepp girls filling salt and pepper shakers at the serving window, she made her way through the crowd. While so much activity and chatter had once seemed like chaos to her, she now understood that these wonderful women had been working since the wee hours and wouldn't quit until after this evening's supper, because they loved her mother. Such support, given so cheerfully, still boggled her mind.

"So how's it going?" she asked quietly. "Can't be easy, deciding to go your own way instead of with your dad."

Annie Mae's eyes were ringed with dark circles. "*Jah*, we're lookin' for Dat to burst through that door any minute to haul us outta here," she replied with a glance in that direction.

"But Jerusalem and Nazareth are watchin' out for us," Nellie added, nodding toward where the Hooley sisters were chopping onions and celery for the stuffing. "And Rhoda's been a real patient roommate while we've done our cryin', wonderin' what's to happen to us."

"But we're hopeful." Annie Mae screwed the lid on a salt shaker with a firm twist. "Even though he's not preachin' today, we think Dat might make a scene during the wedding, to announce how wonderful-*gut* his new colony's gonna be."

"We're happy to spend the day in here cookin'," Nellie agreed as she reached for a fresh can of pepper. "Can't thank your family enough for takin' us in, knowin' how Dat's gonna get back at them for it."

Rebecca looked around, noting the absence of little children. "So . . . how are the twins doing? And Sara and Timmy?"

Nellie sighed. "That's the stinger in all this," she admitted.

"Far as we know, they're with Dat. When we were movin' the last of our stuff on Saturday, he ordered us to stay away from the house until we were ready to beg his forgiveness."

"*Jah*, the dishes and food were still sittin' on the table from that nice dinner on Friday. But Jerusalem and Nazareth marched right on past that to Ben's truck with their clothes, and we followed along." Annie Mae smiled glumly. "It's not the way I'd pictured my life goin', but then I never figured on Dat pullin' such a stunt, either. Whatever he's been doin' since Joey and Josh's wreck just doesn't set right."

"Well, if there's anything I can do, just say the word," Rebecca insisted as she grasped their arms. "Sometimes my being English is an advantage."

Annie Mae chuckled and tugged on a string of Rebecca's kapp. "Ya look mighty Plain to me, girlie," she teased. "But *denki* for sayin' that. Means a lot."

Ya look mighty Plain. And wasn't that a fine compliment for a day when she wasn't wearing any makeup? Rebecca spoke with the Hooley sisters, Hannah, and Lydia Zook as she made her way back to the door, filled with a sense of goodwill and unity despite the way these women's spiritual leader was wreaking havoc on their orderly, purposeful lives.

Be with the Knepp girls, God. And please, please don't let Hiram make a shambles of Mamma's big day.

Up to the old white Lantz house she drove, to park at the far end of it. At the sight of her dad's Buick, her heart beat a little faster—and here came another car up the long lane. When she saw Andy waving through the windshield, she motioned for him to pull up beside her car.

"Rhoda! Rhoda!" Brett crowed as he hopped out, followed by his grinning sister, Taylor.

Rebecca grabbed them in an eager hug, but then gazed into their eyes. "OK, I'm really Rhoda's sister, Rebecca, but

I'm tickled you think I look like her. We're all so glad you've come to the wedding!"

The kids' faces fell, but then Brett lifted the back of her kapp. "Aha! Now we'll know you by your short hair."

"Yup." She pointed to the door that led into the kitchen. "If you go inside you'll find who you're looking for. And I bet she'll come running to see you, too, even though there'll be dozens of people in there."

Taylor grabbed her brother's hand. "Let's go, Brett! I want to see what they all look like in their Amish dress-up clothes."

As the kids hurried toward the door, Rebecca smiled at the older woman getting out of the car with Andy's assistance. "Betty, it's so good to see you again," she said, taking the woman's hand. "Would you like to sit with me today?"

"Oh, I'd . . . like that. I don't know a soul except for . . . you Lantzes," she replied in a halting voice. "But I'm so excited to . . . be here."

"Come on in where it's warm. I'll see how many names I can remember for you, until Rhoda and Miriam can help us out." She flashed a smile at Andy, who looked a little flustered, yet as eager as his kids. "We'll find Dad lurking in there, too. He's really looking forward to chatting with you."

Andy's raised eyebrows made her pulse flutter in anticipation. In her mind, she'd played out how this day would unfold a dozen times . . .

"It's a big day," Andy remarked as they stepped into the noisy kitchen. "Thanks for helping us make the most of it."

Immediately they were engulfed by Mamma's cousins and other ladies from around Willow Ridge, but before she could make any introductions, her mother grabbed her in a tight hug. "Oh, honey-bug, it's so *gut* to have ya here. And Betty, you're lookin' right perty in that red poppy dress, too!

Come nibble a little somethin' before the sticky buns and muffins get put away."

"Andy! There ya are!"

Rhoda's voice rose above the chatter and Rebecca's heart swelled. Her sister's arms were around Andy's kids and theirs were around her, a happy sight indeed. And how Rhoda glowed when she gazed at Andy while he returned her intense gaze. If any couple had ever been more attuned to each other, she didn't know who it would be—except maybe for Mamma and Ben. As her sister began to introduce Andy and his mom to her aunts, uncles, and cousins, Rebecca glanced toward the front room. It still amazed her, how interior walls came down and the men strategically squeezed in so many pew benches to seat the crowd they expected today.

"Aunt Lovinia . . . Aunt Mattie," she said as she hugged Mamma's sisters. "It's so *gut* to see ya again, so soon."

"*Jah*, and it's a fine way to start out the New Year, too," Lovinia replied. "Quite an honor for Mose to be preachin' at his sister's wedding."

Rebecca spotted her dad in a corner chatting with Derek Shotwell, so she made her way through the happily chattering crowd in the front room. As he kissed her cheek, Rebecca felt especially blessed that Dad, too, was welcomed by these Plain folks. "Andy's meeting Mamma's relatives from hither and yon," she said. "I think you three English fellows will be good company for each other. And I hope your conversation goes well."

Derek chuckled. "Whenever I'm consulted about a project in Willow Ridge, it's anything but ordinary."

"Good people here," her dad agreed. "Sincere and hardworking. A solid investment opportunity—well, maybe if you don't count Hiram." He glanced around the gathering crowd of bearded men wearing black trousers and vests with white shirts. "Do you think he'll show up?"

"Every person here is wondering that very thing, Dad." Rebecca caught Andy's eye and waved him over. "Let's get you fellows seated before the service starts. It'll last about three hours before everyone heads over to that big metal building next door for the wedding feast. Good food, good conversation. It'll be a memorable day for us all."

Lord, I'm going to remember this day forever, Andy thought as he gazed out over the huge crowd assembled in Miriam Lantz's extended living room. He and a few other non-Amish guys sat to the rear of the men's side, but when he peered over the top of the male heads with their home-style haircuts, he could see Rhoda. She sat beside Rachel, in the front row of the women's side. Bishop Shetler, Preacher Tom, and Preacher Mose—Miriam's brother from out of town—nearly bumped into her knees as they gave their sermons or directed the church service that preceded the wedding.

Even though all those female faces and kapps looked nearly identical—so nobody drew attention to herself—Rhoda's smile and shining eyes set her apart. As he observed the standing and kneeling, he became even more aware of how much he had to learn. Brett shifted against him occasionally, but he'd found an Amish boy a few rows ahead of them to study. The kid, a bowl-cut blond, was turning to gaze curiously at Brett's red sweater, tie, and striped dress shirt, while Brett probably wondered about wearing a home-sewn black vest and pants with suspenders rather than a belt. But Brett was absolutely quiet, keeping his wiggling to a minimum, mostly because Rhoda had asked him to.

It amazed Andy that these folks fell to their knees to pray

on the hardwood floor, without grimacing. He missed having a piano or any other musical accompaniment to the slow, methodical hymns he didn't recognize. But there was no denying the close attention everyone paid to Bishop Shetler's sermon . . . the quiet joy on these Plain faces as they worshipped God without worldly distractions.

After another hymn and a prayer to conclude the church service, Miriam and Ben came to stand before the bishop, Tom, and Miriam's brother Moses. A murmur rose from the crowd when Hiram Knepp stepped out of the kitchen, where he had apparently been following the service. He strode to the front, nodding to the three leaders. "I'm calling a Members' Meeting to inform you of God's further instructions to me—His blessing that has provided land for the new colony of Higher Ground, Missouri," he said in his resonant baritone voice. "I have run an ad in *The Budget*—"

"No, Hiram, this is not the time or the place," Jeremiah Shetler interrupted. "We're here to marry Miriam and Ben." As he, Tom, and Moses moved in closer, everyone in the congregation shifted so they could see what was going on. Miriam and Ben stood staunchly, refusing to give up their place of honor.

"There'll be no coaxin' folks into your new venture," Preacher Tom continued in a peeved voice, "because ya didn't follow through on your confession—and because of what we've learned about this tract of land in the meantime. We were gonna address this after Sunday's service, but maybe now's the better time. What do *you* say, Ben and Miriam? It's your day."

Silence filled the room as all present gazed at the couple to be married.

"I'm for settlin' the matter right now," Ben replied.

"*Jah*, me too," Miriam affirmed. "Can't in *gut* conscience let any of my friends believe your proposal for a new colony is legitimate, Hiram."

Folks sucked in their breath. Hiram's face turned as red as a raw beefsteak. But before he could protest, Preacher Tom looked out over the crowd. "Brothers and sisters, we are concerned mostly with how our bishop stands before us without havin' been reinstated into the membership. Instead of waitin' for our decision last preachin' Sunday, he told us how God spoke directly to him about startin' up a new colony," he said in a loud, clear voice. "But I've learned, from a fella I trust, that the man who ran into the horse pullin' Joey and Josh's sleigh has offered Hiram quite a nice settlement so Hiram won't take him to court."

An outburst of whispering and exclamations rose from the crowd.

"Thomas Hostetler," Hiram replied in a tight voice. "Are you telling me you trust what some *fella* has told you, over what the God who chose you to be His minister has proclaimed? That's blasphemy, pure and simple."

The women gasped and every man in front of Andy scowled as they muttered among themselves. Andy felt odd, being that source the preacher had trusted . . . and surely Hiram would figure that part out. Yet he'd done the right thing, informing Tom, Miriam, and Ben of their leader's wrongdoing.

Jeremiah Shetler raised his hand for silence. "Because this sort of brazen disregard for the *Ordnung* rides on the coattails of other serious sins Hiram has committed," he continued, "Tom, Gabe Glick, and I recommend that Hiram Knepp be excommunicated from the Willow Ridge district. You'll need to vote on that, of course."

Faces fell in shock, and once again silence enveloped the crowd. Soon, however, heads were nodding and hands were clasped in laps as folks prepared to do what must be done.

"*Jah*, that's the way we've gotta settle this," Henry Zook declared. "The will of God is made known through His People. The Bible tells us that wherever two or more are gathered, the Lord's present, too. He's expectin' us to act on this matter right here and now."

"This is utterly—" Hiram threw up his hands. "How can you accuse me of misleading you? Such unsubstantiated information is—"

"You know the procedure, Hiram. You're to leave the room, along with all those who aren't baptized into the Old Order," Tom countered. Then he looked right and left. "You English guests will have to leave, as well. Stretch your legs and we'll reconvene in a few. Thanks for your understanding."

As Andy rose, the Amish fellow seated in front of him pointed to a door near the stairway. Andy took Brett's hand and shuffled down the narrow row ahead of Bob Oliveri and Derek Shotwell, hoping Hiram wouldn't circle the house to confront him. He would, however, defend Tom Hostetler's accusations if Hiram had figured out he was the source who had reported that phone call at the hospital. It was the least he could do for the man who had been so encouraging—yet so honest—with him about joining the Amish church . . .

The *bam!* of the kitchen door made Miriam inhale sharply, along with everyone around her and Ben. Hiram's anger wouldn't end here. There would be retribution down the road—but Jeremiah seemed unconcerned about that as he tended to the business at hand.

"As we call this Members' Meeting to order, let us pray for open minds that invite God into our decision," the bishop said in a resonant voice. "I've never seen the likes of this. But we believe that all things are part of the Lord's plan, which means that He will use even Hiram's unthinkable behavior to work His purpose out. 'Vengeance is mine; I will repay, saith the Lord.' So we shall leave behind any thoughts of getting back at Hiram as we vote."

Grasping Ben's hand, Miriam bowed her head in silence with all of her family and friends.

After a few moments, Jeremiah gestured for her to be seated with the women while Ben took his place on the front pew of the men's side. "We are deciding if your bishop, Hiram Knepp, is to be excommunicated from his leadership position as well as from membership in the Willow Ridge district," he stated. "An *aye* declares your belief that he should be banished, while a *nay* means he should be kept in good standing. As is our custom, we will begin with the men."

Miriam glanced over at Ben. While she had no doubt how he would vote, his expression bespoke the seriousness of this election. Now and then, folks were expelled from the church for not confessing when the bishop directed them to—or they left because they no longer wished to live up to the stringent expectations of the Old Amish order. But never had she heard of a district banishing the leader God had chosen for it.

"Aye," Wilbert Riehl sang out. As the eldest male member of the district, he was always seated on the front row. Then Ben and the other fellows all followed suit without so much as missing a beat.

As these male voices rang out in her front room, Miriam's heart thudded. What a monumental event, taking place right here in her home. Oh, but Jesse would've been appalled . . .

"The men have voted unanimously to banish Hiram," Jeremiah summarized as part of the proceedings. "What say you women?"

When the bishop of Morning Star gazed at her, as the first person on the front row, Miriam blinked. Even though she had no doubt about her feelings, it still seemed so foreign—so *final*—to excommunicate a bishop. "Aye," she

said, although her vote felt anything but uplifting or victori-
ous, even after all the times Hiram had humiliated her.
Rachel and Rhoda cast the same vote without a moment's
hesitation.

Along the rows behind Miriam, the familiar voices of
female friends and family members echoed the affirmation
that Hiram no longer belonged in Willow Ridge. When at
last the youngest members had voted, Jeremiah nodded
solemnly.

"The People have spoken," he said. "It is finished. Let
us pray before we continue with the day's more joyous celebration."

As they stood outside in the brisk winter breeze, Brett
tugged at Andy's hand. "What's going on, Dad? That was the
man we saw when we were eatin' breakfast with Rhoda,
and—"

"Hiram's done something horribly dishonest," Andy explained as they made room alongside the house, out of the
wind, for the other men who were coming outside. "Sometimes people who have a lot of power, or a lot of money,
use it for the wrong purposes. Or they lie about how they got
that money."

"And the fact that God chose him to be the leader of this
community makes it very difficult for these folks to decide
he's no longer fit to be their bishop," Derek Shotwell added.
Then to Bob and Andy he said, "This explains a few major
transactions he's discussed with me lately in very cloaked
terms. When I said things are never ordinary in Willow
Ridge, I was *not* expecting the bishop to be excommunicated
at a wedding."

"You can bet all these family visitors from out East will
talk this up when they get home, too," Bob remarked.

"Might be a long while before Hiram scares up enough members to get a new colony going, when people hear he's been kicked out of his district."

Rebecca's father seemed amused by something, even though the vote going on inside was a very serious thing. He looked up at Andy and smoothed his thinning hair after the wind riffled it. "You, on the other hand, seem to be the town hero after you came running when Hiram's little boys got thrown from their sleigh," he remarked. "Tiffany—Miriam's Rebecca—says you're starting up a clinic and maybe making house calls in a special horse-drawn wagon."

"I think that wagon's an ingenious idea," Derek chimed in. "I bet you'll draw a lot of patients from all of these little towns hereabouts, too. Not just from the Amish."

Andy blinked. While it was fine that Rebecca had shared his dreams with her dad and the banker, he felt a little exposed. What if he didn't get his house sold? What if he couldn't pull together the funds he'd need for medical equipment? "I hope my ideas don't seem premature or half-baked—"

"Come on back in, fellas," one of the younger Amish men said from the doorway. "We did our business quick and clean."

"We appreciate your patience, dear friends and guests," Preacher Tom was saying as they took their seats again. "And now we can proceed with a wedding that brings us all great joy."

Hiram had apparently lost his membership in Willow Ridge, for he was now conspicuously absent. As the ceremony went on, Andy noted the faces of the women glowing with goodwill and happiness despite the monumental event that had just taken place. Clearly Miriam Lantz and Ben Hooley were dearly loved—and they dearly loved each other as they repeated their vows, beaming.

This will be you and Rhoda someday.

Andy couldn't help smiling as he found her face across the room. She was looking directly at him and having the same positive thoughts, if her expression was any indication. Although there was no music, no exchange of rings, no flowers—no photographers crouching to catch these sacred moments with their cameras—Andy had never attended a wedding where everyone in the room seemed so bonded together, so invested in this couple as they began their new life together. It was a wonderful feeling to be caught up in the love and support that filled this home. He dared to hope that these same people would welcome him someday as Rhoda's husband.

As the ceremony ended and the chattering crowd dispersed, Bob clapped a hand on Andy's back. "I can't recall a wedding that ever pleased me more—even if I couldn't understand a word they said!"

"Didn't have to know the lingo to feel the love," Derek agreed. "What an awesome couple Miriam and Ben make. Pillars of this community—and even more so now that Willow Ridge will be seeking out a new bishop."

Rebecca's father and the banker exchanged a look, and then they stopped in a back corner of the noisy room. "Andy, we'd like to help you in your new medical venture," Bob began, his lips twitching with a grin he was trying to suppress. "Tiffany asked me to look over that building you were considering—partly because she'd like to set up her own business there. What would you think if I bought the place and became your landlord?"

Andy's heart stopped. "It was never my intention to make you feel—"

"Oh, no one ever *makes* Bob invest in property," Derek said with a laugh. "But we admire your willingness to serve the community and to honor Rhoda's religious convictions.

Tiffany—Rebecca—is so excited about the opportunity this gives *her*, too, if you'll allow her to work with you."

"Why wouldn't I?" Andy asked hoarsely. "But I never figured she would—"

"Hah! Good luck at predicting what *that* young woman will do. She's cut from the same cloth as her mother and her sisters." Bob chuckled. "It was my pleasure to acquire Miriam's building so she could operate without fear of Hiram's interference. And because you'll need electricity and Internet service, it makes the same sort of sense for a non-Amish person to install all that worldly technology so you can use it without owning it."

"I can see how an elevator would be in order, too, to comply with the disabilities codes," he continued. "But we're not here to ram this idea down your throat, Andy. A man should make his own decisions."

Who could have anticipated this development? This meant his mother would be able to get between the two levels of their home . . . and if he didn't have to invest in the building, his money could go toward that clinic on wheels . . . Andy grasped Bob's hand and then shook with Derek, as well. "I can't believe this kind of help has just fallen into place—"

"It's like Miriam loves to say." The banker looked toward the bride, who was surrounded by dozens of well-wishers. "All things work out for those who trust in God. And if you're marrying into her family, with Bob backing you, that's all I need to know. You're destined for success."

"How about if I call you early next week?" Bob suggested. "I see a certain young woman heading your way, and you might not want our arrangement to be common knowledge until you're convinced it's a good idea."

"Thanks. I appreciate that," Andy murmured.

As Rhoda approached, holding Taylor's hand and waiting

for his mom to keep up with them in the crowd, Andy felt a welling up of emotions. What a turnaround this was, after the censure they had endured when they'd been caught kissing in his car. Even though Rhoda didn't know about the assistance he'd just been offered, her expression said she believed in him completely . . . wanted to be with him, for better or for worse.

"You look awfully happy, considering that interruption in your mother's wedding," he remarked as she grabbed his hand.

"Puh! Takes more than a run-in with Hiram to ruin Mamma's big day," she replied. Her blue eyes glimmered as she gazed up at him. "And what a way to start the New Year, too. Things are changin' in a big way in Willow Ridge, and it's workin' to our advantage, Andy. Come and meet Ben's family before we head for the feast! Now the real fun gets started!"

Rhoda took her seat at the *eck*, a large corner table where the wedding party sat on a dais so they could survey all their guests. She couldn't stop grinning. She had remembered most of the Hooleys' unusual names as she'd introduced Andy, his mom, and his kids, and as special guests they sat at tables near the *eck*: Jerusalem's twin brother, Jericho, was passing a big platter of the "roast," made of baked chicken and stuffing. Calvary, Corinth, Judea, and their siblings and kids seemed delighted to be attending Ben and Mamma's festivities. There were so many Hooleys, they'd rented two full-size buses with drivers to come from Lancaster County. Jerusalem's and Nazareth's siblings had booked the entire family-owned motel in Morning Star so that Ben's parents, brothers, and sisters could stay in the new house. Mamma's sisters, their husbands, and their kids were bunking in the

main house with Rachel and Micah, as they had done for
Rachel's wedding in October.

When Rhoda's gaze rested on Andy and his family, her
heart danced. Taylor wiggled her fingers before forking up
a big mouthful of gravied mashed potatoes. Rhoda waved
back, pleased that she was wearing the purple polka-dot
Plain-style dress. She was proud of the way the kids had sat
through the long services when they had no idea what was
being said in Pennsylvania Dutch. The English guests had
been seated in this first shift so they could leave whenever
they chose to, but Rhoda hoped the Leitners would stay the
entire day. She wanted them to experience all the visiting
and meet more of her family . . . so her kin could adjust to
the idea that she was in love with a man from the outside
world.

Ben dinged his knife on his glass and stood up, waiting
for silence. "Miriam and I are so happy you're all here," he
began, "and we've got an idea to share with ya."

"Jah," Mamma joined in as she rose beside him. Oh, but
she looked years younger and sparkly with excitement. "The
Lord's blessed Ben and me with many *gut* gifts in the short
time we've been together. So instead of givin' us presents we
don't need, we'd like ya to consider donatin' to the new
Willow Ridge clinic. Thanks to the fine fella my Rhoda has
taken a shine to, we're soon gonna have a trained healer as-
sistin' us with childbirths and injuries."

Rhoda's face got hot. She saw the same amazement on
Andy's face while her mother continued.

"Andy Leitner's completed his nursin' degree. Matter of
fact, he saved Hiram's young sons when they had a horrible sleigh wreck a couple weeks ago." Mamma paused to
let this information sink in. "Most important, he's takin' his
instruction to become Amish so he can someday marry

Rhoda—and ya know what a commitment that'll be for him and his kids."

As folks all over the big room craned their necks to see Andy, Rhoda felt their gazes on her, as well. She noticed a kitty-cat grin on Rebecca's face. Had her sister had something to do with this announcement?

"Andy hopes to set up his office down the road from here. And he wants to make house calls in a special wagon stocked with the medicines and equipment he'll need— which will set him back a perty penny," Ben pointed out. "We've set up a special clinic account with our banker, Derek Shotwell. So if ya care to pitch in on this project, he's the man to see."

Derek stood up to wave at everyone. He had obviously been in on this surprise, and enjoyed playing a part in another venture with his Plain clients.

"We're runnin' an ad in *The Budget* to support the start-up of Andy's practice, too. If ya mention this to your friends back home, we're bettin' Andy'll find out just how generous and grateful the People can be," Mamma said. "He's a *gut* man, and he loves my Rhoda. *Denki* for whatever ya care to share."

When Rhoda could catch her breath again, she went to stand behind Ben and her mother. As she wrapped her arms around their shoulders, she understood the meaning of *love* in a whole new way. "That was the nicest thing ya just did for us," she said with a hitch in her voice. "But ya didn't have to—"

"Oh, honey-bug, the real joy comes in doin' things because ya want to, not because ya have to." Mamma sat taller to kiss her cheek. "There's more than enough love and money in this room to share, ain't so? It'll be fun to see how much Derek collects today, and how much gets sent to that account from folks readin' about it in the paper, too."

When Rhoda sat down to her dinner again, something compelled her to break with their traditional seating arrangement so she could spend this time with Andy and his family. She was gathering up her napkin and utensils when Luke, seated beside her, patted her arm.

"Who knew what would come from that kiss in the car?" he asked quietly. "I'm glad it's workin' out for ya, Rhoda. Ya deserve to be as happy as your *mamm*."

That was certainly something to aspire to! "*Denki*, Luke. The future's lookin' real bright, ain't so?" Rhoda picked up her loaded plate, determined to work on that happiness for the rest of this fine day.

As she approached the table to sit with them, Andy and Betty scooted apart to make room for her. Luke had followed her from the *eck* with her folding chair . . . her cousins were waving at her, calling out their congratulations as though this had turned into a celebration for her and Andy as much as for Mamma and Ben. From the *eck*, Rachel was grinning at her, too—and wasn't that the most wonderful affirmation of all?

"This is . . . so exciting, Rhoda," Andy's mom said into her ear. "I can't wait . . . to see Andy's clinic take off."

As the people in the Brennemans' huge shop finished eating, they came to shake Andy's hand and wish him well with his medical venture. It was almost as though Hiram's leaving had paved the way for a whole new beginning in Willow Ridge. Quite a line of neighbors and Hooley men stood ready to speak with Andy, and then they were writing checks for Derek Shotwell.

"Say—ya wanna come out and play in the snow with the rest of us? Gets kind of slow in here when the adults start yackin'." Levi Zook stepped around from behind his father to flash a hopeful grin at Brett and Taylor. "My little sister Amelia's gonna be out there, too."

"That's right nice of ya to ask, Levi," Rhoda remarked. "This is Brett and Taylor Leitner from over in New Haven, and this," she continued as she addressed Andy's kids, "is Levi Zook. His family runs the market down the way."

The shine in their eyes made Rhoda's heart dance. "Run along and play, kids. There'll be lots of snowball throwin' and relays out there—but no hitchin' up the sleigh for any rides, ain't so?" she asked in a purposeful voice.

Levi grinned sheepishly. "*Jah*, the sleigh's stayin' parked. Mamm told Jonah he was to be our watchdog today, on account of how folks won't want to shop at our store if Cyrus and I keep causin' trouble."

"Can we look at the sleighs and the horses, Rhoda?" Brett blurted.

He and his sister wore such hopeful expressions that Rhoda had to hug them. "*Jah*, go out and buddy up with the kids. They'll show ya the barns and the orchard and what-not. Take a *gut* look around. See if ya might like makin' this neighborhood your new home."

Off they went with Levi to fetch their coats, and their eagerness warmed Rhoda in a way she hadn't expected. She was watching them make their way through the crowd, replying politely when other folks welcomed them, when a familiar voice spoke in front of her.

"Rhoda, I'm mighty pleased with how this is all turnin' out. Let's start Andy's instruction as soon as we can." Preacher Tom stood on the other side of the table, smiling. He leaned closer so they could hear him above the noise of the crowd. "On our walk over here to eat, I saw Hiram's fancy black Cadillac rollin' past. Sad to say, but he's drivin' down the road to perdition, for sure and for certain. But for the rest of us, it seems this New Year's Day is a fine start for a wonderful-*gut* future, ain't so?"

Rhoda's heart swelled as she grabbed the hand Tom offered. Andy took the preacher's other hand as he slung an arm around her shoulders. "That's the way I see it, too, Tom," she replied. "I'm real glad ya want to be a part of bringin' us together."

"I never in my life expected such an outpouring of money and love," Andy chimed in. "A lot of wishes are coming true today, because all things are possible with God. And with Rhoda, of course."

Chapter Twenty-Five

"Over here, I see a reception desk and a good place for the waiting area," Andy said. It was Saturday morning and he and Rebecca stood in the doorway of the building where they hoped to set up shop. Micah Brenneman and Bob Oliveri had joined them for a look around before they told the Realtor it was a go, and Rhoda was putting in her ideas, as well.

"We can build in a workspace for you, too, so you can tend your website business when we don't have patients. We'll have a private entry to the back hall, where you'd have access to the elevator and your office space on the second level. We can have our family entrance on that side, too."

"And if this center wall gets extended and soundproofed, we can separate your living area from the office," Rebecca replied. "Will that work, Micah?"

"*Jah*, that makes better use of the space than dividin' it by levels," the carpenter affirmed. "I'll give ya a rough estimate of Adam Wagler's remodelin' price and finish out the proposal I've been workin' on. Is later this afternoon soon enough?"

Rebecca's dad was walking along the walls, checking electrical outlets and ventilation ducts. "I like your vision of how the space should be used," he remarked. "It still amazes me that Derek collected more than thirty-five grand at the wedding dinner. But I've seen that sort of support in Amish communities before."

Andy did some mental calculating. "That works out to several hundred dollars per family that was there," he said with a shake of his head. "Hard to believe those conservative fellows would cough up that kind of cash, when they'd just met me."

"It helped that a few members of Ben's family and Miriam's two brothers made sizeable donations." Bob flashed Andy a grin that crinkled the skin around his eyes. "It'll be fun to see how much more comes from folks who see Miriam's ad in *The Budget*."

"*Jah*, Micah's family received more than eighty thousand dollars toward his *dat*'s hospital bills after he lost his legs," Rhoda chimed in. "We Plain folks look out for each other."

"This new office will keep my daughter close to home, too," Bob added. "I have Miriam to thank for that, and for Tiffany's entire transformation into Rebecca. All in all, I'd encourage you to go ahead with it, Andy," he continued in a businesslike voice. "This is an even better investment than the Sweet Seasons—and we all know how that place has put Willow Ridge on the map."

Micah came across the room to hand Andy a business card. "Almost forgot about this bein' in my coat pocket," he said. "A fella over in Cedar Creek makes a lot of specialty buggies and carriages. Ya might wanna give him a ring about your house-callin' wagon."

Andy gazed at the simple card. *Graber's Custom Carriages*, it said, and it gave a number for a James Graber. "This is fantastic, Micah," he replied. "I'm amazed at how much help is coming at me from so many directions, now that I've declared my intentions."

"They say your energy flows where your intention goes," Rebecca remarked with a nod. "I've seen that happen so many times in this little town, it's made a believer of me."

The muscular carpenter flashed Andy a grin. "And if you're makin' Rhoda and Rebecca happy, that means Rachel will be willin' for me to work on your place while I'm also fixin' up our house. The three sisters are thicker than thieves, ya see. Please one and ya please them all."

"And upset just one of them . . ." Andy added in a teasing voice.

"*Jah*, we don't wanna go there!" Micah laughed. "*Gut* luck with gettin' all this business settled. I'll call ya later with my figures."

"I think I'll head on home, too. Got some more packing to do before I move into my condo," Bob remarked. "Let me know your decision any time, and I'll take care of the details with Jennifer."

After Rebecca hugged Andy and her sister, she followed her dad outside, which left the two of them standing in the empty building. Andy put his arms around Rhoda. It was a heart-pounding decision, a big leap of faith to have Bob Oliveri invest in a building before he knew the clinic would be a success.

"Are you sure you can live this way, Rhoda?" he murmured. "It'll take a lot of work and imagination to turn this old building into a home."

Rhoda hugged him hard. "Ah, but Micah's got a way of transformin' places, ain't so? Feels like this was all meant to be, Andy. I think ya should do it!"

What faith she had in him. And if the Lantz family stood with him, who could turn against him? "All right, then. Let me grab Bob before he takes off."

Andy loped out to the parking lot, where Bob and Rebecca stood beside the Realtor's SUV chatting through her open car window. He stopped next to them, grinning uncontrollably. "Rhoda says we should just *do* it," he announced. "I've been wanting to say that all along, so—"

"Good man!" Bob crowed. "Welcome to Willow Ridge, Andy. Jennifer and I will get right on this."

"Perfect," Jennifer Bradley agreed. "I'll lock up and get this process started."

Rebecca rushed at him for a hug. "Thank you, thank you, thank you," she murmured happily. "The pieces are falling into place now, for all of us."

Welcome to Willow Ridge. As the three cars pulled away a few moments later, Andy's heart thudded with a feeling of such rightness, such destiny. His life came into clearer focus than he'd known since before Megan had walked away. He hugged Rhoda, who was laughing and crying at the same time.

"I love ya, Andy," she said with a hitch in her voice. "It's been another happy, happy day, ain't so?"

His heart swelled and his throat tightened. He'd been afraid he'd jinx the situation if he said that L word too soon, yet Rhoda had fearlessly stated her feelings. "I'm just beginning to know the meaning of that word. To trust in it again," he whispered. "I can't thank you enough for believing in me—for believing in us. And yeah, I love you so much I can hardly breathe right now."

She rose on her tiptoes to kiss him. "Oh, ya gotta keep breathin', Andy. You're drivin' us home in the sleigh so we can tell Mamma and Rachel about this, ain't so?"

Andy held her tight, closing his eyes with the sweetness of this triumphant moment. It would take some getting used to, the way the Lantz women playfully conspired to get their way. But it was such a welcome change from going it alone, uphill, bearing the weight and responsibility for getting everything done for himself and his family. Here in Willow

Ridge, he felt as though everyone was already pulling for him. Guaranteeing that he would succeed.

The way—his future—had opened like a beautiful door. Andy believed he could accomplish anything if Rhoda stood beside him.

"OK, kids, check one more time to be sure ya got all the ornaments from the inside branches," Rhoda said. "Then ya can show me how this tree folds up. Never seen the likes of that, ya know. We Amish don't have Christmas trees—real or fake ones."

"So how do you decorate, then?" Taylor asked. "Do you have a Nativity scene like ours?"

Rhoda smiled. What a treat, to be here with Betty and the kids on the last day of their vacation before school started up again. They were asking good questions about how their lives would be different once they moved to Willow Ridge, and she was pleased to answer them. Andy was working a shift in the obstetrics ward, grateful that Preacher Tom had given permission for her to be here while Andy worked and his family prepared for their new life.

"We have a real simple set with just Mary, Joseph, and Baby Jesus that my *dat*'s grandpa carved," she replied. "And we have a bigger Nativity scene that Mamma's family gave her when she married my *dat*. Otherwise, we put candles in the windows and fresh pine garlands on the mantels of our fireplaces. For us, it's all about the birth of Jesus the Savior."

"No Santa Claus?" Brett asked. He was gazing wistfully at the two lighted figurines dressed in red with sparkly white trim. "He's really your parents, you know. But we like to keep believing in him so we get more presents!"

Rhoda laughed and rumpled his silky hair. "And I understand that the real Saint Nicholas was a *gut* man whose generosity improved a lot of lives. But nope," she replied. "We give each other simple gifts. Most of them we make ourselves."

Brett considered this as he wrapped the cords around the plastic figures. As he placed them in their big box, he said, "If we won't be having electricity in our new house, we can't use our tree lights or these Santas anyway. Do . . . do you suppose we ought to donate them to the Goodwill store in Morning Star? So some family without much money can have them for next year?"

"That's a fine . . . idea for all of this . . . stuff," Betty answered from her seat on the couch. "I kept out . . . the special ornaments from your . . . first Christmases, but I think we can let . . . the rest of them go. Don't you?"

It was a sobering thought for two kids who had grown up with so many English Christmas traditions, so Rhoda let Brett and Taylor consider their responses without further comment. She was taping a big box shut when the doorbell rang repeatedly.

"Open up! I know you're in there!" a woman's voice exclaimed. The door opened, and with a gust of wind a tall, slender blonde walked in. She looked surprised to see them all sitting right there in the front room.

But *surprise* didn't nearly cover the looks on the kids' faces, or the thundering of Rhoda's heart as this unannounced visitor took off her sunglasses.

"Mom?" Taylor rasped.

"Mommy!" Brett yelped as he bolted up from the floor.

As both children rushed into the woman's arms, a sense of dread swallowed Rhoda whole. She glanced at Betty, who looked as if she was having a nightmare. While nothing could have prepared her for this situation, Rhoda was wishing Andy had told her more about the circumstances of

Megan's leaving the family. Hadn't he said she was living in California now, remarried?

"So it's true," Megan said in an accusing voice. "Your dad has taken up with this—this backwoods Amish girl, and she's brainwashing you into joining their cult along with him. Pack your bags, kids. You're coming with me."

Rhoda's heart was pounding so hard she couldn't reply. Small comfort that Taylor and Brett backed out of their mother's arms then, shaking their heads.

"It's not that way, Mom," Taylor declared in a strained voice. "Rhoda's been taking care of us, cleaning the house—"

"Which proves my point," Megan said as she glared at Rhoda. "If your father is crazy enough to consider joining the Amish church—marrying an uneducated woman who's only fit to cook and clean—he's obviously lost his mind. Not to mention his ability to look after you."

"N-no, it's . . . not like that," Betty protested. "Andy and . . . Rhoda are—"

"And what's happened to *you*?" Megan demanded. "If you've had a stroke, Betty, you're no more able to care for my children than Andy is. My God, this family has fallen apart since I left. Get packing, kids."

"But we need to call Dad—"

"Leave your father out of this. Thank God somebody warned me about this mess before it was too late. And you"—Megan pointed at Rhoda—"get out of my house. Get *away* from my children."

Rhoda swallowed hard. Never in her life had she been spoken to in such a tone, and she didn't know how to handle it. Betty, looking very worried and frail, had grabbed her walker and was heading for the kitchen to escape this craziness, but somebody had to take a stand. Somebody had to talk some sense into this woman, even if she was the children's mother.

*Be with me, Lord, because if I ever needed Ya—if Andy
ever needed Ya—it's right this minute.*

"Let's think about this," Rhoda said, gathering her
courage. It wasn't the Plain way to get angry or argumenta-
tive, but she was the one in charge while Andy couldn't
defend himself or his family. "The way I understand it, ya
left these kids a couple years ago without much thought for
what might happen to them. So what's put this bee in your
bonnet to show up *now*?"

"Do you hear the way she talks?" Megan grilled her
children. "Surely you know better than to believe what this
unsophisticated—why, I bet they don't even have indoor
toilets in Willow Ridge! Why would you want to live that
way? And live without electricity and your computer?"

Taylor's eyes widened. "But, Mom, we've been to Rhoda's
house. They *do* have bathrooms. And Rhoda—"

"I've heard all I need to know about Rhoda—"

"And who told ya all this? Who got ya stirred up so you'd
come and torment your kids with stuff that's not true?"
Rhoda demanded. It was one thing not to fight with this
woman, but another matter altogether that Megan was telling
such blatant lies.

Megan put her fist against her hip. "It doesn't matter
where I heard about you. It's easy to see that every word of
the letter was true. So *leave. Now*, before I call the police. I
will not have my children's minds poisoned with your religious tripe."

Run to the gas station. Call Andy. Bad enough that Taylor
was starting to cry and Brett was gripping his sister's hand,
looking terribly confused. She might have no say in what the
mother of these poor kids was about to do, but Andy certainly needed to know his ex-wife was planning to steal them
away. As Rhoda grabbed her black coat and bonnet from the

front closet, Taylor broke away from her mother to grab the back of Rhoda's dress.

"Please, Rhoda, don't go! We'll make Mom understand—"

Tears erupted from her eyes and all Rhoda could do was lean toward the little girl and lightly touch her face. "Pray hard, honey-girl," she whispered. "We'll get this figured out and then—"

"Out!" Megan ordered as she threw open the door.

Blinded by her tears, Rhoda scurried outside and past a big van in the driveway, as fast as the slippery patches on the pavement allowed her to go. Her coat flapped around her body and the wind made her wet face feel like it was freezing, but she continued frantically down the block. At the intersection where Andy's street met the county highway there was a gas station with a convenience store. She rushed inside.

"Please, may I use a phone?" she gasped as the store's warmth enveloped her. "Got an emergency at the Leitner place."

"Your cell dead?" the man behind the cash register asked gruffly.

"Don't have one. *Please*—"

The attendant scowled but placed the store's telephone up on the counter for her. "Don't be long," he groused. "If my boss finds out you're making personal calls, I'm in big trouble."

Rhoda closed her eyes, desperately trying to recall Andy's cell number. After her fingers punched the numbers, she waited breathlessly while it rang. Her pulse was thundering in her ears and she felt so afraid, but what could she do? Megan was the children's mother . . . and that would never change, no matter how much Rhoda loved Andy and he loved her. And if the tall, pretty blonde had shown up out of the blue today, what would keep her from intruding on their lives anytime she chose to?

Or would Andy change his mind about becoming Amish now? Rhoda squeezed her eyes shut, resigning herself to leaving a voice mail. Either he had his phone shut off during his shift or . . .

"*Jah*, Andy, ya better head home, soon as ya get this message," she rasped. "Megan showed up at the house, and well—she ordered me to get out, and—just please hurry! She told the kids to pack up so they could leave with her."

Rhoda hung up, ignoring the doubtful expression on the attendant's face. Before he could take the phone back, she punched in Sheila's number and prayed her driver wasn't out with another customer, not answering her phone while she was behind the wheel.

"Sheila?" she said. "Can ya come get me?" She told her English friend where to pick her up, thanked the attendant, and then stood in the front window to wait.

She felt as though Jack the Belgian had kicked her in the chest: she couldn't breathe. She couldn't begin to think, what with her mind racing even faster than her heartbeat. Had she done the wrong thing, leaving the kids with that hateful, un-informed woman? Andy would be devastated if his ex-wife disappeared with his kids before he could get home . . .

Devastated enough to give up his future in Willow Ridge?

If it came to his choosing between getting his children back and marrying her, Rhoda had no doubt what Andy's decision would be. And this storm was blowing up the day after he had decided to start his clinic with Rebecca as his partner—after Bob Oliveri had already committed to buying the building for them. So many hopes were going to be ruined . . .

When a familiar van pulled into the station's driveway, Rhoda stepped out into the wind. The door opened and

Rhoda swung herself up into the front seat beside Sheila, still so shaken she didn't know what to say.

"What on earth happened, Rhoda?" her driver asked in a concerned voice.

Rhoda heaved a sigh, hugging herself. "I don't rightly know. Andy's ex-wife got a message that his kids were bein' hornswoggled into joinin' a cult, on account of how their *dat*'s takin' instructions to become Amish. She ordered me out," she added with a hitch in her voice. "If—if this is God's way of tellin' me I'm not to become part of their family, well . . . I don't know what I'm gonna do, Sheila. I just don't know."

Chapter Twenty-Six

"Mom, slow down." The hospital cafeteria was a noisy place to talk on a cell phone, so Andy covered his other ear to hear more clearly. "I can't understand what you're . . . no, Mom, think again," he insisted, now concerned about her mental state. "Megan left us. She got married and went to live on the California coast with—"

"N-no! She's here," his mother insisted in a low voice. "She . . . sent Rhoda away and—and she told the kids . . . to pack their bags. Andy, come home!"

A sudden rush of anger made him swear under his breath. Why, after all this time of minimal communication with him and the kids, would Megan come back? And why was she ordering Taylor and Brett to pack without letting him know?

"All right, Mom, I'm on my way," he said as he hurried away from the table with his lunch tray. "Be careful. I'll get there as fast as I can." He clicked End and then noticed a voice mail waiting for him . . . heard the terror Rhoda was trying to mask as she left a message similar to his mother's. She didn't deserve whatever insults or accusations his ex had hurled at her, but Rhoda could take care of herself. He had to hurry if he was going to keep his kids safe.

Dr. LaFarge was seated a few tables over and Andy was grateful that his supervisor understood the gravity of this emergency. Down the hallways and out the door he raced. He cranked the cold engine of his car and sped along the side roads, hoping to avoid a speeding ticket. How should he handle this totally unexpected situation?

His kids must be so upset and confused after watching Megan send Rhoda away. Megan had always looked down her nose at the Plain folks who lived nearby. She considered them a nuisance when their buggies didn't move off the pavement quickly enough, and she smirked at their old-fashioned clothing.

As he rounded the corner of his street, he tromped on the gas and pulled into the driveway to block the exit of the cargo van idling there. Megan had opened its doors and was urging the kids to get in, while Brett pitched a fit and Taylor stood stiffly off to the side, crying.

Andy shut off the ignition and leaped from his car. "And what is *this* about?" he demanded. Thank God both kids rushed toward him when he opened his arms. They clung to him as he figured out what to say next to the sleek blonde whose sunglasses masked her expression. "You signed over all responsibility for these children when—"

"That was before you began indoctrinating them into a cult," Megan replied coldly. "Oh, I met your little shoofly pie–maker, Rhoda. Sent her on her way so I could restore some sanity to my children's lives."

"But, Mom, Rhoda loves us!" Taylor cried as she clutched Andy's leg. "When you left us, we didn't even know you were going. Didn't even get to say good-bye."

"Rhoda cooks for us and—and she wants us to be her kids," Brett wailed from Andy's other side. "You're gonna leave us again—aren't you? And now that you've sent Rhoda away, who's left here to love us?"

Andy closed his eyes against the emotional wallop his kids' words packed . . . the sting of their accusations. But they hadn't said one thing that was incorrect or exaggerated.

Megan's smirk told him this was going to get even uglier. He leaned down to the children and spoke quietly. "Get in my car. Don't unlock the doors for anyone but me, got it?"

They nodded eagerly and clambered into the front seat. As Andy clicked the locks shut, he heard sirens in the distance, but right now he couldn't be concerned with someone else's catastrophe. He had his own fire to put out, and there was no doubt in his mind that someone was about to get burned.

Lord, thanks for getting me here on time, and please take care of Rhoda. You've got to help me with the right questions, the right actions here. This is craziness, and we need to get to the bottom of it fast.

"So what's this about, really?" Andy repeated. When Megan grabbed for his car keys, he stuffed them in the deep pockets of his scrubs as he stepped away from her. "And why would you care what we're doing? You took off with a guy who provided a much classier lifestyle than a mere teacher could give you. No running the kids to activities. No cooking dinner or dealing with their—"

"What's with the turquoise pants?" she asked with a smirk. "Don't tell me you're a veterinary assistant or a—"

"I'm a registered nurse, thank you very much," he retorted. "Rhoda's family is proud that I've become a healer—"

"Oh, *please*. Ever the idealist, figuring out what to be when you grow up. Going to school again instead of settling into a career that'll make you any money," she derided him. "I can't believe a perpetual student like you would deny your children access to advanced education by making them become Amish. It really is time for me to reclaim my kids."

"Brett and Taylor may choose not to be baptized into the

Amish faith when they're of age, and I'll totally understand that," he replied stiffly. "What brought this on, Megan? You didn't just take a notion to fly in from the coast—"

Andy's words were interrupted by the sirens that had been coming closer. He jumped aside when an ambulance raced up the driveway toward the house, closely followed by a fire truck and a police car that stopped at the curb. What on earth was going on here?

Megan shook with her anger. "If you called these people here to—"

"Hey, what's going on?" Andy asked as the paramedics hopped from the ambulance. They were the same guys he'd worked with when Josh and Joey Knepp had wrecked their sleigh, and that restored a bit of his sanity.

"Got a call from this address," the driver said beneath the blare of the fire truck's siren. "Somebody named Betty. Older lady who said she was having a stroke."

Mom! In the heat of his discussion with Megan, he'd forgotten about her. And here came Officer McClatchey, too, along with the guys from the fire truck.

"We'd better get inside," Andy said as he rushed toward the door.

"But there are kids in this car—"

"And they're right where they need to be," Andy said with a pointed look at the policeman. "I'll fill you in on that situation once we're sure my mother's all right. This way, guys."

Once again Andy's heart throbbed too hard. What if the shock of Megan's return had traumatized his mother? "Mom? Mom, where are you?" he hollered as he entered the house. "Are you OK?"

"Yup," came a quiet answer.

He led the emergency crew into the kitchen and then stopped abruptly. His mother sat calmly at the kitchen table, eating one of Rhoda's sugar cookies. She smiled, a dab of yellow frosting on her upper lip.

"Mom, when I heard the sirens, and then the ambulance and the fire truck came *here*—"

"We had an . . . emergency with Megan. So after I talked to you I . . . called 9-1-1," she replied with a lopsided grin. "Thanks for . . . coming so fast, fellows."

A nervous laugh escaped him as he looked at the EMS crew and Officer McClatchey. Andy wrapped his arms around his mother's shoulders. "Mom, you're brilliant," he whispered. "The kids are fine. Just stay in here, OK?"

She nodded. Took another bite of her cookie.

"So you're all right, ma'am?" the ambulance driver reconfirmed. "Not having chest pains or dizziness or—"

"Not anymore. It's that . . . other woman you need to . . . be concerned with," she replied, gesturing toward the doorway.

Andy went along with his mother's lead. "Actually, Officer McClatchey, we do have a domestic dispute in progress," he said. "Mom called me home from work because my ex-wife has flown in unannounced. I was granted full custody when she divorced me, yet she was loading my kids into her van when I arrived a few minutes ago."

"And don't think for a minute that I'll let this discussion continue as though I'm not here," Megan snapped as she entered the kitchen.

The ambulance driver looked at his crew and the firemen. "If there's no fire and no one needing medical attention, we'll be on our way then," he said. Each of them took a cookie from the plate his mom offered, thanking her. Then it was just the policeman who stayed behind to set this situation straight.

"Shall we go into the living room? Your mom seems very comfortable here." McClatchey eyed Megan, motioning for her and Andy to precede him. He sat down on the couch so he could take notes on the coffee table, motioning for them to take seats, as well. "And for the record, ma'am, your name is—?"

"Megan Zylinsky," she replied stiffly.

"And why exactly did you return to Missouri? If Andy and his mother believe you were planning to take his children—"

"They're my children, too, you know!" Megan's cheeks turned very pink. "And when I got a couple of calls informing me that Andy had taken up with some Amish girl—"

When the policeman glanced his way, Andy quietly said, "Rhoda Lantz."

"—and then received a letter informing me that he intends to join the Amish church and expose the children to such—such a backward, uneducated cult," Megan continued in a rising voice, "well, can you blame me for wanting to protect them?"

"Who called you?" Andy demanded. "Surely you didn't believe just anybody—"

"May I see the letter you've spoken of?" McClatchey asked coolly. "Documentation will help us sort out this situation. And it's only fair for Andy to be on the same page."

Megan's eyebrows rose. "I see no reason to disclose my source. I'm Brett and Taylor's mother, and that supersedes any—"

"Not if you don't have custody, it doesn't." The officer shrugged. "If this matter goes to court, the judge will insist on having this document, so you'll save everyone a lot of time and expense if you'll show it to me, Ms. Zylinsky."

Megan looked from the policeman to Andy, stiffening. "I see how it is. You're siding with Andy. You men will stick together to—"

"No, ma'am, I happen to know Rhoda Lantz and her

family. They're among the finest citizens in the county," McClatchey replied. He leaned his elbows on his thighs, fixing his gaze on Megan. "Rhoda's the reason two little boys got proper care after a nasty sleigh accident a couple weeks ago, because she called Andy to the scene. I can't believe your children are in any danger whatsoever, and I would trust her implicitly with my own children's welfare. Now let's see that letter, or we'll need to go to the station to finish this discussion."

Megan's face fell. She looked ready to protest further, but then dug through her purse and thrust an envelope at the policeman.

"How many calls did you receive? And from whom?" he asked as he unfolded the single page.

Megan cleared her throat. "I . . . he spoke with such authority. Knew enough about my kids to be the real deal. And having lived here in New Haven, around Amish people—"

"You don't know who called you? But you believed a total stranger instead of asking *me*?" Andy rasped. This was more than he could tolerate. But McClatchey had the situation under control, so he settled down . . . wondered how much of this nonsense Rhoda had endured before she'd been sent away. If Megan had told her anything that had set Rhoda against him, he would—

"—I knew exactly what he was talking about. I don't want Brett and Taylor sacrificing themselves to that religion," Megan finished in a huff.

McClatchey read the letter in his own good time, his expression closed. "And do you recognize this signature?" he asked. "I find it odd that someone would type the letter without also typing his or her name beneath such an illegible signature. Unless this person knows you personally."

Again Megan clammed up, looking miffed.

"May I show this to Mr. Leitner?"

"What*ever*," Megan snapped. She crossed her arms, looking around the living room as though gathering further evidence that her children shouldn't be living here.

Except for a few boxes of Christmas decorations that hadn't been taped shut, however, the house looked immaculate. Andy silently thanked Rhoda for that as he looked at the letter, hoping it didn't rattle in his hands as he held it.

Dear Ms. Zylinsky, I regret being the bearer of such unfortunate tidings, but it behooves me to inform you once again that your children, Brett and Taylor Leitner, have come under the persuasion of a certain Rhoda Lantz while she has been performing housekeeping chores for their father. You should be aware that Miss Lantz has gone against the orders of her Amish leaders by becoming involved with your ex-husband, beguiling him into entertaining notions of becoming Amish so he can marry her.

Andy thrust the letter away as though the words were burning holes in his eyes. Suspicions were coming to a rapid boil in his mind, but expressing his exasperation would only give Megan more fuel for her arguments. "This is absurd," he muttered.

"Any notion of who wrote it?" Officer McClatchey asked.

"I have a pretty good idea, yes." Andy exhaled with a hiss.

"Are the writer's allegations true?"

How much should he reveal? His answers would infuriate Megan further . . . but what did he have to hide? He and Rhoda had addressed the issue of that kiss in his car and had moved forward, so he had no reason to hedge. "Rhoda and I plan to marry after I have taken my instruction to become

Amish," he replied, taking strength from the image in his mind of Rhoda's lovely smile. "It's common knowledge around Willow Ridge that I'll be opening a small clinic, offering my medical assistance to Amish and English alike. My children *adore* Rhoda," he added emphatically. "We— we're delighted that she and her family have welcomed us into their lives."

Andy focused on Megan then, feeling a sudden calm . . . a strength he welcomed after this past hour's confusion and strife. "Megan, I didn't contest it when you left us, nor did I challenge you when you admitted you'd been seeing another man before you demanded a divorce," he said quietly. "But if you think you can charge back into our lives and destroy the happiness we've found—the solidarity we've developed as a family—I will fight you tooth and nail. You don't have a legal leg to stand on," he reminded her coolly. "Never mind your total lack of concern for the kids when you left us for another man. A fancier lifestyle."

Megan appeared stunned by the intensity of his stare and Officer McClatchey's. Finally she rested her head in her hand. "But he sounded so . . . persuasive. So genuinely concerned for the kids," she murmured. "Justin told me I should fly out here and bring them back with me."

"Admit it," Andy insisted, closing his eyes against all the memories her appearance had kicked up. The way his gut was rolling, it felt like the bad old days when they had argued so bitterly . . . when it had been a relief for her to go on business trips. "Aren't you secretly relieved to learn that your children are happy and healthy? And that you don't need to inconvenience yourself by taking them into your new life?"

Resentment flickered in her eyes, but rather than fling

more verbal mud at him, Megan reached for her purse again. "I can see I'm outnumbered here—outmanned—"

"No one's forcing you to back down, Ms. Zylinsky," the policeman pointed out. "If you prefer to hire an attorney and pursue this matter, that's certainly your right. Meanwhile, I'm glad your children didn't have to witness this unpleasant conversation."

"Oh! And they're still out in the car," Andy said as he rose from his chair. "They must be freezing—"

"I'll go with you. Say my good-byes and head on back to the airport," Megan muttered. Then she let out an unladylike snort. "This whole idea about you turning Amish is as ridiculous as your getting a *nursing* degree, but hey. Why should I care, right? If you're all so enamored of Rhoda and her type, I should leave you to your ignorance. My mistake, thinking I could save you from your delusions."

Andy watched her go outside, confident the kids would do no more than roll down the car windows.

"What a piece of work," the policeman muttered.

"Can't thank you enough for your support," Andy said as he offered his hand. "You and Mom really saved the day. I saw plane tickets in Megan's purse. She was ready to whisk the kids out of here without me knowing a thing about it."

"Wish all my calls got resolved so easily," the officer said as he headed for the door. "I'll stick around writing my report in the car until she's gone."

Andy shrugged. "I have to move my car from behind hers. I hope I can repair all the confusion and damage this stunt has inflicted on my kids."

And what about Rhoda? Do I still have a chance with her? Or have Megan's shenanigans ruined the hopes and dreams we were building together?

When Andy looked outside to see that Megan was already behind the wheel of her van, something settled inside him. Could it be that once again she hadn't told her children good-bye . . . much less that she loved them? He sighed, then fished his keys from his pocket. He had a lot of questions to answer, a lot of wounds to heal. His kids' anxious expressions stabbed at him as he backed his car from the driveway and watched Megan race off down the street.

"What happened, Dad? What did Mom say?" Taylor asked as she wiped her face with her coat sleeve.

"That was awful." Brett heaved a shuddery sigh. "I want to talk to Rhoda, *now*. I want to go back to how things were before Mom tried to—to kidnap us."

"Best idea I've heard all day, Son. Let's get Gram and go."

Chapter Twenty-Seven

"What if Andy's ex-wife has taken off with the kids?" Rhoda fretted. "It'll look like my fault, for sure and for certain, because I didn't stick around to—"

"Oh, Sister, I can't picture Andy blaming you for that." Rebecca stopped unpacking to wrap her arms around Rhoda's shaking shoulders, as Rachel stepped up to hug her from behind.

"This looks worse than it really is, I'm thinkin'," Rachel assured her. "The way Andy has eyes only for you, Rhoda, it'll take more than a *woman* to chase him outta your life."

Rhoda wiped her eyes on her dress sleeve, wanting to believe her sisters. Mamma and Ben had gone to Clark to visit cousins who couldn't make it to the wedding, so the *dawdi haus*, cluttered with Rebecca's boxes and sparse furnishings, echoed with their voices . . . sounding as unsettled as her heart. She could think of a dozen comebacks for Megan's cruel remarks now, but she disliked the way she felt as such spiteful, vengeful phrases formed in her mind. It wasn't her way to strike back when someone challenged her.

"I'll put on some water for cocoa, and we can help

Rebecca unpack," Rachel suggested. "It's better than gnashin' at the bit, when we don't know all the facts about—well, would you looky there," she said as she glanced out the front window. "Could be your prayers'll soon be answered, Sister."

Rhoda thumbed away her lingering tears and peeked through the new curtains. Oh, but her heart played hopscotch when she saw Andy's car pull in. Better yet, the kids jumped out before their *dat* shut off the engine.

"Rhoda! Rhoda the Reindeer! We're here to see ya!" Brett called out.

"Gram ate all your cookies," Taylor joined in. "So we've come for more!"

Rhoda rushed out the door. She was giggling at the notion that Betty had finished off all those frosted sugar cookies while Megan had been antagonizing them. When the two children rushed into her arms, she crushed them in a hug, rocking them from side to side. Had anyone ever looked or felt so good as these two?

"Silly gooses," she teased, gazing into their bright eyes. "Your gram wouldn't eat that many—"

"Oh, I . . . cleared the plate," Betty assured her. She was taking Andy's arm as she got out of the car, a girlish smile lighting her face. "Shared them with the ambulance crew—"

"Yeah, Gram called 9-1-1 just in time!" Taylor crowed.

"And it was so cool when the sirens were cryin' and the fire truck stopped right in front of *our yard*!" Brett added gleefully.

Rhoda laughed at this lively account, yet when her eyes found Andy's she stilled. His dear face showed such concern—for *her*. He looked so happy to be here after the disaster that had shattered his day.

"Rhoda, I'm very, very sorry," he murmured as he took

her in his arms. He pressed her head to his chest with a tired sigh. "I never dreamed Megan would show up with such cockeyed ideas about—well, if she insulted you, I apologize."

As the kids took their grandmother inside, Rhoda let out a long breath. "I was so worried that if I left them, she might really take them away. And then you'd be blamin' *me* for what happened." She raised her eyes to his. "What *did* happen, Andy? Why'd she show up feelin' so full of vinegar?"

"I've got a pretty good idea, but I'm hoping you and your sisters can confirm my hunch." He stepped inside the *dawdi haus* with her and gazed appreciatively at the freshly painted walls and gleaming woodwork. "What a great place. Hey there, Rachel and Rebecca."

"Mighty *gut* to see ya, Andy," Rachel answered from the stove, where she was putting the kettle on. "Rhoda was plenty worried about these two kids of yours."

"And they were worried about her. We all were." He smiled at the way Taylor, Brett, and his mother were admiring the apartment as they stepped between the open boxes of Rebecca's belongings. He pulled a sheet of paper from his coat pocket. "What do you make of this letter? This, and a couple of phone calls, had my ex flying out here in a tizzy, ready to haul my kids back to California."

Rhoda took the typed page and began to read it with a sister looking over each of her shoulders.

Dear Ms. Zylinsky, I regret being the bearer of such unfortunate tidings, but it behooves me to inform you once again that your children, Brett and Taylor Leitner, have come under the persuasion of a certain Rhoda Lantz—

Rhoda's head swiveled. She couldn't read any further. "So Megan's last name is Zylinsky now?" she rasped.

"She went back to her maiden name after she divorced me," Andy replied quietly.

"This smacks of Hiram's mudslingin'," Rachel muttered. "He always uses his hundred-dollar vocabulary when he's up to somethin', too. Don't ya remember how he called Ben's old girlfriend in Lancaster County to stir up the pot, tryin' to make Mamma think she shouldn't marry him?"

"Hiram?" Rhoda gasped. "But how would he know Megan's name, or her address?"

"A name like Zylinsky would be very easy to track down with a computer," Rebecca remarked as she finished reading the letter. "It's a matter of public record that she and Andy divorced. So once Hiram or his computer assistant found her name, he could have looked up her address and phone number on white pages dot com, or used an online people-finding service."

Rhoda shook her head. "I'm a lot better off not knowin' how all this modern computer stuff works."

Rachel, meanwhile, was pointing to the bottom of the page. "For sure and for certain that's Hiram," she declared. "That same signature is on our marriage certificate."

Swallowing hard, Rhoda had to agree that the name on Megan's letter matched their former bishop's handwriting. She, too, had signed Rachel's certificate, after all. "And we all know how convincin' he can sound when he's tryin' to talk ya into something," she remarked. "But when will his nasty tricks end? What if he keeps on tormentin' us, Andy? Gettin' the kids and Betty all upset while he's tryin' to keep us apart?"

"Keep us apart? That's not going to happen as long as I draw breath, Rhoda."

When Andy wrapped his arms around her again, Rhoda

felt his pulse beating in time with hers as his confident voice rumbled in his chest. He reminded her of the sweet-gum tree behind the Sweet Seasons, strong and solid. Able to withstand the storms and harsh realities of whatever their courtship and the changing of his faith brought their way.

"I'm going to call that carriage maker in Cedar Creek today to talk about my special wagon," he assured her. "Something tells me that'll be the key to my new nursing service."

"Dad says you've gotten another twenty-five thousand from Miriam's ad, plus more donations from the locals," Rebecca said. "Clearly, everyone wants you and your clinic here."

"And Hiram's headin' off to Higher Ground," Rachel said. "He'll be too busy recruitin' folks to bother ya much, ain't so? Nobody from Willow Ridge is goin' with him, so he'll be startin' up that new colony with a bunch of strangers who don't know what he's up to."

Surrounded by these loving smiles and gentle voices, Rhoda relaxed. What a wonderful world she lived in. And hadn't Jesus promised that all things were possible with God? As four shorter arms wrapped around her waist, Rhoda delighted in the way Brett and Taylor embraced her while Betty stood behind her, hands on her shoulders.

"We weren't goin' to California with Mom, you know," Brett assured her. "While Dad had us locked up safe in his car, Tay and I came up with all sorts of ways to escape before she got us on a plane."

"Yeah," Taylor stated. "Once Mom said all those mean things about you, Rhoda, I—I didn't feel like she was our mom anymore. Not like you are."

"Ohhhhhh." Rhoda blinked back tears, but these were the kind that welled up when she was so full of joy that it spilled over. As she pulled the kids closer, smiling up at Andy, it occurred to her that not so long ago she had been wondering what to do with her life, wishing for the love and fulfillment she thought had passed her by.

Well, here they were. Another gift from God, come down at Christmas.

And for wishes come true and prayers answered, Lord, I thank Ya from the bottom of my heart.

What's Cookin' at the Sweet Seasons Bakery Café?

Because I love to cook as much as Miriam and Naomi do, here are recipes for some of the dishes they've served up in *Winter of Wishes*, as well as some that Rhoda makes for Andy's kids. I read Amish cookbooks and the recipe column in *The Budget*, so I can say yes, the convenience foods you see as ingredients are authentic!

Colder weather calls for stick-to-your-ribs soups and comfort foods—and for me it wouldn't be Christmas without cookies! I make hundreds of dozens of cookies to share for the holidays each year, and most of these are favorites I bake again and again. For an even larger selection of goodies, you'll want my upcoming anthology, *An Amish Country Christmas*, which will include a recipe section of nothing but my favorite cookies and holiday desserts!

I'll also post these recipes on my website, www.Charlotte HubbardAuthor.com. If you don't see the recipes you want, please e-mail me via my website to request them—and let me know how you like them! I hope you enjoy making these dishes as much as I do!

~Charlotte

Golden Cream Soup

If you enjoy potato soup, this version sports a few more veggies, and the cheese makes it a real comfort food. For variety, or so your family and guests will consider it a meal in a bowl, stir in a cup or two of diced ham or diced cooked chicken!

3 C. cubed raw potatoes
½ C. celery slices
½ C. chopped onion
½ C. sliced carrots
1 C. water
1 chicken bouillon cube
1 T. parsley flakes
Salt and pepper to taste
2 T. real bacon bits or crumbled bacon
2 T. all-purpose flour
1½ C. milk
½ lb. Velveeta cheese, cubed

In a soup kettle or two-quart pan, mix vegetables, water, bouillon, seasonings and bacon bits. Simmer about 20 minutes or until the veggies are tender. Mix the flour into the milk until smooth and add to the pot, cooking until thickened (don't boil it). Remove from heat and stir in the Velveeta until it's melted. Makes 6–8 servings.

<u>Kitchen Hint</u>: Because this is a milk-based soup, it won't keep long in the fridge and it won't freeze well, so try to eat it all within a couple of days.

Breakfast Casserole

Look in any Amish cookbook and you'll find a dozen different recipes for make-ahead, one-pan breakfasts ready to pop in the oven as soon as the cook's feet hit the floor of a morning. This is a great way to use up bread that's gone stale. The meats—usually sausage, bacon, or ham—are interchangeable, and the aroma that fills the house is guaranteed to entice everyone to your table! Great for dinner, too.

    8 slices of bread, cubed
    1 lb. cooked sausage, bacon, or ham, crumbled
    2 C. shredded cheese, divided
    2 C. milk
    ¼ C. butter or margarine, melted
    6 eggs

Spray/grease a 9-by-13-inch pan. Arrange the bread cubes on the bottom, then sprinkle with the crumbled meat and half the cheese. In a separate bowl, stir the milk, melted margarine, and eggs with a fork until well blended and pour this mixture over the other ingredients.

Stir, if you need to, to moisten all of the bread. Cover with foil and refrigerate overnight or for several hours.

Take the casserole from the fridge about half an hour before baking. Preheat oven to 350°F and bake for about 40 minutes, until the center is firm. Top with the remaining cheese and return to the oven, uncovered, for 5 more minutes. Let set for about 10 minutes before cutting. Dig in!

Famous Name Pizza Crust

If you don't associate pizza with Plain folks, think again! This recipe was in *The Budget*, submitted by an anonymous reader, and after trying it I knew it would be a hit with the kids in this story—and with everyone who likes a thick, bread-like crust for pizza. It makes enough for two individual pizzas or one 14-inch crust.

1 tsp. salt
2 T. sugar
1 tsp. garlic powder
1 tsp. oregano flakes
1 T. dry yeast
2 C. all-purpose flour
1 C. very warm water
2 T. vegetable or olive oil
Cornmeal
Additional flour for kneading

In a small, deep bowl mix the dry ingredients. Measure the water from the tap—warm but not steaming hot—and stir the oil and water together, then pour this liquid into the dry ingredients and stir to blend. Finish mixing by hand until the dough holds together; then knead on a floured surface a few times, just until it's not sticky, and shape it into a ball. Wash the bowl in hot water, spread oil or butter inside it, and put the dough in it, turning it to coat the top. Cover with plastic wrap and allow to rest about 15 minutes. Roll out the dough to cover a pizza pan or stone that's been spread with cornmeal, and top with your favorite sauce, cheese, and toppings.

Bake about 20 minutes at 375°F, or until top and edges are golden.

<u>Kitchen Hint</u>: I use spaghetti sauce, spread it thick, and then put a layer of cheese before adding my meat and chopped veggies . . . and then I sprinkle on grated Parmesan and more shredded cheese. I figure there's no such thing as too much cheese on pizza! Refrigerate leftovers.

Whole Wheat Italian Sausage Pizza

Truth be told, I prefer a pizza crust with some whole wheat flour in it . . . it allows me the illusion that I'm eating a more healthful pizza! But then, when you pile on chopped veggies, tomato sauce, and cheese, pizza isn't really such a nutritional disaster. Makes a fine breakfast the next day, too! This recipe rolls out to cover a 14-to-16-inch pizza pan or stone.

1 T. cornmeal
1½ C. all-purpose flour
¾ C. whole wheat flour
2 T. dry yeast
2 tsp. sugar
1 tsp. salt
¾ C. very warm water
2 T. vegetable or olive oil
½ to ¾ C. pizza or spaghetti sauce
1 lb. bulk Italian sausage, cooked and drained
1½ to 2 C. chopped toppings such as bell peppers,
    olives, mushrooms
2 C. shredded mozzarella or other Italian cheeses
¼ C. grated Parmesan cheese
More shredded cheese, as desired.

Spread cornmeal on pizza pan or stone. Prepare the toppings by slicing, dicing, etc.

In a small, deep bowl, mix the flours, yeast, sugar, and salt. Mix the water (very warm to the touch but not steaming hot) and oil, then pour into the dry ingredients and stir until blended. Finish blending by hand, and then knead the dough briefly on a floured surface until smooth but not sticky and shape into a ball. Wash the bowl with hot water, coat the inside with oil or butter, and put the dough in to rise, turning it to coat the surface; cover with plastic wrap, and let it rest about 15 minutes. Meanwhile, preheat the oven to 375°F. Roll out the dough on a 14-to-16-inch pizza pan or stone, spread with sauce and toppings. Bake about 20 minutes, until cheese is golden.

Kitchen Hint: The more stuff you pile onto the crust, the more time you should allow for baking! And, as with the crust recipe above, there's no such thing as too much cheese on pizza—I like to put coarsely grated cheese on the sauce, then pile on the meat and veggies, and then top it off with a smaller shredded cheese and the Parmesan.

Rhoda's Oatmeal Cookies

Nothing makes your home smell better than baking cookies! I prefer to use the old-fashioned rolled oats in everything I bake, but the quick-cooking version will work fine, too. This recipe is a lifelong favorite of my nieces and nephews, always moist and chewy, with lots of raisins, nuts, and cinnamon.

    1 C. sugar
    1 C. brown sugar, packed
    1 C. butter or margarine, softened
    2 eggs
    1 tsp. vanilla extract
    2 C. all-purpose flour
    1 tsp. each of salt and baking soda
    1 T. cinnamon
    3 C. old-fashioned rolled oats
    1 C. chopped nuts
    1 C. raisins

Preheat oven to 350°F. Cream the sugars and butter/margarine, then mix in the eggs and vanilla. Add in the flour, salt, baking soda, and cinnamon and mix well. Add in the oats, nuts, and raisins—your dough will be moist but stiff. Drop by rounded teaspoonfuls onto cookie sheets covered with parchment paper. Bake for 10–13 minutes, or until just starting to brown. Makes about 5 dozen. These freeze well.

<u>Kitchen Hint</u>: As you spoon the dough onto the cookie sheets, leave it in rounded mounds so the cookies stay moister. Don't overbake! You can also substitute dried cranberries or other dried fruit chunks for the raisins.

Sausage & Cheddar Biscuits

Dense and moist, these scone-like biscuits are always a hit and a special breakfast treat. Maybe it's the salty-sweet flavor combination, or just the little specks of sausage and cheese that lure you to eat just one more . . . If it makes you feel healthier, you can use turkey breakfast sausage rather than pork.

   12 oz. bulk sausage
   3¼ C. all-purpose flour
   ½ C. sugar
   2½ tsp. baking powder
   ¾ C. butter or margarine
   1½ C. shredded cheddar cheese
   ¾ C. buttermilk

Preheat the oven to 375°F. Cook the sausage until no pink remains, then drain on paper towels and break into small particles (a food processor is fastest, or a handheld pastry blender works, too). In a large bowl, stir together the flour, sugar, and baking powder, then cut in the butter/margarine with a pastry blender (or, you can do this step with the food processor after you remove the sausage, and finish the recipe using the food processor) until the mixture is coarse and crumbly. Stir in the cheese and sausage, then add buttermilk all at once and blend until everything's moistened. Turn this (wet) dough onto a floured surface and knead briefly, then pat into a layer that's ¾-inch thick. Cut with a 2½-inch biscuit cutter (or a drinking glass) and arrange the biscuits on a baking sheet covered with parchment paper. Bake about 15 minutes or until golden. Cool on a wire rack. Makes about 1½ dozen. Freezes well.

<u>Kitchen Hint</u>: I don't keep buttermilk around, so I use either commercial dry buttermilk powder, found in the baking aisle, or I stir a tablespoon of vinegar into ¾ cup of milk and wait a few minutes for it to thicken.

Split Pea Soup

This soup didn't appeal to me when I was a kid, but wow, do I love it now! It's an inexpensive meal in a bowl, thick and satisfying, and it packs a lot of healthful fiber.

1 lb. bag of green split peas, rinsed
1 can of chicken broth (garlic- or herb-flavored is
    good)
6 C. cold water
2 C. cubed/chopped ham or kielbasa/smoked sausage
1 med. onion, chopped
Salt and pepper to taste
2 large carrots, chopped
4 stalks celery, chopped

In a large Dutch oven or stock pot, combine everything except the carrots and celery. Bring to a boil, then reduce heat to a simmer and cook, covered, for about an hour. Stir occasionally. Add the carrots and celery and simmer another 30 minutes, or until peas are mushy and the soup is thick. Serves 10. Freezes well.

<u>Kitchen Hint</u>: Does your favorite soup pot have "hot spots" where thick food tends to stick? Be sure to stir this soup now and again to prevent scorching.

Irish Brown Bread

This makes a big, dense loaf of dark, slightly sweet bread that looks impressive sliced into generous wedges on a platter. Warm it slightly before you serve it, and slather it with butter! Yum!

2 C. whole wheat flour
2 C. all-purpose flour
1 tsp. each: baking soda, salt, baking powder
½ C. sugar
½ stick margarine or butter
2 eggs
3 C. buttermilk

Mix the dry ingredients and cut in the margarine/butter with a pastry cutter. Add eggs and milk and mix thoroughly. Pour into a greased Bundt pan and bake at 325°F for about 40 minutes (a toothpick inserted in a crack should come out clean). Cool in the pan for 15 minutes, then turn it out to cool completely. Slice and enjoy! Freezes well.

<u>Kitchen Hint</u>: The old buttermilk trick: stir 3 tablespoons lemon juice or white vinegar into 3 cups of milk and let it sit about ten minutes to thicken.

Holiday Banana Muffins

Here's yet another great excuse to let bananas get too ripe! The fruit, coconut, and chocolate chips make this a very special treat for Christmas breakfast, or bake them in holiday cupcake papers and serve them as dessert!

½ C. butter or margarine, softened
1 C. sugar
2 eggs
1 tsp. vanilla extract
2 C. all-purpose flour
1 tsp. baking soda
1 C. mashed ripe bananas (2 medium)
1 11-oz. can mandarin oranges, drained and chopped
    slightly
1 C. flaked coconut
1 C. mini chocolate chips
⅔ C. sliced almonds
½ C. maraschino cherries, chopped
½ C. chopped dates

Preheat oven to 350°F. Cream the butter/margarine and sugar with a mixer. Beat in eggs and vanilla. Combine the flour and baking soda, then add to the creamed mixture along with the bananas. Stir in the fruits, coconut, and nuts. Spoon batter into sprayed muffin tins, about two-thirds full. Bake about 15 minutes or until just golden and firm in the centers. Cool in the pan ten minutes and then remove to a rack to cool completely. Makes about a dozen. Freezes well.

Kitchen Hint: Because this recipe leaves part of a package of dates, I usually double the recipe to use the whole box. To save time or serve this as a breakfast cake, you can pour the batter into a sprayed 9-by-13-inch pan and bake it about 25 minutes, or until just firm in the center. Cut it into squares when it's cooled.

Sugar Cookies

This is the cookie that turns an ordinary cookie tray into a fabulous plate of Christmas cookies! I usually make five to six batches of this dough, adding paste coloring and flavored gelatin (see below). I bake the cookies one day, store them in a covered container, and then decorate them the next day because it takes that long to finish about 13 dozen of these!

½ C. butter, softened (no substitutes)
1 C. sugar
1 egg
1 T. lemon juice
1 tsp. vanilla
2 C. flour
½ tsp. salt
½ tsp. baking soda

With a mixer, cream the butter and sugar, then beat in the egg, lemon juice, and vanilla. Combine the dry ingredients and gradually add them to the sugar and butter mixture until well blended. Tint with paste food coloring, if desired. Wrap dough in wax paper or plastic wrap and refrigerate it for at least 3 hours. (It will keep for several days, until you have time to bake.)

Preheat oven to 350°F. Work with half of the dough at a time: roll to about ¼-inch thickness on a floured surface, then cut with cookie cutters. Place one inch apart on a cookie sheet covered with parchment paper, and bake 7–8 minutes for softer, chewier cookies and 9–10 minutes or until lightly browned for crisp cookies. Cool in the pan for a minute and then remove cookies with a spatula to a cooling rack. Makes 2–3 dozen.

<u>Kitchen Hint</u>: For flavored sugar cookies, add a 3 oz. package of sugar-free gelatin to the dough! I make green dough with lime, yellow dough with peach or orange, and dark pink dough with cherry gelatin. If you use regular sugar gelatin, reduce the sugar in your recipe by a couple of tablespoons.

Buttercream Frosting

This is the recipe I learned long ago in a cake-decorating class. I love it because it doesn't taste like shortening, and it dries firmly (without getting hard) when you decorate cookies or cake.

½ C. milk
½ C. softened butter (no substitutes)
½ C. shortening
½ tsp. salt
1 tsp. vanilla
1 tsp. lemon flavoring
6 to 8 C. (about a pound) confectioners sugar

In a large mixing bowl, blend the milk, butter, shortening, and flavorings with a mixer. Blend in the sugar a cup or two at a time, scraping the bowl, until the frosting is thick and forms peaks.

For colored frosting, use paste coloring to ensure the frosting will be thick enough to hold its shape during decorating. Makes enough to decorate/frost 6 batches of sugar cookies, or a cake.

Kitchen Hint: I divide my frosting into 4 or 5 plastic containers and color one batch with deep pink, one batch with yellow, one with green, one with sky blue, and I leave some white. Then I get out my pastry bag and decorating tips, the sanding sugars, jimmies, and miniature M&M'S, and I play! Let the decorated cookies dry/set up before you store or freeze them.

Chocolate Date Nut Bread

This dense, sweet bread is a wonderful addition to any goody tray, and great for breakfast, too! Serve with strawberry cream cheese for a real treat.

¾ C. boiling water
1 C. sliced dates
1 C. chocolate chips
¼ C. butter
1 egg
¾ C. milk
1 tsp. vanilla
2½ C. all-purpose flour

1 C. chopped nuts
⅓ C. sugar
2 tsp. salt
1 tsp. baking powder
1 tsp. baking soda

Preheat the oven to 350°F. Combine the water and dates and set aside. Melt the chocolate chips and butter, and set aside. In a large bowl, mix the egg, milk, and vanilla, then stir in the chocolate, the date mixture, and the combined remaining ingredients.

Pour the batter into a 9-by-5-inch loaf pan that's been sprayed or greased. Bake for about an hour (start checking for doneness in the center after 45 minutes). When a toothpick inserted into the center comes out clean, take the bread from the oven. Cool in the pan for 15 minutes before removing it to cool completely.

Hannah's Perty Pink Stuff

I knew as soon as I spotted this recipe I would have trouble not eating the whole bowl before I got it to the table! It's one of those "salads" that's really more of a dessert, but whatever you want to call it, it's really a nice addition to a holiday meal. It would also be yummy made with different flavors of pie filling.

8 oz. cream cheese
1 can sweetened condensed milk
1 20-oz. can crushed pineapple, drained well
1 can cherry pie filling
8 oz. tub of whipped topping

Cream the cream cheese, then add the sweetened condensed milk. Next stir in the pineapple and pie filling, then stir in the whipped topping. Pour into a large glass serving bowl and chill for several hours.

Raspberry Walnut Brownies

Oh, but these dense, moist brownies are the best chocolate fix! The layer of raspberry jelly between the brownie and the velvety chocolate frosting adds a sweet, tangy surprise as you bite into one.

Brownies

6 squares (6 oz.) unsweetened chocolate
1 C. shortening
6 eggs
3 C. sugar
3 tsp. vanilla extract
2 C. flour
3 C. walnuts, chopped

<u>Velvet Chocolate Frosting</u>

2 squares (2 oz.) unsweetened chocolate
4 T. each butter and light corn syrup
2 C. powdered sugar
2 T. milk
2 tsp. vanilla extract
⅔ C. raspberry jelly

Preheat oven to 325°F and spray/grease a 9-by-13-inch pan. Melt the chocolate with the shortening in a double boiler over warm water or in a microwave-safe bowl for about a minute, stirring after thirty seconds. Cool slightly. Blend eggs, sugar, and vanilla, add the melted chocolate, and then stir in the flour and walnuts. Spread batter evenly in the prepared pan and bake about 40 minutes, until center is firm. Carefully spread the jelly to cover the brownies. Let cool.

For the frosting, melt the chocolate, then stir in the butter and corn syrup. Mix in the remaining ingredients until smooth and velvety. Spread on the cooled brownies. Cut in 6 columns by 8 rows to make 4 dozen sinfully rich brownies.

<u>Kitchen Hint</u>: These freeze well; but unfortunately they get messy when you pack them and mail them—not that anyone receiving them has ever complained!

Cranberry Upside-Down Cake

What a yummy way to enjoy cranberries! This coffee cake can also be served as a dessert, but I love it warm for breakfast. The cornmeal cake is dense and satisfying. My husband likes to put his serving in a bowl and pour milk over it, while the cake is still warm.

Topping

½ stick (¼ C.) butter or margarine
¾ C. packed brown sugar
1 bag of fresh or frozen cranberries
½ C. golden raisins (regular raisins are fine, too)

Cornmeal Cake

1 stick (½ C.) butter or margarine (not spread), softened
¾ C. packed brown sugar
1 T. vanilla extract
1½ tsp. baking powder
2 large eggs
⅔ C. milk
1¼ C. all-purpose flour
⅓ C. yellow cornmeal

Preheat the oven to 350°F. Spray an 8- or 9-inch round cake pan. For the topping, put the butter in the cake pan and melt it in the oven, tilting the pan to spread it evenly and coat the sides. Sprinkle the brown sugar evenly on the bottom, then add the cranberries in one layer. Scatter the raisins over the top of the berries.

For the cake, cream the butter, brown sugar, vanilla, and baking powder with a mixer until well blended. Beat in the eggs (mixture might look curdled). On a lower speed, mix in the milk, flour, and cornmeal just until blended. Spread batter over the topping. Bake about an hour, until top is browned and a toothpick inserted near the center comes out with moist crumbs. Cool in the pan for 5 minutes before inverting onto a serving plate. Serves 8–10.

<u>Kitchen Hint</u>: The cooled cake keeps well for a couple of days at room temperature, or it can be wrapped well and frozen. Rewarm in the oven or microwave.

Enjoy another visit to Willow Ridge next month
in a special holiday treat,

An Amish Country Christmas

by Charlotte Hubbard and Naomi King.

*In Willow Ridge, Missouri, the Christmas season is a time
when faith brings peace, family brings warmth, and new ro-
mance brings sparkling joy . . .*

The Christmas Visitors

For spirited Martha Coblentz and her twin, Mary, the snow
has delivered the perfect holiday *and* birthday present to
their door—handsome brothers Nate and Bram Kanagy. But
when unforeseen trouble interrupts their season's good cheer,
it will take unexpected intervention—and sudden understanding—to give all four the blessing of a lifetime . . .

Kissing the Bishop

As the year's first snow settles, Nazareth Hooley and her
sister, Jerusalem, are given a heaven-sent chance to help
newly widowed Tom Hostetler tend his home. But when her
hope that she and Tom can build on the caring between
them seems a dream forever out of reach, Nazareth discovers
that faith and love can make any miracle possible . . .

Books by Bestselling Author
Fern Michaels

___The Jury	0-8217-7878-1	$6.99US/$9.99CAN
___Sweet Revenge	0-8217-7879-X	$6.99US/$9.99CAN
___Lethal Justice	0-8217-7880-3	$6.99US/$9.99CAN
___Free Fall	0-8217-7881-1	$6.99US/$9.99CAN
___Fool Me Once	0-8217-8071-9	$7.99US/$10.99CAN
___Vegas Rich	0-8217-8112-X	$7.99US/$10.99CAN
___Hide and Seek	1-4201-0184-6	$6.99US/$9.99CAN
___Hokus Pokus	1-4201-0185-4	$6.99US/$9.99CAN
___Fast Track	1-4201-0186-2	$6.99US/$9.99CAN
___Collateral Damage	1-4201-0187-0	$6.99US/$9.99CAN
___Final Justice	1-4201-0188-9	$6.99US/$9.99CAN
___Up Close and Personal	0-8217-7956-7	$7.99US/$9.99CAN
___Under the Radar	1-4201-0683-X	$6.99US/$9.99CAN
___Razor Sharp	1-4201-0684-8	$7.99US/$10.99CAN
___Yesterday	1-4201-1494-8	$5.99US/$6.99CAN
___Vanishing Act	1-4201-0685-6	$7.99US/$10.99CAN
___Sara's Song	1-4201-1493-X	$5.99US/$6.99CAN
___Deadly Deals	1-4201-0686-4	$7.99US/$10.99CAN
___Game Over	1-4201-0687-2	$7.99US/$10.99CAN
___Sins of Omission	1-4201-1153-1	$7.99US/$10.99CAN
___Sins of the Flesh	1-4201-1154-X	$7.99US/$10.99CAN
___Cross Roads	1-4201-1192-2	$7.99US/$10.99CAN

Available Wherever Books Are Sold!
Check out our website at www.kensingtonbooks.com

More by Bestselling Author
Hannah Howell

Romantic Suspense from
Lisa Jackson